Paradig

The foun

Jamari and the

Part III

A Novel by

R. Roderick Rowe

Table of Contents

The Founder's Sons (Jamari and the Manhood Rites, #3)............1
Chapter Two..18
Chapter Three...26
Chapter Four...34
Chapter Five..40
Chapter Six..56
Chapter Seven...75
Chapter Eight..89
Chapter Nine...100
Chapter Ten..113
Chapter Eleven...121
Chapter Twelve...126
Chapter Thirteen..135
Chapter Fourteen...143
Chapter Fifteen...157
Chapter Sixteen..169
Chapter Seventeen..183
Chapter Eighteen..191
Chapter Nineteen...210
Chapter Twenty...222
Chapter Twenty-One...235
Chapter Twenty-Two...251
Chapter Twenty-Three...262
Chapter Twenty-Four...276
Chapter Twenty-Five..282
Chapter Twenty-Six..288
Chapter Twenty-Seven...294
Chapter Twenty-Seven...306
Epilogue..310
The End...311

This book is a work of fiction. The society in these pages is built on a different set of rules, laws, taboos, and cultural morals that what we see in our world today.

The characters and events in this book are fictitious. Any similarity to real persons, living or dead, is coincidental and not intended by the author.

While there are hetero and homosexual encounters herein, they are not graphic in nature and are necessary to convey the book's essence to the reader. Homosexuality, while present and approved of, is not the dominant focus of the work.

Acknowledgements

IT'S NEVER POSSIBLE to fully thank and appreciate everyone who holds a support role for a novelist. I'll try to touch on the ones who I feel had the most impact on this work.

One of the most amazing Beta Readers I never deserved gets top honors here. Tom McConnell gave far more than any Beta Reader ever has, offering top-notch critiques into character motivations, scene set-ups, believability, plot development and overall impact. No one has yet 'gotten' all the full depth I've built into this trilogy. Tom came the closest, though, and gave me insights into the characters that helped me to flesh them out into living, breathing humans.

I took the 4th Draft to a Developmental Editor. This was the first time I'd ever used anyone in that role. Sarita Lynn Edwina Brown fleshed out some very important scenes, calling me to task for having one of the characters act in a way that was completely opposed to his every other characteristic in the novels. She then worked with me to get that necessary, even vital, scene fleshed out again with a re-work of who did what and why.

Her response to that last sleepless night when she finally reached the ending is one of the strongest affirmations I've had. It was a post-midnight summons to the phone where I read the response to those summarizing paragraphs.

"Holy Brother/Mother/Father/Sister of God! Randy, you are not a writer, you are a prophet! And you have delivered the message with courage and love. Blessed be. I am in total Awe! Namaste' my friend."

In Retrospect

IT'S BEEN FIVE YEARS since I published this work and now, as I sit down to look it over again, I have decisions to make. Do I bring the entire novel into line with my writing style and ability today? Or, do I fix the most glaring errors and move on? I'm settling on a heavy do-over of the first chapter along with a strong clean up of Chapters Two and Three. The rest I'll simply look for grammar and clutter. And then move on.

What I struggled with for the longest time is that there are elements of the trilogy that have not been perceived. I take the blame for that in full measure.

I must confess, though, that a recent set of reviews renewed my faith in the vision I set out to achieve. I'm going to share some snippets of those reviews and then talk about what I intended. I suspect this is very unusual from an author. Most, I'm told, put their book out there and then leave it in the hands of the readers, reviewers and various other types of folks who encounter it in some way to draw what they will from the words.

From the review of **Jamari and the Manhood Rites**:

> "This story reminded me a bit of the way I felt on first reading some of Ursula K. LeGuin's stories, like The Left Hand of Darkness that made me stop short when I was younger and wonder what would happen in such a society where cultural norms have been turned around. The same sense of discovery was there for me in this book as I read on wanting to find out more about what trials Jamari would go through, how he would react to them and what he'd be like on the other side."

From the review of **Jamari Shaman**:

"I was curious here to see how the spiritual aspects would come more to the fore. The first book reminded me of Ursula K. LeGuin in the sense of experimenting with culture/world building. This book reminded me of some of the reasons I was attracted to the work of Tony Hillerman and the way he could explain Native American beliefs and rituals along with the mysteries.

From the review of **The Founder's Sons**:

"Whew, this one had a lot going on and an Epilogue that I found chilling and perfect. Jamari is going to need every skill he possesses, as the greed that caused the original devastation, causes eyes to turn once again to his lands and forests. He fully comes into his power here, finds allies both human, spiritual and in nature. Here the Manhood test and rituals reach their culmination and it is a must-read to see where Jamari, the people, and the land end up. Knowing the ending now, this is one that will bear rereading at a slower pace to savor the world building and the spiritual aspects more fully."

I'm not sure who **Susie Umphers** is, but this reviewer is the one person who has come closest to "getting" my intent as I wrote these novels. And, being compared to Ursula LeGuin? Oh-My-Gawd! What a thrill that was – so far from any reality I could have imagined, and so perfectly accurate as well. I would never have thought to compare myself to LeGuin and question whether I earned that spot or not, BUT, Umphers captured perfectly what I set out to do:

What would happen in a society where cultural norms have been turned around? In this trilogy, I turned them around with great deliberation and purpose!

I've never read The Left Hand of Darkness, but I'm going to as soon as I finish this update! I don't want that reading to influence what I leave in or take out of this original series.

Paradigm. What is entailed in this one word that IS my world? A paradigm is how someone looks at something. It describes how the myriad layers of a person's life color their view of a thing they want to perceive. "Through rose-colored glasses" describes a view of someone who sees things in the best light. Their entire world-view is colored "rose" and they often find the best of any situation.

Think back to "The Wizard of Oz" and your exposure to that world. It was a bright, colorful, lively, and dangerous world Dorothy found herself transported into. She faced many dangers on her quest to find her way home. As they entered the Emerald City, she and her companions were told they must don the green tinted glasses to protect themselves from the dazzle of this fabled city of wonders. From then on, everything was emerald.

The city was a wonder, but what happens when you peek behind the curtain?

Paradigm Lost.

Our culture sees things through a prism that has been built over hundreds of years; through countless revolutions and exodus events; from the blood, sweat, and toil of untold generations. One can't simply lift those blinders and suddenly SEE clearly. But, what if a society marching along a deep rut leading over a cliff could be forced to see something from a new light? Could there ever be a change in paradigm? Could a tiny sliver of fresh light find its way through a crack in the lens?

That crack isn't going to happen from some little, suggestive, whining voice saying we gotta do better. That crack will only happen when someone is bold enough to say this shite sucks! When a seed is planted in some few people who then grow up to maturity with the thought of something different from how it's always been. That's when a work mattered. How many people who hold that seed within will be necessary to begin to jolt the human march out of a rut and onto a fresh path?

Want to find out? Read this trilogy with a mind toward close examination of the points where it offends you; the areas where it reinforces you; with a mind open enough to change so that you don't immediately discard this strange new culture. Then let that seed settle into fertile ground.

Paradigm Lost.

Chapter One
Something Awry

"I am too damaged by the extensive programming of dis-belief brought on by the church and its teachings. I can't do the things that I know mankind can and should be able to do, simply because they took my belief away. I don't believe strongly enough."

Justin Earl Knight, Founder of the Elk Creek Tribe

JAMARI, DRESSED IN the finest shaman attire he had with him for the expedition, looked down on the still body of his lover. We had already folded Shane into position to be interred under the chosen tree. His icy blue eyes were closed forever.

Suppressing his grief, Jamari the human brought forth the Jamari Shaman-self and looked up into the sky through the overhanging limbs of alders, maples, and firs. Jamari Shaman lifted the handful of salmon fillets, their orange-red meat dangling to either side of his upheld arm. "Use this meat for sustenance on your journey to your next self," he said. "May that next iteration on the great wheel be more forgiving than this one. Goodbye, my friend. Goodbye, my lieutenant. Goodbye, my bright beacon of hope."

And goodbye my husband, his deeply buried self cried out silently. Goodbye my lover.

He relaxed the uplifted arm to settle the offering into Shane's arms when a shadow darkened the shaft of sun, which pierced the looming branches. Then he tensed as Eagle descended, gliding between limbs, trees, and bushes to hover over his hand.

Eagle turned his will onto Jamari, and Jamari fell into the great eye which focused on him. He then sensed the brightness of his "self-spirit" called forth and that self-spirit, thralled into the summons, emerged to greet Eagle.

Then Jamari felt a sundering as the recently fragile connection of soul-essence to physical form snapped ... and he felt himself taken in. Taken in and away as Eagle ascended through the overhanging trees, carrying Jamari-spirit and leaving Jamari-vessel gaping emptily up at his receding self.

JAMARI AWOKE IN A SWEATING, thrashing panic. He lunged to the side of the bed, seeking the night's bed-mate and found no one. Then he rolled back to the other side, seeking there. There was no one there either and his panic hurled him out of the bed amid a tangle of blankets where the cold stone floor woke him completely. He recalled himself to his own room where his friends had been leaving him alone at night so they could sleep. His nightmares had become a constant factor. They accepted the bruisings his thrashing administered as he awakened, but they couldn't stop them. So, he slept alone. And woke and cried, alone.

He banished the sadness that engulfed him. Jamari forced that part of himself down into the subconscious once again. He shivered on the floor, fighting off tears before crawling once more into his lonely bed to finish out the long night.

They had hustled him home to Elk Creek Hall and to the young men's hearth with Shane's body fresh in the grave. The streamside longhouse they built to keep Christian safe during his recovery from his wound still had sap seeping from the rough-hewn planks, and the boughs of thatching were still green when Jamari they forced Jamari to say his last goodbye to his lover.

He had no say in the matter; he had, in fact, tried to sleep out his life right there in the soil of Shane's tree. They hadn't allowed it, and he wondered why he didn't care as much as he thought he should. His lover, his declared life partner, had died in a short and bloody conflict with a rogue band of Outsiders, and now Jamari skulked around the halls in his underground home, avoiding nearly all contact with anyone outside of his immediate friends and hearth mates.

The Elk Creek Tribe were his people. Other than some short travels and his participation in the recent summer expedition down to the coast, Jamari had spent his entire life in this one community. He loved his people with all he had in him.

He simply couldn't accept the adulation his fellow tribesmen seemed to give him, though. Jamari had nothing to do with Eagle having descended onto that grave scene. It wasn't Jamari who had called in that Spirit. But, oh boy, did it impact him!

Simultaneously, he shuddered with both awe and fear when he remembered Eagle's weight settling onto his uplifted arm to take the offering of salmon flesh Jamari had meant for Shane's ritual travel ration to the great beyond. Still, he had felt something enter him through Eagle's steely gaze and, most of all, felt as if something, some very important piece of *him*, had left with Eagle when He had withdrawn His gaze. He felt bereft, as if some very important part of *him* had soared off into the azure heights through the boles of the maturing firs. Oh yes, he still felt that gaze!

Jamari felt like a charlatan when they called him Jamari Shaman. He had not felt the Spirit within him since that fateful day three weeks ago. Even the most intense of meditation sessions were simply quiet interludes, with only his own thoughts rattling around in his head. There was no reaching out to follow the flight of a hawk. No sensing of his mates. No calling to the higher power.

He was a charlatan. Pure and simple.

His rooms in the back portions of the underground fort of Elk Creek Hall were both a welcome and a rebuke. Here it was where Shane had taught him the intricacies of the Night Studies. Here was where he had first felt the deepest stirrings of love and forbidden attachment to his mentor. He often imagined the bed coverings still held Shane's musky scent. The old elk hide was getting ragged as it lost hair, but Jamari couldn't let it go. Wandering into the bathroom they had shared so often in slithery shower time; he saw himself in the mirror.

Jamari was no longer the slim stripling who had first moved into this set of rooms. His body had muscled up significantly from the summer expedition. Daily rowing, lifting, and salt processing built a physique, he supposed. His mop of light blond hair had darkened, looking more like it would go all brown soon and his blue eyes were under-shadowed by a darkness no amount of sleep could seem to dispel. He still had the prominent brows, darker than seemed likely for his level of blond, and the long lashes that seemed to attract more than a fair amount of amorous attention. The chiseled abdominal muscles from the daily exertion were receding and becoming simply a fit and trim belly.

He looked past his reflection to the double shower he had shared so intimately with his blond-haired and blue-eyed lover and considered a cleansing, just one more attempt to dispel the gloom, but decided he'd go seek Haloki instead.

Haloki, his onetime trainee, did not currently have any assigned role as mentor since, finally, the Hall had more potential Night Studies mentors than they had trainees. Hopefully, Haloki would spend some time helping him dispel the empty longing that seemed so much a part of Jamari these days of his twentieth year of life.

THREE MORE DAYS PASSED, and Jamari was still an aimless mess. Jahangir was still mopping up the problems down at Tom Folley, where all the trouble had been with the Outsiders. Christian, his onetime Night Studies student and the second of three young men involved in that skirmish, was recovering from the arrow wound to the back of his left shoulder. Word was he would regain some use of it, but he might never draw a bow again.

Jamari heard gossip in the dining lounge that the final stand-off had been anti-climactic. Jahangir had surrounded the hovels of the rogue settlement high on the switchback ridges above Tom Folley Creek. When the erstwhile leader of the group had defied the order to stand down, running in a pointless charge towards the militia who surrounded his village, only one hapless soul had followed his lead. Jahangir's soldiers shot and killed both. The rest of the villagers capitulated.

According to the rumor, Jahangir was proposing to settle the group into Hancock Valley as a new tribal holding. To Jamari, it seemed absurd. He hoped ... well; he didn't know what he hoped, really. Could he hope for such a clean ending to the strife that had ended with only one tribal death? Even if it was his lover, could he wish for the destruction of all the enemy villagers? But he wasn't sure he could approve of having them as a part of the Tribe either. Or to give the outsiders the gentle and beautiful valley at the eastern foot of Hancock Mountain.

In these aimless days of wandering, he wondered about his relations with his fellow young men. He had purposefully turned down an assignment to be a mentor for the current batch of newcomers, yet he still had the opportunity and need to share eros with his hearth mates.

During his recent session with Haloki, he remembered being almost brutish in his single-purpose drive to finish, driving mercilessly on during the afternoon tryst. Haloki had taken it, panting under him, his hands clenched into fists at his sides as Jamari finally finished. When he had offered a quick apology for his roughness, he had realized he couldn't seem to really care as much as he knew he should have.

He was sensing something was wrong in himself, but the only thing he could attribute it to was the loss of Shane. He told himself he would get over it, eventually. That this was his first time experiencing the loss of a loved one, and as bad as it was, he had no way of knowing what he was going through was something very different and far more horrible than just emotional loss.

Jamari was dying inside. His fitness level and physical state were at the peak of youth, but the inner *self* he had worked so long to develop was dying. He no longer felt the pull of the Numinous during his daily meditations with the inner spirit.

Looking for a new place to wander, Jamari walked up the stream and explored the halls deep within Milltown Hall, the other main building of Milltown Village. In a near-deserted labyrinth several levels down from the busier areas, he walked in endless pacing, head down, not paying attention to turns or dead-ends. He rounded a dark corner and bumped into another wandering soul.

"Sorry," he heard from a voice from a year ago. "I wasn't looking where I was going and have seen no one down here in ages." He hadn't thought of Lynn in months. They had transferred him abruptly almost a year ago from his post as a mentor to Jamari's group of young men trainees. Though they still lived in the same village, the two simply hadn't crossed paths much since the unexpected transfer.

Now, as he saw Lynn in the subterranean passages, his face dimly lit by the energy saving setting of the underground hallways, he realized something new. Even though he didn't sense his internal energies being drawn away and into Lynn as he had in the past, neither did he sense the emanation of soul. Lynn was simply a neutral now. Jamari noted his attractiveness now that the undertone of spiritual revulsion was absent.

Lynn was a blond. Not a blond in the normal sense, like Jamari was. Or Shane had been, with yellowish hair. Lynn had light brown hair, too light to call brown, too dark to be true blond. Was there even a name for this color? Lynn also had blue eyes and longer-than-normal eyelashes framing them, and he was taller than Jamari at six feet.

Jamari wondered what Lynn might be like in eros. After all, the repulsion Lynn had once emanated had deterred him before. He looked at Lynn with the eyes of one lonely man to another.

Lynn seemed cautious. "Jamari, how are you?" he asked. "It surprised me to hear about Shane being killed by Outsiders."

"I guess I'm doing okay," Jamari answered, wondering at the word "surprised" instead of "sorry." He saw Lynn's eyes tracing a path down his body. And he noticed when that gaze came to rest where his breech clout loosely held his manhood. Jamari returned the roving glance and appreciated the fold of Lynn's indoor trousers. He saw a shift in shadows as the wrinkles realigned from a swelling presence.

"I'm still trying to get over Shane's loss," he told Lynn. "I should be down at the young men's hall now. But I was avoiding it because of the memories." He paused as the shadows and highlights shifted into a full rise. "I treasure the memories he and I built together in my rooms there," he said, acting as if the visual communication hadn't happened. "But sometimes, I just can't get past the feeling he's still there and will step out of the shower anytime to ask what we're doing for the evening."

"I'm sorry," Lynn said, reaching out a tentative hand.

How have I made him so cautious? Jamari wondered. But then he remembered the last time they had been alone together. Lynn had almost forced himself on Jamari, and Jamari had been on the verge of physically throwing Lynn out of his room when Carson had come in and interrupted the tableau. Deciding to forgive him, Jamari took a cautious step closer and felt Lynn's warm hand settle onto his shoulder.

"My rooms are near here, if you'd like to stop by," Lynn said as he rubbed Jamari's shoulder with his hand.

"I guess I could," Jamari answered. "It's not like I've got anything to do. Or anywhere to go right now."

When they reached Lynn's rooms, they shocked Jamari. His own set of rooms in the young men's hall were much more expansive and open. Lynn's place comprised a single room which served as both bedroom and living room, with a small shower and bathroom in a side alcove. Jamari and all his hearth mates had assumed Lynn's transfer up to Milltown Hall had meant his promotion to full citizenship. This tiny little hovel, not even good enough for a troglodyte, didn't match up with those assumptions at all.

There would be no room for a shared shower in this space. Lynn reached out to hold him in his arms, letting their combined bodies come into intimate contact. Jamari let all the suppositions and wild thinking fade and let his body experience the moment.

He felt Lynn's desire against his belly and his own lifted in response. Lynn untied the laces at the neck of Jamari's cloth jerkin and lifted his arms to pull it over his head and off, discarding the garment onto the floor.

"It's kind of weird," Lynn said after a bit. "I usually feel this 'presence' from you. It's what really made you irresistible to me in the first place, yet I don't feel it now."

"Do you want to stop," Jamari asked. "We don't have to share eros together. It may have seemed like a good idea when we first saw each other out in the halls, but we aren't obliged to follow through now we're in your room."

"No," Lynn answered as he wrapped Jamari in his longer arms, "I want to share eros with you. I don't think you realize how very attractive you are. There's not a guy in the village who would turn down the chance to share eros with you!"

Jamari felt the truth of Lynn's desire as Lynn pulled him close and gently turned him away, caressing his backside as he moved close. Jamari felt the warmth through Lynn's lounge pants and felt Lynn's hand reach around and into his breechclout. He gave in to the moment and shifted himself back to meet the physical touch, which seemed more than anything else to put Shane's memories at bay. When Jamari felt Lynn's lips on the base of his neck, he reached down and unfastened his belt. His breech and the belt thumped onto the stone floor and he stopped thinking about anything.

Well into their trysting, Jamari realized Lynn was not making love with him. Instead, he was punishing him. The ferocity of his driving, pounding action did not contribute to shared joy. It was an assault. It seemed as if the worse Jamari felt, the closer he was to crying out in pain, the greater Lynn's pleasure.

Lynn was a soul stealer, Jamari realized. This was an exercise in endurance: holding himself still so those deep, driving thrusts wouldn't do him any more damage than necessary; concentrating on keeping his strained muscles relaxed so he wouldn't seize up.

In suffering through it himself, Jamari realized what he had been putting Carson, Haloki, Elan, and the others through in his own recent eros sessions. Tears were falling from his eyes and he had his own hands clenched into fists at his side before Lynn finished pounding him into submission.

The tears weren't from the pain of Lynn's rough penetration nearly so much as the from realization of the pain he had caused others.

"Is that how you always *share* eros?" Jamari asked as he dressed himself.

"Usually, no," Lynn answered. "It's just I really felt nothing until I started really pushing. It was only then that you started sharing your essence with me."

This confirmed Jamari's worst suspicion. Lynn was a soul-eater.

Was there a name for someone who thrived on consuming the essence of others? Was it possible Lynn had never felt the movement of the Great Spirit in his life?

This was something beyond even a zombie, which the tribe recognized as a near-human entity but lacking a soul. This thing actually sucked the life essence from its fellow humans!

"What do you do during meditation time?" Jamari asked impulsively, shocked he had spoken aloud.

"I don't know," Lynn answered lazily. He still hovered possessively near Jamari. "Isn't it, really, just time to do nothing? I mean, there's really nothing listening if we meditate, is there? I mostly just think about the things I've done; the things I hope to do. Sometimes, I just masturbate thinking about someone I've been with or someone I want to be with. Like you. I've fantasized about you a lot." Lynn reached his hand over toward Jamari, apparently intending to rest his palm on Jamari's face.

Knowing Lynn fantasized about him at such an intimate moment was too much. He was close enough to dressed, he decided suddenly. He shrugged away from Lynn's touch and picked up his shirt. Lynn's hand briefly rested on Jamari's shoulder as he walked out the door.

"Don't," he told Lynn. "Never think you'll be with me again!"

The look on Lynn's face astonished Jamari to a new level. The anger Jamari felt fed him. Lynn's face was shining in apparent bliss. Jamari retreated then, racing down the hall. Away from Lynn and his hunger.

Away, perhaps, from the part of himself that told him he deserved it. And most important, away from the self that seemed to finally have found him again after a long absence. He could feel a tendril of his spirit again and was deeply ashamed.

He pulled his tunic over his head while storming down the halls toward escape.

In his twisting, jolting run, donning his pull-over shirt, Jamari felt a sudden, stabbing pain in his lower left ribs. It was exactly where Cougar had scathed him with her back claws the year before.

He came to a stop and puzzled over the spot with questing fingers. There he found a sharp point of pain, but no specific bump or protrusion. He resumed his walk down the hall at a more sedate pace, lacing the front of his tunic as he walked. He still fumed from everything he had learned about Lynn. And about himself as well.

Chapter Two

Jamari's long spirit walk

Peter, the Second Knight Shaman, and Terry, his successor and current, Third Knight Shaman, shared tea in the Knight Shaman's quarters in Milltown Hall. They had separate cushioned chairs which Terry had placed to look out the view window into the waters of Lake Yoncalla.

Each gazed absently out the window as they began their wake-up routine. Neither would have objected to see a trout or catfish swim by. Terry often scoffed that the fish had somehow reversed roles, checking on their kept-humans in the terrarium, seeing that their air-breathing captives were still alive.

The two men wore homespun night pants and grey sweat shirts against the chill of the concrete edifice they called home. The bed over in the room's nook showed rumpling from the night's occupants. Being the first week of October, it was at least a month until the salmon would be returning, so they certainly weren't expecting those, but it would be interesting to see a returning steelhead passing by on the long route back down Elk Creek to the ocean.

"I'm glad Jamari suggested we try to save some of the salmon brood stock from last year," Terry mentioned, sipping his morning tea. "His observation and suggestion showed a great deal of personal insight, strength. And empathy with our world. His determination in following up was the driving force which had the council set up the hatch box systems again."

"It was even more important the council agreed to it, even though they never believed it was a real problem," Peter answered. "Nearly all the returning fish showed injuries. And the netting operations the Outsiders had set up had severely damaged what few remained. They were grateful they had made the motions to make Jamari feel appreciated and valued."

Terry looked away from the dancing rainbows ringing the sun-dazzled window and looked Peter in the eye. Terry was a youngish man given the power and status he held within the tribal hierarchy as Knight Shaman. This was a position created shortly after the Founder's death, intended to be the primary guardian of the spiritual essence Founder Knight had set as a tribal goal. Besides Knight Shaman, he also had earned the position as chief judge of the tribal court system.

At thirty-eight, he looked a young thirty, with a fit body which was, at five foot nine, just under the tribal average. He had a long black braid which, while hanging unheralded now, he fully adorned with awards and mementos of a life's achievements for ceremonial events. He possessed dark, dark eyes and a firm chin and nose that highlighted his near-full Native American genetics. "Do you think Jamari would sense the same thing today?" he asked. "Do you think he would go to the effort of mentioning it; following up on it; pushing for it, if he saw the same condition today?"

"Do you suspect something?" Peter asked as a long-nagging suspicion blossomed in his own mind. Peter's secondary tribal role was as a licensed physician with a doctorate from the Oregon Health Sciences University up in Portland.

Peter had been one of the first students to attend after they cobbled it back together from the ruins of the Fall. He was well into his sixties, the original color of his gray hair undetectable. He wore the dignified mass bundled into a ponytail instead of the braid the warrior types used.

Being a medical student from his very first days out of the young men's hearth, back when the Tribe was still occupying just the Milltown Village and casino areas, he had never undergone the militia training that was now mandatory for every tribal member. Peter had brown eyes, dark and flashing, and he carried a facial structure reminiscent of a Pacific Islander. His once muscular physique was fading into the sinewy build of an older man.

"How can I not?" Terry answered. "I was out of town for the first couple of weeks after Jamari came back and didn't get to see all his behavioral changes, but what I've seen in the last week is enough to be alarming. Did you know Jamari had a tryst with Lynn yesterday?"

"That seems ... very abnormal," Peter reflected. "We all recognize Lynn as one of the unawakened, most likely never-to-be-awakened. No one with the level of empathy of a shaman could ever feel a need to engage in eros with such a person."

"Yes, it seems to be a telling point, doesn't it?" Terry offered. "How could Jamari Shaman bring himself to have sexual relations with a soulless one?" Terry looked deeply into his old mentor's eyes.

"Unless something has happened, and he is no longer Jamari Shaman, but just Jamari," he said pointedly.

Peter's eyes widened as he lifted his head sharply and turned away from the window to look directly at Terry. "What could have caused such a thing?"

"You were my teacher. I was hoping you would have some thoughts," the Knight Shaman answered.

Both paused and sipped their tea, taking in the aromatic smell of freshly harvested mint. They watched the morning sunlight playing beams of rainbow arcs through the water and over the bottom of the sill and onto the slate flooring.

"You took what I could teach and built it far beyond anything I had ever done or suspected could be done," Peter finally answered. "As I took the things Rodney taught me and built upon them far beyond anything Rodney suspected could be done." Both watched a pair of brood trout glide majestically across the expanse of the glass.

"There is so much of shamanism which has been lost to the ages," he continued. "Rodney, once he had taught me up to the level he had direct knowledge of, often lamented the fact the old ones were so reticent to share the secrets of their spiritual practices."

"Maybe not so much reticent as responsive to the purges Christianity started every time the initial settlers saw evidence of heresy," Terry answered.

"Regardless, we're in a bind right now," Peter said. "I agree there's something ... not right ... with Jamari. I had hoped it was simple grief over Shane's loss, but my suspicion has been building that it was much more. Your questions now make it almost a certainty.

"He slept with Lynn!"

"A hylic!" Terry filled in.

Both watched as a trio of smaller trout wandered across the old acrylic glass viewing area, their speckled bodies undulating in effortless waves. When the aquamarine waters were clear once again, Terry looked over at his old mentor. "Can we try to trace back to when he seemed normal and maybe find some clue what happened? Then we may have some idea how to restore him to himself."

"I think you've said more than you may realize," Peter replied with sudden animation. "We know he could spirit walk while also carrying on with his more mundane activities. What if his spirit-self got caught up somewhere and lost contact with his physical self?"

As the Knight Shaman, Terry was stunned at this possibility. "It would be a whole new level of risk and danger to our spiritual practices if it were even possible," he said. "But what we're seeing right now could be evidence of that phenomenon.

"It's becoming clearer now, as well. I've noted an almost-emptiness when I've been around him lately. And I'm ashamed it hasn't been enough time. I've been avoiding him: not because I disapprove of anything he's done, but just to give him time to grieve."

"Let's hope it's not an irreversible mistake," Peter said gravely. "I think I know where to look, though. Let me describe to you again what happened at Shane's death and internment. The incident with Eagle may well be the place and time where this whole mess started."

"I've heard the story in bits and pieces," Terry reflected, "but not all in one cohesive telling."

"We were walking up Elk Creek," Peter said, "taking the route which loops the long way around the hill at the old tunnel. Jamari and Eric were talking about using the tangled pile of old river-washed logs at the big bend in the river to build a longhouse. We heard a gunshot, followed shortly by another.

"All of us focused on getting Jamari to a safe place, and he kept resisting. He wanted us to sprint up ahead to help with whatever was going on. The sergeant got him into the stack of logs with Eric and me. But only by threatening physical force. It pissed Jamari off being treated like a youngling.

"We had no sooner gotten into an opening in the tangle of logs when a runner brought us news that hidden archers had hit both Christian and Shane with arrows. And Shane had killed both of them.

"As soon as Jamari heard the news, he sent forth his spirit-self and proclaimed Shane was dead, and Christian gravely injured.

"Then he did something I still don't quite believe. I saw the strength of his 'sending' as he projected his will out. He shouted: 'Watch out, there are more coming,' and then fell into a faint. I can't imagine the strength of will which must have been necessary to project himself: to propel his very *self* out to warn the others. It had to have been extremely taxing. With his spirit still questing out, to Zach Shaman as it turned out, he fainted." Peter paused in telling the story, reflecting, and remembering the details.

"In any case," he continued, "when Jamari recovered, he seemed pretty much intact. I could sense his spirit once again inside of his body. He seemed sad, but, at the same time, proud he had gotten a warning out in time."

Peter sipped his tea again, finding the cup empty. "I could use a refill," he said. "How about you?"

"Yes, I think a warm up would be good," Terry said, standing to take the cup from Peter. He turned to the back of the room, away from the view window, and set up two metal tea strainers with the freshly chopped lemon-mint leaves and poured hot water over them for steeping. "Is there still some honey in the bowl there?" he asked Peter as he dipped the strainers to stir the beverage.

Peter lifted the lid on the glazed clay dish, looking inside and lifting the wooden honey-spoon to trail a golden tendril of syrupy sweetness. "Yes, there's plenty," he answered.

Terry brought the still-steaming cups back and handed one to Peter as he settled himself into his chair.

"So, I think the self-projection isn't when he got himself lost," Peter continued, "but could it have weakened his attachment to his body? Could the effort have caused him to be only loosely connected, like a rope which has been used beyond its capacity, many of the small fibers of connection having been frayed, so the next time it's used, it fails?"

The question seemed rhetorical to Terry, so he simply stirred his tea as he watched for more fish in the window.

"We got through the first night," Peter continued after getting his own tea mixed and sweetened to taste and testing it for warmth, "taking care of Christian, setting up a semi-permanent camp. I knew he couldn't survive any movement, much less a wilderness trek, in his condition. It was a close call, too. We almost didn't save him at all. I don't know how many times I thought I had lost him. When I couldn't sense his spirit inside at all. Jamari and Zach both helped to keep his spirit inside as I opened the wound for cleaning and then stitched him back together. I know the more scientific doctors preach that only purely physical actions truly make up healing, but Christian would have died in the night if it weren't for the psychic support the three of us brought into play.

"Anyway, the next day, we set about getting ready for Shane's burial. I convinced Jamari he would have to be Jamari Shaman and not Jamari-the-man for the ceremony, and doing so would be the best way to honor his love and commitment for Shane; would ensure he got a proper sendoff.

"I didn't even think about whether his spirit-self could have become unanchored. But I still would have had him perform the ritual if I had thought of it as a possibility. I would have reasoned that the ceremony, the spiritual investment, would have restored him back to himself. Here's where I think it happened." Peter looked over at Terry to make sure he had his full attention.

"Jamari added an extra step into the ritual. I agreed, thinking it would be a restoration of some of the older ways. He wanted to make an offering of food to the spirits, to have Shane comforted by including spiritual sustenance as he departed this world.

"When he held up the offering of salmon strips, Eagle took the offering Himself. The Great Spirit answered a summons in physical manifestation.

"Here is what I saw: Jamari looked deep into Eagle's eyes as Eagle accepted the offering. His arm settled, what I thought was from the weight of Eagle landing unexpectedly on his outstretched hand. What if it wasn't from the weight? What if what actually happened was his spirit-self had gone into Eagle and flew off with Him?"

"It's an amazing event," Terry said. "I think you may be right about *when* it happened. The question is, what can we do about it now? Is it even possible to restore a travelling soul to a still-living body? How do we even find his soul to restore it?"

"I think we rely on Jamari to find it," Peter answered. "Even if there isn't as much 'soul' living in him as there once was, I still see the spark of self buried deep down inside. He'll need to use that spark as an anchor to hold himself in place while he searches."

Chapter Three

Dream Walker

J amari listened when Terry and Peter presented their thoughts to him in the Knight Shaman's common room. It embarrassed him to learn Lynn had bragged about his conquest. And the elders and teachers he respected most were witness to his shame.

"I can feel my spirit slowly returning," he told them. "It's much too slow, though, and I don't know if it would ever fully return by just waiting for things to get better. I can 'feel' again. What it seems is that I'm growing a new spirit within to fill the emptiness of my original soul-spirit. I feel the shame of your knowing of my interaction with Lynn. I feel the pain of having put my hearth mates through physical misery similar to what Lynn visited on me." He paused for a moment of reflection, watching the placid blue-green waters of the lake through the view window in this outer chamber.

There was no rainbow dancing its game of tag over the floor today since the sun hid behind a wall of cloud, but he always anticipated seeing the fish swim by. "I still can't connect to the Other World during my meditations," he finally admitted. "I never realized just how lonely it would feel being limited to only my own thoughts as they bounce around, echoing in my head with no answering sensation; to not have that sense of connection with the piece of God which lived in me as, or with, my spirit." He looked at the two senior shamans. "I agree something must be done. I have no wish to continue as a near-soulless one."

The next afternoon, the shaman contingent present at Milltown Village gathered in the Knight Shaman's room. There, working with

Jamari, they all decided that if they were going to bring him back to himself, location would be paramount. It would need to be a spot where Jamari felt more in-touch with his inner self, more open to the spirit world. Jamari suggested they make the trek up to his spirit's place in the hills above the next morning. There, they hoped Jamari could enter his meditative trance state and seek his missing self.

"Let's take a tent," Peter suggested. "We don't know how long Jamari will need before he finds what he seeks. He'll likely be cold if it passes into evening or night."

"Good idea," the Knight Shaman answered. "We'll bring a big one so we can all fit in during the awakening."

Jamari had had little time with Zach since the expedition had returned. They had assigned him to the courthouse as a judicial assistant, and Jamari had been moping in Milltown Village. Zach, as a practicing shaman now, was to be a part of the ritual. He and Zach had shared some very special times during the coastal expedition. Both amorous and as partners learning the arts of shamanism together under Peter Shaman's tutelage.

The remembered interactions, the interest which twitched his manhood, were at least a beginning, he thought to himself. He still acknowledged all those connections should have meant more to him than just the simple physical aspect.

The next morning, a warm one for late October, they all gathered their packs and set off. Jamari led the way, pointing out where to duck under brambles, remembering where they needed to shift away from the game trail to get past the thickest of the forest growth.

When they reached the meadow, he paused and looked around in memory. Looking at a clump of brownish grass drying from the summer drought, he recognized the exact spot where he had sat to begin his meditations less than a year ago. Looking up, he saw where Hawk had come over the ridge hunting. "Let's set up here," he suggested. "This is the exact place where I was sitting when Cougar came to me."

He felt a shiver of anticipatory dread at the memory, simultaneous with an awakening spiritual surge he hadn't felt since Shane's death. He still wondered if all he needed was more time to get over his loss. The building fear the slow return would not complete the process spurred him to continue their plan.

"It's important you firmly direct your dream state," Terry told him as they set out blankets prior to pitching the tent. "Even more so than for a normal shaman quest. There is only a fragment of 'you' living in-house, and you don't want to wander around letting your attention be caught in random events. Let the hawk go by. Let the bobcat run alone. Guide your intent to meet your spirit. It will be much like when you were first seeking others you knew. Like the time you sought Shane on the river while you were over the mountain. You knew vaguely where he was." Terry paused here, looking closely at his protégé. "My fear, though, is you won't know exactly where to look in this case. Just put out sensing feelers and seek for your 'self'."

"Will you need a challenge to enter the dream state?" Peter asked.

"Let's hold off until I try entering the spirit realm first," Jamari answered.

"You have a choice, you know, of who awakens you and brings you back," Terry said.

Jamari, recognizing Terry's concern in his disjointed comments, stood and embraced the Knight Shaman. "Yes, I know. I think it is best if it is Zach, though. I may need your more advanced experience if something still doesn't seem right as I'm returning. You couldn't provide the same level of insight and help if it were you awakening me."

Terry looked at Peter over Jamari's shoulder, obviously wondering if he should mention Peter as an option as well. Peter returned the look, crossing his hands in front of his abdomen and then splitting them apart in a throwing away gesture, obviously communicating that Terry should leave it alone.

"We all care about you and how you come through this, you know," Terry continued as he held Jamari in his arms.

Jamari felt the warmth of his lean and muscled body through the jerkin. He held Terry closer to him before letting go.

Jamari turned to see a leather cover settled onto the browning grass for him, and he sat cross-legged on it. He looked around the hilltop meadow as he prepared himself for entering a directed-dream state.

The others settled in a square, with himself occupying the north-most corner, Zach at his left and making the eastern corner, Peter opposite and making the south corner and Terry on his right making the western corner of their square. He looked up at the sky and realized what was missing. "We should do the clearing ceremony," he said. "Do we have sage and sweetgrass with us?"

"Yes," Peter answered. "I had thought of it, but I wanted to see if you remembered first." He dug into his carry bag and pulled out sage, sweetgrass, bowl, and a striker. They often considered strikers a "cheat," Jamari thought. Instead of using skill and élan in striking steel against flint, this device had a piece of flint mounted on one end of a bent spring arm and a roughened steel surface on the other side. It formed a sideways "V" from where it was bent.

Jamari watched as Peter set out some tinder in his bowl and then clenched his fist around the two sides, bringing the flint sliding rapidly along the steel releasing a shower of sparks. He had the dry tinder aflame in short order, and he lit a slow taper with the quick-burning fuel before it flared out. He then used the burning taper to ignite the sage for the Smoke Bowl Blessing.

Peter smudged the burning sage, leaving the bundle smoking more than burning. He surrounded himself with smoke. Then he also smudged the circle of participants. When he had cleansed the circle, he then blessed above, below, and the four directions. He then raised the smoking herb up to the heavens. "With this smoke, we banish all evil from this place. We banish negative energy from our endeavor."

He used a feather fan in his other hand to direct the negative energy away and then crushed the smoking sage out in his bowl before lighting the sweetgrass. He smudged the sweetgrass bundle, leaving a smoking remnant, and then bathed himself in the cleansing smoke as he had done with the sage.

"With sweetgrass, we bless this space and welcome positive and supportive energy," Peter intoned, and then he used the feather fan once again to sweep the smoke all around the circle, wreathing fully over and around each participant before finally concentrating the remaining smoke on and around Jamari. "Bless this endeavor. Bless Jamari, that he may find himself in the otherworld, that he may make himself whole again," he finished.

Jamari felt ready for meditation trance, and as Peter smudged out the sweetgrass, he closed his eyes and sought the spirit realm. It took intense effort, far beyond what he was used to exerting, but he could finally feel the separate realms of spirit and flesh. Once in the spirit realm, he looked about through spirit-eyes and saw sparks of life all around him, exactly as Terry had warned, including a small rodent at the far edge and a doe and fawn pair on the opposite side. He turned from those distractions. Because the Knight Shaman suspected the problem originated from Shane's interment ceremony, he sought that memory.

In an instant, he was there again. As difficult as it had been to establish trance over the past few weeks, this voyage was becoming alarmingly easy, as if some greater force was compelling him along a path. He watched himself as if from a height as his past self once again raised a handful of cut salmon strips up to the sky to seek the spirit's blessing for Shane's internment. Only now he looked down from on high, but dropping at an alarming rate, seeing his own upturned face, yet feeling the dance of wind past wing and feather.

He was seeing the scene as if he were Eagle.

Once again, Jamari heard the shrill "kree" as Eagle descended onto his arm to take the offering. Only now it was his own hunger slaked in the dripping morsels of flesh. Once again, he looked into Eagle's great eye: greater now in this vision even than it had been when he lived it. This time, though, he was also looking back, peering deep into the soul behind his own startling blue eyes, sensing the brightness of "self" emerging to greet Eagle ... and he felt himself taken in. Taken in and away as Eagle ascended through the overhanging trees.

Jamari felt a bolt of energy jet away from the clearing, darting away to the north and east even faster than Eagle could go. It disappeared before he could understand what it was. He thought he felt Shane for a quick instant, and then the spirit was gone. Was this how Shane's spirit had left the Dream World?

He was with Eagle now, soaring on sweeping wings, dancing through bole and shadow and limb, watching his memory-self continue the ceremony through the openings in the trees until Eagle carried him over a ridge and away.

A long journey happened in an instant, and he was passing over Yoncalla and then descending onto a glade near his home of Milltown Village. He recognized the point where the stream bent around the shoulder of the mountain. The bend marked where Eagle had carried him up to the heights. He felt a sudden lurch of descent as Eagle carried him down into a copse of firs that held one lone oak, young and small, fighting to reach up to the light, which only haphazardly broke through the upper branches.

He remembered just a few snippets after finding himself with the tree, chiefly Eagle descending onto the upper limb of the young oak tree that was largely overwhelmed by the surrounding firs. But this oak had life pulsing through it in glowing green bursts, and Jamari felt the life force within embrace and envelop him as Eagle set him into those branches. And then more fragments.

He felt himself called back into his mundane world and his spirit self fought the summons. After a struggle, Jamari returned, but with only disjointed memories of his time in the spirit world: the Founder as a man-tree, the spirit of the glade; his essence, which had been a looming light of presence in the spirit world, much stronger and more powerful than the individual components of the combined spirit there. He perceived a visible thread binding the Founder-Spirit to the glade.

Eagle, as an avatar of the Great Spirit, God, Jehovah, outshone the pulsing glow that was the Founder. And himself. The greatest single revelation of all: him being chosen as a companion of the Spirits. Somehow, he *was* Forest, in all its pieces, great and small, somehow encompassing all of it. And yet, he was still just Jamari, shaman of the Elk Creek Tribe. He buried himself in Zach as he awakened, crying out the loss. Knowing even as he placed his seed deep into his lover that this journey was but the beginning of a much longer path.

What had seemed to be but an instant of passage to Jamari turned out to have lasted out the day. It was fully dark, and they had raised the tent around him as he had sojourned in the upper world.

Between the four of them, they captured some of the essence of his spirit walk as Jamari had been still communing with the glade even as they brought him, reluctantly, back into his own body. He had been voicing his thoughts as he had cried out his loss at being brought back to the mundane.

But Jamari was whole again. He could sense those around him, could sense the small animals outside the tent they all shared, and he could feel a distant welcome from the copse of firs that bounded this meadow. His tears were not only for the separation from the perfection that was the spirit world, but also for the harm he had done while his spirit had been wandering. He hoped his beloved companions in the young men's hall could understand and welcome him back into their fold.

Even as he mourned the loss of his connections to the God's Glade, he was whispering out his impressions and memories. It would be a long time before those halting sentences would be fully understood!

"It is slow lightning. Dancing from root to root. It is slow lightning, and the trees are listening."

"Eagle is in dancing flight. Looping over and through the branches of the oak, he is nipping with unseen claws. And the Founder is awakening!"

"The forest awakens as slow lightning runs through the roots. Only where the fungi are missing are there trees not awakening. All in the lightning realm are awake and answering the call. The animals are listening too!"

"Under the green blanket, the secret lies. Only listen and you will hear! The forest is talking!"

"We wondered what message Eagle, the messenger of God, carried. We were wrong to think so narrowly. I was and am the message!"

When the group of shamans returned from this endeavor, they shared the tale of Jamari's voyage with God with Chief Elk Creek and Chief Milltown. They all decided the story of this passage needed to be shared. Jamari Shaman was again a topic of choice in the Tribe's collective deliberations. Besides a Spirit Walker, he was now thought of as a God Walker. He was the only known human to have walked with God.

And returned.

Chapter Four

Acceptance

The Knight Shaman took Jamari into his own rooms for healing after they returned from their trip up the mountain. It took Jamari most of a week to get used to being whole again, to being apart from the Great Spirit again. To just being human again.

He woke often in the long nights, shaking from dreams that weren't nightmares but certainly weren't wholly "human" dreams either. He remembered more snippets of images, words, and emotions from his dream-walking sojourn. Terry was always there to hold and console him, to talk him through being human again, to teach him human need and satisfaction again.

One night, Jamari awoke quietly, just a simple awakening with no dreams or visions. Terry's arms were around him from behind, his warmth a comfort in the deep of the night. There was no internal calling of messages or demands. He was simply Jamari again.

There was an other-worldly glow to the room, which made him wonder about his connection to reality. It was a soft glow, bluish light gently dancing from a point along the wall he was facing. As he was trying to separate dream from reality, he worked to identify the glow, to place it in a realm he could comprehend. Gradually, his vision focused, and he realized he was seeing moonlight dancing through the water and beaming in shattered blue prisms onto the floor and sill of the underwater view window. Of all the many wondrous things he had beheld in the real and other worlds, this one moment in a quiet night impressed itself on him as one of the most magnificent.

The next morning over breakfast with the Knight Shaman, he opened the discussion about returning to his life in the real world and how he was contemplating joining his lovers and friends in the young men's hall down the river.

He thought most of Haloki, who still didn't have anyone he was mentoring. Jamari wondered if there was some guidance from the hearth leaders which left Haloki in hiatus the last few times there had been new young men being indoctrinated into the Night Studies. Or was it Haloki's choice? A part of his nature, knowing he wasn't comfortable being the active member of a relationship? A facet of his known but seldom-discussed attachment to Elan? They had assigned Elan, Haloki's declared life partner, out of town for the last few months. Elan would return sometime around the upcoming Fall celebrations.

Jamari left the comfort of the Knight Shaman's rooms after the healing week. "I'll return if I need the healing," he reassured Terry. "I need to be 'me' again."

Jamari returned to his own set of rooms down in Elk Creek Hall. He sought the company of his friends; rugby and wicket ball, and long, hot soaks in the tubs and showers to wash off the dirt and sweat of hard labor and play. He sought exuberance, which had been missing from his existence since his encounter with Eagle.

Since Shane's death.

Jamari was nervous as he walked the halls of his underground fort home. He hoped Haloki had forgiven him. He hoped to make up to him for the horrid way he had treated him during his dream days. Once he got there, he stood outside the door in uncertainty for a while.

What if Haloki spurned him? What if he didn't, but was fearful anyway? What if ...? He gave up all the "what ifs" and knocked on the simple wooden door. He waited, thinking to himself all the worry was for nothing. Haloki wasn't even in there. Then the door opened.

Haloki stood there in his lounge wear, a pair of loose hemp fiber pants roughly dyed in a greenish-gray tint, tied at a narrow waist, and a simple pull-over sweatshirt in gray. Haloki had the features of a Native American, but softened by some Polynesian mixed in. He was Jamari's height at five foot nine, slender yet wiry-muscled. He looked expectantly at Jamari as he stood in his doorway.

"I'm sorry to bother you," Jamari said. "I was hoping I could come in." He waited in painful anticipation, hoping against hope Haloki would invite him in. He had just about decided to leave when Haloki stepped aside and motioned him in.

When Jamari got inside, he turned to see Haloki shutting and locking the door. He still hadn't said a word. "I'm so sorry," Jamari said painfully. "I wasn't myself for a few weeks after Shane's death. I treated you poorly, and I don't deserve to be back in your life, but I hope for it, anyway."

Haloki simply motioned Jamari over to the couch. When Jamari went to settle there, Haloki finally spoke. "Not there, my friend. In the bedroom. We can talk there."

Tears started involuntarily in Jamari's eyes as he realized Haloki had indeed forgiven him already. He stumbled into the bedroom as instructed, navigating with tear-blurred eyes. When Haloki wrapped him in his arms, he couldn't hold it back anymore and broke into quiet but racking sobs.

"I'm so sorry," he kept saying as the sobs continued to break past his reluctance. "I'm so sorry."

It wasn't only how he had treated Haloki that had finally caught up to him. There was the shame of how he had treated his other friends during his dream-walking time as well. It was the memory of how Lynn had punished him for "withholding his essence" during their horrid tryst. It was the regret of leaving the Great Spirit behind when he had been called back.

It was fear that, as Jamari Shaman, he would have to make such a trip again, and he wasn't sure he'd be able to find his way back, despite the reassurances of his mentors.

He also cried for Shane.

Finally, he cried for Shane.

Haloki just held him until the sobs subsided. "I knew that already," he told Jamari. "We heard about your extended vacation from reality. It hurt me when you were so callous, but just like all the others, I assumed it was because of Shane's death. I would take roughness from you for as long as you needed. But yes, it hurt.

"It's behind us now, though. I know what happened, and I forgive you."

Jamari bent down to place his head into the lee between Haloki's head and shoulder, letting the weight of his regret pull his head into a closer embrace. "I don't know how I can deserve such great friends," he whispered.

The winter months sped by in a blur. Jamari still allotted the crucial two hours each morning for his sojourn into the inner world of the spirit. He achieved contact with his elusive inner spirit only rarely and he marveled that he once took such connection for granted.

He was starting to feel the voice of his inner-self again, even if he hadn't quite managed any of his previous skills. He still spent many an afternoon up in the Knight Shaman's rooms.

When the gray days began to recede and allow a rare sun-warmed day, he often made his way up into the woods for communing with the Great Spirit. Fear and anticipation warred inside him as he pushed beyond what most others had done once more. He feared he would find himself in the spirit world, that he would be caught up there again. And he anticipated he might once again feel the warm touch of God.

One sunny morning, Jamari made his way up the hill above Elk Creek Hall. It was winter falling and spring rising, yet the morning was warm enough that he had already built up a mild sweat of tickling tiny rivulets down his back under a light-weight leather jerkin.

He appreciated the leggings he had attached to his breech belt for the protection they offered against the blackberry brambles. He brushed a drop of blood away from his right forearm where a small puncture from an encounter with one of the pernicious thorns was still stinging, wondering to himself if he should have donned the heavier leather jerkin with its longer sleeves instead of the lightweight one, which the warm day had lured him into.

He paused to carefully grip a bramble stem in a narrow stretch between thorns. He was dealing with the woody vines of hardened thorns left from the prior season. Even the undersides of the leaves were barbed with the mature growth. He worked the stem back onto itself and used the thorns against other bramble vines to hold it out of his path. He might need to bring a machete along on his next trip with all the questing vines crisscrossing the already-narrow path, he thought.

After his months-long recovery, his only assignments had been to heal himself, to strengthen the connection of body and spirit that had been riven during his unprecedented encounter with Eagle, the messenger of God.

He also needed to think about an inward drive that seemed to be shadowing his dreams since his spirit had found its way back. It seemed as if there were some driving force goading him to do something. Something important. He felt there was something he must remember from his time with the Greater Spirits. Something he was sure he had mumbled about as he was leaving the spirit world behind. Yet it remained just on the outer edge of recall, where it haunted him with teasing fractal memories that time had hidden behind consciousness. He could barely recall the reluctance as he pulled away from the bliss of his sojourn with God.

His wood carvings had been well accepted so far and he had been asked to create a totem for the spring celebrations just over a year away. Having agreed, he had just over one year and two months to get this project completed. And he hadn't even selected the log he would use yet!

His first, personal, totem had been completed last spring just before leaving on the coastal expedition. A tall wooden mask consisting of a hawk's face formed the lesser spirit at the base, and a snarling cougar formed the dominant of his own two spirits at the top.

He had some thoughts for how to build his ideas into the village totem pole: how to mount the wings symbolizing the traditional Eagle spirit. He fully intended to add Salmon totems to the pole this year. The contemplation of the salmon was the focus of his thoughts as he continued his climb up the mountain behind his fort-home. Others had never considered the value, perhaps even the foundation, the salmon brought to his tribe. Recent developments, however, had shown him just how important this seemingly inexhaustible resource was.

Could he pull it off? Could he capture the essence of his tribe's connections with their world? Could he express the final element of water, as well as land and sky? Could he someday fathom a way to include fire and complete the list of elements?

Chapter Five

Laughing Trees

A top a lesser ridge, he felt the energies of the land build. He no longer thought about this "sensing." It was just a fixed part of his "self."

With the subtle pull of those energies calling, he found himself a grassy patch with a base of green moss next to a darkling glade of fir trees. A small meadow edged it all, and in the transition space, ferns made a solid band along the edge. He settled on his back in the open meadow, looking up into a clear spring sky.

Clear, at least, of clouds: there was a sky track up there. The arrowing plume of cloud streaked across the clear blue, blazing its way to the south. Tracks like these were the exhaust trails from high-flying airplanes. Like a wagon, he had been told, except these rode the wind. He thought of them as Sky Walkers: braving the elements to break free of the bonds of earth.

Once, there had been many of these planes seen every day, carrying the busy people of those times from one place to another. Some would fly from Portland, way up north in Oregon, south over his state of Lincoln, over the state of Jefferson, and into California for a day. Then fly right back the very next day.

The Tribe owned a smaller version of one of those planes, which they landed on the old freeway up near Curtin to deliver supplies from the outside world. Jamari would travel to Curtin and to the Curtis Creek dam and mills the following week, mostly looking for the right log for the totem pole. He hoped to see the plane then.

As the arrow of white passed over the hill, he settled into his meditations. These were a bit troubled as he pondered his sketchy memories from his time of walking with Eagle, of a forest still sleeping, but coming awake ... whatever that meant. He scuttled to seat himself at the edge of the clearing, keeping the dense copse of firs at his back. Inside the line of ferns, there were some pasty-white mushrooms peeking up from the moist shade under the blanket of moss, small and unhealthy looking, with fragile stalks supporting tiny little heads.

When he sat down on his own patch of mossy bed, he disturbed a section and saw the lace-work of fungal roots interlaced with the dark soil. The fresh loamy smell of healthy earth drifted on the air. Thinking nothing of it other than the momentary cooling sensation as the upturned earth took in the heat of his palm, he settled into trance.

Did the Founder give me a clue? he wondered. During Shane's internment ceremony, he remembered being fascinated with the story the Founder had written on how to become a tree. He concentrated his essence on becoming a tree as he dropped into a meditative trance.

Jamari entered a communications network he could never have imagined. The trees at the edge were celebrating the light that was reaching them at the base of their boles. They were telling the inward trees (who had long been blocked away from this warming sensation) what it felt like to have light-energy-warmth seeping directly into their toes. They were talking about the human who was listening in on their conversation and wondering why he wasn't talking to them.

Don't let it alarm me, Jamari admonished himself, remembering the last lines from the Founder's note: *"What! Don't lose it just because a bird landed on you! Now, start over!"*

Jamari almost startled out of the communion once he realized what it was. He was hearing the trees talk to each other! But how? How was it possible? Could he answer?

He sensed the trees laughing at him as he returned from the trance where the entire day had passed and dusk falling. When he suddenly sat up and lifted his hand from the broken patch of mossy overlay, Jamari felt himself disconnect from the grid of knowing. He looked at his hand, where the dark soil and the white traceries of fungal root clung. He lifted the hand for closer inspection and smelled the rich, yeast-like essence of healthy loam.

It was an important moment; he was sure: he just didn't know what it meant. Jamari had to get back down the hill before full dark caught him. He brushed his palm against his leggings as he stood and felt the grainy texture of soil and web-like mesh of roots rub off his skin. It felt like pulling a short thorn from his skin as the fungal roots pulled free.

The separation from the forest entity was complete, but he was now looking at a set of tracks amidst the meadow grasses that set the hairs on his arms to standing painfully against the inside sleeve of his jerkin. He saw a tracery of bent ferns leading up to within two yards of his meditation spot, a wide swath where something had settled as it had watched him. Saw one clear print in a bare patch of dirt.

A very large cougar had come to the meadow's edge and sat watching him as he communed with the glade.

His fear had him covering ground too quickly to reflect on just what had happened on this momentous day: listening to trees laughing in the sun and knowing the stronger of his two totem spirits had paid him a visit while he was in trance. Dominating his thoughts was the certainty the Knight Shaman would be very disappointed in him for allowing himself to fall so deeply in trance he hadn't noticed either the passing of time or the visiting predator. It went against everything they taught him, everything he had cautioned himself against. He feared even more reaching out to the Other World.

Could he ever safely spirit-walk again?

Jamari told the Knight Shaman about his experience. The next day, Terry introduced him to a couple of new companions. "I need you to take a walk with me," the Knight Shaman told him when Jamari showed up at his quarters for his morning lessons. "I'm going to introduce you to a couple of men who I'm hoping you will get along with." The Knight Shaman led him out of his quarters, turning to close the apartment door behind them. "After your various adventures, I want you to have accompaniment on your daily trips up to your meditation spots."

"But, don't you think having 'company' would simply interfere with the spiritual awakening I'm trying to gain?" Jamari replied as they headed down the long hallways towards the front entrance of Milltown Hall.

"You know I've already been having trouble in attaining spiritual trance. Do you think having others fidgeting around and about while I'm working on my internal balance will make it even more difficult?" Jamari tried not to sound too peevish as he voiced his concern, but a quick glance at the Knight Shaman quickly showed he had been unsuccessful.

Terry looked over at him as they continued to walk side by side down the hallway. The two stepped into a small alcove between two massive concrete pillars. They watched a trio of other men traveling in the opposite direction go by.

"I admit this may not work out," Terry said. "But losing you would be very costly to the Tribe. Losing you to another extended trip walking with the Great Spirit, one from which we can't call you back, would be even worse."

"There are a lot of dangers involved in this quest I seem to be on," Jamari answered. "I'm frightened to piddling of losing my 'self' again. Every time I remember just how close I came to being one of the soulless ones, I cringe. I feel as if there is a path I must follow. A path which involves even deeper spirit-walking than I've already done. I've heard it said I'm now known as Jamari God-Walker. I don't know whether the description fits, but I know I am following a fresh path." They slowed as they approached the stairway that led down to the main level, the level that housed the boys' crèches and the youngling's hearths and the main exit to the outside.

"I understand your concern, Jamari," Terry answered as he led the way, single-file, down the narrow stairway, running a hand along the banister as they went. "Will you try this arrangement while we work on another, hopefully better, solution?"

"You know I'll always follow where you lead," Jamari answered. "I've seen and felt your caring for long enough to recognize you're doing this to protect me. I'll take whoever you want on my sojourns with the spirits. And I'll hope doing so turns out to be useful."

"Thank you," Terry answered as they reached the bottom of the stairs. "We're going to a meeting room attached to the mentor's quarters," he said as he led them down a hallway very familiar to Jamari from his years in Jahangir's hearth. They walked past the entrance to the shower area, and Terry opened a door.

Inside, Jamari saw a communal shower area composed of a broad ovoid room with several alcoves to either end, each containing two showerheads on opposite walls, sized for two men at a time. The floors were concrete, with tiling in the shower areas. There were benches and alcoves with wall hooks for hanging clothes. It was a simple area with doors in the back.

"Most of the doors lead into the mentor's individual rooms," Terry told him. "This one, though, leads to their conference room." He opened it and led Jamari inside. There, Jamari saw two men sitting in wooden chairs at a long table.

"Jamari, this is Lon," Terry told him as he introduced the nearest of the two, who quickly stood. Lon was about five foot ten, stocky, without being overly muscular. His glossy black hair, just long enough to tie back in a short ponytail, framed hazel eyes with long dark lashes. His hair length suggested he had only recently completed the Manhood Rites and had not yet had time to grow his braid. The Native American heritage was obvious, but he had a more Asian-like nose, a nice little nose, not a button nose like Jamari's, but not the beaky protuberance of the Native American line, either. Overall, the combination of features, which seemed both innocent and bold, beguiled Jamari.

"Lon and Joshua will be your companions on your daily trips up to the groves and glades." Jamari looked Joshua over as Terry introduced him. He shook hands with the pair. Joshua was Jamari's height, with the same glossy black hair as Lon, long enough to be worn in a man's braid. He had a more prominent, not quite Roman nose so often associated with the tribal heritage, but distinct in how it formed a steep declivity straight down from full brows, leaving the dark eyes in shadow.

Each of them wore leathers: leather breech clouts with leather leggings attached and tall moccasins. They were both wearing off-white long-sleeved hemp tunics open at the neck, with the cloth laces that could either pull the openings shut or leave them open to allow cooling. In the cooler climes inside the hall, they each had the laces partly drawn and loosely tied. Both were attractive, with wide shoulders, narrow hips and muscular arms and legs.

"I want all of you to understand what this companionship means," Terry said, drawing their eyes to him. He motioned them into chairs around the table large enough to seat fifteen or sixteen men. Once they seated themselves, he continued. His tone of voice showed he was now the Knight Shaman, and not just a friendly teacher and guide. "Jamari is a shaman," he said as he looked at each of the two. "He is working on developing some new skills in his role as a shaman. These new skills often leave him vulnerable to the elements as he sojourns in other realms."

"Your role is simple," he told Lon and Joshua. "Don't let any physical harm come to him while he is in his meditation trance. It is also complicated. Jamari will need to act in ways that may seem dangerous to your perceptions. You are to defer to Jamari's decisions when he is working on the spiritual aspects of his endeavors. If he tells you to hold back, or that he needs to take an action which you are concerned about, you are responsible for ensuring he understands the basis for your concerns. He is responsible for listening to those concerns and then doing what he can to work with you to ease them. *But,*" he looked at all of them again, "if he tells you he needs to take the risk, you are to allow it. Your responsibility will be to safeguard him as best you can without interfering with his spiritual judgment." Terry paused again, this time looking straight at Jamari.

"You, Jamari, are charged with accepting these two as companions and guardians as you seek to fulfill your spiritual calling. You are to defer to them regarding safe conduct and activities until and unless you must deviate due only to your needs as shaman." Terry paused again, considering.

"Jamari's spirit animal is Cougar," he continued. "Cougar visited Jamari the last time he was in his meditation trance. Cougar, as an avatar of the Great Spirit, approached Jamari and sat with him as Jamari visited with a glade of trees."

These revelations visibly intrigued Lon and Joshua, tightening their focus on Jamari with interest.

"*If* Cougar had sought to harm Jamari, He would have done so," Terry continued again, a revelation that somewhat settled Jamari's own concerns. "What I suspect is Cougar, as spirit-animal, was guarding Jamari, perhaps simply sharing Jamari's vision with him. So, the reason I bring this up: if Cougar should approach again while

Jamari is in meditation, or even just traipsing along through the woods with you, you defer to Jamari's judgment if he is aware, or you set yourselves up in a defensive position between Cougar and Jamari if he is in trance. You do not have permission to harm Cougar until and unless it's very obvious what you're dealing with is a simple cougar-as-predator *and* that it intends to harm Jamari.

"This may mean you will have to wait until it strikes you. Jamari already bears the scars of just such an attack. He ate the lion, killing it with a blade while it was trying to kill him. You'll see the scars he still bears from the incident." Terry paused again, glancing from one to the other assuring all three were attentive. Joshua and Lon were looking at Jamari with fresh interest now.

"Yes, there is danger in this endeavor," Terry continued, "just as there is danger in taking a canoe down the river, in hunting a bear with a bow, or in swimming across the lake. The dangers need to be faced, but you will work to minimize those dangers where you can.

"Are there questions?"

Jamari was looking at his new keepers. His new keepers were looking at him.

No one had questions.

"I know none of you are ecstatic about this arrangement," Terry said. Look at it as a chance to get to know someone new; to learn and see things you would not have learned and seen otherwise. Neither of you has had much involvement with the shamanic arts. Jamari, these are both men who have completed the Manhood Rites. You can learn from them as well. You're all young men who can enjoy your time together." He looked at all of them again. Perhaps waiting for a response. Perhaps not. His expression was perfectly neutral. Jamari knew him well enough to know he was expecting comments at this point.

"Knight Shaman," Jamari said, "I will welcome these two as companions and, hopefully, as friends. As you say, we all have things we can learn from each other. We all are young men and can learn and enjoy each other's company."

"I agree, Knight Shaman," Lon said. Joshua quickly parroted his agreement.

"Well then," Terry said. "Since you're all so happy with this arrangement," - the dry humor of the remark *could* have been simple imagination - "I've planned for a set of rooms in the back halls. They are suitable for one of Jamari Shaman's status, and there will be plenty of room for all of you. "Why don't we check them out?"

They all rose, Lon and Joshua picking up rucksacks from under the table.

"Lon and Joshua were going to be assigned 'somewhere' today," Terry said. "Their terms as monitors were over when the last of the boys from Robert's hearth transferred. We only needed to see whether the three of you could accept the terms of this very unusual arrangement." He opened the door and motioned them to precede him out.

"It's back towards my quarters," Terry told Jamari. "It's another room which has view windows looking out into the lake. I've seen how much you've enjoyed the view from my rooms." He placed a companionable arm over Jamari's shoulders as they walked, subtly slowing Jamari to let Lon and Joshua get a little ahead.

"I hope you'll accept this as a positive development," he told Jamari quietly. "Your continued presence in the young men's hall has become a bit of a distraction lately."

Jamari tensed as if this were condemnation, but Terry quickly clarified. "Not that it's any of your doing," he said. "There's been a contest amongst all the new trainees to have the famous Jamari Shaman as their Night Studies mentor. I'm sure it makes the other mentors feel second-string. And given the direction of your explorations lately, you should not commit to a mentorship when you could likely be called away." He squeezed Jamari's shoulders briefly before releasing him from the impromptu hug.

Jamari pondered as he watched his two new companions sauntering up the hall ahead. "I understand," he finally answered, as Lon and Joshua began striding up the stairwell to the next level. "When you first told me I might have some talents of a shaman, I was nervous: concerned it would cause my newfound friends to be uncomfortable around me. I didn't expect trainees would seek those out in a potential mentor."

Terry chuckled, dropping his arm down Jamari's back in a familiar caress, landing on his rounded rump for a gentle and teasing squeeze. "I suspect *this* might have as much to do with the whole competition thing as your status as a shaman," he husked. "I don't think you fully appreciate your more physical attributes."

Jamari enjoyed his caress as they continued their slow stroll up the halls. "I wish you could have my back during all these explorations, but I know you have other duties." He looked at Terry as they approached the steps. "You know I will still want to share eros with you occasionally, right?"

Terry stopped at the base of the stairs. "I'm honored, Jamari. As one man to another, yes, I want to share eros with you as well. When we can." He put both arms around Jamari and pulled him into a full hug, letting their two bodies come into close contact before placing his head down into the lee of Jamari's shoulder and planting a kiss there. Then he stepped away, motioning Jamari to precede him up the stairs.

Jamari found his eyes watching Lon as the muscles of his legs and buttocks drove him up the last of the stairs to the next level. With his simple enjoyment of the view and driving, bunching action, he fully understood Terry's comments.

They found Lon and Joshua waiting just down the hall when they got to the top steps. There was a cross hall here, and they were obviously waiting to see which way they were to go. "I'm having your belongings brought up from Elk Creek Hall, Jamari," Terry told him as they came up to the pair. "We will do the transfer after the midday meal. This way, gentlemen," he said as he took the lead, turning to the right, towards where Jamari knew Terry's own set of rooms was located.

When the hall came to a "T" section where they would have turned to the right again to reach the Knight Shaman's rooms, they turned left instead. Jamari knew they were traveling along the stretch of the granite wall they anchored the dam to, passing sections of carved base-rock intermingled with concrete reinforcement, getting farther away from the concrete dam itself with each step. They passed two doors to the right, obviously rooms that would be next to the water as well. Then Terry opened the third door along the hall. Jamari was looking farther along the hall in his normal sense of wonder as Terry worked the lock. It was curving back to the left, following the contour of the ridge that they built Milltown Hall into. *Where will it lead?* he always wondered. And this time, he vowed to himself to find out.

Inside, exactly as he had discovered on his first visit to the Knight Shaman's rooms, was a watertight door standing open, situated to swing shut and stop any water incursion into the hallways.

"I'm going to leave you here," Terry told them. "Jamari, this is your new quarters for as long as you are a member of the Tribe. After you've seen what's here, after you've gotten your belongings settled in, you can pick some furnishings. Lon and Joshua, you are here because of some unusual circumstances. I hope you'll treat this as your home for now as well, yet with the respect due to Jamari's personal quarters." He motioned them in again before turning to walk back down the halls towards his own quarters.

Inside, it amazed Jamari to find his new rooms were more spacious and open than even the Knight Shaman's rooms were. They saw a similar-sized view window looking out into the lake waters. Terry had sent some of his things he'd been keeping in the Knight Shaman's rooms to his new quarters already, he saw. His first wood-carving project, a carved face adorned with the stern beak and head of Eagle (he'd tried to make the face of himself but had failed utterly) sat on a marble pedestal on the left side of the view window. On the right side, hanging on the rock wall, was his carved two-totem mask, the lower of two spirit animals represented as a hawk's face in bas-relief, topped by the snarling face of Cougar carved into the wood. It was called a mask, but Jamari, having carved it out, knew its weight would make it impossible to wear as a part of any costume.

Lon and Joshua were standing in stunned silence in the doorway as Jamari realized he should welcome them into his home so they could all explore what this wonderful place offered. "I'm sorry," he said, turning towards them. "Please, put your bags down by the door here, and we can explore together. When we have a better idea of how things lay, we can put them wherever they need to go."

Joshua kept his eye on the view window, entranced much as Jamari had been on his own first viewing of the underwater world as seen through acrylic windows as he set his bag down beside Lon's. "Don't you worry about the water coming in here?" he asked quietly, his eyes wide as he contemplated being overcome by a sudden influx of water.

"Not really," Jamari answered seriously. "If you look, they built the room with ceilings higher than the highest possible water level. So, even if the acrylic gives way, you won't drown. Unless you never learned to swim." He looked questioningly at Joshua at this point.

"I know how to swim," Joshua said quietly, still entranced by the view through the window. Jamari looked at Lon now.

"I could probably out swim any other man in the Tribe," Lon said.

Jamari looked around the room again before continuing. "Also, these same windows withstood the shock of the cataclysm of the Fall decades ago and have held up ever since. *If* they were to break, we would be uncomfortable, but not in any real danger."

Joshua was still staring out the window as a catfish wandered up it before turning and suddenly darting back down into the depths. He shook himself, obviously reminding himself he was supposed to be the guardian here. "Well, let's explore the new digs," he said bravely.

"Sure," Jamari answered. He looked over to see Lon gazing at the carved head wearing Eagle's visage as a cap. "Do you want to see it closer?" he offered.

"Yeah," Lon answered almost reverently. "Who carved this? Do you know?"

"That was one of my first completed projects in my art," Jamari answered.

"Wow," Lon said as he stepped over to look more closely at it.

His close inspection made Jamari examine it again from a fresh perspective. He had thought of it as a somewhat amateurish effort when he had completed it, but he had sanded it smooth, and polished it to a fine gloss anyway in respect for his first completed project. The face was about a foot above the base and appeared to be held up by long, flowing locks of free swinging hair, unbound from any braid or restraint. He had charred it to darken the hair from the reddish tint of the fir wood. Down at the broadened base, he saw the one knot that had given him a special challenge in trying to smooth out the finished product. As the small statue had ended up, the little knot now looked like a simple whorl in the hair. The face itself, with a small nose under a heavy brow, seemed very much like a Native American visage. The Eagle cap had the beak closed and pointing straight ahead of the stern mien. Overall, the statue stood about a foot and a half tall, with an eight-inch-thick base. "You can pick it up," Jamari offered.

"Maybe later," Lon answered quietly. "It's very well done, Jamari Shaman."

Jamari paused for a moment in sudden realization. "I think when we're in quarters, we should simply be three young men together," he said. He immediately recognized the words as Shane's close to two years before, when the two of them had met and spent a night with Zach during an overnight trip to Yoncalla. He pushed down the sudden pain of memory, looking at his two new companions, hoping they hadn't seen his weakness, hoping they would say nothing if they had.

"I can call you by your name," Lon answered. He looked over to where Joshua was still standing beside the main entryway.

"I as well," Joshua said.

"Well," Jamari said briskly, "let's explore." He looked and saw doors on either side of the guest area. A sudden sense of disappointment thrilled through him when he realized there might be bedrooms on two different sides of the room. He had never been required to spend a night alone in any bed and had often wondered how the Knight Shaman did so, and even now, Terry seemed to have taken for granted Jamari would enjoy a solitary bed as he himself so often did.

In his ruminations, Jamari realized he had been hoping to share sleeping quarters with the two of them. He'd have to figure something out if there were two bedrooms. Some excuse that would justify all of them rooming together. He hastened to the right, where he thought there shouldn't be too much space between the other door they had passed in reaching the door to his new rooms. *If it is a room*, he thought, *I can say it is much too small for a bedroom.* As he opened it, he found instead a large closet, much like the one in his room in Elk Creek Hall, with rods for hanging coats and outerwear, along with shelves below for boots and other supplies. He left it ajar for the other two to inspect as he turned towards the doors at the other end of the room. He noted in passing there was no furniture in this main room yet and wondered how he would go about finding a couple of chairs and table to sit in out here.

Behind the door on the other end of the room, he found a bedroom. Like the main room, this one was at least half again as large as the bedroom of the Knight Shaman's quarters. The bed, located to his left, was huge, at least as wide as it was long, covered with a luxurious bear-skin over the other more mundane blankets. There was no need for a headboard since they set the entire wall with upright hardwood planks, smoothed down and varnished to a warm, welcoming walnut color. The window on his right looked out into the lake. He could imagine himself lying abed some morning and watching the daylight penetrate through those waters to light up the room.

Past the bed, there were three doors along the next section of the wall. He passed through the entry door and into the room after his first quick perusal, Joshua and Lon following along as well. He walked around the bed in front of the window, where he reached for the door closest to the lake-wall. When he opened this door, he fumbled around on the wall just inside the door for a switch, first on the right side, closest to the outer wall and then on the left before he found it and turned the light on to reveal a walk-in closet, wrapped on three sides by empty rods which were hung beneath shelves that would hold far more stuff than he could envision himself ever possessing. He felt a body close behind him and realized he had been staring.

"Sorry," he muttered, turning to find Lon standing close behind him, so close he could smell the mint of his breakfast tea on his breath. "It's a lot to take in. These quarters are very generous."

"No problem," Lon said as he peered over Jamari's shoulder. "But I'm guessing Joshua might want to have a look in here as well." He pulled back from proximity to let Joshua in for a peek.

"Well, there are two more doors," Jamari said with a strained laugh as he felt Joshua move to stand close behind him. He stepped away, leaving the light on for them to look in if they wanted before going to the middle door. When he opened it, he found the light switch on his first fumbling reach and lit up a generous shower room with a multi-nozzle affair, four nozzles here instead of the two in his rooms down in Elk Creek Hall. One showering stall behind swinging glass doors held what he thought of as a wonderfully communal arrangement. They had placed a bench on either side of the entryway. Above each bench, the designers had placed wall hooks. He saw his own lounge wear from the Knight Shaman's rooms hanging on one set of hooks, with his furry-side-in leather slippers under the bench.

The third door revealed a latrine area when Jamari opened it. He wouldn't have to invent a reason for all of them to share the bedroom, since there was only one.

He turned and looked the bed over. "It looks like we're sharing," he said, trying not to let his relief show. He tapped the surface questioningly with his hand. It was firm yet yielding to pressure as well. Tentatively, he sat down on the bearskin, feeling the luxuriant brush of long hairs against his hand before swiveling around to lie back and let those same soft, welcoming hairs brush against his neck and ears.

"I could get used to this," he said with a sigh. When he looked up, he saw both Joshua and Lon watching him intently. "Well, do we break the bed in first or get the two of you unpacked first?" he asked.

In very short order, he learned there was plenty of room for all three of them on the bed, and he rediscovered the sensuous pleasure of bearskin fur against naked skin.

Chapter Six

First Flight

In a pique, Jamari opened his eyes, and pointedly looked at Lon, while doing his level best to imitate the Knight Shaman's oh-so-effective emotionless stare. Jamari had a difficult time getting used to having Joshua and Lon hovering while he was trying to reach his internal spirit. He tried to temper his angst with their presence, even though neither could sit in quiet contemplation for over five minutes at a time. And even then, they could rarely synchronize their individual five-minute limits. One would always fidget, or fuss, or stage whisper to the other.

Lon was completely oblivious to the meaning of the stare.

"Oh, you're back," he said. "Are we headed down to the hall soon?"

"No," Jamari said. "I'm still trying to break through to the other side. Do you think the two of you could move over to the far edge of the clearing?"

They were crestfallen at the implied rebuke. But they stationed themselves further from him so he could keep trying.

If he were truly honest with himself, he had to admit the real barrier was the re-awakened fear of falling too far into the spirit world and not finding his way back. He still woke sometimes with the shuddering shakes as he dreamed of those days when his spirit had been away. He still fought to access the internal God, even though the fear still haunted him.

The nights back at his new rooms in Milltown Hall more than made up for the distractions, and he wondered about simply engaging in those same distractions out on the meditative sojourns. Lon and Joshua were inventive, lean, and enthusiastic in their night sports. That was an element he wouldn't give up readily.

He went down Elk Creek with a group one afternoon, and they spent a night at the permanent camp beside the dam at Curtis Creek. It was a much smaller dam because of a much smaller creek. The entire site was too small to call a village, so they simply knew it as the Curtis Creek Camp. They used the energy from the dam to process logs during the rainy season. Then, the higher stream flows could power the equipment. During the warm season, the camp members spent their time repairing their complex equipment and bringing logs in to be decked. It was a logical and efficient use of the seasons since they did not damage the forest trails as much during the drier season and the logs cured to better quality while awaiting the power-up of the water-driven mill.

When the team Jamari was a part of had inspected the equipment twice and deemed the mill ready for the next season, they all went out into the surrounding hills seeking deer, elk, bear, and other game to bring down and smoke or cure for winter rations. They kept some sheep in the meadows and a small herd of goats wandered the surrounding hills, watched over by their contingent of goatherds. It was a hard, yet rewarding life and Jamari thought he might enjoy the lifestyle himself had he not accepted his place in Milltown Village as shaman.

There was a simple generator installed in the outfall, providing the camp with electricity, unlike so many other tribal settlements. They had a hydrogen generator like the one at the Milltown Hill Dam as well. With the hydrogen generator, they used some of the excess electricity from hydropower to generate hydrogen, which they then used to power a small boiler with an attached steam turbine. It wasn't nearly as large as the main one up at Milltown, but overall, the

Curtis Creek Camp had amenities that made it a much sought-after posting.

Jamari met the enormous horses specifically bred for hauling logs and other heavy loads. The Tribe had their antecedents from a local logger back in the founding days just after the quakes took down all the infrastructure that the culture back then had depended on.

The giant Shires were gentle, accepting grain from his open palm during a break between loads. The frilly fur of their lower legs fascinated him. Five of the six draft horses were black, with some white and gray in their leggings. One standout, a brown mare who seemed to stand aloof from the others, showed the poise of a herd leader.

Jamari had noted an apple orchard with a storage shed not too far from the mill area, so he made a quick trip over and dug out some apples from their beds of straw. There was enough for two each. They seemed pleased at this offering and let him pet them while they crunched the welcome treat.

After feeding them, he watched a fresh pair of horses laboring up the oddly rutted road, dragging a log behind them. He understood then why the road up to the dam had three furrows, with the center as the deepest. Once they delivered the log, he watched the lumberjacks use peaveys to roll it into position under a set of swiveling tongs. The tongs attached to a long beam that was built to pivot and swivel the log up and onto a pile.

Jamari could see several stacks of logs being set up and separated by size. There was a lot of space in the log deck area, since this was the tail end of the sawyer season. There was plenty of room. The camp would be busy waiting for the fall rains. They released the working drag team into the field after dropping their load, and they went out into the grass and rolled, scratching their hides clear of the mussing from their cushioned harnesses. Two of the horses he had befriended took their places in the harnesses and trotted contentedly down the lane for another log.

Before he left, he had the chance to look over the log deck for interesting pieces in search of a likely log to start his totem pole project. The timeline was narrowing. Even if he understood what he wanted to accomplish with a carving project of this size, he still needed to find the right log to start with. They had trimmed all the logs at the mill site down to carting size, though, and none seemed to possess the qualities he was hoping to find.

He considered simply giving up the grand plan he had in mind and building a more mundane totem pole. Then he remembered the tangle of logs gathered on Elk Creek downstream from where the Outsiders had killed Shane. Those logs were whole, with broken limbs and full root wads. Thinking of Tom Folley Creek, he asked if they could follow the contour of the stream as they left the Curtis Creek Dam area. Matthew, knowing what Jamari was looking for, agreed. He added the caveat that the travelers needed to be at Curtin before darkness fell.

They worked their way down the stream bed in search of the right log. There was nothing to see for the first couple of miles. The constant activity around the mill site assured any likely trees taken down by flood or wind would be transported to the mill for conversion into lumber.

Right before the confluence of Curtis Creek and Elk Creek, Jamari saw a tangle of downed trees. These gave him hope, but once he got to them, he realized they were all too small to allow the carving necessary. With only a little time left before they would have to leave the stream-bed and hit the trails, the creek made a dramatic bend, resulting in a good batch of debris gathering at the outside of the turn. Intertwined into this tangle of logs, Jamari spotted the one he wanted. The storm that took it down had broken it off about thirty feet up from the base, but the key was that it had sufficient girth to allow him to carve out the features he wanted and, most important to his vision, it still had the root structure.

Crawling through the tangle and reaching up with his left hand to pull himself up to the root structure of this tree, his left side came into abrupt contact with a smaller protrusion from the tangled mass. His phantom pain, the residual from the scathing he had received from the cougar who had marked him, was immediately back, and he paused his climb, bending over as well as he could to take tension off the sore point in his lower left rib cage. He pretended to be looking into the mass as he glanced back to see if anyone had noticed his sudden cringe of pain. The continued pangs from his long-ago encounter with Cougar were his own business, and he didn't want the others to think their shaman trainee was any less the man than they were.

With studied nonchalance, he continued his examination of the root mass. His plan required those roots as a part of his carving, so he gave specific instructions to Lon and Joshua, who hurried off to carry the request to the mill. Jamari asked the lumberjacks to load it onto a wheeled carrier and take it to the courthouse. There, Jamari would work on the project during evenings and meditation times while he was also working as an aide to Terry, in his role as Chief Justice of the court.

"This is where I head back to my village," Matthew said once they had climbed back up to the main path. "Safe travels to all of you."

"Be safe yourself," Peter replied. "Do you want to wait until either Lon or Joshua can go along with you?"

"I can make it back to the courthouse in time for an early dinner and then up to Milltown Village well before dark," Matthew answered. "I'm pretty sure the Knight Shaman would express displeasure were I to take one of Jamari's new escorts along with me." He said this last with a wink for Jamari, who suddenly remembered the same wink on the day Matthew had sent him and Shane off to the guest house in Yoncalla with Zach as their militia escort. *He doesn't miss much*, Jamari thought to himself with a smile for Matthew as he turned away to the east.

"Do you really think the constant escorts are necessary?" Jamari asked Peter once they had regained the main trail and started their walk along the stream to reach the trail over the Salt Creek Pass. Lon and Joshua could cut across the meadows and should be waiting for them after carrying their message to the camp. "Not that I'm disappointed in their company," he qualified. "I like them. A lot. It just seems to impede my sense of serenity, is all."

"I don't think my opinion matters," Peter answered. "The Knight Shaman thinks it's necessary, and he didn't give anyone any options or leeway for variance."

"Well, I hope I can convince him to give me some personal time at some point," Jamari said, somewhat peevishly.

"I'll talk with him and see what his actual concern is," Peter said. "Maybe we can meet his expectations without actually burdening you with two escorts all the time."

"Thank you, Peter," Jamari said. "I think I know what the concern is. He told you about the episode when I was communing with the trees, right?"

"Yeah," Peter answered. "It's something new for all of us. Not just that you let yourself go deep enough into trance where you let a full day go by without noticing or because you were so far gone a cougar came almost right up to your knees and sat watching you. It is all that, *plus* the idea you were communing with a forest glade — well, it is amazing and concerning to me, to all of us who value you and your abilities as an important part of our lives. We care, Jamari, and don't want to lose you to some unforeseen adventure." He paused for a couple of steps. "Again," he said quietly, probably not intending Jamari to have heard at all.

"Well, you were the one who read 'How to become a tree' during Shane's interment," Jamari answered. "I was thinking of becoming a tree as I was settling into meditation then. I even remember telling myself to not startle away from the connection when I realized I was in the story exactly as you spoke it."

"That bears some thinking," Peter said as they continued at a good pace along the trail. "The Founder often railed about the spirit of man being robbed of connection to God by the church, the very agent which purported to put man in closer touch to God. He lamented he could feel the power of the spirit, felt he could call it into being. Yet each time he was close, the fears planted by the church overcame him and kicked him out of communion." He paused here for a bit, breathing heavily but evenly as they ascended a long slope. As indefatigable as Jamari often saw him, he realized Peter was older than he let on.

"I think even though he couldn't claim to have been as close to his spirit and the Other World," Peter continued eventually, "he was very prophetic in his 'imaginings' of what could happen when man finally overcame the crippling conditioning which the church had imposed."

They walked in relative silence for a few minutes, listening to the swish of their leather breeches as they passed by the occasional brush or vine. "I'm not sure the spirit walking is of a concern right now, anyway," Jamari said as he reached out to put his arms around both Zach and Peter in an awkward hug as they continued walking. "I haven't been able to fully enter spirit trance since the day I heard the trees laughing about the sun on their toes. Every time I start my meditations, every time I feel myself slipping into trance, I jolt back out of it. I think I'm just as scared about all those things as you are. And the fear keeps me from the meditations I need to perform."

Peter contemplated this as they continued the climb up the pass. Lon and Joshua, running at a controlled jog, caught up to them as they reached the halfway point up the long curving freeway section. It was one of the rare stretches which remained intact through the eighty years since the Fall. Apparently, the pair hadn't thought to cut the triangle and had gone all the way back to the streamside trail.

"I need to think about this, Jamari," Peter finally said as they all took a short breather. "Sometimes fear has kept some, if not all, of us from entering shaman trance. The problem we're encountering now is you've gone so far beyond where any of us have ever gone before. You'll remember the Founder mentioned his 'feel' for there being a greater spirit in the hearts of old trees."

Jamari nodded his agreement as he took a good drink of water from his canteen and then he passed it on to the others.

Once they had started up the pass again, Peter continued. "The idea of you leaving your body and not finding your way back again is of concern. Not so much to us anymore as it seems to be to you. We've found the more times we transition from body to spirit and back, the easier it is for us to find our way to our physical bodies. For you, it severely weakened the link when you projected yourself out to warn Zach of the approaching band of outsiders back when they killed Shane. No one has ever extended their essence in such a way before. We suspect projecting yourself strained the connection. Then, the encounter with Eagle injured it even more. Almost beyond the breaking point. I say almost. There was barely a difference between you and one of the soulless ones for a few days there. I sensed it, but attributed it to sorrow from Shane's loss." The deep look he gave Jamari then was compassion, love, caring, and concern all in one, and it rocked Jamari to see it all displayed so openly. Then the impassive mask once again covered the well-loved countenance.

"It took the Knight Shaman's observations after getting back from his mission down to Roseburg," Peter continued, "to key all of us into the fact your spirit was away. There used to be a joke at one time. 'I have two brains. One got lost, and the other is out looking for it.' It was funny for a lot of years. And then we began to re-learn the skill of spirit-walking, and it had a much deeper meaning."

"I actually was sensing something wasn't right," Jamari said as they continued their walk up the now gentle incline. "I think my spirit-self was slowly returning because I remember beginning to feel the shame of some things I had been doing during the empty time." He paused here and looked at Zach. "I was with you only one time during that period. I remember being very abrupt and almost uncaring about you while we were sharing eros. Did you notice anything while we were together?"

Zach contemplated as they continued to walk. "I felt something 'off,'" he answered after a couple minutes. "I remember thinking you were far more forceful while you were with me than you, or anyone, had ever been before. I remember thinking it felt like you were punishing me for being alive when Shane was dead." Another pause as they walked farther along the freeway, navigating around a spot where the underfill had eroded away, leaving a small gully cut into the pavement. "Like Peter, I thought of you as grieving and you would get over it in time." Here, he stopped as they reached the other side of the gully. The five of them stopped for a break, and Peter opened his canteen to share around.

"I have been thinking about sensing spiritual presence," Zach continued as they took turns downing the water, "and I confess I haven't been able to pull it off yet. I suspect it was because I was so often assigned to spend watches and night sessions with Scott. I've learned what he is since those days. If he's not fully hylic, then he's as close as one can get. I think I unconsciously dampened my ability into latency in self-defense. As a result, I never noticed a lessened spirit from you." Zach looked over at Peter. "Maybe I could use some lessons about sensing spirit-self?"

Peter motioned them up from their rest and answered as they continued. "I'll ask the Knight Shaman if he can help you. It is one of his strongest skills, the self-regulation and the directly connected ability to recognize the emanation from others."

"It was one of the first lessons he taught me," Jamari interjected. "I'll never forget the fear I felt when he first animated the Eagle Avatar, when I simply 'knew' I was alone in his room. He spent the next couple of weeks showing me it could be done and then another two weeks teaching me how."

They could see the top of the next rise ahead as Jamari continued. "I remember taking it one step further on my own. He wanted me to practice dampening my self-emanation. Somehow, during my first attempt, I split a piece of my consciousness off and watched as my physical body sat on the floor next to the view window in his room. The spirit-self slipped through the window and traced a couple of fish up to the surface. I remember watching them as they sipped a couple of small mayflies which had landed on the water. I was amazed to see how they could suck the flies down with only the slightest of ripples, and how ripples seen from underwater can capture the sun like a prism and build little circular rainbows.

"Then Terry interrupted me and asked me what I had just done. 'I thought I was dampening my emanations,' I told him, 'but I think I split off a part of my essence and became two selves for a bit.' We had some initial concern, but then we worked out what I had done, and he learned he could do it as well. It was harder for him."

The travelers were near the top of the next rise, looking down into the next shallow valley, when Peter spoke again. "Terry told us about that. He was concerned you had gone far beyond anything he had ever done. Rodney was looking very smug when he heard it. He told Terry the same thing had happened when he was teaching me before they made me the Knight Shaman after Rodney. And then the same thing happened with me when I was teaching Terry. When he surpassed my skills and had reached his full citizenship, we helped him transition into being the Third Knight Shaman."

They think I am going to be the next Knight Shaman! Jamari suddenly realized. *I don't think I'm ready to be the Knight Shaman.* But remembering past times when his councilors and teachers had led him into things he had thought of as "beyond" his abilities, he kept silent about his concerns. He looked at Peter in understanding but left the topic closed. Both recognized Jamari had acknowledged the possibility.

"Everybody down!" Joshua commanded from his vantage up ahead. They all ducked to the side of the road and found cover. Where, just a moment before, there had been five individuals traipsing along a well-worn path, now there was just the slightest quivering of branches to show where they had been. As those last branches settled, they all watched through various vantage points while Joshua motioned for them to remain concealed as he slipped out of his place in the ditch to creep up to where he could see down the trail ahead.

Eventually, he signaled them all to rise and come up to where he was. Jamari brushed some leafy debris from his legs and breechclout as Lon hurried past him from his trailing position. He walked up to where he could look down the next sloping hill. They saw a couple of leather-clad men carrying bows, one of whom also carried a large leather bag hung over his shoulder. "It's just the daily couriers," Lon said.

They waited for the couriers to reach them at the top of the rise. Once they were all together, the seven men settled in for an evening snack. It would be a couple of hours before they reached Curtin, probably just as twilight was settling in. They could get a small meal then, as they would miss the evening dinner.

The couriers, two men who looked to be in their thirties or early forties, were happy to spend some time chatting as they shared a meal. Jamari learned they were full citizens who had chosen the life of a courier in order to be constantly on the go and not tied down into any single place. They were a part of a broader career known as Rangers. These were true representatives of the wandering urge that had once led the westward expansion of a nation. These two were carrying messages that the Tribe's small airplane had delivered, and they carried them to the courthouse and tribal center.

Rangers. Wandering the wild ways. Patrolling the tribal forests. Scouting out Outsider and Wildling incursions. An interesting career, indeed.

"You'll be long after dark getting there," Peter observed. "Are your messages so urgent?"

"We're planning on calling on the camp at Curtis Creek," the younger of the two answered. He and his partner were of the Native American genotype, with long braids and broad cheeks. The younger had a bit of Pacific Islander showing, and the older had a bit of the Asian with slight epicanthic folds at the eyes.

Once they started out again, there wasn't much conversation until they reached the last rise from where they could look down into Curtin. Jamari and Zach both saw the strange-looking device that was the Tribe's airplane. From afar, it simply looked like a shiny white cross with a strange little secondary cross at the narrow end in back. As they got closer, perspective showed a tube-like apparatus with fixed wings sitting on a tripod of wheels. They tied it down to the concrete of the old freeway.

"We'll get a closer look tomorrow," Peter said as the day's light was fading away. "We should introduce ourselves to our hosts for now and get settled in for the night."

Curtin was by far the smallest full village of the Tribe Jamari had ever visited. A single longhouse internally divided into two main areas, one for men and the other for women. Peter introduced Jamari and Zach to Chief Curtin, who was an older Native American woman named Ginny; shortened from Genevieve, she informed them. She and Peter seemed to know each other very well.

"How do you know each other so well?" Jamari asked.

"We were children together back before the Tribe decided to separate the boys and girls as a part of their cultural re-design. We became much closer than we ever should have," Ginny said with a smile and a twinkle in her eye.

"We did, didn't we?" Peter answered with a gentle smile that took years away from his stern visage. Both Jamari and Zach stood in stunned silence.

"It wasn't as bad as you're thinking," Peter said, laughing, noting their open-mouthed wonder. "We never experimented together sexually until we they allowed it. But we made a couple of babies together." He said this last with a fond look between the two.

"It's just so...different," Zach said finally. It was obvious he had substituted the word "different" from another choice, possibly the word "wrong."

They guided Lon and Joshua over to the barracks during this interchange. When the room had emptied to just the three shamans and Ginny, she reached over and put an arm around Zach's shoulders. "This was long before we had set the current culture in place," she said. "You've both traveled a bit and seen how the non-tribal communities still raise boys and girls up alongside each other.

"We purposely chose a different way, for reasons of our own, and spent many years defining how we, as a tribe, would face our own moral, ethical, and cultural upbringing. Surely, you remember reading about how communities were organized back before the Fall?"

"Well, sure," Jamari answered for a nearly speechless Zach, who didn't look comfortable at all with Chief Curtin's arm spanning his back and pulling him into a one-armed hug. "It's just, well, it seems like it was always this way," he finished lamely.

Peter looked at both youngsters with concern. "One of the most important parts built into our culture has always been the imperative that we face new circumstances with new ideas. I'm wondering if we shouldn't concentrate on teaching innovation and openness during our indoctrination years after seeing your reactions. Back then, we saw the need to rear children in an entirely new way when we realized each pair of parents was instilling different values in their individual children. This was resulting in differing cultures all trying to co-exist together."

They followed Ginny's gesture to the table for their late dinner as Peter continued his explanation. Ginny let Zach go from her one-armed hug long enough to be seated. Then she held him again, to his obvious discomfort, once they settled.

"Also, just like you noted down at Tahkenitch, Jamari, we saw children of more prosperous parents receiving a much different and more supportive upbringing than those of less prosperous parents. The result was those children were often better prepared for adulthood than others in the same community. This although a child's potential for human intelligence and ability had absolutely nothing to do with whether his or her parents were 'rich,' or 'influential,' or any of the other reasons which often separated and segregated children into various strata within the community.

"Even more important," he continued, with a look across the plank table at Ginny, "we saw youngsters becoming emotionally attached and even carrying their attachment so far as sexual activities when their genetics made it unsafe.

"Is it important to tell them about those days?" Ginny asked.

"These are two future leaders of our tribe and culture," Peter answered. "They both saw some of the physical attributes when people bred too close to the hearth." He paused here and looked across to Zach and then to his left at Jamari. "What you didn't see," he continued in a far more serious voice, "was the mental deficiency which has and will develop from a narrow gene pool. We have selected you for fathering at various times. You'll remember it is always the women who choose who they mate with. The deeper story, though, is there are historians in each village who check the lineages of every member of their community and then exert the right to veto a woman's choice based solely on whether the relationship is too close." Peter paused for a moment's reflection.

The dinner comprised generous portions of roast elk smothered in gravy and on a bed of sourdough bread. Jamari and Zach dug in with young appetites, attempting to pay attention to the two leaders while satiating their hunger.

Ginny obviously caught the gist of where the conversation was going. "We saw they denied the children of less influential parents many opportunities, and the absence of opportunity and expectation made them more likely to remain less successful than children of influential parents." She looked over at Peter for a minute, obviously remembering their shared youth.

"We were the first generation raised separate from direct parental control," Ginny continued. "There were hits and misses as we developed our process, but we survived and grew as a community from those. Though Peter and I didn't act on our mutual attachment, there were other youngsters who did. The problem, we quickly recognized, was individual attachments and 'romances' couldn't consider the recognition of genetic potential. When two pregnancies happened in our age group, the Tribe re-evaluated our approach and built what we have now."

Here, Peter stepped back into the conversation after finishing a few bites from his plate as well. "Ginny and I, as young adults, were among the first of the mentors and monitors. Those roles were the most valuable of the developments which finally allowed us to develop the hearth system where one man or woman raises a group of younglings with the help of others. It was a team which designed and supported training to build our cultural ethos. You've both seen each hearth leader assisted by mentors and monitors. You may not have seen just how many people work as a dedicated team to raise up our youngsters. It really takes a village."

Ginny finally relented and let Zach go from her one-way hug. "It looks like you're through with dinner. Why don't we get you settled for the night?" She gestured to one of the Curtin tribe members. "Charles, why don't you take these two over to the men's side and set them up in an alcove together? I suspect they've got some talking to do before they go to sleep. They seem a bit shocked at recent revelations."

"Maybe a bit shocked," Jamari said reflectively, "but it all builds a more complete picture. It appalled me when I saw the differences in how they raised the Tahkenitch younglings differently based on their parentage. I even asked for some changes to be made there as a part of our treaty. Learning just how recent a development it was has been a shock is all." He let Charles lead him and Zach away from the central commons area and over to the men's hall side, where they settled into a small alcove, separated from others simply by a hanging tapestry on one side and a rough-woven blanket on another. There were a couple of sleeping pallets, which the two young men wordlessly moved to the center of the space and set up their bed together for the night.

The next day, they took a tour of the community. They saw where the old freeway had fallen away into a ravine just north of town, leaving a near-impassable barrier that separated tribal lands from the Outsiders just north of them. It was only a few miles to where the State of Lincoln ended and the State of Oregon began.

The most exciting moment of the day, and of Jamari's life so far, came when they settled him into the interior of the four-seater plane, where the pilot gave him a quick ride up into the sky. Lon was also along, relegated to a back seat but thrilled none the less. It astonished Jamari at how fast the land below sped by. One main thing he saw was a revelation and relief for him. When the plane was just a mile north of Curtin, following the path of the old freeway, still climbing from the take-off, he saw a wide crevasse that bisected the road. "What's that?" he asked the pilot.

"That's where the built-up boulder and sediment they used to level the land for the freeway fell away during the 'quake. It looks bad now," he said of the ragged edges and steep drop down to a rocky arroyo, "but it's one of the main things protecting us from the ravages of the outside lands. They can't get here with their harvesters and excavators, hopefully for a very long time yet."

Jamari contemplated this as he rode. He had his face up against the window most of the time, watching the lands below shrink into featureless forest as they climbed ever higher into the sky. He was in awe when the pilot turned the plane around, seeming to stand it on its side, making it seem as if he could simply fall out and down to the ground below. Lon gasped aloud at this maneuver, but Jamari took it in stride. It might have been less climactic for him due to how often he had enjoyed the view from on high many times before as he had shared visions with Hawk in his spirit-walking sessions, but being there himself was certainly a whole new experience!

Once he was on the ground again and watching as Zach and Joshua took a ride, he turned to Peter. "Why are we being shown this?" he asked. "Why are we being offered an airplane ride when no one else I know of has ever had the pleasure?"

"Let's wait until Zach gets back," Peter answered with seriousness. "There's a reason, and it's a very good one."

"Sure," Jamari answered as the plane sailed out of sight over the ridgeline north of them. "I can wait. I always have."

Jamari was obviously referring to the many times they had coaxed or cajoled him into agreeing with the guidance of his mentors.

Once Zach had returned, they invited all of them to share lunch with Chief Curtin and Peter on an overlook with a view into the ravine they had seen that morning. Over lunch, they answered Jamari's question. "It's a part of our future," Peter told them. "The outer world is encroaching more each day onto our lands. We're always working to help those who approach us to understand our ways. Not always with success.

"You're both going to be working in the court for the next year, learning what you can about that aspect of our community. Over the last few years, our interactions with the Outsiders have involved more and more legal challenges. When some come into our lands, they accept our position as owners and administrators and our overall hegemony. Others seem to resist, insisting their standing in the outer world should somehow protect them from learning our ways. We work to educate and assimilate, but sometimes, we have to bring the two governments into play, sometimes with treaties and agreements, others via the courts. The tribe sent ambassadors up to Eugene and Salem to help educate the Oregon citizenry about our ways and laws. We have had to send up our judges and legal representatives as well.

"You were both given rides today to see how you responded to being in the air. Whether you would get airsick."

Jamari remembered his days down at the coast that summer, when he had ridden one of the Tahkenitch Tribe's heavy ocean-going canoes out from the river mouth and onto the ocean, where he had felt the rise and fall of the ocean swells. He remembered the initial sensation when up and down and side to side seemed to disagree with his sense of balance, but then he remembered getting over it quickly and enjoying the hunt.

They had been hoping then to get close enough to a sea lion to harvest one for the meat and hide, which was used to make winter-wear. The only one they had gotten close to, though, had been too small and young, so they had returned to the river mouth before the tide had turned and the resultant choppy waves resulted. There had been a few of the expedition members who had not been so fortunate, who had been sick to the point of throwing up before they got back to the protected waters of the bay.

"You are both likely going to be asked to travel with one judge or lawyer as a part of your introduction to our courts. And you'll be learning how we interact with the outer world," Peter continued. "You did well on this introductory flight, so you'll both be taking more trips over the next year as a part of your court assistant duties."

Chapter Seven

Spirit Walking Visitor

Jamari and Zach returned to their rooms up at Milltown, knowing they had just a few days to prepare for their year-long move down to the courthouse. Thinking about all the changes he'd been through, Jamari realized he had been churning through the Manhood Rites for close to two years. Even more challenging to grasp was that the most intense parts of the militia training were done. He would enter his last period of the Manhood Rites as a court assistant down at the casino/courthouse.

He wondered at the sense of loss he felt as he contemplated leaving his rooms in Milltown Hall after only a couple of weeks of living in the homey comfort they provided. He mused what the rooming arrangement would be down at the courts.

It seemed he wondered a lot about what things were going to be like since he began the Manhood Rites. He didn't regret any of it, though. Each extra step had been a learning experience, and he was feeling as if he were reaching a point where he could encompass the many strings and machinations built into the culture he was a part of.

He reflected about how the courthouse, first established as a tribal casino, had been placed strategically beside the freeway to bring in the funds needed to help as the Elk Creek Tribe was first beginning the massive construction projects at Milltown. They had built it large, with an immense open area meant for slot machines and other games of chance, a three-story hotel, an indoor pool area and a small golf course arranged around it.

Most of those luxuries had disappeared after the calamitous events triggered by the great 'quakes of 2040. The swimming pool, where the roof had given way during the second and strongest earthquake, they had filled with soil and planted useable crops. Most recently, instead of crops, which were now being readily farmed in the adjacent fields of Scotts Valley, they planted decorative and soothing plants and the area had become an oasis of calm amidst the activity of the tribal activities hosted in the structure: an embassy of sorts where visitors checked in prior to visiting other tribal lands; a courthouse where all tribal conflicts were heard (and which had recently become a county courthouse for the State of Lincoln's own Lincoln County); the home of the Scotts Valley villagers, with Men's, Women's, and young men's halls and young women's halls; and still-available rooms for let to the occasional visitor.

Amidst all the turmoil, Jamari was still having trouble with the meditations. He hadn't truly felt the Great Spirit since he had come back from his dream days. The one session where he had inadvertently talked with the trees up above Elk Creek Hall had been his last genuine connection with the spirit world. He was missing it, and he wondered if he had the strength or the courage to let his control free enough to allow the essence of God to move within him again. His two escorts were always there, as well. Their presence could certainly be a contributing factor.

They made the move down to the courthouse with little fuss. Jamari packed up his clothes, leaving the militia leathers behind, taking care to bring his ceremonial leathers and, most especially, the new dress pants and shirts issued to him in his first days in the young men's hall but which he hadn't even had occasion to wear yet. The memory of Shane helping him try them on when they had finally arrived came to him in a quick flash. They had made a fun game of it until both had given in to the desire and taken off the fancy duds and enjoyed a quick interlude. Though the memory brought a moment of peace along with the pang of loss, Jamari realized the pain was fading.

Zach and he said goodbye to their hearth mates in Elk Creek Hall after breakfast and picked up their bags for a quick trip down to the stream-side. There was too much to carry on their backs for the long walk, so they used a canoe for the trek down, Lon and Jamari in one, and Joshua and Zach in another.

When they pulled the boats out of the water at the back of the casino/courthouse, Jamari saw his totem log dragged up behind the building, with the roots and a couple jagged limbs still propping the rest at an awkward rest. It was looking somewhat forlorn and neglected, splaying raggedly truncated limbs and root sections out and around. It was, despite Jamari's imagination, more like a dead tree than the graceful totem he hoped to make of it. He would have to find a place out of the weather to set it up for carving since he didn't relish the thought of carving in the fall rains or winter snow. He fully expected to take right up to the next year's Spring Celebrations to finish the project.

The four young men set their multiple bags at a back door and went in, looking for someone who could tell them where they would be rooming.

Jamari and Zach, as court assistants, would share a decent sized room together. The chamberlain gave them the afternoon to get set up, and one of the more experienced court assistants walked them through the pertinent areas of the building. The court rooms, the waiting rooms, the dining halls, and common areas were all fitted into one over-filled afternoon.

Joshua and Lon would be court bailiffs for a while. Their escort took them into the barracks area of the building. A few short weeks of near-constant companionship seemed to have built a stronger connection than Jamari had realized. He held his emotions in check as the man led them in the opposite direction of where his escort took him. He knew they'd still be his keepers when he found time to set out for the woods and meditation sessions, and the thought helped to subdue the regret of parting.

The next morning, clothed in black pants, shiny black shoes that pinched his feet, and a blinding white shirt, Terry led Jamari into one courtroom through a back door. When they came into the courtroom, Jamari saw the same judge who had interviewed him on his declaration of Manhood Day. He wasn't in his robe, just the black trousers, white shirt, and tie, along with his glossy black leather shoes. Jamari noted he had lost weight in the time since he had last seen him.

"Ah, you're here," the judge greeted Terry.

"Yes," Terry answered. "This is Jamari. I don't know if you remember him or not, but you were his judge on his declaration day. Jamari, this is Rory. I'm sure you remember him."

"It's a pleasure to see you again, sir," Jamari offered, reaching his hand out for a handshake.

Rory put on a visible show of reluctance, reaching out and then pulling his hand back and checking to see if his arm still functioned. They all laughed at this obvious reference to Jamari's reaction to the Proposition, the first of the tests of reason included in the declaration-day challenges.

Then Rory reached out to take Jamari's hand for real and shake it, putting the other over it in emphasis. "I'm glad to make your acquaintance again, Jamari Shaman," he said. "It's been a pleasure hearing tales of your feats and achievements over the past two years. Believe it or not, they had admonished me for making your declaration rites so 'easy' for you. But you have justified my decision in every way imaginable."

It took Jamari aback that Rory would make this pronouncement and, once again, embarrassed him at being praised for a talent he felt he hadn't mastered even yet. Especially after his recent episode, when his spirit had mostly been away from his corporeal self, when he had treated his friends so horribly. "I appreciate your praise," he said. "I always strive to live up to what folks think I already have mastered."

"Well," Rory said, "I think you'll come to terms with just how phenomenal of a young man you already are, and then just accept the accolades you've earned in 'striving to live up to it all.'

"Thomas, meet Jamari," Rory said to the other judge. "Jamari, this is the newest judge of the court. He's here to help carry the load and to allow those of us who were over-burdened before to have essential time for exercise and spiritual renewal."

Looking over this newest addition, Jamari's first impression was he was far too young to carry the title of judge. No older than twenty-eight or twenty-nine, a Native American with a strong nose and dark eyes, Thomas looked like someone Jamari might want to get to know. "A pleasure," he said, reaching his hand over to shake. Thomas had a powerful grip, which held Jamari's hand a little longer than was necessary.

"The pleasure is all mine," Thomas answered. "I've heard many tales about you and have to say you are far too young to have accomplished even half of what I've heard."

The expectations of his reputation seemed to confront him with every new acquaintance. *Can't I just meet someone someday and have them get to know me instead of already knowing so much before we've ever met?*

Along with other introductions, those first days at the court introduced him to his duties of just what things were associated with being a "court assistant." Jamari ran errands. He relayed messages. And fetched meals when it was inconvenient for a judge or other officer of the court to take time out and visit the dining room. He escorted citizens, accused and witnesses, to their various appointments within the halls.

There were still rest days, though, and half-days when he could have some time to himself. One such day, he decided to visit the hills around the courts, which he had never explored before. Setting out with the two keepers, as Jamari still thought of them, although they had names and shared his living quarters when he was up in Milltown Hall, he reflected it was becoming much more difficult to find meditative peace when they were traipsing along.

He had always assumed stealth (quiet, peaceful passage) was a standard practice within the Tribe. Lon and Joshua, however, seemed completely immune to such niceties. He resigned himself to his fate, leading them to the south, away from the casino/courthouse, to reach the first small rise that held some semblance of a wild place. He was always more comfortable, more relaxed, and more able to reach his inner calm and feel the God-within when he was in a place less sullied by man and his passage. Hence, the sense of resignation knowing these two were sure to disturb any level of peace and tranquility he could hope for.

He found an inviting spot, a meadow edged with a small copse of alder, and settled down on crossed knees to lean against the trunk of one. "Do you think you two could settle quietly?" he asked them peevishly after the branch breaking ground-shaking journey up.

"I'm sorry, Jamari," Joshua answered for both. "We know how much you need quiet and solitude for your shamanism. We also must ensure your safety as well. Quiet, we can do. We can find a place of comfort where we shouldn't need to move. We can't go far enough away where you won't be able to sense us in your spirit walk, though."

He looked suitably impressed at what was a challenging feat these days for Jamari. With his continuing reticence about going too deep into trance, just reaching his inner spirit was a challenge. It didn't get any better when these two were hovering.

"I apologize," Jamari told them. "I'm still getting used to the fact that I have minders, and I'm taking out the resentment on the two of you. It's not your fault, and you're doing what the Knight Shaman assigned you to do. Probably with far more patience than I deserve for all my grumbling and grouching."

Lon took a step closer to Jamari and squatted, letting his loin cloth fall between two tightly muscled thighs. At face level, he leaned forward and placed a kiss on Jamari's forehead.

"You have shared your life, your home, and your bed with us," he whispered. "We are one in more ways than you know." He stood, bringing his waist back level with Jamari's face. "Don't think of us as an intrusion," he suggested. "Instead, think of us as an extension of your very self. That's how I think of the three of us." He turned and strode off on surprisingly light feet, lifting himself up on his toes with every step, bunching up his amazingly rounded butt. He barely scuffled the grass as he lightly tiptoed around sticks and twigs, and then he settled into a crouch beside a nearby brushy enclave as Joshua also crept away on silent feet.

Why all the noise when we were traveling up? Jamari wondered. *When they can ghost into silence and disappear with such ease? Was all the noise on purpose? Meant to scare off any predators who they could have surprised by a stealthier approach?* He hoped not, since he enjoyed seeing the squirrels gracefully dancing along limbs; the deer daintily stepping amongst the ferns and roots, and even the wrens and voles who put the finishing touches to life in the world he sought.

He let his suspicions fade as he contemplated a glimpse of bright clouds, cumulous and rising, capturing the sun at their edges and thus highlighting the darkness of the internal mass. As he settled himself against the trunk of a Red Alder, he let his awareness flow out to the surrounding area as naturally as breathing in the rich smell of healthy forest humus. He did sense Lon and Joshua and he purposefully included their essence as a part of his own and found that helped him reach his spirit-self.

He was just beginning to feel the essence of the alder copse when another presence brought him to alertness. He opened his eyes to see Joshua, bow drawn, an arrow aimed towards a large cougar.

His totem visited again, only this time, Jamari had sensed the approaching presence. "Hold your shot," he quietly ordered Joshua as he saw Lon in the background coming silently up from behind the predator.

Joshua's response was to draw the bow back even farther, obviously preparing to release an arrow at full draw. Jamari reacted with unthought instinct, reaching down to his side and grasping his knife from its sheath. In one fluid motion, while still seated, he drew and flung it as a missile to hit the hand holding the bow.

If he had gauged the distance correctly, the butt of the blade should hit and deflect Joshua's aim. If not, the point could well encounter and severely damage his friend's hand.

The thud of impact sounded out a blunt hit, and the impact deflected the arrow. It flew past Cougar, piercing the ground just to the left of Lon's approaching feet.

Cougar let out a caterwaul of complaint, a mix of a woman's shrill scream and the bass roar of a lion. As the roar abated into a series of purring rumbles, She looked to Jamari, Her tail flicking in annoyance before turning a baleful glare to Joshua through tawny eyes slitted to piercing anger as the predator studied the prey.

Joshua was holding his bruised hand and shaking it to get feeling back into it, maybe to shake out the sharp pain of bruised, but hopefully not broken, bones. He looked up to see those deep eyes studying him with ears pinned back and tail low-slung and twitching. Joshua involuntarily stepped back a couple of paces into the ferns.

Jamari unconsciously reached out with his mind to soothe Cougar from her wrath, much as he had reached for the bobcats that had run rampant through the rooms of his youngling crèche.

She raised Her ears from threat to curiosity as She turned Her head once again to face Jamari. He watched Her pupils expand from the narrow concentration of intent into the wider, more open look of tentative welcome.

With deliberate steps, She approached as Jamari signaled to Lon and Joshua not to interfere. Jamari waited, still cross-legged and seated, fighting off the memory of a wholly different encounter nearly two years ago.

He had occasionally felt discomfort approaching fear when the nearly domestic bobcats had mock-stalked him in serious play those many years before. He'd carried the marks of their teeth and claws through many days as one of the few younglings brave enough to engage their play mode.

With the evidence She had felt his admiration. Even with the widened eyes showing more interest than predator intent, even with the tail held higher in greeting, even with all this, he felt more than uncomfortable as She approached.

They were all tense as Cougar stepped forward and reached Her head out to sniff his outstretched hand, never allowing Her lambent eyes to stray from Her solid lock deep into his own. He felt the heat of Her breath along with the soft brush of chin whiskers for only a moment before She lapped his palm with one swipe of Her spiky tongue and then turned and leaped away, bounding through the copse of alder until She faded back into the forest.

They all shared several moments of stunned silence, watching the ferns settle back from their swaying dance from Her passage. "I think you broke my hand," Joshua finally accused as he continued to shake and wring out the pain.

"It's not broken," Jamari answered harshly. "I very specifically told you to let down your bow, yet your response was to draw it even tighter. Did not the Knight Shaman order you to yield to my judgement regarding things spiritual?" He leaned forward from his cross-legged seat and stood in one fluid motion to stand in confrontation with his guardian.

"I couldn't help myself," Joshua answered. "It shocked me She had gotten so close before I saw Her, and was so afraid She could so easily have taken you into death with only the barest of efforts."

"Do you not remember me telling the Knight Shaman of my last encounter with Cougar?" Jamari asked, his pique relentless. "She came and guarded me the last time I was in meditation. She sat beside me as I wandered through the laughter of trees, and She did me no harm. I knew as soon as I sensed Her She intended no harm this time either. This is my totem! You knew that!"

"I'm sorry," Joshua answered lamely as he bent to pick up his bow from the carpet of ferns and mosses.

"It was a mistake," Lon inserted. "We've all learned something here. I, for one, never really understood what it meant to have Cougar as a totem, to have the spirit to sense Her intent, to have the courage to face Her wrath.

"I, too, was intent on taking Her down if I could. The only reason I didn't have my bow drawn was because I didn't have a shot without also endangering either of you."

They all still shook from the intensity of the encounter. The shrill scream, which could have frozen prey from yards away and which they had experienced at arm's reach, still seemed to rebound around inside their heads.

Lon stepped to Joshua and bent down to retrieve Jamari's blade from a bed of ferns. Lon stood and took the steps to reach Jamari. Then, holding the tip of the ten-inch blade in his hand, he proffered the hilt to his shaman. Jamari noted the visible tremor, magnified by the length of the blade, and made a show of chasing the hilt in a little circle before taking it from his friend.

"I don't know how you do it," Lon said huskily. "How can you be so untouched by what just happened? You're still as steady and solid as if nothing had happened at all."

"It means something different to me, is all," Jamari answered as he sheathed his blade. The three young men stood in uncomfortable silence as they each contemplated differing perceptions of an amazing encounter. Finally, Jamari stepped past Lon to reach for Joshua's hand. He held it in his own, feeling how cold it was, feeling the quivering residue of emotional overload as he bent it and gently moved each bone. "It's only bruised," he concluded as he dropped the now lax hand.

"I'm going to find another place to settle," he told them. "Joshua, you stay here. I'll deal with you later."

From his new place, with energies quickened and turned into roiling currents of emotion, he finally acknowledged the truth of the day to himself. *There's no way I'll be able to get back into meditation*, he admitted. With reluctance, he pulled himself away from the dappled patch of shade/sun he had found. He looked around to see Lon hovering.

"We may as well start back," he said. He looked at the sky to see where the sun was. "It's only been a short while, and we have until this afternoon before I'm called to other tasks. I guess I can work on the totem for a while."

When Joshua stepped around a small copse of tight-grown maple, he just looked at him. "You can guard the rear as we go back," Jamari ordered in a harsh tone, relaying lack of forgiveness.

He made no progress at all on the totem pole. He recognized he had no ideas, no thoughts of what he intended with any part of it. In fact, he hated the very thought of the endless project hanging from the eaves. If there had been some fire starting material available, he realized, he might even have burned it.

In their room later, he came as close to being rough with Zach as he ever had since his travels with the Spirit last fall. He realized the still-rampant emotion before he did any harm, though. He rolled away, giving himself to Zach, and felt his lover's relief before settling into a troubled slumber.

Days later, with Jamari constantly putting Joshua on "rear guard," Lon forced him to bridge the wound his anger had become.

"You have completely forgotten the emotional intelligence classes of our youth!" Lon accused. "If this is the best that a shaman, even one still just in training, can do, then we're doomed to fail as a tribe!"

"What would you have me do?" Jamari shouted back at him as they continued their walk, loud enough that Joshua surely heard them from his following position. "What reward should I give him for trying to kill my totem? What smarmy words should I give him to make him feel better about it?" He felt hot tears building at the corners of his eyes and turned away to dash them off, hoping Lon wouldn't notice. Knowing he would anyway.

"I would have you admit that he's human!" Lon replied, the very first time he had ever raised his voice to Jamari. "As I would have you admit that *you're* human!" His voice rose even further, spittle spraying from his mouth as he shouted, "You can't go on with this irrational anger eating away at you!"

Lon paused, looking back to see Joshua dashing tears from his own eyes as he witnessed the argument. "Try to remember the emotional intelligence lessons," he cajoled in a lower, slower voice. "You've been so tightly self-contained for so long you're bursting out now, releasing all that pent-up anger-grief-fear-frustration onto someone who loves you more than you'll ever know." He paused again, stopping their walk at a shady declivity in the trail, set up against a rising bank, sheltered from the heat of the mid-day sun.

Incongruously, he removed his shirt, pointing to the tattooed rank of First Lieutenant on his upper left arm.

"This," he said with emphasis, "says you'll listen to me, Ensign Jamari Shaman. You will sit here with Joshua while I step up the path. You will talk with him. You will *be* with him. If I step back down this path as the evening falls and you haven't found a way to forgive him, to bring him back into your confidence, to bring your emotions back into control, my only recourse will be to take this matter to the Knight Shaman."

Jamari looked at a dejected Joshua as Lon stepped up the trail after seeing them settled into the small opening. Joshua's head hung low, unwilling to meet Jamari's eyes. Jamari could see the brighter patches where tears had washed away the dust of the trail. Joshua's shoulders slumped in defeat, and his very inner spirit sang out his pain. Being forced to see the result of his actions, Jamari couldn't help but feel shame. Emotional intelligence, he scoffed to himself. It has departed me for sure, along with my ability to be a shaman.

He remembered the memory from his early training: Emotion is not wrong. It's what you do with it that becomes wrong. Open yourself to the emotion. Let yourself feel it. Identify the cause and then let it go. Let it go.

It was a slow realization, but one he comprehended as the woodland animals rustled about again: he couldn't be angry and spiritual at the same time. They have taught me emotional intelligence. This is just the first time I've ever needed to apply the training and internal insight to anger.

Misplaced affection, I've been through.

Sex thought of as love I've dealt with.

Attachment become bond.

Grief of loss.

Those I've dealt with and been able to control. Most of the time. Anger is new. Why am I holding it so close? Nursing it into a rage? Why am I so angry in the first place? Was it really Joshua's disobedience?

Looking back, that fear response was perfectly natural. Fear! I was afraid during the encounter. Afraid of the lion. Afraid of the danger to my totem. Afraid of the havoc a lion would wreak with an arrow through it. And most of all, afraid that my keepers and lovers would see that fear.

Holding onto his own irrational anger was hurting himself even more than it was hurting Joshua.

"I'm sorry," he said as he reached to put his arms around his friend. The anger, once identified and questioned, lost its power.

"We've built too much between us for me to destroy it now. I value you. I value your insights, your perceptions, your faithful watch over my well-being." He could feel Joshua beginning to soften his tense rejection.

"Please," he said. "Let me hold you at least," he begged of his lover.

"I'm so sorry," Joshua cried in quiet pain as he leaned into Jamari's arms. "I was so afraid. So scared I would lose you."

"I was scared too," Jamari whispered into the dark hair where Joshua nested his head into his shoulder. "I was afraid of too many things all at once. And the biggest fear of all was that you had seen."

"I saw no fear," Joshua exclaimed, lifting his head. "Lon was right when he asked how you could do it. How you could be so calm facing the wrath of the largest cougar either of us has ever seen."

"Yes, I was afraid," Jamari answered, reaching a hand up to trace a tear down the face next to his own. Then he looked into those deep brown eyes and fell in.

When Lon came back down the trail, Jamari had settled his clout back into place and they were brushing the dirt and twigs out of their hair and clothes. They were once again in alignment with each other.

"Good," was all Lon said. "Good."

Chapter Eight

Outside World Peeking In

A land of Law cannot be a land of Justice.
Similarly, a land of Justice cannot be a land of Law.
We will not accept this!

Justin Earl Knight,
Founder of the Elk Creek Tribe

Near the end of April, with a lull in the court activities, Jamari found a few days free to get up-river and relax in his rooms in Milltown Hall. Terry also made his way up to spend some time in counsel with Chief Elkhead, Chief Milltown, and Chief Elk Creek. Nearing noon on their third day at home, Jamari had stopped over in Terry's rooms for a morning of lessons and togetherness. They were sharing tea when a messenger banged on the door. The messenger told them Terry needed to get down to the courthouse for an emergency meeting. A flustered few minutes later, they dressed for the damp spring day and headed down the halls to the front entrances of Milltown Hall.

"What could it be?" Jamari asked as they hurried down the halls towards the front entrance.

"I don't have any idea," Terry answered, "but it'll be good for you to see one more of the myriad of things we ask the Knight Shaman to tend to." This seemed like yet another reference to his likely role, and Jamari let it pass. If they offered the position to him, he would decide to accept or not at that time.

They quickly set up the canoe for the trip down the valley. It was the quickest way to reach the courthouse, but Jamari always felt guilty knowing it would leave someone the chore of carting it back upriver along the trail so it would be ready for any future summons. Paddling a canoe up this portion of Elk Creek with its rushing rapids was not something one did other than for the simple exercise of the attempt.

After a spirited trip down, with Jamari in the front and Terry in the back, both driving their paddles with determination, they landed at the docks next to the courthouse and saw nothing out of the ordinary at all. There were no extra people, no visible tension in those who awaited them, nothing to show what the urgency was about.

They made their way from the back entrance to the courts section of the building. "So, what's the deal?" Terry asked when they reached the main courtroom, looking around at the members of the court: Jamari's friends Joshua and Lon, along with one other court bailiff, a court recorder, three assistants, Judges Thomas and Rory, and a few whose role Jamari still didn't know.

"News from Salem," Thomas answered solemnly.

"Well," Rory interjected, "what we have is some alarming news from up north. "The eastern heirs of one of the timber companies have filed for repossession of the Milltown Hill forest lands. They filed in the state court in Salem last month and we just got notification today from the weekly couriers. We may need to increase the number of trips the plane makes!"

"Whew!" Terry exclaimed. "Not only do we have a lot of folks living on those lands, but it's also home to the Founder's Grove and the Founder's Grave." He stopped to look pointedly over at Jamari, knowing the little he knew about Jamari's spirit dreams of the Founder's Grove and his belief that the Spirit of the Founder was still living there. "This will take some thought. Did the couriers have any documentation we can look over? Is there a timeline for a response?"

Jamari still didn't have a clear idea of just how to express his still-nebulous thoughts regarding the Founder's Grove, and he suddenly felt an increased pressure to get on it.

In the ensuing discussion, Terry, as chief judge and as the tribal legalist with the most experience in the outer world's courts, would be the Tribe's chief representative for this challenge.

By the end of the next day, they had managed a meeting of council members and set some directions and research in progress. They dispatched Thomas up to Salem to gather as much information as he could find on the filing. They took Terry from all court appearances and put him full time on researching the claims and background of the Wearehauses Timber Company, which had sued. Jamari, as his assistant, stayed busy fetching the molding remnants of files from the darker recesses of the courthouse storage rooms.

Trips up to the woods became short and trivial. Work on his totem pole came to a virtual standstill. And he learned way more than he ever wanted to know about just how valuable a paper trail could be. The two even made a surreptitious trip up to Milltown Village and to the darker catacombs of Milltown Hall to do some research in the electronic archives. It was surreptitious because there were those who still didn't even know of the presence of the server rooms and the vast resources of tribal lore and knowledge contained there.

As he entered the cool rooms, he felt and heard the slow rustle of fans and towers, and he looked up at the large wall monitor on which he had first witnessed the recording of the Founder presenting Jamari's first video presentation. That monitor remained dark for this visit, though, and the Knight Shaman led him into a small alcove of a research room with two smaller monitors, each with keyboards on accordioned leashes connecting to wall plugs and into the vast database of the central system.

Pictures on "microfiche," whatever that was, occupied his entire day. As Terry rapidly scrolled from one page to another, enlarging some for no reason Jamari could discern and discarding others with barely a glance, Jamari couldn't even fathom what his role in this room might be. Terry was so intent on his search that Jamari didn't dare ask for guidance or instruction.

Nearing noon of a long morning, he saw movement out in the primary space and quietly exited the alcove to seek some human interaction. What he found was an acolyte of the I.T. world, an otherwise perfectly normal man of indeterminate age with a balding pate. A truncated braid announced a very unlikely membership in the warrior set of tribal members. He wore a set of homespun trousers, a rough-side-out set of shoes with some edges of sheep fur showing through, and a woolen sweater to ward off the coolness of this sepulchral monastery. All this unlikely apparel matched with a set of spectacles. Jamari had seen these devices on rare occasions, mostly on older men who would put them on to read smaller print. This individual seemed to need them always, and Jamari's eyes watered when he tried to look through the lens to make eye contact. The eyes appeared over-sized behind the glass lenses, eyelashes seeming to be the size of pencils from the magnification. "Um, hello," Jamari greeted him. "I'm here with the Knight Shaman, but I'm feeling useless right now. I'm wondering if you could help."

The man looked up from the pad of paper he was carrying, the new angle distorting the picture of his eyes even more. "Hmmm?" he asked.

"I'm Jamari. I'm here with the Knight Shaman." He pointed over to the alcove and the back of Terry's head.

"Oh!" the man exclaimed. "Jamari Shaman! I'm so glad to meet you!" He reached out to grasp Jamari's hand, dropping his tablet, remaining completely uncaring of the scatter and rustle of pages fluttering down on the floor.

"Sure. Th-thanks," Jamari stuttered, trying in vain to free his hand from the clammy, clinging grip. "What's your name?"

"Oh. Sorry. I'm Jerry. Still just studying the I.T. Arts. Should be a journeyman in the next couple of years, though!"

"Well, Jerry, the Knight Shaman and I are here to research some very important documents about a court case up in Salem and I don't have the foggiest idea of how to help him, much less how to follow along with what he's even doing. Can you help me learn enough of this whirring monstrosity to contribute something?"

"Oh, sure," Jerry said, finally releasing Jamari's hand. "Look, it's really easy. You just put the cursor over the first menu, click it, and type in the database you want to research in. Then you enter the file types you're looking for. Then you highlight from the menus and open the files you want to read."

Jamari's eyes had glazed over long before this string of arcane and cultish-sounding utterances ended. It seemed on the surface to be in the English language, yet he couldn't put any of the words into play in his mind for just what they were supposed to mean. "Um. Thanks," he muttered back. "Do you think you could show me how to, what was it, 'Type'?"

Jerry stuttered back a couple of steps in seeming amazement at this demonstration of complete ignorance. He looked around the room as though searching for someone lurking behind a tower or in one of the whirring alcoves between rows of square boxes stacked atop each other in tall, long rows, looking for someone to spring the joke on him. To laugh at him and this ignorant shaman. Seeing no one, he turned back to Jamari. "Are you sure you're supposed to be in here?" he asked quizzically.

"Well, the guard out front let us in," Jamari answered. "And then the Knight Shaman" - emphasizing the title to encourage some cooperation from this apparition of a person - "got all tangled up in that researching and let me know I was annoying him by trying to offer help." He pointed again to where Terry had leaned back in his chair.

"Oh! THE Knight Shaman!" Jerry exclaimed on seeing Terry's face. Suddenly, he darted off and over to where Terry sat, offering the same stammering near-worship he had offered Jamari, only with more groveling involved. Jamari stepped over just as Terry told Jerry he had found all he needed so far. To please "print out" the "queue" he had put in and said he would send Jamari back for the documents after they had eaten lunch down in the main hall.

Terry motioned for Jamari to follow him out through the labyrinth. "Don't ask," he said when they got outside. "I got the information I needed. It'll be ready in an hour. You'll come back there to pick up the documents." He pointed to a side door just down the hall from the entryway into the server room. "Then we'll go to my rooms for the afternoon, and I'll show you what I'm looking for in order to get this trial going our direction."

The whir of the sudden case left Jamari missing many of the prime points of the year. Spring celebration at the first of May came and went as they continued their diligent search of records and files. The year, 2117, was racing by and now nearly half gone. Peter Shaman had conducted the tribal ceremonies, as he had for many years before Terry had taken over as Knight Shaman. Zach had been his assistant, reaching a point where he was taking part in some of the more important spiritual rites.

The hurry of the research behind them, their case finally in order, and the date up at the Salem State Court still some time off, Terry and the others had found all they needed to refute the spurious claim. After the intensity of those three weeks, Terry and Jamari had decided a brief break from the courts was in order, so they had journeyed upriver to their true homes in Milltown Hall.

They walked the short distance down to the footbridge, over the creek, and then back up to the fish ladder. There, Jamari learned the joy of meditating and communing with the inner God while ensconced inside the viewing area. With windows on three sides, the rush of winter flows had subsided, and the water, which had been a muddy brown through most of the winter, was settling into an emerald color that brought a glowing and flickering green to play on the walls of the view rooms.

The constant susurration, altering in pitch and tone as the currents washed and swirled past the viewing windows, was very conducive to a peaceful meditation, though the constant flow noises had at first kept him from the necessary disconnect from the physical. Jamari found that through just listening, feeling, being, the journey inward was easier. The cacophony of the roiling water outside cycled into a repetitive and soothing pattern. The longer he sat, the longer he just *was*, the deeper he felt himself going into his inner self.

Still in a bit of a daze as they left the view rooms, he came back to reality during the short walk down to the footbridge and then back up the creek to the Milltown Hall side.

"I've arranged for someone to help with your spirit walking," Terry told him as he shut the door to his common room behind them. The main foyer offered a placid view of the lake waters behind his window, which was a soothing silence. Terry motioned Jamari to a seat against the wall, where they could gaze out the window. Jamari shifted the chair so he could watch the light-play as waters, stirred by the wind above, formed small ripples and built a prismatic dancing rainbow along the floor.

"Especially the aspect you've recently discovered of communing with some trees and forests," Terry continued. "You will be surprised, but I think pleased as well. She has been training in the shamanistic arts a few years longer than you have. She showed a special affinity with the wild woods very early in her life and has sought positions which put her in outdoor activities nearly continuously. Just a minute."

Terry paused as he stepped over to the door to his personal quarters. When he opened the door, Jamari was stunned to see Sophie, the first woman he had ever fathered a child with. He straightened from his casual slouch in the chair as she stepped into the room. It was the same woman, only more so.

Besides having developed more of the classic hourglass figure, with a slimmish waist and slightly wider hips, she seemed to have a presence beyond what she had exhibited in their brief encounter on their assignation day over a year and a half before. He still remembered his very first encounter with her, way back when she was still a child and he was still in the youngling's hearth, with Jahangir as hearth leader.

"Hello Jamari," she said as she walked across the room to him, "I am called Sophia Shaman now." Attired in full leathers, pale, almost white, with a beaded skirt under a fringed blouse, her blue eyes seemed a shade softer under the effect of the water-filtered light dancing along the floor. She braided her brown hair into a single long braid that reached down to her waist.

Jamari stood to greet her, accepting her hug gracefully. "Is it appropriate to ask about our child?" he asked.

"Of course," she answered with a smile. "We have a daughter who is doing well in the infants' crèche. She got our blue eyes, but at this point anyway, she seems to have found a gene which gives her glossy black hair. She seems very inclined to use this combination to woo anyone who'll be tempted into giving her special treats in reward for being 'just so cute.'"

Jamari laughed at the description. "Of course," he said, "she would have to be beautiful given who her parents are.

"But what of you? Terry says you may help me as I'm learning my talents and the demands which seem to arise from them."

"I'm sure you remember the very first time we met." Sophia became serious. "I've had a calling to the natural world for as long as I can remember. They recognized it early on and the Tribe has set my tasks to keep me in touch with the wild world through all the other processes I went through as a child growing into a fully functioning citizen.

She had just let him know she had completed the Womanhood Rites, Jamari realized as she continued.

"Believe it or not, we in the women's hearths have developed stronger spiritual ties into the spirit of the wild places than the men."

"Why would I find that hard to believe?" Jamari asked.

"Why, because you are a man," Sophia laughed. "Ego-centric, testosterone, conquest, and all that nonsense."

Jamari laughed with her. Terry said his goodbyes. "I've got to go meet the chief," Terry said. "Please, make yourselves at home here. Lunch will be down at the main cafeteria in about an hour. I'd be honored if the two of you could join me there."

"Of course," Sophia answered. "It would be a pleasure."

"I'll look forward to seeing you then," Jamari added as Terry left the room.

"Well, should we sit?" Jamari offered. "And I'd love to hear what ideas you have to aid me in understanding what my talents are taking me through now."

Sophia laughed quietly at his description as she sat in the other plush chair beside Jamari to view the quiet waters of the lake. "Well," she said as they both got comfortable, "although we women have developed a closer affinity with the wild woods and their creatures, we've never experienced being called by those same woods to do something as seems to happen with you. Nor have any of us fallen into the God's embrace for as long as you have."

"What is it the Knight Shaman hopes for by having you help me out, then?" Jamari asked.

"He speculates you are hearing the trees, but he doesn't know if they are hearing or recognizing you. Other than the comment you made after your first contact with the grove above Milltown Village, anyway."

"I'm not sure I remember the comment." Jamari grew pensive as he tried to remember the day. "I saw the tracks of a very large cougar which had come close to me, and I could see where it had sat watching me during a lost day of 'communing,' but I don't remember what else I might have said."

"He said you had mentioned the trees were laughing at you as you pulled away," Sophia answered.

"Oh." Jamari paused for a moment. "I still don't get it," he said.

"Well, I will be available to watch over you while you're in trance. I won't be trying to kill any of the forest spirits who may seek you out while you're communing, but I won't let any of them harm you, either. Any other help I can be is less obvious. With my affinity with the forest, he hopes I'll be able to sense any response from the trees and then help you understand more about what to 'feel' for or what sense to use, or anything else I can do to help actually communicate with them. If it's possible."

"Well, I think the whole 'Cougar thing' is settled anyway," Jamari said. "Did he tell you about the last time I was out? With the two escorts? Just as I was entering meditative trance, I felt Cougar approaching again. This time, I sensed Her presence and returned from meditation to see Joshua getting ready to shoot Her. I could barely keep him from killing Cougar, but he missed his aim, and Cougar flounced off through the woods on Her way. Then we all pretended nothing had happened as I attempted to visit with the trees. I felt nothing at all from that copse, though. Just a time of quiet contemplation under a peaceful canopy."

Their conversation covered what they could about Jamari's exploits, what he felt the compulsion might be regarding the talking woods, and back around again to their baby before the lunch hour came along.

Chapter Nine

An Unexpected Ally

"We're going to a dinner tonight with a special group of tribal members," Terry informed them over lunch. "This is an initiation for you, Jamari, and some others as well. We call it the 'welcoming of the awakened.' The term is from some of the oldest Gnostic texts. When we recognize someone has awakened, when they have 'left the dream state of normal existence behind,' we welcome them into the community of other awakened ones.

"Even though we've taught you about Gnosticism, along with other spiritual systems, we have talked little about the various levels of human existence recognized by the Gnostics. I want you to understand those differences now, before we go to the dinner this evening." He put his meat and cheese onto a slice of bread, which he topped with some lettuce and tomato before smearing another slice of bread with mayonnaise and building his sandwich.

"The 'awakened' is the level you'll be initiated into," he continued once the sandwich assembly was complete, and he mashed it down so it would fit into his mouth. "There are fewer people who reach this level. Though, with our constant focus on the inner spirit from the earliest age, there are far more now than ever before. As 'awakened' we have reached a place where our spirit-self is aware, and we are seeing the world from fresh eyes and perceiving things in new ways. We have gotten deeply in touch with our inner spirit. This is the first of three broad categories. The 'awakened' were called pneumatics in ancient times. It was a recognition of the 'spirit' as being airy."

Terry took a bite of the sandwich. "Not bad," he commented after a sip of juice.

"Another level comprises those who are awakening. They have begun to perceive their inner-self as recognizing the world around them in new ways. These were called psychics. The vast majority of humanity falls into this category.

"The last level of human existence, as identified by the early Gnostics, comprises those who have no hope of awakening. They are called hylics. The Tribe, after many years of observation, has observed a further stratification within the hylics, finding a subgroup. Those are soulless.

"The ancient texts didn't describe them as such, but it's the best categorization we can find which also helps us to recognize an inherent danger they pose. I know you've had some experience with a couple of people who fit into this category. Scott, the corporal you met in Yoncalla, seems very much like one, but he has shown signs to those of us who watch that he may bring his soul out from deep hiding. He may not, which would make him a true hylic, or he could manage it and then be a psychic." Terry took a couple more bites of his sandwich as Jamari and Sophia were finishing up their own.

"Lynn," Terry continued again, "who we've been observing for many years, is almost certainly never going to awaken. There doesn't seem to be anything inside of him even trying to connect to the world around him. His actions seem to show he is simply looking to see what's in it for him.

"I've told you before, when the Tribe was first founded, there was a much higher incidence of hylics, the soulless ones. Something to do with the cultural lack of spirituality of those times is what we suspect.

"Anyway, tonight, we'll be presenting you as an awakened one." He stopped here to look over to Sophia, who shook her head slightly, an unspoken "no" to an unasked question.

"There will be other presentations as well," he continued. "You'll want to gussy yourself up with your Cougar cape and your best leathers. I'll let you head on over to your rooms to get ready. I suspect Lon and Joshua are already there waiting for you." As always, Jamari assumed this meant the Knight Shaman had directed them.

Jamari hugged Sophia as they stood. "It's been great to spend some time with you," he said. He watched Terry and Sophia walk out of the dining hall together, and then he turned to his own rooms and an afternoon with two friends.

At the dinner, Jamari had yet another shock in store. With full pomp and circumstance, the spiritual leaders of the Tribe paraded in. They introduced Rodney as the first shaman and the First Knight Shaman. They presented Peter as a shaman and the Second Knight Shaman.

They presented one lady as Lillian, the Sophia Shaman, the second of that line. Jamari hadn't even been aware there was such a position, but once he heard it, he realized it made perfect sense. The approach to spirituality was different between male and female, so why not also have a supreme level of female shaman who was guide and goad to female shamans as Terry was to male shamans? Then they introduced Terry as the Knight Shaman.

After the introductions, the Sophia Shaman stood from her seat to the left of Chief Elk Creek at the head of the table, showing her age in the care behind each step, yet looking regal at the same time. He found it odd that his friend had the same name!

"I have been the Sophia Shaman for over thirty seasons," she announced to the assemblage. "As many of you know, the name 'Sophia' comes from the first of the Aeons, who sprang from the dream of the Monad. It was Sophia who wanted to create something of her own, and from that need spawned the Creator God. We took on the mantle of Sophia Shaman to work mankind back into the grace of the Highest One." She paused as she considered whether to repeat the full legend, which had carried forward through the centuries from over two thousand years before, when the Gnostics had still been a spiritual influence on the tides of man. It was obvious when she reached the decision to not share the story yet again, as she looked back out at the diners with new determination.

"Now one comes who surpasses my skills and will assume the mantle of Sophia Shaman. Sophia, please rise."

From the women's side of the table, Jamari's Sophie rose to step forward. He hadn't picked her out from the gathering, but as she strode forth, he saw the confidence with which she approached this new role. She was wearing the mantle of Wolf, her totem animal, over her ceremonial leathers.

Lillian Sophia Shaman lifted the strap of a leather pouch that had hung unnoticed at her side, as if it were such an integral part of her it simply was unseen until removed. In fact, the dress leathers she wore showed shiny indentations of long-held contact where the pouch had rested for many years. The Sophia Shaman lifted the strap over Sophia's head and placed the pouch at her side.

"I abdicate my role as Sophia Shaman in favor of one who is better able to perform these duties," the old Sophia Shaman announced in a voice that held the quavery quality of extreme age as the pouch settled in at his Sophie's side.

"I accept this role," the new Sophia Shaman answered. "You can step aside from this burden, Lillian Shaman, but I hope you will keep yourself available to me as I learn my fresh duties and challenges. I hope you will assist me where you may." Lillian Shaman marched down the table to Sophia's previous seat after seeing the new Sophia Shaman into the chair at the left hand of Chief Elk Creek.

Jamari, seeing a transformation right before his eyes, recognized his Sophie was gone forever, subsumed into this new role. He understood the subtle denial she had made at lunch. Terry had been offering to share the information with Jamari prior to the actual assumption, and she had declined.

Once the transfer of the spiritual mantle had been completed, the attendees enjoyed their dinner in amiable conversation. Near the end of the dinner, the Knight Shaman arose to address the assembly.

"I welcome you here tonight," he addressed them as a whole, "with a special welcome to those few new members attending their first evening's camaraderie with their fellow pneumatics and psychics. It is you, the newest members, whom I address first.

"In the earliest days after Christ departed to the heavens, during which spiritual practices were being developed which would define the next few millennia, there became a schism between two dominant factions. These factions ranged over a broad array of spiritual practices and beliefs. All were trying to base themselves on what Christ taught us during his time on Earth with our ancestors. On one end of that broad spectrum were the beginnings of the Catholic Church. Originally, the term 'catholic' simply meant 'of broad base' and was used to describe an all-encompassing set of spiritual guidelines.

"Over the first few centuries after Christ's departure, those on the far right of the spectrum limited the spiritual practices they qualified as serving Christ. One of the most basic of these limitations was that the new 'Catholic' (now defined as 'of relating to the Catholic Church') set a tenet decreeing only the supreme pontiff (in those days a bishop over an entire city or regions combined faithful, and not the pope as today) could speak to God on behalf of man. They developed a creed which became a driving mantra: when man is away from the bishop, therefore, he is away from God.

"On the other end of this wide spectrum (the founders would identify as 'the far left') were the Gnostics. The Gnostics believed any man or woman who was 'awakened' could represent him or herself to God in prayer and practice.

"This divide eventually developed such a schism that the Catholic Church declared all practitioners of Gnosticism to be heretics and ex-communicants. As you may surmise from our existence here today, Gnosticism survived. This was only barely. Gnosticism had all but died out before the discovery of some ancient, long-hidden texts which gave justification to some widely separated and tiny groups of adherents who had survived the centuries of purges. The discovery and translation of these documents allowed a re-birth of the practices which we in the Tribe employ to this day." Terry motioned to another member to stand.

"One of the main tenets of Gnosticism was any 'awakened' member could assume the mantle of priest or bishop for the duration of one of their celebrations of mass. They tempered this by further understanding each individual in attendance would hear, evaluate, and decide for him or herself the validity of any inspiration or thought offered. Tonight, we will hear from Paul Shaman of the Yellow Creek Village." Terry welcomed Paul to the place of honor at the head of the room and then took his seat again.

Paul was a man of middle years, with strands of gray in his black braid, which swung in an undulating wave down to his hips as he moved. He wore fringed leathers with beaded enhancements sewn into patterns on his breast. One pattern seemed to depict the masked bandit, as if Racoon were his spirit guide.

"Why do some spiritual leaders say, 'The man who conquers sex becomes a God'?" Paul began. His voice was deep and resonant, carrying throughout the room with ease.

"Because enlightenment is when an individual recognizes their 'self' as containing the whole. The body-self, which is the identity-self. The spirit-self, which is the gained-self through enlightenment. The soul-self, which is the self which some do not possess. Perhaps even the totem-self if one is chosen by one of the many avatars of God. All as one complete self: the God-Self.

"It's when someone has dropped the deep sense of separation of self, not that they don't recognize their body and its individuality but more that they deeply recognize the conglomerate self as a part of their 'whole,' so the urges of the body-self are only a small part of the conglomerate self." Paul paused in his oration for a moment, taking a sip from a hardened-clay mug before continuing.

"They are a witness, not a thinker. So why sex? Because sex is one of the hardest desires to overcome, the deepest sense of ego-self wants to dominate another individual's illusion of self. A very selfish emotion: ultimate domination of another.

"Someone in the first stage of enlightenment, (what we call 'awakening' or 'psychic'), which is when they recognize all their 'selfs' as one but still haven't integrated all those aspects fully, will still have the physical desires of sex more than the spiritual and social desires of sex because the physical self is still so much a part of their existence. When they see a sexually attractive person, it may pull them out of their recognition, out of selflessness. They start to desire and lust. One minute, they are in full center, recognizing the oneness, and then the next their 'I' is back, thinking about all they would do with that person or object if given the chance. Recognition gone.

"Not that sex is evil. It's a beautiful thing, but the lust involved is what makes a difference. Watch the mind at that moment and you can tell.

"Think of recognition: it's like if you were to be looking at a portion of a painting or motif, perhaps only partly reflected in a mirror, or as seen through a set of hanging drapes flapping in a breeze, and you can't recognize what it's supposed to be. Then there's a moment of clarity, and you finally see enough to grasp what it is, holding the recognition of what is. Recognizing the whole as one is just like that, only, as soon as the thinking mind is back, the recognition is lost. So, sex, the physical lust, pushes back the thinker, the deep sense of spirit-self.

"The day the recognition stays is also the day you have achieved God. Enlightenment does not mean the end of sex. It is the beginning of a new kind of sex. It's of the moment, not something of the mind, not a thought. If you fully welcome all your varying 'selfs' during sex, you can reach the deepest states of meditation because, during the orgasm, a kind of death happens. In that moment, you lose yourself totally." Paul paused here, looking around the assembled.

"And *that* is also when you find yourself so completely you will never even hope for simple sex as an act of lust again, because you've found a spiritual match and made something together that can never be bettered except as the deepest of sharing found only with another awakened soul." Paul reached into the leather carry bag that hung at his side and pulled out a page, yellowed with age, which seemed to have actual typed letters on it! In an age where typewriters were only now being developed again, this paper was decades old at the least.

"I want to offer you the words of one of the other founders of our community," Paul said as he moved that paper up to where he could read from it. "Russell Cullen joined the Tribe as one of the first wave of adoptees, after they had already granted us recognition as one tribe of indigenous Americans. He helped to develop the culture and community we enjoy to this day. I offer you a poem he wrote decades before joining with the Elk Creek Tribe. Evidence of his philosophic questioning long before he helped to use philosophic reason to build our culture."

INSTINCT

From my porch,
I look up to the mountain
And listen to the night.
Then I'm drawn up into the darkness.

The night pauses,
Waiting for me to pass.
Finally, one rodent
Rustles the underbrush,
And the night breathes on.
The air is alive
As I breathe the shadows in.
The hairs on my arms
Stand painfully erect.
A soft flutter
From a high perch,
Then silent wings,

   And a rabbit scream calls the night.

As the cries echo,
Rebounding around the wood,
I stand frozen at the edge –
Waiting to run,
Waiting to merge
Into the night.
With suddenly heightened senses,
I can almost taste the musk smell of blood
And of rutting.
And I stand
And stand erect.
Nose flared,
I roll my face up
To taste the hungry air.
The wind in my breast
Aches to let go,
To screech out
In a lonely howl.
But I can't let it go.
Because then
The night
Will own me.

IT WAS MORE OF A PERFORMANCE than a reading, as Paul ranged his voice from high to low, adding excitement at key phrases, near-whispering in others. Jamari almost felt it as a shamanic performance given the impact it had on him from the inside out. His own arm hairs were standing as the reading completed!

"Think about those words," Paul said into the silence of the room. "Think about what you felt as I awakened those words from their page.

"Russ was obviously talking about the power of sex. It's scattered throughout the work in subtle ways. 'Because the night will own me.' Use care as you enter this endeavor! We in the Tribe teach sex as one of the most valued and valuable of all human pursuits, yet at times, it is still almost a casual thing!"

The presentation gave Jamari a lot to ponder. He recalled his days when he had been nearly hylic, when his spirit had been sojourning in the glade with Eagle, the Founder, and the Great Spirit and he remembered, once again with deep shame, the callous bedding he had inflicted on his friends and lovers.

After Paul's presentation, Jahangir stood and made his way to the front of the room. "They selected me to be first to make this announcement," he said, looking around the assembled. "But I think others should also share the front place with me as I do. I would call Rodney, the First Knight Shaman and hearth master in the Young Men's Hall; Peter, the Second Knight Shaman, Matthew, chief of Milltown Village, and Terry, the Third and current Knight Shaman, to share this moment with me. If you would, please come up and join me as we all share in this well-earned achievement."

What can these have to do with any announcement? Jamari wondered. He hadn't long to wait, though, so he sat farther forward in his seat to be sure not to miss whatever momentous occasion this might be.

Once they were all at the front, Jahangir looked around again. "I think I've forgotten someone," he said. "Jamari Shaman, would you join us as well?"

Unsure of what this could represent, Jamari looked at Sophia for inspiration. She simply waved her hands in a shooing motion, encouraging him to go up front. He did, passing behind some and in front of others from his seat closer to the back of the assembly. Finally, he was at Jahangir's side, wondering what all the commotion could be about.

"Thank you, Jamari," Jahangir said with a smile. Then he turned to the full audience. "All of us here have helped to raise young Jamari Shaman up through the steps of the Manhood Rites. Each of us has observed a very active mind, constantly seeking to connect with himself and with the people and broader world around him. Each of us, as his advisors, teachers, and guides, has fully agreed that this moment, though early by many standards, meets not just the basic requirements, but surpasses most by far. It is with great pleasure we wish to present Jamari Shaman as a man and complete citizen of the Elk Creek Tribe!"

Everyone in the room stood in respect, and some wit started clapping, so of course, everyone else joined in as well. Jamari himself was flummoxed and bewildered. Two years in the young men's hall, and he was a full citizen already! He hadn't even thought of it as a remote possibility. He was flustered and flushed when the applause died down, and he started to return to his seat, but Jahangir restrained him with a gentle hand on the shoulder.

"We won't ask Jamari to make any momentous speeches or any such," Jahangir said, "but we will, all of us, escort him to his new seat in this council."

Jamari wasn't sure where he would fit, but he allowed himself to be led down the table.

The first person he passed, sitting at the head of the long table, was Chief Elk Creek, who stood and embraced him.

"We need to meet soon," the chief said to him as he held him close. "There will be much to say to each other."

Jamari felt a sudden fear at the contact. It seemed as if Chief Elk Creek had a diminished spirit, far less than the spirit of a tribal citizen, certainly less than what he would expect of a vigorous leader. He looked intently at the Knight Shaman in sudden surprise. Terry simply shook his head. It was a very subtle negation, invisible to the surrounding crowd as the two shamans made a quick decision to not mention this sudden revelation.

"Yes, Chief," Jamari stuttered out in surprise.

They next passed an empty seat where the Knight Shaman had been seated at the right hand of Chief Elk Creek before being called to take part in the ceremony. Jamari looked across the table from the Knight Shaman's seat to see Sophia where she sat at the left hand of Chief Elk Creek. Then they came to a seat where Jacelyn, the chief of the women's hall in Elkhead Village at the head of Lake Yoncalla, sat. She stood as well, giving him an even stronger embrace. "We are so proud of you, Jamari. We expect many great things from you."

Matthew took his place in the next seat after embracing and congratulating Jamari on his completion of the Manhood Rites. Then Peter did the same right beside Matthew. The next seat had been Jahangir's, but he continued farther down with Terry and Jamari. They passed two council members and then saw someone else stand and move farther down.

They placed Jamari in a seat just on the other side of Lillian. When the member who had moved down the table gave him a look of incredulity, perhaps even envy, he realized he was being seated amongst the elite of the Tribe. He accepted Jahangir's and Terry's congratulatory hugs before taking his new seat. Jahangir and Terry returned to their own places at the table.

After some final visitation time, he could say goodnight to Sophia and seek his bed. He would share with Zach tonight and hopefully be able to start a search for his own internal purity of self.

The next day, curious about the key speaker the night before, Jamari asked Terry about Paul Shaman.

"He was actually being considered for the role of Knight Shaman just before I manifested my talents," Terry answered. "While he could see and read the soul/spirit in others, I was the first to learn to suppress and then enhance the emanation of that presence within myself. He still surpasses me in some shamanistic skills. The key difference between us is in how we come to our understanding. I approach from the spiritual side and develop the intellectual interpretation, whereas he approaches from the intellectual side and then works his findings into the spiritual. They are two different approaches which both work to enhance the tribal collective spirit."

"Now, what is going on with Chief Elk Creek?" Jamari demanded. "I know what I felt when he embraced me last night. I've been around him before and never felt such a diminished spirit-self."

"We're still watching closely," Terry answered. "I've noticed and spoken with some other shamans. Peter Shaman, as physician *and* as shaman, is looking into it for us."

Chapter Ten

Conversing with a Glade

Like many shamans, Sophia took on a role as the newest judge of the courts. This had the benefit of allowing her to spend time with Jamari on his still-undefined mission. There was no intention for the Sophia Shaman to spend her career as a judge. It was an important aspect of all spiritual leaders of the Tribe to have experience and participation in the court.

They both suspected it had something to do with her role as Jamari's spiritual mentor. Regardless of why, though, they enjoyed many an afternoon reflecting and meditating together.

Jamari had difficulty allowing himself the same level of camaraderie they had shared before. This was no longer just the mother of his first-born; no longer the companion from his youth; no longer anything simple at all.

This was the Sophia Shaman, with power and influence beyond imagining. Yet he was constantly aware of her sexuality: aware and afraid, remembering the deep soul searching he had endured after his first coupling with her in his first breeding assignment. He remembered pondering far into the night if he were going to be a breeder after their assignation. He looked forward to their days together.

On a day in June, the two met for lunch in the diner in one corner of the vast chamber that had once been the vault of the casino's main concourse. Of the three establishments set up to cater to the throngs who often found their way to the tribal governing center, Jamari found this one somewhat plain, with sandwich opportunities heavy with veggies. "Thank you for agreeing to my favorite place," Sophia said as they found their seats. "I know you enjoy the meatier offerings over on the south side more."

"I've always been told I should eat a more balanced selection," Jamari said. "I can't eat all those fried meats just because I like them." They both watched their server approach. She passed by several other tables to reach them. Was it because those tables had already placed orders? Or, as he suspected, did she recognize the pair and wanted to be sure they had the best and quickest service? Jamari wondered at the level of attention everyone paid when he and Sophia dined together. A new judge and a fledgling shaman who was still trying to find his way. Okay, the new judge was THE Sophia Shaman of the entire tribe and they knew him as Jamari God Walker. There was that.

"Where do you think we should start our investigations of your calling?" Sophia asked once the waiter had departed, leaving glasses of water on the table.

"I think to save time, we should concentrate on places where I've had encounters already," Jamari said. "But the best opportunity seems to be the glade up above Milltown Village, and that's a good hour's walk from here."

"Maybe on a quiet day when we can devote the whole day to the project," Sophia said.

They chose the place where Jamari had first experienced a communion of sorts with the trees of the wild-land.

"We know it's a place where you felt the spirit of the glade," Sophia said. "It's also the only place where you've felt as if a Forest Spirit communicated back to you."

"What makes you say it communicated to me?" Jamari wondered as they set out. The warm weather had arrived, and Jamari was wearing his lightest leggings to protect from brambles on the trail and had elected to carry a shirt in his carry bag instead of wearing it. He wondered at how Sophia could be comfortable in her leather shirt and leggings, with an added leather skirt swaying along with her gait as well.

"Terry told me you felt they were laughing at you as you returned from the spirit world," Sophia replied. "Even if it's not a communication you comprehended fully, given they didn't communicate in a language you know, it was a communication. We just need to figure out how to understand more." She paused as they clambered over a downed tree crossing their path. "Well, understanding is what I'm interested in, anyway," she continued as they set off again. "It's the main reason I agreed to be a part of this exploration when the Knight Shaman asked it of me."

They shared a companionable silence through most of the trek, following the old road up almost to Milltown Village before taking a side path to the south and up into the rising hills. He enjoyed the feel of the tall grass sluicing across his legs, wading through the ferns edging the meadow, seeing and hearing the insects set wing at the invasion, watching the pollen puff up and float in yellow clouds. The ferns were a lush and deep carpet traveling back into the wood as far as they could see.

Jamari led, as he knew where the specific glade was, and they reached it at just after mid-morning, right around the same time he had started his meditations the first time. As he turned to Sophia, he realized he hadn't been called to mating in quite some time. He found his mind remembering with pleasure his one day with Sophia during his first servicing session. He put those thoughts aside as he felt his face warm. "Do we stop at the same spot," Jamari asked, "or go back, trying to find the center of the glade's spirit presence?"

"I think we try the same location," Sophia answered thoughtfully. "It almost feels as if the glade is welcoming you already!"

"I have felt nothing," Jamari said as he looked over at her. "I had to sit still for a long time before I sensed them."

"I don't think I perceive the same things you do," Sophia said. "Even though I can easily sense a broadcast feeling, I could never transmit thought, nor feel anything so specific as what you did last time you were here when you felt 'as if the near trees were bragging about the heat of the sun on their roots, conveying what it felt like to the ones further back who couldn't experience it for themselves.'"

"I did hear, or sense, their celebration," Jamari said in wonder. "So many things I just don't understand, and I blithely overlook one of the most wondrous of all. I heard the trees 'talking' to each other!"

"Well, show me around," Sophia said. "I want to know as much detail as you can recall. Where were you sitting? Where did you see Cougar's imprint? What position were you sitting in? Leaning against a tree or not? We will need to know as much as possible as you attempt to go into their realm again; so I can attempt to follow and understand."

Jamari showed her first where Cougar's imprint had been. All the bent grasses had recovered in the ensuing weeks, but he could mark it closely by where it was in relation to where he had been sitting. He sat in the exact spot, legs crossed in the same way, leaning down in the same way to allow his hand to rest on the soft carpet of moss.

"What's the opening in the moss?" Sophia asked, pointing just to the outside of where his hand rested palm down beside his leg.

"It's where my hand was then," Jamari answered. "When I shifted position, I displaced a section of the moss and then my hand rested in the cool soil underneath while I started my meditation."

Sophia leaned over, carefully lifting more of the moss. In doing so, they both could see a lacery of white filaments lining the dark, almost black, soil. She reached a careful hand out and opened a hole deeper into the loam, finding more and more layers of thread-like substance. "The roots and trailings of funguses," she ventured. "Put your hand over this opened area again and see if you can start your meditation."

Jamari complied, settling into meditation with ease, almost as if something about this area was assisting him into the Other World. Once again, he sensed the trees telling each other what they felt. Only now it seemed the ones closest to him were sharing their impressions of him, of his attempts to commune with them. He had a very vague and distant sense of "hello" and then he was back out in the mundane world where Sophia was tapping his shoulder repeatedly, trying to bring him to focus and awake.

"They said, 'hello'!" he exclaimed as he was rousing.

"Yes," Sophia answered in excitement. "I felt it as you awoke. It took a very long time, though, and you had disappeared from my awareness through most of it."

"Why?" Jamari wondered. "What did I do? What made you think I had disappeared?"

"I eventually figured it out," Sophia answered, still bubbling with excitement at the discovery. "You slowed your mental process down: so slow you became almost a tree yourself.

"How long do you think you were out?" she asked.

"It only seems like a few seconds," Jamari answered. "But my body feels as if it hasn't moved in hours." He shifted himself around, stretching muscles sore from holding a single position for so long, absently brushing his hand against his leather legging. He felt as if he had to rub a bit too vigorously and then realized he was scraping off tendrils of the fungal filament which had clung with tenacity to his palm. They both stared at white tendrils in dark humus soil spotting his legging. The healthy scent of forest soil wafted up and made him recall many earlier sessions when he had "sensed" something from other tracts of forest. Touch. Smell. Thought. Another yet un-named sense that allowed him to be aware of a forest spirit. All these sensations obviously meant something. But what?

"You were in trance for over six hours at least," Sophia informed him. "I used most of the time to realize what you had done. I couldn't slow my thinking down enough to follow what was happening, but I could still sense the wonder this glade felt at interacting with you!"

"How can I have so little to share after such a long time?" he wondered aloud. "They said 'hello.' That's all I get from six hours?"

"I suspect your 'slowing down' matched your thought-speed to their resonance," Sophia speculated. "You took some time to match resonance with them. It's amazing you could do it at all. It's awe-inspiring that a human can hear and speak to trees! But, you're right. It doesn't leave much to communicate when 'hello' and 'hello back' takes six hours!"

"Well, we'd best be heading back down the hill," Jamari said as he stood shakily on legs gone all tingly from inaction. "It looks like we've got an hour of light left. We may be on the road back to the courthouse before full dark falls."

"Perhaps you should say hello to your other escort first," Sophia told him, angling her head to where Cougar rested in nearly the same depression of grass as She had before. Her head lay on Her forepaws as Her eyes sought him out and followed him.

Jamari took a couple of unsteady steps towards Her. She stood, twitching Her tail in a sharp flutter. Her ears remained up and swiveled forward as though to welcome him to come closer. He took those final three steps to where he could reach a tentative hand out. As She leaned into his touch, he wondered at the silky smoothness of Her soft hairs. Did this somehow relate to the cougar that had attacked and tried to kill him almost two years before? *Will I ever feel right wearing the Cougar cape again?* he wondered as he knelt beside Her. On one knee, his other leg propped before him, his head was level with Hers. Her head had nearly twice the mass of his own. Six feet long, not counting the tail, and he was petting Her like one of the tamed bobcats in the youngling's crèche! He reveled in a wordless bonding for a few minutes.

Then Cougar turned Her gaze on him and he felt drawn into Her very being. In a sudden panic of remembering, he recalled the sense of falling into Eagle's eyes at the start of his out-of-body time. He quickly shut his eyes and blocked his connection. Cougar twitched her ears back in seeming annoyance, then turned and leaped out of sight in two bounds, covering twenty feet in long arcs.

"What just happened?" Sophia asked. "I sensed an invitation and then irritation bordering on anger before She turned and leapt away."

"I panicked," Jamari said. "Her welcome seemed very near to the falling in and away that happened with Eagle back at Shane's burial and when I started to connect, it seemed almost instinctive that I pulled back."

"Wow," Sophia said. "I understand the reaction, yet what I would do to have had the same offer!"

Jamari stood in quiet contemplation for a moment, watching as the swaying grasses settled back into their drooping poise. "I feel a coward," he said. "Will I always fear that deepest connection to the avatars of the Great Spirit now?"

"I suspect you'll have the opportunity again someday," she said. "When you're ready, you'll see that you're less likely to fall away from your corporeal self like you did when that first time caught you unaware of and weakened from your exertions." She turned away from the glade, motioning Jamari to begin the trek back.

"Are you hungry?" Sophia asked as they started down the trail. "I had some pemmie from my pouch while I was waiting, but you haven't eaten anything since breakfast."

Jamari thought about it for a bit. "As I think about it, I am hungry," he said. "I hadn't even noticed until you brought it up." He dug into his own carry-bag and broke off a sizeable piece from his brick of pemmican. He munched on handfuls of pemmie while they walked, occasionally stopping to drink from his canteen.

"I hope I can figure out a way to carry on these extended and weighty philosophical conversations while still eating and drinking," he offered dryly.

Sophia, who had remained silent in contemplation, answered in a more serious manner. "That was a relatively young glen," she speculated. "I suspect they had recently harvested it just at the Fall. Eighty or Ninety years ago. I'm wondering if an older forest, one with a stronger sense of spiritual 'self,' might communicate at a different pace."

"Hopefully, a faster pace," Jamari offered. "I don't know if I could stay in trance long enough to visit at an even slower pace than what I managed today."

Chapter Eleven

A Grave Offense

L ynn had been walking past the boy's hearth as one of the night monitors was talking with one of his charges.

"Lynn, can you watch over the boys for a bit while I get this one settled?" Tim asked him.

Lynn agreed to watch over the remaining boys who were sleeping while the monitor walked the boy up the hall to a room set aside for calming and quieting raucous young souls.

When Jamari happened by later, he was intent on getting down to the courthouse before the day's sessions started. He saw Lynn with the boy in a quiet alcove where he didn't expect interruption. When Jamari saw what was going on, he immediately sent Lynn to his rooms.

"Please pull up your pajamas," he requested of the boy. Then he held him in his arms as he asked how this had happened. "It's not your fault," he reassured the confused and trembling youngster. Then he walked with the boy over to the room where Tim was still talking with the first boy.

They settled each boy for the rest of the sleep period. When the boys were sleeping, he told Tim what he had seen. They then found another monitor from another boy's hearth to watch over the two in the time out rooms. Jamari went to awaken Devon, the hearth leader, while Tim resumed his duties watching over the remaining boys in the hearth.

Jamari never learned what event had left Tim alone to watch over the eighteen youngsters in Devon's Hearth. He never heard where the other mentor assigned to work in tandem with Tim had gone, nor why. When Jamari reported his discovery to Devon, he promised the first thing he would do when he got down to the courthouse, where he was late for the morning session already, would be to swear out an affidavit of what he had witnessed.

He was late and the Knight Shaman, as a judge of the court, gave him no chance to follow through on his promise before the noon hour. After receiving a quick yet firm upbraiding for interrupting the court's session, he asked for some time with Terry in his role as legal counsel over the lunch break.

"What is it, Jamari?" Terry asked coldly, obviously still peeved with him for being late for the court session. Not that the morning's case was terribly important. A simple disagreement between two of the ranchettes over in Kaffee Flats between Yoncalla and Drain villages. It seemed more like he felt betrayed by his favored acolyte, who had failed him.

"I was witness to an abuse this morning on my way down here," Jamari answered. "In Devon's Hearth, there was an altercation which required Tim, the monitor for the morning stretch, to pull two boys aside. Tim saw Lynn passing by on some errand or other and asked him to watch over the remaining boys while he settled one boy into a calming room and sent the other back to bed in the dorm.

"When I came by, I saw Lynn being sexual with one boy. I think one of the two who had been involved in the altercation, but I don't know for sure. I sent Lynn back to his rooms and told him to stay there until we sent him for him. He could still be there now for all I know. Then I helped Tim get things straightened out in the hearth before getting down here as fast as I could."

Terry was silent for a few minutes, obviously contemplating the enormity of what he had just heard. "You know, making this accusation puts you in the same amount of danger as Lynn, right?"

he asked after a moment. "You remember that from your own days in Jahangir's hearth?"

"Yes, Knight Shaman," Jamari answered firmly. "That detail of our tribal law is clear. I even understand why it exists, and I accept my risk is the same as Lynn. I will not, however, allow a molestation to go unpunished."

Terry stood and paced around the desk in his chambers. "We'll have to hope the boy will testify honestly," he finally offered. "I'll have to recuse myself from the case and let a lottery determine who will preside.

"I'm sorry Jamari. I had no idea of the gravity of what made you late. Just to be sure, knowing Lynn's history over the last few years, he is going to be facing the death penalty. If they find your claims true. It means *you* will face the death penalty as well if your story isn't corroborated."

"I know I face the same penalty if I'm lying, Knight Shaman," Jamari answered stoically. "It has been on my mind since I started my trip down the river. I'm doing what needs to be done. For the Tribe. For the boy. Even for myself. If I fail, I won't go into the next cycle with regret. If I say nothing and Lynn does something similar again, I'll have much more on my conscience. This is what I must do."

"Do you know how many people Lynn told about your sexual encounter?" Terry asked pointedly. He paced around his desk again as Jamari, shocked at the revelation, contemplated a wholly unexpected question.

"I have no idea," he finally answered. "I didn't even know he had told anyone. Why does it even matter?"

"Because, along with what Lynn described doing to you, those stories will discredit you. Tear down your testimony. Make it look as if you're making this accusation in revenge for how he treated you!"

Jamari finally realized the genuine danger of his situation now. If the boy was less than forthcoming. "But why would Lynn be facing death?" he wondered aloud. "They have applied death to a tribal member one time. Back when the council removed Chief David James from office. That was almost sixty years ago!"

"I can't answer that, Jamari. I'm afraid I've already said too much." He stepped to the door, opening it with such suddenness the air pressurized the room, generating a breeze strong enough to displace loose papers on his desk.

"Bailiff!" he called in a near yell when there was no one there to greet him.

Shortly, Lon came bolting around the corner. "I'm sorry, your honor, I was visiting with Judge Rory and Joshua."

"Get all the other judges rounded up for a meeting in my courtroom. At least the ones who aren't in court proceedings right now, anyway."

"Yes, Knight Shaman," Lon said with a penetrating look at Jamari. He turned back the way he had come, running back down the halls. Jamari heard him enter Rory's chambers, and shortly after, he heard a scuffle of feet as others dispersed out to summon the judges. Hard-soled shoes told an obvious story in an echo chamber of a hallway, he thought.

"Well, let's get in there," Terry said resignedly. He pointed Jamari around the hallway, showing he should enter from the main door of the courtroom while he, as judge, would enter through the judge's door in the back.

It was a very long walk through the halls to the front doors. He met several others, also converging in response to the summons. He held the door for Judge Thomas, known as Thomas of Elkton, where he had grown up, to differentiate him from Thomas of Milltown up at Milltown Village.

When all were present, Terry rapped them into silence with a sharp clap of his gavel. All the folks were looking at him, wondering what could be going on to have them all summoned at such short notice.

"We have a problem," Terry said without preamble. "Jamari was witness to an incident up at Milltown Hall this morning, which is going to have repercussions. I don't have all the details yet. There's still a lot to learn. But this is a very serious situation."

Chapter Twelve

Trial By Tribe

Thomas drew the lot to be the presiding judge. One of the first things Judge Thomas emphasized to Jamari was the jeopardy of the False Accuser.

"I'm surprised so many of you even think my risk matters," Jamari replied. "Are there any among us who actually believe in our God? In our promise of an afterlife?"

"So be it," Thomas responded gravely. "Trial begins tomorrow morning at Eight A.M."

The judges, knowing Jamari would be called as a witness, but also knowing he was on trial as well, arranged for him to sit in a side room with the door ajar. He could hear the testimony offered without impacting the witnesses' testimony.

He learned there was, as Terry had said, far more history than just this one incident.

Some key moments caught Jamari's interest.

They questioned Tim, the Night Monitor, first. "I saw Kevin and Bradley quarrelling during the night. I pulled both boys from the sleeping dorm to counsel them."

Tim seemed shaken, not just by the gravity of his place in the trial, but also by the outrage committed on his watch. "I needed time to get Bradley settled into bed in the calming room and had asked Lynn to watch over things while I was absent."

Having a name applied to the boy Lynn had mistreated seemed to make it even more real. Kevin. A young boy of twelve, ready to move to a boy's hearth out of the youngling's crèche.

THEY HEARD OF THE NIGHT in the young men's hall when Lynn had deserted his own Night Studies trainee, hoping to be with Jamari.

Carson had overheard the last part of Lynn's interaction. "I heard Jamari tell Lynn 'No' three or four times," he told the court. "Jamari was handling it perfectly, being firm in his refusal without forcing it to blows. When I heard what sounded like the bed moving as one or both hit it, I went in. I told Lynn they had assigned me as Jamari's mentor for the night and he had his own trainee waiting out in the common room for him." Carson was strong in the witness chair, offering just enough information without overly embellishing.

DAN, LYNN'S NIGHT STUDIES trainee at the time, was called in next. "Lynn knew that Shane, Jamari's assigned mentor, had been called down to the court to finish out a case he had been involved in prior to being transferred up to the young men's hall. He told me he was going to talk Jamari into all three of us sharing a night together."

Jamari felt for him as he heard the emotions of the memory and of the trial itself near overcome him in his shaking voice and many pauses.

"I overheard the entire exchange after Lynn made me wait out in the commons. Those rooms don't have doors, only curtained hangings, and I heard everything they said. It wasn't Lynn trying to get the three of us together; it was Lynn trying to get a tryst with Jamari."

The court established a history of Lynn pushing others beyond their limits and then deflecting or re-wording any accusation as if the target of his amorous advances had asked for it. Later in Dan's testimony, he described another incident from when he had been Lynn's trainee.

"Lynn was trying to have full intercourse with me from the start. We both knew they proscribed penetrating interaction for our early Night Studies lessons. He kept hinting that if I asked, it would make it okay. I had experimented with others in my boy's hearth and knew I could enjoy it. I was just nervous because we had been told to wait until we had our initial training first. Lynn finally convinced me to ask him for it, and I did." He paused, and Jamari could hear his voice cringe at the memory.

"Being with Lynn was nothing like I'd ever experienced before. He was almost savage as he took his need out, and I had to bite my hand to keep from crying out." Jamari could hear the pain in his quavering voice. "A month after they moved Lynn out of the young men's hall, the night before Jamari was going to have his first breeding assignation, we set up a training session to help Jamari know what to expect and to do. Part of the rehearsal was having Jamari be with me as if I were a woman." Jamari couldn't help himself and got up to peek around the doorjamb. Was he really going to tell that tale?

Dan paused again, looking around the room to see the reactions at the admission. "That night, when Jamari was in me, was the first time I ever experienced the ultimate finish with another man. He was gentle. Caring. Loving. Even with Shane and Carson offering pointers while we were engaged, I could feel Jamari's intent to please me." Dan looked directly at Judge Thomas, his gaze passing by the darkened door Jamari was peering out of. Jamari ducked back and sat back down.

"It was like night and day, the differences between the two of them."

LATER, THE KNIGHT SHAMAN testified they had removed Lynn from the young men's hall because of his violations of the guidelines given to mentors.

Oddly enough, the Knight Shaman seemed to speak out on behalf of Lynn. Not against Jamari per se, but he told how they had often relied on Lynn's innate sense to determine the strength of spirit-self in others.

"Lynn is overly drawn to those whose spirit shines the strongest. We used his attraction as a first sign his target may have shamanistic leanings. We always emphasized to Lynn there was never any toleration for abuse, either sexual or physical, and we were very specific with him about it." He paused for a moment to reflect.

"Lynn never told us about Jamari. We found out about his latent ability in a much more dangerous way when Jamari went spirit-walking on his own."

As Terry had explained to Jamari at one time, he now explained to the court: the only way to prevent a soulless one from harming humans is to convince the soulless one there was far more danger to them in doing the harm than there was in any potential pleasure the soulless one stood to gain from the act.

"It appears now, Lynn recognized something special in Jamari and sought to harvest whatever it was for himself."

FOR KEVIN'S TESTIMONY, Judge Thomas seated the boy in the witness chair with himself in a chair on a level with the witness. It quickly became apparent that the prosecution and defense had worked out a set of questions that Thomas could ask, since sometimes Thomas would stop the questioning and call the two attorneys back into his office for a conference.

"Can you tell us what happened yesterday morning?" Thomas asked Kevin.

"I only wanted to have some closeness with Bradley. I wasn't trying to force him into anything, just trying to convince him it was okay. Tim took both of us out into the hall and then sent me back to my bed. He walked Bradley over to the timeout room."

"Well," Thomas answered, "we need to protect our young ones. I hope you can see that you need to take 'no' for an answer and we will pull you aside for some calming time while you learn how to contain yourself."

"But I didn't do anything!" Kevin answered.

"No, you did nothing wrong," Thomas answered kindly. "Sex is perfectly natural. How we, as humans, express sex can be one of the most sacred things in our lives. You were getting ready to be moved up to a boy's hearth when all this happened. That's where you will learn more about this sacred part of your being. This incident will not change that. You'll be making the move as soon as we have learned as much as we can here. You'll get to be with some of your friends who have already started their training with a new hearth master. We just need to find out about Lynn first. Can you help us do that?"

"Yes, Thomas. I can do that."

"What made you get up from bed and go out into the hall where Lynn was?" Thomas asked.

"I couldn't get back to sleep," Kevin answered. "I heard Tim ask Lynn to watch over us. I thought I could talk with him like I have with other monitors when I couldn't sleep. He seemed understanding and offered to help me where Bradley wouldn't." Kevin was silent for a moment, looking down at his hands in his lap.

"I didn't think there was anything wrong with it until Jamari came around the corner and told Lynn to go to his rooms and stay there.

"I've seen Jamari around before. I've heard him talking to others. He always seemed nice and easygoing. Never too pushy. Never bossing anyone around. When he told Lynn to go to his rooms, though, it scared me. I don't know why, but when I heard his voice, I knew something had upset him."

Over the questioning, Kevin told exactly what Lynn had done with him. Much to Jamari's relief.

WHEN JAMARI WAS CALLED in, he didn't even have a moment to answer the first questions, as Lynn's defender peppered him with questions. "Isn't all this really about how Lynn treated you when you agreed to have sex with him in his own room?" the defense attorney asked.

"Do you harbor resentment against Lynn for his part in being with you? For being rough with you? For mis-treating you?"

He lanced these questions at Jamari one after the other.

"Enough!" Thomas interjected in a harsh voice, shaking the gavel at the man. "You have a job to carry out in defending your client. That gives you no license to badger the witness. I can and will find another to represent Lynn if you can't conduct yourself in a seemly manner!"

Jamari watched the two perform their roles from the witness chair, looking out over the packed courtroom, glancing at Lynn, where he sat in his finest outfit: a rather garish get up. A light green shirt with blooming sleeves and darker-green, tight pants, seemingly fit for a character from an old play but not the tense setting in a courtroom. Jamari sensed the power of the players at a deeper-then-visual level, the life and death at play.

"I never even thought about Lynn or any of my interactions with him after we were together," Jamari finally could answer. "I recovered from my unexpected spirit-walking shortly afterwards and spent a good deal of time simply trying to come to grips with what I had been through."

There was a susurration amongst the spectators in the courtroom as his statement reminded them this was Jamari God Walker.

After calling for silence, Thomas banged his gavel so firmly the head separated from the handle and clattered across the room. Even this didn't immediately work to restore order amidst the upwelling of surprise and awe.

"I will clear this courtroom," he nearly shouted. "Every trial of every tribe member is open to all witnesses to avoid the suggestion of anything underhanded in the proceedings. That can and will be suspended if you cannot restrain yourselves!"

He waited for a quick moment for calm to settle again and then nodded to Jamari to continue his answer.

"I was surprised to learn others even knew what had happened," he said as he looked Lynn full in the eyes.

"Yes, it was unpleasant. Yes, I felt that Lynn had sought pleasure from me without sharing pleasure in return. Yes, I think he tried to take something of my essence from me." He looked over at Thomas.

"No, I do not harbor resentment or anger. I consented to the interaction and chose not to fight free of his attentions when I realized he wasn't even trying to share pleasure with me so much as to take his ease on me."

IT WAS NOT THE TRIBE'S way to draw trials and repercussions out. Get the information together. Gather the witnesses. Present the evidence and the defense with accurate information. Then carry out any judgement in as humane a manner as possible.

It was over in an afternoon. At the close of the one-day trial, Lynn and Jamari both stood at the defendant's table, side by side, accuser and accused, one to be found guilty, the other to be freed.

"All rise," Lon, as the bailiff, called out as Thomas entered the courtroom in his black robe and took his seat.

"You can be seated," Thomas said to the room at large. "The defendant and accuser will remain standing to hear the verdict." He waited for the room to settle and a hush to descend. Looking carefully at the two young men, he spoke to them. "Lynn of Milltown Village, formerly of Yoncalla, you are accused of the sexual molestation of a child.

"Jamari, as the accuser, you face the exact penalty if we have found Lynn not guilty. We, the Tribe, have this law because of pre-tribal days when false accusations became common: when one person was angry at another; when a prosecutor needed a perpetrator in order to close a case; when a detective felt a particular suspect simply 'must have done it.' There were multiple incidences when the system imprisoned someone for years, decades even, and then later found to be innocent: when a key accuser came clean or when DNA analysis was available, or many things which could exonerate the falsely accused."

He glanced around the crowded courtroom. "It was always the hope that accusations of wrongdoing would drop, and they have. It was never intended, though, to allow a perpetrator to be set free simply because a witness feared to face the consequences of a false accusation." He paused again to look directly at Jamari. "It takes great courage to face a charge of this nature. It takes great personal integrity to know bringing a charge could imperil the accuser as much as the accused. We set it up this way because we trusted in the honor and courage of our citizens."

He paused again to look at Lynn, this time with the icy stare of judgment. "Lynn, the charges against you are confirmed beyond any

doubt. You stand convicted of sexual molestation of a minor child."
A general hubbub of mixed relief and outrage ran through the large
room, and Thomas gave one sharp rap of the new gavel to call the
room to order.

"You are exiled from the villages of the Tribe. Henceforth, you
will patrol with the various militias for the rest of your life without
surcease, without rest, without relief from fire, flood, heat, cold, rain,
blizzard, or ice. You are exiled. You will remain under watch for this
night, and your first patrol will begin at dawn.

"Get out of my courtroom!" He waited as Joshua and another
bailiff escorted Lynn out of the room, not yet releasing the general
court just yet.

Once the spectators settled again, Jamari remained standing
alone at the defendant's table. He was feeling shame at the level of
relief he felt. He worried for Lynn. His role in the Tribe had long
kept him from regular patrols, had allowed his fitness level to taper
off. Knowing the first patrol would be a challenge as he regained lost
skills, he anticipated the pain of the challenges ahead for Lynn. Until
he felt Thomas's eyes on him. He looked up to face the judge of the
court.

"Jamari, as the accuser, I laud your personal strength of character
in how you steadfastly refused all hints and warnings in order to
bring this act to justice. You knew you were facing stiff penalties had
the evidence not worked out, yet you kept your stand, kept your
honor, and upheld the highest standards of the Elk Creek Tribe. I
give you one last duty. You, as a shaman, will accompany Lynn on
his first patrol. You will assure justice is done. I will ask you to my
chambers to discuss this patrol." He looked around the courtroom
again, seeing perhaps some disappointment from so mild a sentence,
perhaps some sadness at the loss of a prominent participant in the
tribe's many plays. "This court is adjourned," he announced with a
final rap of the gavel.

Chapter Thirteen

Deadly Consequences

As the sun settled toward the hills, the group of hunters paused at a small pass to taste the air of an open meadow. The meadow was a remnant from a long-ago forest fire and an anomaly among the densely forested hills.

This dream again, sleeping Jamari thought to himself. I've had this dream before. So many times. Why?

They had traveled through a dark glade of fir trees throughout the long climb from the Elk Creek Valley, now far behind them. The next nearest village was fifteen miles to the east, and the land they stood on had reverted to wilderness with even the ancient blacktop crumbling into ruin as the roots of grasses and shrubs ate away at every weak spot until only a serious study would show the remnants of a ribbon of pavement under the triumphant growth.

From this point, they were to patrol for incursions into their lands. The pass marked the eastern boundary of the Tribe's original land grant from the state and federal authorities.

Even in my dream I remember the history, he thought. Dream was further identified by a lack of sensation. Jamari remembered feeling a bit too warm when they stepped out of the forest and into the bright sun after the brisk pace up the pass. Dream Jamari only remembered the sweating warmth without feeling it. I need to view the dream, Jamari realized. There's a lesson here that I'm missing. Maybe guide the dream in new ways.

Jamari could see that Lynn desperately needed a break. He was suffering from the rigors of the journey.

How am I knowing Lynn's thoughts? Jamari-Dreamer wondered. I've never "remembered" his thoughts! How many times have I dreamed this same dream, and here is a first?

Jamari's friend and companion, Lon, was the lieutenant in charge of this patrol. Joshua was also along. They both still guarded Jamari against harm.

They all stopped and dropped their packs, settling bows and quivers to the ground. They were setting up for a dry camp when Lon asked Lynn to gather some dry wood for the fire.

Jamari looked the leader in the eye. Then he drew one special arrow from his quiver and handed it over. They had discussed this in depth before beginning this mission. Jamari, as the key witness against Lynn, would normally have the role that Lon now assumed. Jamari, as shaman, could not be the executor of this assignment.

Can't I skip this part? Sleep-Jamari begged of himself. The spirit-response seemed no. He would need to relive these moments yet again.

Jamari watched Lon nock the arrow and draw the bow. They shared a look of deep regret and understanding.

"Lynn," Jamari called loudly, turning to face the moment.

Lynn turned from where he had stepped up the trail. He looked at Jamari in answer to the call and then to Lon, wondering about the bow aimed straight on at him.

"You've been judged," Jamari stated firmly.

Lynn had one quick moment of understanding before he saw the bow, slackened in release, now discharged, empty, still held in Lon's upheld arms. He didn't even feel the arrow as it flew into his heart. For the shortest moment, he felt the sting as if a large bee had stung and bit him at the same time. He looked down to see the fletched end of an arrow standing out of his chest. He stared at it in amazement for a moment, tried to turn around, then sank to his knees. A thin but insistent spout of blood issued from his nose and mouth. He held there for a moment and then leaned over to lie on his side.

They didn't forgive me; *he thought to himself. His legs thrashed a bit when he settled, struggling for a comfortable position amidst a short patch of fern. Then he was still.*

Jamari Watcher saw a transformation then. It was Lynn's face settling into the soil, and then it was Shane's! And then it was ... a younger Shane? The face of a boy who could be Lynn or Shane, far too young to have been from a time when he knew either of them. It was Lynn's face and then Shane's. One more cycle in the dream.

There it was, Dream Watcher realized! He remembered seeing Lynn's legs twitching in the ferns, the blood beginning to spread out from under him.

He had seen the place where Shane had fallen a year ago. A patch of ferns along the river's edge. He remembered seeing some ferns thrashed just like these. He remembered thinking of how his lover's legs must have churned, hoping to find a place of relief. Comfort in a place where there was none to be found.

Watching Lynn's last moments had triggered something of Shane. One a craven being put down. The other, a hero, having saved lives through his sacrifice. Why would they compare? Was it a lesson he still hadn't learned? Would he have to relive this dream even more before he got it?

Lynn's hunting mates gathered around him as his blue eyes grayed out and faded.

"Lynn," Lon said, kneeling next to him, "you committed a crime against another human being, one so appalling the Tribe has determined you are soulless. As you pass, your partners of the hunt are giving you this opportunity: if you have a soul, bring with you to the next cycle of life the knowledge you cannot harm a child as you did and still survive. As your executioners, we pray with you, hoping there is some remnant of a soul left to redeem in these last seconds."

Lynn's eyes went wholly blank and Lon reached out to shut them from the world that had rejected him. The men laid their hands on him, calling on the spirits to reclaim a damaged soul, asking for a better cycle of life for Lynn in the next round.

The Elk Creek Tribe was a sovereign nation. It negotiated treaties with the United States and other governments and set its own laws.

The price for violating tribal law could be immense, as Lynn had discovered. Another lesson, Jamari wondered to himself. So many lessons lately. Anger as spirit-killer seemed to recur. Was it anger from the entire tribe, which condemned Lynn? Was this truly the only way to ensure he would never offend again?

They dug a shallow trench next to a large boulder, rolled Lynn's body into it, covered the body with rocks, and covered the rocks with mosses and grasses.

Dream Jamari noted his early self had stood back from those last moments. Dream Jamari remembered the memory-thoughts that had spun through his mind. This had been his very first assignment after becoming a full citizen, and he couldn't shirk his responsibility. Lynn had felt betrayed when Jamari reported him. Lynn had acted as if he deserved something different from Jamari because of their past comradeship.

Jamari was troubled because Lynn had thought he was getting a new pass at life when he'd been exiled to the patrols.

To Jamari, it seemed wrong somehow that Lynn had not known his fate until those last moments, but Jamari wondered if sparing Lynn the fear of knowing had been the right thing to do. They had spared Lynn the hours of fear that would have followed had he known his fate. They had taught Jamari that people afflicted as Lynn was, with a complete lack of a sense of empathy for "others," could not benefit from punishment. Those like him would perceive punishment as torture, since the soulless one could not alter his or her basic nature.

Was advance knowledge of his fate punishment? What was feeling fear for a few hours compared to the price Lynn's victim would pay for the rest of his life? Lynn had inflicted a life of emotional pain on the boy.

He wondered what he himself was becoming if he could even think of inflicting punishment on another. The months he had spent in the courts had not prepared him for an ending so final as death. He had watched as judges decided and settled cases that now, in retrospect, seemed completely irrelevant. Losing one's life, even absent the suffering, was an enormous price. He was glad it was the court, in the person of Judge Thomas, that had decreed this end. And he was glad he did not have the decision on his conscience.

As the party turned away, Jamari regretted it was his quiver light by one arrow. Since he was the accusing tribe member, it had fallen for him to deliver the final sentence. He was glad the shot had been true, that Lynn's death had been quick. He shuddered with relief yet again that there had been evidence to support his accusation.

Finally, Dream Jamari realized something. Something important.

Jamari didn't agree with the tribe on this issue. He acknowledged that there had to be a solution which would prevent further harm when someone showed they would continue to harm others without remorse. Without accepting an "Other" could be a human self. Death probably was the ultimate solution, and he accepted that.

Being declared soulless was the pang he was experiencing. How could any man see into and judge the soul of another? None could. Man could not step into the place of God to make such a judgment.

He knew Lynn, if he held a soul, had it buried so deep that it couldn't be sensed by the most sensitive of shamans. How could a man, a man of the tribe, make such a horrible and permanent judgment?

Of course, he had had no actual choice. If there was one thing the tribe was most opposed to, it was forcing another into a sexual interaction. Forcing a child was even worse.

Lon was leading the way down the path when Joshua placed an arm around Jamari's shoulders, urging him forward.

"You did the right thing," Joshua told him. "It was a quick end to a nasty situation."

Should I have been the one to offer the ultimate gift of compassion Dream Jamari asked himself? The acknowledgement that he could have a soul; could be redeemed in a future cycle? But, no, he recognized the words would have been empty coming from him. He knew all too well Lynn had lacked a soul. It was best that Lon, in his role as first lieutenant and patrol leader, be the one to offer the benediction. Lon could not sense souls, nor sense spiritual connection. He had a soul himself, as Jamari knew from long interaction, but he lacked the shamanic capacity to sense it, or the lack thereof, in others.

The group continued through the pass, descending to a spring that bubbled up and drained into a ferny dale below. There, they settled in for a fireless camp. No member of a tribal hunting party would ever build a fire, no matter how small, in the dry days of fall, before the rains lessened the chance of conflagration. The patrol members used this small spring to wash themselves of their recent past. Cleansed, they all settled into a common tangle of bodies for the night, with Jamari as the center, his companions still giving him moral support.

Observer Jamari watched that cuddle with fondness for his band of brothers. He realized now he had reached the realizations that would let the dream pass and fade away. He could follow dream-memory to its finish as observer and not try to find any further lesson.

It was on the journey back, five days later, that they passed by the cairn again and found it scattered and Lynn's remains naught but some scraps of desiccated flesh still stubbornly attached to a few of the bones. The party stood over the remains, looking at the signs which told of a large cougar having worked the body away from its rest and consuming the flesh as smaller predators and scavengers feasted as well. Jamari looked up from the scene, waiting for Lon to look up and make eye contact.

"Should we re-bury him, do you think?" Lon asked quietly.

"I think not," Jamari answered. "I remember when I was first presented as a shaman to the Tribe. After the cougar wounded me and I killed the cougar that attacked me in my meditations, during the ceremony where they recognized me as a shaman, the Knight Shaman said, 'Blessed is the lion which becomes man when consumed by man. Cursed is the man who is eaten by a lion and becomes a beast.' Somewhere in the Gnostic Gospel of Thomas, I remember."

He looked at the tattered remains and saw a gathering of crows eyeing the remaining scraps. "Cougar has consumed Lynn. Maybe it will be a step up for him in his next cycle."

One last observation for Dream Jamari here. His early self, in these words, had acknowledged that Lynn had a soul to be consumed and taken in by the lion. It was a benediction of sorts, he felt, as he became Dream Jamari again.

The group turned and made their way down the ridgeline path for a late afternoon return to Milltown Hall and a warm shower after a six-day patrol that had begun with Lynn's last act.

The final closeout of this chapter in his life was a crossover from earlier days under Terry's tutelage. "Remember the story about the lady in Chicago?" Terry asked him as they sat in the easy chairs in Terry's rooms.

Jamari thought for a moment, remembering the lesson Terry was referring to. He remembered the vividly written description of a room in a house in the tenements that had been bathed in blood from several murders done inside. He remembered the description of a police force and their tactics as they entered the home, more like a military action than a police action. Most of all, he remembered the questions he had asked Terry as he had been trying to understand the lesson to be learned from that reading.

"You said it was like the lesson of the lemmings," Jamari said shortly, "that it was a parable." He thought again of the end of the story: how the woman refused to divulge information about the perpetrators of the multiple murders in her home. How they arrested her for criminal indifference, a law that they passed as a last-ditch effort to break the hold of an unwritten law of silence that ruled those streets, to force unwilling "citizens" to cooperate in taming the streets of the pre-Fall inner cities.

Jamari contemplated the lesson of that day with his recent experience with Lynn and his crime. He remembered just how many times they had warned him of the danger in continuing with those charges, how being the accuser would subject him to the same risk of life that Lynn faced. His own clear understanding dominated though: regardless of personal risk; he went ahead with the testimony because it was the right thing for the tribe. For his community.

"You said it is one of life's lessons that must be felt, must be experienced in order to 'live the lesson.'" He looked at Terry again, this time with understanding. "That culture was doomed," he concluded. "Their 'citizens' had no respect for the community, for anything other than their own survival. Writing and enforcing that law was a last-ditch effort, which only broke up the community even quicker in the end."

"You live it now," Terry had said smugly. "We all do. The tribe has never had an internal police force. We've never needed a separate body to regulate our laws, which we also have very few of. We are self-regulating because of citizens exactly like you."

Dream Jamari had made the final realization and could sleep comfortably. The nightmare would never bother him again.

Chapter Fourteen

An Other Glade

The preparations for the court hearing in Salem were complete. The hubbub around Lynn's sentence had settled.

With some days available to concentrate on his projects, he started the work on the totem.

Chief Walter and some others had helped Jamari tuck the tree into a curtained nook inside the highest room of the main casino floor. It hung from the rafters with a set of scaffolding built around it, looking as if someone had taken a tree from the forest and hung it up for some bizarre butchering. One man devised a swiveling hanger that held the totem upright with the rooty base just above the floor level, yet allowed the totem to revolve with the simplest of efforts while he worked.

There was still a haunting sense from his days in spirit form. A nagging sense suggested that deep in his most forgotten dreams, there was something to be discovered out in the wild woods. It still pulled him from his dreams at night. Something needed to be done, and he needed to discover not just what, but also how.

The compulsion drove him, along with Sophia, out one morning sans guardians. The absence of Lon and Joshua was a recent capitulation by Terry, who had agreed with Sophia that she would be an adequate guardian. As an animal-spirit shaman, she expected to be of help when he entered the deep shaman trance and needed protection or assistance.

Terry made it clear he didn't consider only one guardian to be an ideal situation. He told Jamari that he'd return things back to the safety of a double guard pair if something untoward should occur.

Jamari enjoyed Lon and Joshua's company on other outings, and they still visited each other's rooms during the court week, but on this day, he was free of further escort.

They walked north up Scotts Valley, toward the old path that traveled over the ridges and into London. There was a burial site there where many of the residents of both Scotts Valley and Lane Creek had gone to rest under their trees. Though neither had visited this glade before, the elders told them it was an entire copse of thirty-four trees, all guarding the remains of various tribal members from over the years.

Early in tribal founding, laws from the outer world had designated only assigned areas as graveyards. Some trees in this glade dated from those years and times, years before the Founder chose his own spot in a glade far across the valley and up another set of ridges. They still guarded Founder's Glade against trespass, against knowledge of even where it was.

Their instructions were to walk for about an hour before they found a small fork branching to the left off the London trail, shortly after the crossing where one path turned right for Lane Creek Village and the other went straight on for the climbing, weary way to London Village. They paused where they were supposed to and poked around the brush and shrubs, looking for such a trail. Eventually, they found it by stepping farther up the London trail and then turning left.

The little trace skirted up a steep draw, falling away in heart-stopping precipices on one side and giving tenacious holds on the upper side by grabbing onto Scotch broom shrubs. After an arduous climb, they finally could see why this had been a preferred spot. They could look down into Scotts Valley and see the courthouse as if they were looking down on a little doll village. Jamari had not been aware of two long houses tucked into the little wood in the field to the east of the courthouse itself. The surrounding trees perfectly screened them from view while down at ground level, but from their current vantage, the two long dwellings stood out like barrows in the ancient Scottish Highlands.

"I wonder why the longhouses," Jamari said as they stopped for a breather.

"I think it's where the militia members stay when there are gatherings in the courthouse area," Sophia answered. "When there are outsiders gathered in our main building, we don't show our full hand."

"No, I guess we don't," Jamari said. "How much further do you think it is?"

"You don't feel it already?" Sophia asked.

Jamari closed his eyes in concentration, opening himself up to the inner world, looking for his link to the Other world, listening for the voices of the ancestors. He found them. Faintly, he could feel a steady subliminal whisper, as if a hive of bees maybe swarmed over the next ridgeline. "What is it?" he asked. "I've never felt such a thing. It's like buzzing, yet too quiet. Like whispering, but as if only dogs would hear."

"I think this glade has a more powerful presence than any other we've visited," Sophia replied quietly. "It feels as if they are chatting with each other!"

They followed the unheard voices around one more outthrust rock pillar and found a small indentation on their right, with a nearly level bottom where a small pool, dammed by the lip of the path, rippled from the murmur of a small stream dripping inexorably into its upper bank. The small draw worked into a slow rise to the ridge farther into the glade. On the left side of the road, the precipice dropped off in a sudden fall. There was a quiet stream chuckling along just here, splashing a coolness into the dusty early September air, seeming to defy the heat of a summer day with a moist kiss on their parched skins. Just a few steps up this stream, they stepped into the copse of oak.

There seemed to be a sudden hush as they entered the tree-dappled vale. The earlier subliminal buzzing had died into an expectant silence. "They may not want us here," Jamari ventured in the sudden stillness.

"No, I think they're just seeing what we're about," Sophia answered. "See if you can talk with them."

He looked around, not sure what he was looking for. No mossy blanket covered this forest floor like he expected in the fir forests. There was grass, tall and browning in the summer heat. There was a patch of blackberry brambles with berries heavy with nectar hanging from the vines.

Farther up the small rivulet, he saw a gathering of small shrubby plants, no higher than a couple feet tall, with woody base and shiny leaves tucked over small blueish berries. The berry brambles hung here as well, some dangling their fruits down into the leafy shadow of the woody shrub.

Salal. A berry that once was the source of sweetener in teas and compotes long before the white man came to these valleys. Under the shade of the salal, Jamari found what he was looking for: a light bed of mossy cover. Not the verdant green of the fir woods, but a grayish blue with small round-headed periscopes jutting up from the sparse tufts. He lifted a small hummock and found a lacery of fungal root.

"Why do you always look for the fungi?" Sophia asked.

"I don't know why specifically," Jamari replied, "only that I've always felt most connected to the enlivened glades when I'm in contact with these strands of white."

"There must be something to it," Sophia observed, bending down to peer under the salal leaves.

Jamari watched as she carefully twisted a few of the ripened black berries off into her palm. She set them on her tongue and crushed them against the roof of her mouth, obviously enjoying the burst of sweetness. Jamari, strangely aroused at the sensual pleasure she showed while enjoying the fruit, turned away and looked up the draw and into the glade of oaks. He could see where the salal bushes faded away under the canopy. He could also see the grayish moss, maybe more like a lichen, still creeping up and under the eaves.

He rose and walked those few paces, adjusting himself as he traveled, and ignored her throaty chuckle. At the top of the salal patch, he found a softened spot in the soil, shaped almost perfectly for his butt as he settled into it, absently placing his hand just under the moss.

It did not surprise him too much when he looked back down the trail to see Sophia and Cougar conferring at the salal patch. It fit perfectly with the spirit-world drive he was sensing. They both turned and sauntered their way up to him. He let Cougar come to him, only a little jittery at Her size and closeness. She reached Her massive head out and rubbed cheek to cheek with him, marking him as Her own. He felt and heard the bass rumble of Her purr as She greeted him.

Sophia followed behind Cougar with a troubled look on her face.

"She wants you to use the dead man's skill to take energy from Her," she reported to Jamari.

Jamari left off petting the luxurious fur, who had Her head draped over one of his shoulders, the two of them neck to neck, sharing warmth and love in a way he had never known before. "What?" he exclaimed. "How can you know that? What does it mean? What dead man? What skill?"

"I don't know, Jamari," Sophia answered, still troubled by the request. "She doesn't speak to me in words. Not even images, really. I just get an idea of a walking cadaver with great hunks of decaying flesh dropping off. I see an emanation being drawn from someone - I think it's you - and into the apparition, as if the emanation is feeding the monster."

"That's not even close to what I was asking," Jamari replied, resuming his caressing of Cougar, who still had Her head over his shoulder, and even seemed ready to wrap a foreleg around him to get even closer. "How can you even know those things?"

"I told you when we were first assigned to work on this project together that I was very sensitive to the wild-wood-world," Sophia answered sharply. "I also said you were an arrogant male who would likely never see beyond his own nose." She stopped and controlled herself before sitting down on the other side of Cougar, where she became a voice hidden behind the immensity of Cougar's shoulder.

"I thought you had proven me wrong about the 'not seeing beyond your own nose thing' with the sessions we've shared while exploring the forest spirits. Yet you never once had the curiosity to ask what I meant when I told you about my ability."

"I'm sorry," Jamari answered while still trying to deal with a massive furball playfully pushing him onto his back. "She's heavy," he complained as Cougar lay over him before rolling over to languish between the two.

"It's okay," Sophia answered as she, too, started petting and caressing Cougar as if She were simply an oversized bobcat. "I'm pretty sure there's something important here we need to understand far more than to snipe at one another over a petty misunderstanding.

"So," she continued, "I've been able to sense something about animals for most of my life. When I was with the goatherds as a girl my first time, I could sense when the bell-nanny became alarmed about something. It was that sense of alarm which woke me from a deep sleep one night, and I found a wolf stalking the edges of the herd. The nanny projected her alarm to me. She moved to the side nearest the wolf, urging the herd as a group away from the threat, calling out to me in my mind for help.

"When I came awake, I had my sling loaded with a stone before I even saw what was happening. Even as I stood, I was beginning the back swing to give momentum to the stone, and as I saw the shape of the wolf in the darkness, barely fifteen feet away, I let the stone fly. It should have been sheer folly, but the stone entered through his eye and brained him where he stood.

"That's how I got my Wolf cape. That's when the other shamans began to train me into my own powers. The result, as you saw last spring, is my position as the Sophia Shaman. The sensitivity training helps me sense more clearly when an animal, and now, apparently, an avatar of the Great Spirit, wants me to comprehend something."

"Okay and wow," Jamari said, nearly stunned to silence, distracted only by the bass purring of Cougar. "So, now, what can we make of Her message to you? Can you give me any more detail of the monster in the vision? How long ago? Still a threat? Is *that* what She is warning us about?"

"Not still a threat," Sophia answered firmly. "I think She consumed the flesh from it herself after you struck it down."

Jamari froze into silent immobility, remembering those ultimate moments as Lynn lay bleeding out on the rocky soil in front of him. "Lynn," Jamari whispered huskily. "We placed a cairn of rocks over him when we left him. After our patrol, we came through the same pass on our way home and found his bones taken up and scattered by scavengers."

"What would Lynn have to do with the dead man's skill and taking energy from Her?" Sophia asked.

"Remember, Lynn was a soul-eater," Jamari said quietly, still absently caressing Cougar where She lay splayed out on Her belly between the two of them. "I don't even know if there's a name for what he was. We know he was a soulless one. A hylic. Destined to never come awake spiritually. But what no one else knows, because I only told Terry, is he could draw the spirit-force out of someone. I could feel it happening. It's one of the main reasons I could never really stand to be around him. Except for ..." He paused, remembering his days of dream-state when his spirit-self had been wandering with The Great Spirit. Trying not to remember what happened one lonely afternoon in the deep recess of one hallway in Milltown Hall.

"Except for what?" Sophia asked after a bit.

Jamari rolled onto his side to face Sophia, lifting himself up on an elbow to see over Cougar's reclining body. "Some of this came out during Lynn's trial. When my spirit was walking in the spirit world with Eagle and the Founder, along with The Great Spirit, my near-hylic self encountered Lynn in the back ways of Milltown Hall. I was lonely. Avoiding going back to my rooms in Elk Creek Hall because I felt haunted by Shane's memories there. Because my body wanted to be sexual with my friends, but had realized there was something wrong with how I was treating them in my grief and loss.

"Anyway, when I ran across Lynn, I didn't feel the sensation from him. In fact, I felt pretty much nothing and recognized him as a good-looking guy who was interested in me. We went to his room. What happened there was very unlike sexual sharing. During which I realized he was drawing my essence into himself while he was taking me. I began to come 'awake,' could feel my spirit coming back to me, but somehow, I could also feel Lynn growing stronger in drawing the spirit-energy out of me as it returned.

"Our parting was not amicable. I grew angry with how he treated me. He seemed to relish the anger, to feed off it. He seemed more satiated by my anger than he was while taking me in the rough way he did." Jamari paused again in pained reflection.

"It was then realized he was a soul-stealer, and he was feeding on me as we continued to share the same space. I fled in anger, in shame. I got away from him as fast as I could. The next day, Terry and Peter worked with me to set the plan for how to find and retrieve my spirit from the long walk with God."

"You're a legend from that adventure," Sophia said as she reached over Cougar to lay a hand on his arm where it lay over Cougar as well. "I don't know just how far the telling has gone, or how much it has grown, but I don't think anyone will ever see you the same since. You're called Jamari God-Walker, probably more often than Jamari Shaman."

"I didn't need to know that," Jamari said plaintively. "I'm just Jamari. It seems as if the Great Spirit has seen fit to use me, that it may task me with doing some nebulous thing I still don't understand. I know it's related to talking to the trees as we've been working on." He looked into her eyes.

"I'm frightened to piddling sometimes with the thought of it. I well remember what it felt like to lose myself in that greatness. Even as I sought the return of spirit to body, I remember not wanting to come back. The memories of what I was, and who I was, and what I was doing in the spirit world are hazy. Like looking across a valley on a hot day, when the air itself shimmers and changes what you know you see into something else. Some other shape of mountain over there. Something other than a tree crowning a far ridge top.

"Some message I was supposed to bring back but lost along the way."

Sophia sat up, disengaging from the three-way hug-and-cuddle session. "Well, what we have now is an invitation. To tap into Cougar's strength like Lynn tapped into yours. But to do what? That's what we don't know."

"Nor just how to draw from the source," Jamari said. "Or how to get past the repugnance I feel at the thought of it."

They both looked to Cougar as She lay on Her belly, forepaws spread out in front of Her, hindquarters tucked in underneath and long tail slowly twitching.

"She's picturing this grove of trees," Sophia said suddenly. "This grove of trees we heard as if a distant whispering but a short time ago and now gone silent. But, of you laying your one hand on Her, and the other into that mass of fungal root you've uncovered and then communicating with the grove."

Jamari looked into Cougar's eyes. She wouldn't meet his gaze but twitched Herself closer to him to ease his touch. Tentatively, with a visible shake in nervous hands, he placed his left palm onto Her shoulder and reached with his right down to the tracery of fungal root. He looked into Sophia's eyes as he closed his own and "thought" out to the glade. The instant connection was like none ever before. He remained in human-time and somehow brought the slow sap-like flow of the grove's essence into the full light of time.

They were awake! He reached to them with a question, but they ignored his query. Instead, they drew on the link to take Cougar's strength and transform it into some other thing. He felt an essence flowing from Her and into the soil. He could almost envision the fungal roots as a mass of neurons, spreading the spirit-energy out to the Grove.

Then he felt something else. Something familiar. Something so well-known he it horrified him beyond words. He felt an essence of Lynn flow out of Cougar, flow through himself and pass into Grove to become a part of the new awareness. He shuddered.

Lynn had not been soulless, only so far separated from his spirit and soul, so deeply buried that the spirit could never interact with others around him, so submerged he simply could not see a soul in himself and therefore couldn't comprehend that others might have such a thing.

Suddenly, Jamari was aware, tears streaming down his face, looking down at a sleeping Cougar and over at a stunned Sophia. With sudden concern, he reached to lay his head on Cougar to listen for a heartbeat. She was so still. But as he lowered his head, he saw Her flank twitch and Her chest expand with indrawn breath, and She settled Her head more comfortably onto Her forepaws.

Sophia waved her hand to get Jamari's attention and then signaled him to silence. They both struggled to rise quietly lest they disturb Her rest. With careful steps as learned from long practice in stealth and the hunt, they took themselves down the short stretch of rivulet and over the small pool, where incessant ripples still lapped at its banks and spilled out and over the precipice. His tears fell off, but the stunning knowledge of what he had learned lay as a leaden regret deep within him.

Then they stepped onto the wisp of trail. Once they were around the rocky scarp, and several steps on, Sophia finally whispered, "I sensed the spirit being drawn from Her. I sensed Her falling into a trance and then sleep. What happened?"

Jamari waited a few more steps as he contemplated his quick-set of image-memories. "The Great Spirit has entered the grove for some purpose," he finally answered, as they rounded yet another bend.

"I could sense the regard of those individual trees, and then suddenly, there were no individuals but only one entity, the Grove. The Grove as another avatar of the Great Spirit. And I could sense It studying me, and then It turned its attention away and to some other purpose."

"Why the tears?" Sophia asked. "You know I can sense your pain, your regret, your deep remorse. I just can't tell why."

"She truly had consumed Lynn," Jamari answered as they carefully worked their way along the narrow trace. "Not just his flesh, but somehow, his spirit, too. She passed his spirit through me and into the copse. It was then that the copse of trees became the Grove, all as one united essence.

"Lynn goes on. Not as a monster, but as a part of this larger work that the Great Spirit has set before this Grove.

"And I feel as if it has returned part of me to where it belongs.

"That is all I know. At least for now."

"Jamari God Walker, indeed," Sophia answered once they were far enough away and their voices less likely to disturb the slumber of Cougar Avatar. "A newly awakened Glade! The spirits of our ancestors brought to life again in new form! Oh, the stories that could be! Yet She cautioned me to silence as the essence of God faded from Her."

"Perhaps that's a relief," Jamari said as they strolled down from the heights. "I feel charlatan enough with all the accolades turned my way without adding yet another feat."

"What can be wrong with having people acknowledge your accomplishments?" Sophia demanded.

"Mostly because, while I am the conduit for these happenings, it is still God who is working in me, and not I who is doing these things. I fear the people may not see the distinction and I am not ready to be Jamari God when I am yet working to be Jamari Man."

Sophia reached across the interval of their walk and held his hand for a few paces while they were in a wide spot on the trail. "You'll always be Jamari Shaman," she said to him. "Even if, or when, they think of you as more, your true self will know.

"Now tell me about your regret regarding Lynn. When did you think there was something amiss in what happened? What did you do about it? What would you change if you could? I can sense an unfinished bit of business within you."

"On the day of the trial," Jamari answered. "It was late afternoon when Judge Thomas banged the gavel on the case and asked me into his chambers. It was there that he told me they sentenced Lynn to

die. He reminded me that with a soulless one, it was best if the...
'monster' actually seems a good word even though he didn't use it
then...didn't know about it until it was done. There was no chance
Lynn would understand the existence of another human as anything
but an empty shell. No chance he would recognize the hurt an 'other'
may feel. None could ever be so important as his own self."

He continued the story as they worked their way down the cliff
edge. He realized clambering down a treacherous cliff was far more
challenging than climbing up one.

"At first, Thomas suggested I be the one to send the arrow into
Lynn's chest. I knew right away it was a deep wrongness. Knowing
I was a witness against him, a part of the last judgement over him,
I could not be all: judge, jury, executioner. My first thought was to
have Lon, who had already been selected as patrol leader, do it for
me. I realized I needed to face the decision more openly, though.
This was not a decision which could I could make in secret. This
would impact the future of the Tribe! I told Thomas of my concerns,
and he finally agreed to the plan, so long as I could convince Lon of
the necessity.

"I spent the evening talking with Lon, explaining about the
sentence, the idea of him carrying it out with me as 'judge' over the
affair.

"Once we had the plan set, I left him and went to talk with
Zach. I couldn't give my doubts to the man who had just agreed to
carry out the execution! I told Zach it was one of the most final of
solutions, something which could never be taken back, but I couldn't
see a way around it, even though the very fact of the decision made
the tribe something far less in the doing. It wasn't the death, I've
realized. It was the judgement that a man was soulless. No entity
other than Great Spirit should ever make that judgement!

"I don't know if I'm expressing any of this at all well. It tore me
up inside. Right up to today. And now I know for a fact there was a

soul hidden deep down inside. If only we could know how to draw it out if we ever encounter another soulless one! Think of all the fear and hardship we could stem!"

Chapter Fifteen

At the Court in Salem

J amari climbed the scaffolding of his project every morning. He felt his internal spirit flowing again after the awakening of the Grove. The muses were driving him with whips and chains; he told Sophia when she ventured into the curtained space one morning and peered up at him, wondering when he would venture out on another quest with her.

When he worked the early carving on the totem, Jamari made a rain of wood chips fall around the base as he removed negative spaces from the characters he envisioned. Instead of dead features needing hours of work, though, it felt as if he were freeing them from long imprisonment. Working himself into a sweat with the physical labor, his mind churned over his many adventures, tossing up random images from early shamanic visions.

The perception of the fungal roots as ganglion for the trees seemed to affirm a very faint memory he carried from his awakening moments after his Walk with God.

"The forest awakens as slow lightning runs through the roots. Only where the fungi are missing are there still trees not awakening. All in the lightning realm are awake and answering the call. The animals are listening too!"

This was a blurb Peter had written of Jamari's indistinct utterings as he was coming back into his own. Jamari could almost piece it into the place in his conscience where he held the suspicion there was something important he must remember from the spirit-traveling days.

Then it all came to a stop with one request he couldn't deny. His quest to explore the intuition that some "thing" needed remembering would be delayed again.

The Knight Shaman, as chief justice of the Tribe's courts, decided Jamari would be his aide during the trial in Salem. "This is an important part of our future," Terry told him as he stood under the chip fall and near-shouted over the incessant scraping. "These happenings will define your future role in the tribe. You must come up and away from our land and this project."

Jamari stopped and looked down to see the Knight Shaman's court finery covered in wood shavings. "I've promised to have this ready for the spring," he said. "And I've only just begun the most rudimentary steps. Leaving it now will break the momentum."

"And it will give you a taste of the life-balance you must achieve in order to be a future leader of this tribe," Terry answered. "Come down and make yourself ready. We will leave in the morning."

On the trip up in the Tribe's small plane, after taking off from the Curtin Airstrip and heading north, Jamari saw how the Outsiders treated their lands. As the plane reached the southern edge of Cottage Grove, that first view stunned him. All his life, he had taken the forests of the tribal lands for granted. He assumed they were just as natural and wholesome throughout the rest of the wide world as they were in his home-lands.

The Outsiders stripped the hills. The rains carved brown-red cuts of runoff into the dead soil. Piles of char dotted more recent cuts. Skeletal remnants, gray in the brown land, where the less desirable trees had simply been cut and abandoned, marked older cuts. "What has happened?" he exclaimed at one point. "Where are all the trees?"

"They've harvested them all," Terry answered. "There are only a very few left in the hills of Oregon, and those are under constant threat from the same companies we're going to face off with tomorrow. Remember, the outer world lacks the deep spiritual connection with the world around them. We spent many years developing our connection in the Tribe. This" - he gestured out the window at the denuded hills - "results from losing touch with the natural world around you. If we can't win our case, it'll be that much sooner they'll come looking for our timberlands."

"But why?" Jamari wondered as he looked out and down at the dead, brown lands passing below, at the dirty runnels where rain water had cut into the unprotected soil. "Why can't they see the harm they've done?"

"I'm sure you've heard this before," Terry said, "but they're still a rapacious lot. Despite of all the years of deprivation and pestilence they've suffered because of their actions, they still only see trees to be harvested and sold."

The roads he saw below were neglected, small and few. They would need to be developed enough to allow coordinated forces to pass before the Outsiders could bring their danger to the tribe for the next few years. But they were coming, and a trace of road coming down out of the hills below had a couple of cars casting dust in swirling tails behind them. Then they were over a small city.

"That's Cottage Grove," Terry pointed out, also noting the dust plumes below. "Last time I made it up this way, the road had not extended into these south hills yet." It put a new perspective on this court case, and on the overall progress of road building, which seemed to bring "civilization" closer and closer to tribal lands from both north and south. East was still safe. The treacherous lands coming down from the Cascade Mountains would not soon be breached by man's engineering renaissance.

The flight took just over two hours from take-off to landing. Other than the denuded lands, it was otherwise uneventful. Jamari had seen sporadic patches of intact freeway gradually give way to longer and longer stretches of developed roads. Most of the bridges were fully intact, and he mentioned that to Terry.

"The pre-Fall civilization was in the middle of a massive infrastructure upgrade," Terry told him. "In the years prior to the big quakes, the state invested hundreds of millions of dollars in rebuilding Oregon's bridges, bringing all of them up to a higher standard of seismic endurance. The result was these standing bridges ... which had approaches on both sides completely devastated."

They had built the bridges at higher elevations than the land around to ensure they would be above the water level in any flooding situation. In order to connect the roads to the bridges, they had filled the land under the roads with boulders, rocks, and gravel to reach the new elevations. When the 'quakes had hit, a process called liquefaction had subsumed the approaches. The bridges then became standing forts for many years after the Fall. The communities that had lasted the longest were the ones who had moved onto the bridges the quickest and defended their heights against interlopers.

Landing at the Salem Airport had been educational as well. It was big enough to hold some twin-engine planes on the tarmac and he got to see one of those take off as they were getting their travel bags out of their own smaller plane.

There was a mix of automobiles traveling the roads and Jamari got to ride in a fully enclosed one, without even an open space to carry things in. They had put their bags in a space called a "trunk" where they closed the lid down on them. He saw some new vehicles darting and mingling with older ones looking to be on their last legs, much as their one pickup down in tribal lands. The ride to the motel was quick and revealed a mix of housing areas. Shanty-laden fields bordered stately mansions with gated access and guards.

Jamari and Terry shared one room while the pilot and co-pilot shared another. The two pilots planned to spend the next day finding spare parts and getting the plane serviced. Once they unpacked their court clothes into a closet to air, they spent the afternoon walking around the safer areas near the motel.

After a restless night, the two shamans dressed in their court best and walked the two blocks to the assigned courtroom. There were very few preliminary remarks. "All Rise. Be Seated. Does the plaintiff have an opening statement?"

"Your honor," the plaintiff's attorney said to the court, "I would submit that this gentleman cannot represent the defendant in that he is not a recognized court official in the State of Oregon."

The judge looked over at the defense table, where Terry and Jamari sat alone, dwarfed by the many representatives from the plaintiffs' team. "It seems a reasonable point," the judge said. "Does the defense have a response?"

"If it pleases the court," Terry answered as he stood, "at this point in the proceedings, we're only establishing the bounds of the case and defining the terms of discourse as we work towards a resolution. The court should be aware the plaintiff has offered terms for a settlement and the Elk Creek Tribe is still considering those terms. Could we not table the question of jurisdiction until we either enter an actual contest before the court or settle?"

"Granted," the judge replied. He then looked over at the plaintiff's table. "We'll continue with preliminaries and address the question of eligibility of the defendant's representatives at a later time. If it proves necessary."

Jamari, still an innocent with plots and counterplots and intrigue and suspense, worried about this first thrust from the plaintiff. *This is the land of the Founder's Grove! This is the identity of the tribe*!

Terry, obviously sensing Jamari's stress, reached a hand over, subtly pressing down on his shoulder in a message: relax; don't show any emotion at all. Then Terry withdrew his hand as the plaintiff's attorney once again addressed the court.

"Very well, your honor. At this time, my client would like to submit evidence to support our case, specifically, of ownership of the lands in question."

The judge looked over at the defense again.

"It would be interesting to see what they have," Terry noted. "Obviously, we believe we have legally attained ownership, but in the interest of justice, we agree to review their offer of proof."

The plaintiff's attorney paused for a quick look over at Terry, put off by the low-key response, but he still proffered a stack of old and yellowing pages. "We have here, your honor, the original land grant in which the State of Oregon deeded this tract of timberland over to the Wearehauses Company. We would suggest this original document be taken in by the court for safekeeping and, since it is obviously in poor condition, the court accept the copies we have made as an acceptable replacement instead of poring through the original, which has the potential to damage those frail pages."

"Objection, your honor!" Terry exclaimed as he rose from his seat. "We will not accept any substitution without verifying it is indeed an exact copy of the original."

"The court would tend to agree," the judge answered. "To preserve the original, and in getting all evidence entered, the court assigns the court secretary to review the original, page by page, with the offered substitution. If the secretary finds them to be identical, then the substitution will be accepted as evidence. Bailiff, please accept the documents from the plaintiff and place them in the witness box for transfer."

Somehow, there was a fluster during the transfer. The original made it safely to the box, but the substitution document somehow got dropped and ruffled and shuffled into a scattered mess. "It's okay, your honor," the plaintiff's attorney stated. "We have another copy right here." Whereupon, he handed a new, still intact set of papers to the bailiff.

"If it pleases the court," Terry said, standing again, "the defendant would like to take possession of the set of documents dropped so precipitously. We will use it as our own review copy for comparison with the set submitted to the court."

"Objection, your honor." The plaintiff's attorney turned from picking up the mess. "We have a perfectly good copy right here for the defendant." Somehow, in his turn and objection, his cup of tea got overturned to land on and soak the pages of the original copy where they were still in a rumpled, now soggy, mess on the floor.

The judge looked over the top of his glasses at the plaintiff's attorney, taking special care to look pointedly at the mess made by the spilled tea. "I think the court will accept those dropped papers for comparison," he said. "It could well be enlightening to see just what all the hooraw was about."

The plaintiff's attorney put on a good show of disbelief and scoffing. "Your honor, we have nothing to hide, but as you can see, this copy is soiled and torn, and with the tea stains on it, it would certainly offer no enlightenment beyond the un-soiled copy we're offering to the defendant."

"If it pleases the court," Terry interjected again, "the defendant is prepared to accept the proffered replacement of the original copy with no hesitation. However, we feel it is time now to enter our own objection as to jurisdiction."

"Absurd," the plaintiff's attorney spluttered. "Even though I'm from out of state, we have three members on the team who are licensed and recognized by the State of Oregon."

The judge turned to Terry with a questioning look.

"It's true the plaintiffs are well and truly represented," Terry answered the judge's unspoken question, "However, the jurisdiction we question is not the plaintiff's, but that of the court itself. The land in question is not within the bounds of the State of Oregon, but is within the bounds of the State of Lincoln. The defense makes motion to have the State of Oregon dismiss this case as mis-filed."

"Objection!" the plaintiff's attorney nearly shouted in a voice that reverberated in echoes around the courtroom, "the defendant could have submitted this motion months ago instead of waiting all this time! Also, the original ownership was established in an Oregon court; therefore, regardless of whatever political shenanigans the defense may have contrived decades ago, this court should therefore rule that an Oregon Court has jurisdiction!"

The judge looked over at Terry for a response.

"If it pleases the court," Terry said before then taking a moment for reflection.

"We must first respond to the accusation that we undertook the forming of the State of Lincoln as a part of a long-standing plot by the Elk Creek Tribe. The Tribe was only a small percentage of the populace of the region when, with no consultation with us, the other surviving communities in southwestern Oregon took the steps to secede from the State of Oregon and form the State of Lincoln. We could not have been involved in the decision at all since most of our neighbors at the time were fomenting war against us as the secession was proceeding. They used the secession as cover to take over our lands, properties, and settlement.

"They included us in the geographical bounds of Lincoln, not because we sought it for ourselves, but because our enemies wished to take over the resources we had developed. The Elk Creek Tribe built our village, our dams, and our community in anticipation of the social collapse our Founder saw as imminent." He paused here, seeming to need time to decide what to say next.

"The surrounding communities, having ignored all the signs which proclaimed that the Fall was imminent, sought to take from us the resources we had developed. They made war on us in the failed attempt.

"To now go back and re-write history, to say we were complicit in a conspiracy to defraud a corporation which has been long dissolved and defunct, that is the travesty. We had no way of knowing anyone from this corporation had survived. In fact, we undertook a long and exhaustive search of the deeds and wills and found the company and all of its owners, formerly known as Umpqua Timber Properties, had ceased existence because of the quakes, tsunamis, and subsequent social upheaval. There were no surviving owners."

"Your honor," the opposing attorney interjected, "since we're not building a case, do you think the defendant could come to some point?"

The judge looked long and carefully over his half-glass bi-focals, his mouth in a downward turn, inside eyebrows drawn down, graving deep lines above the bridge of his nose.

"What would please the court," he finally said in a deliberate, low, and hissing voice, "would be for the plaintiff's attorney to be silent and allow an answer to the question said attorney presented." He continued his quelling glare until the man sat carefully in his chair, draping an arm over the back, sitting facing slightly away from Terry, dismissively crossing one leg over the other in practiced stoicism.

"You may continue," the judge informed Terry once the show was over.

"All of this we did before ever filing for ownership of the abandoned lands in both the State of Lincoln and the State of Oregon," Terry continued, as if there had been no interruption. "You'll note we list the owners as differing from what the plaintiff suggests. When we reach the proper court, we're sure we'll be able to provide evidence of later transactions which led to transference of the property under question to Umpqua Timber Properties and then into tribal ownership.

"What we also will address, once we have this case in front of a duly recognized court, is just *how* the Wearehauses Company found any set of documents at all to show acquisition and ownership of our lands.

"Now, as regards the plaintiff's objection, as stated, we request this court recuse itself from participation on the grounds that this court does not have physical jurisdiction over lands in the State of Lincoln."

As the plaintiff's attorney stood to reply, the judge abruptly signaled him to re-seat himself with a down-turned hand, slapping a sharp bang onto his rostrum. "This court finds for the defendant in this ruling. The case of the Wearehauses Company versus the Elk Creek Tribe is dismissed with prejudice."

Despite the wishes of the judge, the plaintiff's attorney leaped to his feet once again with a scatter of papers and the now-empty tea cup shattering to the marble floor. "Objection, your honor! We request a restraining order on the Elk Creek Tribe, forbidding them to use, access, or otherwise dispose of any properties under dispute until and unless relieved from this order by an appropriate court of law!"

"I'm on the verge of finding you in contempt," the judge replied levelly with a quelling glare. "We have already ruled we do not have jurisdiction over those lands. We do not have the authority to issue any order, even if it were of interest to us. Insofar as the use or disposal of said properties, the Elk Creek Tribe has managed those lands admirably over the last eighty years and the fact they are defending them from the likes of you and your sponsors tells this court those same lands will be in far better safe keeping than placing them into conservancy with your handlers in control.

"This case is dismissed. It is over. Refile down at Roseburg, the capital of Lincoln, and you'll get your day in a duly authorized court."

"Your honor, there is no way for a civilized man to reach Roseburg," the plaintiff's attorney spluttered. "There are no roads. No bridges. No path to get there from here."

"I can answer to that," Terry offered amiably. "While noting and affirming there are no bridges, paths, or roads, it leads me to wonder just how the plaintiffs expect to transport their ill-gotten gains up to market." He watched this dart settle over the plaintiff's table and over the watchers in the room. The Chief Judge of the Elk Creek Tribe waited in vain for a response other than the reddening of the lead attorney's face. He gave a slight smile before wiping it away and turning to the judge again.

"Setting those minor considerations aside, there are flights between Salem and Roseburg at least once a week. I'm sure the plaintiff can arrange with the airline to get one of their people onto a flight to file their false complaints. I wouldn't even suspect an east coast robber baron such as his exalted self would ever allow himself to enter the jurisdiction he finds so offensive and uncivilized."

During all this squabbling, Terry was picking up papers and packing them into a valise for transport. Once the plaintiffs had departed, a court bailiff asked the Elk Creek delegation to meet with the judge in his chambers. Jamari found the title "chambers" to be somewhat ostentatious when compared to the tiny and packed room the bailiff led them to. The judge sat behind his desk, motioning them to chairs on the other side.

"Terry," the judge said, "why did you ask for a recusal? You and I both know they created their evidence from imagination only. You would almost certainly have been granted dismissal overall if the case had continued."

"I agree Oregon would have granted dismissal, your honor," Terry answered. "But even if Oregon granted a dismissal, finding in favor of the Tribe, it would not have been the end of the matter. The plaintiff's attorney is obviously working under orders to attain our land; in whatever manner they can attain it. He would simply have filed in federal court and we would all have battled in another farce of a case up in Seattle.

"Now he must visit the lands in question. He'll have an opportunity, one I'm sure he won't take, to learn more about those lands, more about the Elk Creek Tribe and its stewardship of those lands. It will force him to fly over properly maintained land as opposed to land stripped bare by centuries of over-harvesting and mismanagement. I'm certain he'll, under orders from above, still file in federal court after the Lincoln Court finds in our favor, but we will have bought precious years in the meantime to find a way to permanently thwart their ambitions."

It reminded Jamari of a document he had studied while still in Jahangir's hearth as a boy. He couldn't remember the details, who was speaking or when they had made the statement, but it was a written record of those times during the formation of the Tribe and its cultural and legal mores. He remembered it being a part of the many meetings of the First Grand Council of the newly formed Elk Creek Tribe.

"A nation composed only of laws cannot be a just nation. A nation composed only of justice cannot be a lawful nation. We need to form a nation of balance. Was someone treated unjustly? Regardless of what the law says, there needs to be action to compensate them, as well as to prevent that injustice from happening again. Did someone break the law? Regardless of whether they did or not, was there just cause to do so? Did they harm someone or the nation? These things must be weighed and balanced. It will take a very special person to form that balance. How do we find them? Our judges."

He looked at Terry with a newfound respect. With all his many roles, it seemed he held the key to the Tribe's future even more strongly than did Chief Elk Creek himself.

Chapter Sixteen

The Social Life of Trees

When they got back to their room just after the noon hour, the plane was still out of commission for maintenance. The pilots had thought the case would take up more time and had scheduled an important annual inspection of the engine. It wouldn't be complete until the following Monday. With time on his hands, Jamari wanted to walk around the village of Salem to see if he could locate a good place for meditation. Terry agreed, but only if he could go along as well.

"You still have been lingering overly long in your meditative trances," Terry told him. "And you still have inadequate guards in place to alert yourself to approaching danger during your journeying."

Jamari couldn't help but agree, and it was with relief that he accepted the condition. He very much doubted he would have Cougar's strength and support in this barren and bereft land.

With no sure destination in mind, he asked if Terry knew where some trees could be located. Any representation of Nature at all, really. He missed the natural spirit around him and there seemed no place for spirit at all in the absence of the tribal forestlands. Terry knew of a place with a few trees they could reach on foot, but he cautioned they may not offer the peace of "Nature" that Jamari was seeking.

They set out after lunch, two men in casual clothes, except each had elected to wear moccasins for their comfort instead of the strange "tennis shoes" others around Salem were wearing for casual strolling. Their shaman bags would draw far too much attention to them, so they found a couple of small backpacks in the store across the street to load some of their necessities in.

No one wore so much as a belt knife in this community, so they carried their pistols in their backpacks. The two debated carrying their knives openly, but even if it made them stand out, both were too naked without that most basic of tools readily available. Jamari hoped they didn't stand out too much with their knives on their fancy dress belts outside of their trousers. He was wearing simple khaki-colored chinos and Terry had on a pair of forest-green ones. Each wore the tribal standard homespun hemp shirt that used leather ties to hold the front of the off-white tunic closed.

"We'll look like any other member of the tribe from over toward the coast come up to visit the big city," Terry guessed.

When they finally reached the park, Terry remembered, they found a lane where some trees had been planted into openings in the sidewalk. The keepers allowed no other growth in these isolated islands, so there was just a tree in each tiny pothole. Jamari found the one with the broadest canopy, a maple, leaves a golden yellow and brown, not quite breaking free for the winter's nap yet, but the promise of "soon" sang out in the color. He settled into the shade alongside the trunk, leaning back against the bole. This street the locals seemed to avoid. There was no one to interrupt him as he entered the meditation routine. It was much easier than he had expected, possibly because he knew Terry was standing guard nearby.

It seemed only moments later that Terry aroused him with a firm shake of his shoulders. He was near to tears from the sorrow he felt from the tree. "This tree is insane!" he exclaimed aloud. "It's been alone and bereft for so long there is no peace to be had in its shadow."

"Well, you got some time for meditation, anyway," Terry said.

"What do you mean?" Jamari asked. "I couldn't get into my inner place at all in those few moments."

"You've been in a trance for over an hour," Terry answered equably. "Did you not feel anything at all?"

"Only a sense of confusion," Jamari answered. "I felt the briefest touch of an awareness but it rebuffed me and pushed me back into the mundane before I could sense anything else."

"What did you mean when you said, 'This tree is insane' then?" Terry asked.

Jamari sought within for an answer. "When I communed with the trees of the grove above Elk Creek Hall, I sensed the individual trees visiting amongst themselves," he finally answered. "The forest was a focus. Like a protective umbrella of the whole. It held the individual trees, and the shrubs, mosses, birds, voles and even the mice burrowed into the soil. It also existed and communicated at an entirely other level." He paused and reached out to touch the bark of the maple, trailing his hand down to rustle through the dead soil at its base. "This tree has never communicated with another. It has stood here isolated from contact with any others. It has lost the ability to even think for itself."

"You may have sensed far more than you knew," Terry told him. "Let's walk around a bit while you're remembering your short time with Maple. Maybe as you concentrate, you'll realize even more."

What Jamari realized was there was far more life in the trees in the Tribe's forest land than there was in this fenced-in soul. Now that he was aware of it, he sensed the same isolation from each of the other trees lining the avenue. "What does it mean?" he wondered.

He didn't even realize he had spoken aloud until the Knight Shaman answered. "Apparently, it means your sojourn with the Great Spirit over those three weeks last fall imprinted more on you than just a confusing collage of broken memories. I know it's possible to feel the life of trees. As the Founder worded it, to feel 'the sense of peace, comfort, welcome, and tranquility to be found under the boughs of an ancient forest cannot be denied.' You seem to have come away with the ability to actually commune with the trees themselves."

"How would I know if I actually communicated anything to one of them?" Jamari wondered. "I keep learning more and more about myself and the spirit world around us as time goes by. Yet, it feels as if there is a deeper message there. Some 'thing' I'm called to remember. To do."

"Well, it will come to you in time, no doubt," Terry said as he turned their steps back towards their motel and the evening meal. "I'm thinking we'll take advantage of an opportunity to get you more lessons tomorrow," he said as they walked down an avenue of living dead trees.

"What would that be?" Jamari wondered.

"We can attend a session at church!" Terry announced jubilantly.

Jamari looked sidelong at his mentor, wondering if he dared to ask the burning question, and then he decided it was inevitable. "Okay, what would be the point in attending a church service up here? I'm pretty sure they won't be open to our spiritual practices, so what's being gained?"

"You're going to see another aspect of religious services tomorrow, Jamari. I'm certain you'll find it distasteful, if not outright invasive and offensive, but there is something here you need to learn as you continue to grow into your role as a tribal shaman."

They were in sight of the hotel by then, and Jamari's belly was grumbling a bit, letting him know supper wouldn't be a bad idea. "I'll go, then," he told the Knight Shaman. "Will I get to take my knife there?"

"No," Terry said, laughing, "that wouldn't be a good idea!"

AS THEY WALKED TO THE church the next morning, Terry shared some advice with Jamari. "It's important to remember this church teaches a vastly distinct set of life lessons than what we teach and practice in the Tribe. There will be a time during the service when I will pinch you. And I will probably pinch you very hard. I will want you to remember what you were feeling just before I intervened, as well as what you might have been thinking right before I pinched you. And then, I want you to work to separate your emotional and spiritual self from the sermon. After that point, I want you to concentrate instead on what the preacher - that is what they call their shaman - is attempting to do with and *to* his congregants."

"It sounds pretty serious," Jamari said as he stopped to face the Knight Shaman. "Are you sure this is something I have to do?"

"Yes. I'm sure. Just as sure now as I was on the day I convinced you to consider the path of a shaman. Against your objections, as I recall it." He turned towards the imposing building just down the block and started walking again.

Jamari, left behind momentarily as he pondered a sensation of dread, quickly followed along and caught up to the Knight Shaman. As they came along the walkway, he was noting a stream of people entering the double-wide doors at the front of the building.

They found seats near the back, and Jamari could scan the rows of cushioned benches. Each wooden bench could seat up to a dozen people, and they had to maneuver carefully past each other as they scooted sideways into the interior portions of those benches. They set the seating out in three columns with two aisles separating the three-wide arrangement. It looked like there were ten rows in each column, so about 120 people could fit into one of those columns, making the capacity somewhere near 360 people. Doing all this estimating helped keep him from fidgeting as he settled into a new environment while anticipating some unknown yet threatening development.

Three hundred and sixty strangers were more than he could ever have conceived of as being in one small place, but this "church" was only a quarter the size of the main room in the Tribe's casino/courthouse. And even smaller when compared to the vast meeting hall tucked into the inner recesses of Milltown Hall. He just had never seen either of those rooms even approaching the level of "fullness" this church was showing.

Eventually, as the last arrivals were shuffling in to find their seats, a roll of musical notes sounded around the high-ceilinged room. At first, Jamari had a hard time locating the source, but then he saw a lady way up front seated at a strange-looking piano. It had a completely unfamiliar sound compared to the pianos he had seen and heard before. He listened in wonder to the soaring notes rising and falling in a set rhythm that captured his attention. It was like an accordion, he concluded, but lacking the breathy and sharp notes. This was air blown over pipes, yet the outside casing was of a piano.

As those notes were cycling into a repeating motif, a balding, fattish man ambled in from the back and traversed down the right-side aisle, stopping and greeting certain individuals as he made his way to the front and stepped up the two steps to reach the oddly shaped table there. This man reminded Jamari of Rory, the judge who had determined his readiness to face the Manhood Rites on his declaration day. Well, the belly did anyway. Even at his worst, Rory couldn't have matched the fullness of the chubby face of the round little man who finally reached the lectern and turned to face the congregation. The pulpit was highly polished wood and came up nearly to the man's chest, hiding most of his ample belly. Jamari saw him reach down behind a false front to shuffle a set of papers as the piano-like device softened into silence.

"I want to welcome all of you today," the man said in a baritone voice that reached back to the far walls and bounced around the chamber in quick reverberation. "As we begin, let us bow our heads and pray."

Jamari watched as all those rows of people in front of him bowed their heads as one. He was looking around to check if everyone was complying when the Knight Shaman reached a quick hand over and signaled Jamari to bow his own head, too.

"Lord, we come before You today with thanks and gladness for the beauty of this day. For the bountiful lives we lead in Your glorious name. For the strengthening of our community as we work to recover from the trials You have set for us. We ask You to give our leaders strength, wisdom, and the will to carry out those actions necessary to continue this recovery. We ask you to guide us as we build up the children of God to a level that pleases You as we once did.

"Father in heaven, we pray for Your continued guidance as we pick our way through the challenges You have placed for us and strengthen us in endurance.

"I want to thank You, God, for those unfamiliar faces I see in this chamber today. I ask that you move their hearts to join themselves to You and to serve You and Your cause in bringing Your word to the masses.

"Thank you, God, for the chance You have given me to minister Your word to these, Your people.

"In Jesus' name, we pray. Amen."

All the congregants sounded this last word in quiet harmony, and Jamari heard the rustling of motion again and glanced up to see if it was okay to raise his head up. It seemed like a lot of begging for God to fix their problems and not a lot of working to fix those problems themselves.

"If you'll open your hymnals to page thirty-five, we'll begin today's music fellowship with 'Amazing Grace.'

"Lois, if you please." He looked over at the lady at the piano-shaped instrument.

The soaring notes of music and melody rang out again as Jamari was looking down on the pages of the hymnal held by the Knight Shaman.

Amazing Grace

Amazing grace! How sweet the sound,
That saved a wretch; like me!
I once was lost, but now am found,
Was blind, but now I see.
'Twas grace that taught my heart to fear,
And grace my fears relieved;
How precious did that grace appear?
The hour I first believed!
The Lord hath promised good to me,
His word my hope secures;
He will my shield and portion be
As long as life endures.
When we've been there ten thousand years,
Bright shining as the sun,
We've no less days to sing God's praise
Than when we first begun.

The sound of the congregation singing along with that instrument was a pleasure to behold. Jamari wasn't used to this type of singing at all. His experience had all been in bass notes hummed or sang out in a wordless melody as he led or assisted in tribal celebrations.

As the last words were fading, the preacher/shaman began speaking, repeating the words as the music died away. "'His word my hope secures,' the Lord says to us. 'He will my shield, and portion, be.'" The preacher paused here for a moment and then shouted out: "'AS long as life endures!'"

"Praise be to God we have such a merciful countenance to watch over us and shield us from the toils of this life and 'WHEN WE'VE BEEN THERE TEN THOUSAND YEARS we've no less days to sing God's praise.'"

"Praise God. Praise God," he chanted, holding his arms up in entreaty to heaven above.

"Amen. Amen," sounded the congregation.

Is he ever going to say anything? Jamari wondered.

"And now page one-twenty-four," the preacher directed. Jamari watched as Terry shuffled and riffled to the new page. He heard pages shuffling all around the room and watched the pianist riffling through her music notes to find the pages as well. Then the notes rolled out in sonorous bells, and the preacher opened up in his deep baritone voice.

Just as I am, without one plea,
But that Thy blood was shed for me,
And that Thou bid'st me come to Thee.
O Lamb of God, I come! I come!

Just as I am, and waiting not
To rid my soul of one dark blot;
To Thee whose blood can cleanse each spot,
O Lamb of God, I come, I come!

Just as I am, though tossed about
With many a conflict, many a doubt;
Fightings within, and fears without,
O Lamb of God, I come, I come!

Just as I am, poor, wretched, blind;
Sight, riches, healing of the mind;
Yes, all I need, in Thee to find,
O Lamb of God, I come, I come!

Just as I am, Thou wilt receive,
Wilt welcome, pardon, cleanse, relieve;

Because Thy promise I believe,
O Lamb of God, I come, I come!

Just as I am, Thy love unknown

Has broken every barrier down;
Now, to be Thine, yea, Thine alone,
O Lamb of God, I come, I come!

"Onward, Christian soldiers, Lois. You folks won't need to turn the page for this one," the jolly old man at the front purred. "I know you know it by heart!" The tune and key of the music changed into a more martial beat with heavy bass accompanied with a light and fainting treble. Jamari watched the musician's hands dance across the control board with complete fascination before the singing started.

"Onward Christian Soldiers," the preacher sung out in sepulchral and bass tones, not singing per se, but speaking the words in time to the music. "Marching as to war. WITH THE CROSS OF JESUS going on before." The music seemed to cycle again to a repeating motif and at some unheard signal, the entire congregation burst out into song. Bold. Daring. Challenging the world to defy them!

Onward, Christian soldiers!
Marching as to war.
With the cross of Jesus
Going on before.
Christ, the royal Master,
Leads against the foe;
Forward into battle,
See, His banners go!
Onward, Christian soldiers!
Marching as to war.
With the cross of Jesus,
Going on before.
At the name of Jesus

Satan's host doth flee;
On then, Christian soldiers.
On to victory!
Hell's foundations quiver
At the shout of praise:
Brothers, lift your voices,
Loud your anthems raise!
Like a mighty army
Moves the Church of God:
Brothers, we are treading
Where the saints have trod;
We are not divided,
All one Body we—
One in faith and Spirit,
One eternally.
Crowns and thrones may perish,
Kingdoms rise and wane;
But the Church of Jesus
Constant will remain.
Gates of hell can never
'Gainst the Church prevail;
We have Christ's own promise,
Which can never fail.
Onward, then, ye people!
Join our happy throng;
Blend with ours your voices
In the triumph song.
Glory, laud and honor
Unto Christ, the King;
This through countless ages
Men and angels sing.

Actual tears were running down the preacher's face as he waved his arms to the rhythm of the song. He held both hands out to the congregation, palms down, lowering his arms, an obvious signal to stop singing as the music soared on. Jamari was caught up in the moment, his senses ringing, his blood singing, his energy peaking and his path to his inner self opening wide to take in this beauty.

Then the Knight Shaman pinched him. It was indeed a very hard pinch, exactly as promised, and he closed down his pathways and settled into his seat along with the rest of the congregation. The music still poured out and around the room, begging him to open himself up to it again. To let the music of God take him over and away. Again, the pinch. And the preacher started his sermon to the beat of the martial drums.

"With the cross of Jesus going on before, Satan's host doth flee. We aim our battles to take on the enemies of the Lord. But what, I ask, what signs do we have that tell us who those enemies are? Well, they build their own religions. They set up their own rites. They practice evil ways in fornication and debauchery! These are the ways we know them!

"And they hold vast wealth in reserve when there are those without homes. Forests full of trees, ripe for the taking, standing tall and ready for the blade. Yet the heathens to the south keep us from them!

"Just this week, in a court of law, under the eyes of God above, these heathens tricked the army of the Lord. After months of wrangling, time wasted when we could have been gathering needed planks for building, the barbarians in the Elk Creek Tribe, those wretched souls who practice the basest of vile pursuits, they kept the righteous from those needed resources."

This time, Jamari needed the pinch for a different reason. He had been ready to stand and protest when the Knight Shaman pulled him down and signaled him to watch and see what was happening around him. What he saw was a congregation spinning up into righteous wrath. His own red and angered face was mirrored in those around him - fortunately, since he would have stood out as the enemy otherwise.

"Our warriors in the law will set out to file again, this time in a new court, in the very seat of the devil himself! They have to go down to Roseburg, capital of that heathen land that separated themselves from our righteous ways. They have to face the devil in his den, and they'll need all our prayers to prevail in that wicked land!

"Well, those heathen masses don't know the power of God as they soon will! We will pray them into submission as we build our mighty army to face that evil challenge!"

The sermon went on for much longer than Jamari wanted to listen. He was absolutely amazed that a source of such beauty as had risen in song could also be the voice of evil, proclaiming some right to take what rightfully belonged to the Tribe! And to talk of warriors facing down the heathens! When it was finally winding down, as the last prayer ended, Terry tugged his sleeve and they rose and joined others who were calmly leaving.

"What -" Jamari began to ask. Terry immediately shushed him. Jamari looked at him questioningly, and Terry turned to one parishioner, who was also traveling the same way, close enough to have heard any conversation they might have had.

"How are you today?" Terry asked the plainly dressed man. "Did you enjoy the service?"

"Uh. Sure," the man answered awkwardly. "What did *you* think about the message?" His question seemed *very* pointed to Jamari.

"Well, my friend and I are just passing through on business. We were thinking about heading south to see those tribal lands, but I think we're going to change our plans after what we heard. Praise God for the impulse to go to service this morning; otherwise, we could have been caught up in all that mess!"

"Yeah," the man said with narrowed eyes, "praise God for timely warnings. Where you folks from, then?"

"Oh, up Dallas way," Terry answered. "I have some background with the Grande Ronde Tribe, even though they dis-enrolled my line long ago."

"Well, you would be best to head back that way, then," their erstwhile friend offered.

"Surely," Terry responded amiably. "We'll be heading back that way by this afternoon. This is where we turn to get to our camp," he said as he motioned Jamari to take a left at an intersection that would lead them in the opposite direction from their motel.

"Well, good day to you, then," the man answered. "God bless your journey."

"Thank you, my good man," Terry replied. "May God protect you from harm."

Chapter Seventeen

Spirit Feathers

They had walked a few blocks in quiet before Terry talked openly. "So, what did you pick up from all that?" he asked Jamari.

"By all the spirits," Jamari answered, "are we going to be at war?"

"Good question," Terry answered. "I don't know for sure whether this is just one church with one preacher who has financial or family ties to the timber company, or whether it is something more widespread. I'm going to be sending some folks up this way in the next week who can attend services at other churches in order to find out.

"What I really meant, when asking about what you picked up, was spiritually, during the songs, especially near the end of the singing as the preacher was starting his sermon, what did you pick up? What did you feel and learn?"

"I was pretty open, spiritually speaking, from the songs," Jamari said. "It felt almost exactly like when I purposefully seek within for the inner spirit and God, but somehow more powerful and opened up. Perhaps 'vulnerable' would even be a better word."

"Very good observation," Terry praised. "What would you have been vulnerable to, exactly?"

"Whatever spiritual message that man would have wanted me to experience," Jamari answered in sudden fear. "That entire congregation has just been pre-disposed toward hating the tribe!"

"I think, given the point of the message, you would have been immune to the programming," Terry said. "It almost certainly would have introduced a great deal of self-questioning, though. What if the message had been against homosexuality? Or promiscuity? Or selfishness or greed? What would you have been inclined to do because of having been so spiritually unshielded during the final stanzas of music? Would you have been able to withstand the pressure? Or would you have fallen under the sway of the message and thought of yourself as unworthy for having felt or practiced whatever thing the message was against?"

"I think I'm more resilient than that," Jamari answered. "I'm pretty sure I would have endured some internal dialogue, but I would have kept my bearing and self-value. Is it always 'against' something, though, this 'message' after opening up the spirits of the congregants?"

"I think it only works when it's 'against' some specific thing," Terry answered. "The goal seems to be to make it immoral to exist at all. The easiest and longest-standing target has been sexual expression. For centuries, the churches have taught that sexual activity is immoral, maybe even evil. They offer the guidance that, if a man simply must do something about his sex drive, he should marry and confine his lust to only one woman.

"It is the most powerful element of human existence, and by making it evil, making the individual 'guilty' of sexual desire, they then offer him redemption, if he only follows the guidance of the church and its representatives."

"It seems like they're the evilest thing in the entire picture," Jamari observed, "using a person's inner spirit, their most basic need for connection with God, to manipulate them like that!"

"Well, in that sense, we do the same thing," the Knight Shaman responded quietly.

"What?" Jamari exclaimed. "I've never seen anyone use our spiritual rites to manipulate anyone!"

"You haven't?" Terry replied. "Think about it for a minute.

"I think we can turn here and get back to the motel," he said shortly. "I've been watching, and it doesn't look like anyone is following us anymore."

"What do you mean, 'anymore'?" Jamari asked warily, with a quick glance behind them.

"Do you think the man we talked with was just accidentally following so closely behind us?" Terry asked. "He was staying so close that he would overhear anything we said."

"Are we in danger?" Jamari wondered.

"I don't know," Terry answered, "but given the sermon's message and the attempt to follow us so closely afterward, I suspect someone may have suspected we have ties to the Elk Creek Tribe and was checking us out to learn more."

They had made a couple of turns and finally headed back to their rooms when Terry pursued the lesson again. "Have you thought of any time you might have witnessed anyone from the tribe using spiritual openness during a ceremony to manipulate our members yet?"

"I can't think of any," Jamari answered.

"Hmm. During the salmon return two seasons back, when we noticed the damage to the fish from nets, do you remember us altering the normal message associated with the celebrations?"

"Yes," Jamari answered, "we took enough of the fish to provide for the evening's feast, and then, during the celebration afterwards, you had me work the drums while the tribal members chanted our welcome of the returning migration. Then, while I was still drumming, you gave a lesson about frugality and preservation of the runs in light of the damage to the fish and the potential impact on their continuation."

"True," Terry answered. "I was preaching for conservation, reaching into their inner spirit to invoke their deepest emotions so they would then work to preserve the salmon run for future generations as well."

"But that was an important message!" Jamari objected. "It was a necessary action we needed to take as a united tribe!"

"Yes. It was 'for' something instead of 'against' something. But I, and you as well, used my spiritual position to manipulate the psyche of my congregation.

"What, for the sake of this lesson, is the difference?"

Jamari walked in silent contemplation for a block as he considered.

"We'll turn here again," Terry said. "This should get us back to the rooms in time for a late lunch." He looked at Jamari sidelong as they continued to walk along. "Any thoughts?" he asked.

"I have to admit, we used our positions as shamans to influence the Tribe," Jamari answered. "But it just seems so different from what the preacher did. He was using his position to influence his congregation towards condoning an act of evil. We used our positions to influence our 'congregation' towards an act of preservation."

"The difference could well be in who is considering," Terry replied. "Would the Outsiders who placed the nets think of our influence as just and proper, had we immediately focused our intent on building the tribe up for battle against their trespass? Yes, we did eventually end up in conflict with them, but we did *not* bring on the conflict so much as stumble into it.

"And yes, I recognize you suffered an extreme loss during the conflict.

"What I'm asking is, do you see the need to influence the citizenry towards or against any single act, or even thoughts?"

"It feels kind of repulsive right now," Jamari answered glumly. "I took part in something that closely parallels the evil I just witnessed today."

"I want you to understand more about it before we leave off talking about it," Terry said, as he put an arm around Jamari's shoulders and shared a walking hug for a couple of steps. "When we welcomed you at the Ceremony of the Awakened, did you think every single tribal member should be a part of that group?"

"No," Jamari answered quickly. "There are some tribal members who will never be adults based on their aptitude and ability. There are others who will be adults, but not recognized as full citizens, also based on their aptitude and ability. Even among those who attain full citizenship, many will not be truly 'awake' in the full spiritual sense that we in the group already are. That is a necessary stratification in a society where each earns his or her place in our culture via their aptitude, ability, and effort."

"What is one of the key things we discussed at the awakening ceremony?" Terry asked. "I talked about it specifically before we heard Paul's message."

"Each of the attendees can take in any message and deliberate on it before choosing to believe it or act as if it is true and relevant to themselves," Jamari answered.

"Yes," Terry said. "In that light, where does the guidance for the non-citizens, the non-adults even, come from?"

"Our spiritual influence is used to give guidance to those who may not comprehend or build their own cultural foundation," Jamari realized.

"The guidance we offer from our position becomes the glue which holds our society and culture together," Terry said. "Our Tribe is different in one key way. There is a section of our society which we recognize and empower as also 'awake' and therefore able to influence and guide cultural decisions and morals. They are our monitors. Even I, as the most powerful shaman in the tribe, am subject to oversight from the community of awakened. The key difference between 'us' and 'them' is you and I have oversight from our peers. The preacher in that church today has no oversight in how he uses his position to program the congregation members who entrust their souls to his keeping. He probably has convinced himself of the righteousness of his position. He likely truly believes that he is doing God's work when he influences his congregants towards prejudice and hate."

They constantly watched for signs of surveillance throughout the rest of their time in Salem. With so few hotels available, if the nebulous "enemy" really was thinking about it, they could locate them quickly enough. The next morning, with the airplane back in service, they all four departed before daylight for the walk to the airport and the return to their own lands.

The only remaining revelation for Jamari came as they were walking alongside a section of road used by faster-traveling vehicles. He noticed an excess of animal carcasses beside the road and in the ditch. There were raccoons, still bloody from their recent deaths, along with skunks, possums, and a bobcat. Skeletonized remains evidenced the number of years this had been occurring. "Why are there so many dead animals?" he asked at one point.

"They don't have a defense against the vehicles on the road," one pilot answered. "They have no way of recognizing the danger of a speeding car until it is on them and it crushes them under its wheels. If you could see the freeways up north of here, you'd see it even worse. The cars are very little damaged, but they decimate the animals until there are no more living within range of the road itself. Even then, some migrate away from overcrowded areas and find themselves under the wheels. And deer. Those do some damage to the cars even though they give their lives in the doing."

"How can they allow this to continue?" Jamari wondered, aching for losing life.

"It's all in the name of progress," the other pilot answered. Jamari looked at the Knight Shaman but found him deep in introspection as he was walking along, almost unaware of the conversation. He dropped the topic but was certain he would remember if there ever came a time when he could do something about it.

He, too, was deep in thought when one pilot grabbed his arm and pulled him into the ditch as an oncoming truck roared by them in a cloud of dust. They were all left coughing and sneezing from the stir. "What was that all about?" Jamari wondered when he got his breathing back under control. "Why was he staying so close to us and not swerving away?"

"I don't think he even recognized we were here," the co-pilot said as they stepped back onto the road to continue their walk towards the airport, now visible in the distance.

They were less than a mile away from the airport when Jamari heard a squabble on the road ahead. As they closed the distance, he could see some crows and a couple of hawks gathered over the carcass of some hapless animal. It was no longer recognizable, only a lump of reddened flesh and gray fur.

He was just realizing the birds were feasting on the remains of another of the many road kills when he saw another truck bearing down on the gathering. It looked like the truck was speeding up to get to the feasting birds quicker. Suddenly, the pilot pulled him to the side of the road again.

In a time-frozen blur, he watched all the crows take flight and scatter away. But one of the heavier hawks was a bit too slow.

The passenger side of the windshield of the blunt-nosed behemoth swatted the unfortunate hawk out of the sky. Jamari worked hard to convince himself it was only imagination that made him see a maniacal grin of pleasure from the death machine's driver.

The hawk fluttered in an arc straight towards Jamari, who instinctively reached out as if to catch the lifeless and flailing body. Instead, it dropped to the ground at his feet, tumbling in a flutter until it came to a blood-spattered stop up against his leather shoes, soiling his court-fine pants.

He kneeled and lifted the warm bundle. Its head and wings lolled lifeless, changing its dead balance, so he fumbled to not drop it, somehow fearing he might harm this representative of his lesser-totem.

"They've completely forgotten what their souls are for," he whispered huskily of the senseless death, not just of this bird, but of all the animals littering the ditch behind and in front of them. His tears tracked dust trails down his face as the whirling dust devils settled back into their restless ease on the road. The crows were settling once again onto the further-tattered bloody mass. A new dust storm engulfed them as another car sped up from behind.

"I think you should keep it," Terry said of the dead hawk in his hands. "When your totem sacrifices itself for you, you hold on to and cherish the physical parts the Spirit has left behind. You've earned your own feathers long before this, and the Great Spirit has granted them to you now."

"Hawk did not sacrifice Himself," Jamari answered bleakly as he held the limp, warm body in his hands, feeling blood dripping down his palms. "They murdered Him."

"And maybe He was murdered," Terry answered calmly. "But of all the ways that tattered body could have gone, it landed at your very feet. Remember, we don't tell God what language He can speak to us in. Instead, we work to discern His voice from the tempest around us."

Chapter Eighteen

Invasion!

J amari cured the hawk's skin and hardened the base of the wing-feathers, building the whole into a feathered headpiece. The head, with opened and threatening beak, became the front of the cap, with wings bent into a dive on the side and a red-flared tail at the rear. He wove a small piece of turquoise into the diamond pattern of cobalt-died porcupine quills in the front piece. It was a singularly ugly piece, he thought as he looked at himself in the mirror. But then he re-imagined it as a sinister and foreboding mask to wear when presenting a darker story with some threat of danger.

The weeks passed in quiet activity as he continued his work on the totem pole and his forays into the wild woods with Sophia. He enjoyed making good progress on all fronts. The overall shape of the totem came into rough focus, with the innovative carvings using the roots of the tree to hold carved salmon, and a segment of the upper portion already pinned in place as the wings for Eagle. He had finally relaxed his over-vigilance while meditating. As a result, he had reached a deeper understanding of the forest spirit, even feeling a strong sense of connection to one glade above the Casino/Courthouse which had conveyed a sense of welcome to him though not much else.

A ranger rushed into the courthouse, asking for the chief. They summoned chief Scotts Valley from a trip to the winery and chicken farm on the ridge above the community. When Howard arrived, the young man gasped out his tale. The lands around the tribal village of London, the only settlement the Tribe owned within Oregon's lands, were under assault! Mercenaries accompanied a logging expedition, which had taken down a large swath of timber before they being discovered, opened fire, killing several tribal members as they approached.

Howard, Chief Scotts Valley, sent a messenger to Chief Elk Creek up in Milltown. He tasked the messenger with assuring Colonel Jahangir and Chief Matthew of Milltown, and Chief of Elkhead, Jacelyn, should make haste down to Scotts Valley.

The original runner, a young man of obviously tribal heritage, took advantage of an offered place to rest and recover from his journey while they waited for the village chiefs to arrive.

Jamari and his closest companions waited in the large commons area for the various chiefs and war leaders while two court aides tended to the collapsed ranger. He, while not injured, suffered from over-exertion from his run over the mountain.

Once everyone finally gathered late in the afternoon, except for Chief Jacelyn, who had further to travel, Chief Elk Creek pre-emptively ordered Jahangir to take the militia to the site of the invasion.

"We're officially representing the Lincoln National Guard now," Jahangir answered. "Even though our members have ownership of that land individually, via long-ago treaty and deed transference, the land is in the State of Oregon. They have not recognized tribal ownership of the land. We can't go in with our forces. It would void all treaties and be a potential trigger for civil war with one state against the other."

Chief Elk Creek's face creased in anger, going redder than Jamari had ever seen. "'When any community of people allow themselves to wait in time of crisis for help to come to them, then that community becomes a community of victims.' That bit of wisdom comes down to us from Justin Earl Knight!" Chief Elk Creek shouted. "You'll remember him as the Founder of the Elk Creek Tribe," he added in obvious scorn. Chief Elk Creek paused and looked with obvious rancor around all the members in the room.

Jamari looked over to the Knight Shaman, remembering his own struggles with anger, and remembering Lon taking him to task. *Who was there to confront the Chief of The Tribe*, he wondered to himself? *Who could check his anger and make him pause?*

"What are our options, then?" Chief Elk Creek finally asked. "It is an abomination. Our tribe should not sit out this atrocity without a response!"

"Colonel Jahangir is correct," Terry answered as Chief Judge and the Knight Shaman. "We can send a delegation to Salem to protest and request aid from their legal system, but, even if we prevail on a field of battle, if we act unilaterally now, we stand to lose any good will we've built over the years in one spectacular failure. I know we would decimate this crew of loggers and their guard patrol with ease if we set out to do so. It may even be exactly what Wearehauses wants us to do. It would give them justification for a full-scale invasion of our heartland, maybe even with the support of the Oregon National Guard."

"What is your advice, then?" Chief Elk Creek asked of his councilors.

Terry and Jahangir exchanged glances. Terry nodded to Jahangir to go first in his reply. "I think we need to do a strategic withdrawal from London," Jahangir said quietly. "If we can't legally defend the surrounding lands, it seems to follow that the same restriction would apply to defending the town itself, since it, too, is in Oregon."

Chief Elk Creek winced visibly at this pronouncement. "Now *that* is going too far!" he exploded in anger. "That land is owned legally and with complete moral authority by this tribe!"

"Not accurate," Terry said, his face crestfallen, eyes narrowed, with shoulders slumping.

"The individual plots of land were deeded to individual tribal members long ago. Remember though, Lincoln seceded from Oregon near that same time frame. We have since been granted hegemony over all the lands up to the Oregon/Lincoln border by the State of Lincoln as a tribe, but Oregon has never recognized the fact of 'tribal' ownership under their courts. We will certainly fight to keep ownership of the plotted and deeded lands in and around London on behalf of our individual members who are heir to those properties, but, despite decades of management and maintenance, we don't have *tribal* title to the timberlands. Oregon never granted that."

"Well, we should fire all you legal eagles!" the chief raged. Jamari, while still angry himself, couldn't remember ever seeing Chief Elk Creek so near to out-of-control.

"This is completely untenable!" the chief continued to rage.

Chief Elk Creek glared at Jahangir after running a quelling glance around the room. "I should have known a general who brought our enemy into our fold and gave them the land at Hancock Valley in exchange for peace would back down from an actual fight!" He turned to glare at the Knight Shaman. "And I listened to you when you recommended him!"

Again, Jahangir and Terry exchanged worried looks. It looked as if they, too, were concerned about the chief's irrational anger.

"I think it's a moot point where to assign blame in this matter," Rory interjected. "We should withdraw the community from London, true. *But*, we should then have tribal militia, *not* in the Guard's uniform, post there as their base of operations. They will hold the village against the invaders. We might not repel them from our forest lands, and we'll never be able to replace the trees or even renew the spiritual connection to the graves they protected, but, we have every right under the law of the land to protect our deeded properties from the adventurers."

"Well, Jahangir, can you at least do that much?" the chief asked with a sneering dismissal.

"We can evacuate the villagers through Lane Creek Village and down to Milltown Village," Jahangir answered carefully. "Milltown Hall is vastly under-used right now with our recent expansions into those lands to our west. And we can man and defend the village of London as owners. *But* we can't wear the uniform of the Lincoln National Guard while we cross the state border."

The chief snorted with contempt, spraying saliva onto the table in front of him as he spit out his anger.

Before he could further inflame the situation, though, the Knight Shaman intervened. "Chief Elk Creek," he said, invoking the balance of power between them with the title, "control yourself!"

"Chief Elk Creek, indeed," the chief blurted out. "I'm on the verge of overturning all of your appointments in this matter. All it would take would be one look of encouragement from any of you here, and I'll take this matter into my own hands!"

Chief Matthew answered with quiet force. "You will do no such thing!" he said between clenched teeth, in a voice he fought to keep under control. "If you can't, as the Knight Shaman has suggested, 'control yourself', we have sufficient members of the council present to convene a quorum and take the next logical step down this path! Will you be the first tribal chief since David James to face the ultimate solution? I do not want to ascend to tribal chief over your dead body, but I will if that's what it takes to get a voice of reason in this matter!"

Jamari was stunned to silence as he watched this battle of wills. Studying how Chief David James gave up his life in order to achieve something of true import to The Tribe was a far cry from seeing a similar event right in front of his very eyes.

"Obviously, I have no support here," Chief Elk Creek lamented. "Colonel Jahangir, dispatch your troops as you've suggested. Chief

Matthew, prepare your village to receive refugees. I'll be awaiting developments in my quarters here in the courthouse."

He paused in turning away, speaking over his shoulder. "And send out messages to all the villages. We will convene the entire Tribal Council in emergency session as soon as each village has sent their representatives." Brow pinched and eyes narrowed in scorn, he stormed out of the chamber.

"Colonel Jahangir, I apologize for this," Chief Matthew whispered. "We can hope he'll settle from his temper before this goes too much further. He is a powerful chief and I do not relish the thought of replacing him, whether with myself or with some other person the council may choose."

"I'll set up two response brigades," Jahangir said. "The ones to London will represent tribal interest, wearing militia leathers, and I'll instruct them that the defense of London and associated tribal member properties is their only mandate.

"The others, I will range along our northern borders, in the uniform of the Lincoln National Guard, and will direct to repel all invaders with extreme prejudice."

"We're all emotional right now," Virginia said in a low voice which countered the high tension in the room and helped to bring the volume down. Her comment had the agreement of everyone in the room. "You have a tough assignment," she said to Colonel Jahangir. "Know that the council backs you. You have made an onerous call, but it was the right one." She paused and turned to Terry.

"Knight Shaman, you may have an even more taxing assignment. Do you think you can reason with him and help him face this crisis in a more balanced and reasonable manner?"

"I've worked with him for many long years," Terry answered. "He's never lost his temper this way. I will give him a couple of hours to reflect and process through the points we've made. He should settle on his own. If not, I will do my best to reason with him."

They all set about their tasks. Jahangir dispatched all the members of the Lane Creek, Scotts Valley and Milltown militias on a rout march to London with orders to get the villagers ready to evacuate down to Milltown Village. Then he sent out a series of messengers to gather his soldiers. Milltown wasn't the closest village to London, Lane Creek having that honor, but it was the most logical choice given the many halls of Milltown and Elk Creek Halls had enough room to house them.

Riley, who had recently assumed command of the Young Men's squads as Shane's replacement, took command of the London Relief Brigade as captain. Bill, Jahangir's current deputy, accepted a promotion to Major and took command of the two-brigade border patrol force. Colonel Jahangir would remain at Scotts Valley, where he would command the expected forces from throughout the tribal lands.

Virginia sent messengers to the Women's Hall, upstream from Milltown Village at the tribe's second dam, to gather all the militia squads their village could spare.

During all this preparation, Chief Jacelyn arrived from Elkhead Village. She was quickly brought up to speed and concurred with everything done so far.

Terry sent out two messengers by horse to get word down to Roseburg and the capital. They unanimously selected Terry to be dispatched with messages to the State of Oregon, directly to the governor's office. Chief Elkhead and Chief Milltown had conferred and decided Terry's skills would best apply in Salem. Terry ordered four horses to be saddled and equipped for a night ride. "I really shouldn't do this," he told Jamari when they got a moment together, "but I'm bringing you with me for the visit to the governor's office. Get Lon and Joshua ready to accompany us up."

Terry talked with Chief Matthew about approaching Chief Elk Creek after he had time to cool down. No one wanted a change in tribal leadership at such a time, but no one wanted to force the Tribe into a war, either.

"But why?" Jamari asked as they were walking out of the courthouse. "I still have command authority within the militia. I'm actually a Second Lieutenant with the Lincoln National Guard, right?"

"Your current assignment is as a court assistant," Terry said. "You'll go with me as assigned. And, sadly, neither of us will be in uniform for this venture. We'll be representing the tribe as civilian emissaries while awaiting word and participation from the Governor of Lincoln."

They made it to Curtin just as darkness descended on the embattled land. The pilots were concerned about night flying. The tribal plane did not have the most recent navigation equipment. Terry was adamant, though, and cajoled them into compliance, emphasizing this was an invasion. If the plane wasn't ready for this contingency, he said, then there would have to be some changes made soon.

Jamari found night flying to be singularly unpleasant. There was darkness below. Darkness to the side. Darkness in the cloudy skies above. From his seat in the back of the four-seater plane, Jamari wondered at just how the pilots were coping with it all.

Once at the Salem airport, Terry immediately sent messages to the Governor's office; to the home of the tribal ambassador to Oregon; and others to various military and government officials. He didn't want any time wasted on protocol or niceties when members of The Elk Creek Tribe were preparing for battle.

The distance involved, though, over roads still torn up and cobbled together would almost certainly cause delays enough to assure loss of life regardless of whether Oregon engaged. They got one room with two beds for all four of the travelers due to such a late arrival. They set themselves up in the room, fully expecting to do only wait until at least noon or later of the following day.

The governor surprised them when he sent a car for them within only a couple of hours of their arrival. Terry and Jamari, still unkempt and disheveled from their long day, took the ride to the state house and met with the governor. The tribal ambassador and the two-star general, General Tempson, who commanded the Oregon National Guard, were also in attendance.

There, Terry reported what he knew: a large group had invaded lands owned by the Tribe; there had been a report of gunfire from the ranger, but he hadn't known how many died. The governor dispatched a squadron of helicopters to London to reconnoiter and to be onsite to allow for communications between the responding forces the next day. At the very least, a squadron of war choppers should work to deter the invaders from engaging any further, he asserted.

The helicopters could also get a quicker report of conditions to update the information Terry had, which was over twelve hours old. The Elk Creek Tribe Ambassador largely listened with a frown at the news. Jamari could see his expressions cycle as the story was told. His only response came at the end of the conference. "I hope you know, Governor, General, the Elk Creek Tribe has shown considerable restraint. I would have expected a far more aggressive response than what we're hearing about here."

"It's a very good thing Colonel Jahangir was in Milltown Village when the word came down," Terry said. "I don't want to get into detail about the intensity of the discussion and the outright anger we had to quell in preventing the exact response you were thinking of.

"If Matthew, Jahangir, Jacelyn, Virginia, Rory, and I had not all been present, I'm afraid Chief Elk Creek would have dispatched the troops with a far different agenda."

Terry and Jamari accepted individual rooms in the Governor's mansion. They were both glad the rooms had an interconnecting interior doorway and, though they could get a full night's sleep, spent most of it waiting for updates which never came. In the end, they fell asleep in the same bed, both too tired for eros, but holding each other close in their sleep.

The next morning, a polite knock at the door awakened them. A porter invited them to breakfast with the governor and the commanding general. They hadn't had time to pack clothing for the company they were keeping. The porter found a clothier able to bring suitable wear to the mansion, and both were presentable for the working breakfast well after the land was lit up through the still lowering clouds.

"How can I wear my clout with these pants?" Jamari asked indignantly as he attempted to make it work.

"Take the pants back off," Terry instructed him.

Once Jamari was naked again, Terry reached over to the bed where Jamari had discarded a small cloth thing he didn't understand. Terry held this blindingly white garment up, fitting his finger through an odd little arrangement on one side. "This is the front of this pair of underwear," Terry told him. He then reached his hand through the folds to show the labyrinthine path to access whatever would be inside. "If you need to urinate," Terry said with a smile, it comes out here without having to pull everything down." He tossed them over to the naked Jamari. "Try them out. You might end up liking them."

Jamari struggled, trying to figure out the near-incomprehensible openings and folds before he finally got the blinding white garment up.

"Now turn around for me," Terry ordered.

Jamari felt Terry's eyes as he turned around a full circle. "Oh, you need to see what that does for you," Terry mumbled. "The steward must be gay to have found such a perfect fit and cut for you. Come over here to the mirror. Now turn sideways and just look."

Jamari stepped over as instructed, looking himself up and down in the full-length mirror. "Okay," he said finally, "I guess I don't get it. It's my butt." He turned to look at Terry to see what he was missing and couldn't help but notice a rise tenting Terry's pants.

"It's much more than just your butt," Terry said huskily. "It's a highlight, an amplification, a showing-off, of a wondrous asset."

Jamari turned to look at the mirror again. He had never really considered 'looks' when he was deciding to share a session of eros with someone. There was always so much more to take into consideration. He remembered catching himself looking at Lon's derriere occasionally, though, and now looked to compare. He looked back over at Terry. "Maybe we should have shared eros last night," he said. "I thought you were too tired."

"I was," Terry answered as he strode over to take Jamari into his arms for a body hug. "I should show you how to use that little fold, though," he said.

Then Jamari felt a hand enter through the opening and, with remarkable ease, he was standing free.

"What about breakfast? And the governor?" he whispered huskily.

"The Governor, and the rest of the world, for that matter, can wait while we bring a little love into it," Terry answered as he guided Jamari back to the bed. "I hope you'll forgive me for neglecting you and let me make it up."

"Of course," Jamari mumbled into the side of Terry's neck as they settled into the folds of blankets and pillows. "Always for you."

Later, after a good shower, the porter guided them down the halls to the breakfast room of the mansion.

"I apologize for our tardiness," Terry said. "We slept late and wanted to be sure we had a good shower before presenting ourselves."

The governor looked them over, and Jamari felt his eyes settle on their still damp hair. "I'm glad you found our hospitality welcoming," he answered. "General Tempson has an update for you on conditions down in London."

"I have to say that your Colonel Jahangir is hell-on-wheels," General Tempson said. "He had his battalions on the state borders and was ready to respond to a potential incursion in an amazingly short time. The colonel commanding our recon battalion said he hadn't seen such a classic defensive effort since advanced combat operations training up at Fort Lewis as a captain."

"Well, it seems possible they had the same course, General," Terry said as he sipped a beverage called "coffee," which Jamari had found far too bitter until a steward had shown him how to add cream and sweetener.

"Jahangir also attended the war college at Fort Lewis," Terry continued, "as well as the major who is commanding the response force. I think the captain commanding the militia force that made the overnight trek to London is scheduled to attend the course soon as well. One thing we've always tried to keep up with has been our militia training."

"And done very well," Tempson replied. "We have some updates from London to share." Terry and Jamari both set their coffee down, leaning forward to listen carefully and fearfully to what might come next.

"Not as bad as feared," Tempson said, noting their responses. "There were two deaths in the first of the exchanges when the timber company's escort forces fired on the Londoners when they approached. From what we've been able to determine, none of the Elk Creek Tribe responders had offered any armed offense. They had simply shown up and demanded the logging operation stop."

"As they had every right to do," The Governor interjected as Terry protested. "You can be sure the State of Oregon will do everything in our power to get this incursion stopped, mopped up, and the responsible parties tried for Murder, Assault, Trespassing, Theft and any other charge we can put them under. Tell them where things stand for now, Tempson, so we can enjoy our breakfast."

"Yes, sir," Tempson responded carefully after observing the tense posture and responses of their guests. "The escort forces did fire on the first chopper that went over their operation this morning. Those six individuals were the last ones to offer any resistance. The missile the weaponeer launched KIA'd the entire squad. All the remaining forces threw down their weapons and surrendered. The loggers and surviving escorts—"

"Why don't you just call them as they are, mercenaries," Terry interjected. His face had reddened as he heard of the deaths, his eyes narrowing to mere slits and his brows lowering, making it obvious his efforts to remain calm and rational were at the edge of failing. At least it seemed as if he could contain the rage unlike Chief Elk Creek, who had called the full Tribal Council for when they returned.

"Yes," the governor said, "Mercenary is an appropriate label. There's no reason to sugarcoat anything here. They'll be labeled as such in the charges.

"Go ahead, Tempson."

Nodding to both the governor and to Terry, the general continued his report. "As I was saying, the loggers and mercenaries are all in custody. All of their equipment is confiscated and every one of them is being interrogated to determine who, which company, which officers in the company, was involved. We've already taken some officers of Wearehauses operating under the guise of Umpqua Timber Management Corporation into custody for questioning. This, based on the recent court case, but not having any actual evidence to connect them to the case. I understand their lead counsel is not comfortable sharing a cell with his sponsors.

"We will sort this mess out," he concluded.

"What of the citizens of London?" Jamari asked. "Was their evacuation conducted as planned? Are they safe?"

"I don't know about an evacuation," Tempson answered. "We didn't cross the border ourselves, so didn't have time to see if there were folks traveling on the trail over the pass. If they were, I'm sure they're all safe. If not, I know they're safe, because there was no hostile action in the village itself."

"I suspect the village of London will no longer be tenable to us," Terry said. "To have such an act perpetrated is simply barbaric. The culture from which this act originated, whether or not these specific offenders are punished, is not a culture we can entrust our citizens to."

"I don't know, Knight Shaman," the ambassador interjected. "the Oregon response is everything we could have hoped for. They averted the crisis. There will be no war. No further loss of life. No further loss of property."

"Really?" Terry answered, shifting his narrowed gaze to the ambassador. "Did you forget that Chief Newell was interred in that copse of woods? And a good many other of our ancestors from over the last 100 years? Can they be repaid? Will their graves be un-desecrated? Can the spirits of our ancestors be appeased so easily, do you think?"

Jamari was feeling some concern over Terry's reaction, even as he felt the impact of invasion, death, and war himself.

"I am sorry, Knight Shaman," the ambassador answered. "I was simply trying to see the positive in this mess." Terry stared at him for a moment before visibly deciding not to pursue the matter any further.

Jamari was certain the Knight Shaman would replace this ambassador if he had anything to say about it. And that the only person in the Elk Creek Tribe who would dare to stand up to the

Knight Shaman was Chief Elk Creek, settled the question before they ever placed it.

"Knight Shaman?" the governor inquired politely. "Is that a title of some sort?"

Terry glared again at the ambassador before answering. "It's a symbolic position," he lied, "an honorary offered to the tribe's highest ranking minister."

Jamari was smart enough to not even look surprised at this bit of fully accurate disinformation, and the ambassador hid himself behind his coffee cup for the next few minutes as everyone settled from a scuffle which most in the room hadn't even noticed. Jamari could see from the governor's intense look that he had caught the import of the exchange, but, politician that he was, he would say nothing, either.

"Please, enjoy your breakfast now," he invited them. "The fracas is soon to be settled and we can decide this with passaging time and appropriate deliberation."

Tribal custom was to conduct interment as soon as possible after death, even while the vacated vessel was still warm. This followed with what the Founder had decreed for himself and also agreed with the oldest rites from ancestors in virtually all of their varied backgrounds. He offered, and Terry accepted, transport to the town of London in a military helicopter to gather those villagers who remained behind after the evacuation and summon them to what had been Chief Newell's Grove: could still be such if any of the trees still stood; if the spirits would remain in that savaged land.

The helicopter, black and ominous, stuttering and roaring, settled them in an open landing amongst the harvest equipment and banks of gathered logs. They could see a dirt road which had been carved like a red-brown snake into the hills in undulations which contoured the land in a gradual climb up to the higher vantage where they stepped down from the chopper. Down the hill, tribal members were following this path of desecration to ascend through the freshly razed and barren slopes.

The hope was two-fold in choosing this location. First, to appease the ancestors and attempt to show their spirits they were still welcome in this ground, and then to re-establish growth in the recently denuded land. Of the two men killed in the encounter, one, Brandon, had been tending a tree of his own, readying for his end. He was an older man but had still expected to live for another ten to fifteen years, so his chosen tree was still a young sapling alder.

The other, Paul, was a much younger man who, though Jamari had not known him, was of an age with him. Paul, like Shane the year before, was going to get a sapling maple selected from nearby and brought to the internment site.

This was the first time in the tribe's history an interment tree had been lost. Terry selected a small fir, the same species as had been Chief Newell's totem tree, to plant amongst the remaining roots of the dying stump to house the spirit of that valiant ancestor. Neither of the two shamans knew whether the spirits would accept this action, but both agreed something had to be offered, and this was the best course they could think of.

The land undulated as they worked their way through downed and discarded limbs, over logs not yet dragged out. There, they found a gentle incline set into a steep hillside, which allowed a view down a small draw. A once-chuckling brook now hosted a further tangle of bleeding branches.

When they approached the stump of Chief Newell's spirit tree, walking through a forest razed down to a stubble of stumps, both of them felt a spirit essence still abiding in the stump. Though the stump oozed viscous moisture from its scabrous wound, and it was obvious the tree would never recover, the spirit essence still abided.

I think I would want a maple, Jamari thought to himself, *or an oak, either of those being able to grow a new trunk from the remaining roots of a beheading.* Unlike the fir, which would never survive this wound. The oozing sap filled the air with a fresh fragrance of fir, the freshness of an inviting forest in stark contrast to the spectral vision of a land laid to waste around it. The sense of spirit essence was faint and seemed damaged with the loss of its anchor point, but there was hope they could share the newer spirit trees amongst the three souls, two new and one long established.

They were missing their regalia: Terry, his Otter cape and Jamari, his Cougar cape, but they had their leathers from the ride to Curtin, and made do with paraphernalia supplied by the villagers of London. Terry used a carved wooden chalice as a smudging bowl to start the rites. He lighted a taper, which he then used to ignite a bundle of sage. He let the sage burn until a base of char had formed, then he smudged it out in the bowl, leaving the charred section still smoldering and smoking.

"We bless this land," the Knight Shaman began, waving the smoking sage over the ground and overhead in the air, "with this blessing we cleanse this ground, this sacred site, this air we breathe to aid these souls in safe passage into their next journey. With this sage, we banish all negativity. Let smoke from sage attach itself to all negativity and carry it away to another place."

Looking around at the freshly logged site, with the sap still bleeding from the stumps, seeing the crater where the missile had struck the mercenaries who had fired on the Oregon Guard Helicopter, feeling the sense of emptiness in the denuded landscape, Jamari prayed fervently that the sage could carry all this away.

The Knight Shaman dipped his off-hand into a basin of water and continued. "With the negative spirits cast away, we call upon the four elements: Earth as represented by the sage and this chalice; Water as it drips down to the ground; Fire as represented by the flames; and Air as represented by the smoke. Each of these externals we call upon to bring us the fifth and final element: Life energy within." Terry lathed himself in smoke, then starting to the north, turning clockwise to the east, thence to the south and then the west before also carrying the smoke down to ground level, cleansing the soil that would hold the remains before finally lifting the smoking herb up high and wafting the sage smoke away, "carry that which does not belong up to the sky, to disperse into the ether," he finished.

Then Terry smudged out the sage for real, grinding the rest of the bundle into the wood bowl until all hint of smoke was gone. He shared the ash carefully into the three holes where the trees would stand and then lit the sweetgrass.

"With negative forces banned, we use sweetgrass to bless this site," the Knight Shaman continued as Jamari maintained an incessant beat of the small drum. "We bless this ground. We bless this wood. We bless these trees that, if it be so willed by our Great Spirit, the spirits of our departed can have a welcome home here amongst our sacred lands. We bless this air that it might carry you on to God. Unto the will of the Great Spirit, we offer these souls, for whatever you deem their next step in the circle of life."

The Knight Shaman and Jamari both paused for a moment as they sensed the rushing flight of spirits leaving the site. Those last words had been a release and a benediction. The three spirits had departed. Jamari, with a slightly more refined ability to sense, felt three sparks sail away to the south, toward tribal lands and Milltown Hill Village.

Looking at the Knight Shaman, Jamari resisted the quick release of tears as he felt the departure, leaving an already empty and dead glade even more bereft. Jamari resumed the beat on his small drum and The Knight Shaman continued with the ceremony, recognizing this process was now intended to comfort those who remained.

Chief London read the same passages from the Founder as at Shane's interment. Finally, they lowered bodies of the two men into their graves and planted the trees above them. The Londoners, all militia members who had remained behind the evacuation to defend their homes, began their trek back down the hill. Several remained behind to attend the three lone trees.

Terry and Jamari rode the same helicopter back to Salem. After they gathered up their things for the flight back down to Curtin, Terry met with the tribe's ambassador to Oregon.

"You are still ambassador," Terry told him. "As such, I fully expect you to spend every bit of your energy convincing Oregon to grant the lands around London, lands we have stewarded for over 75 years, to the Elk Creek Tribe. This grant must be complete, turning over full sovereignty to the tribe, and must also include adequate compensation for the losses we sustained in this regrettable incident. I will send our troops to commandeer all the equipment used in this assault. You would do well to have ownership of those granted as a tiny first step toward reparation.

"I would strongly encourage you to work on your meditations as well. Your attempt to white-wash the loss of Chief Bryan Newell's sacred place shows it has been far too long since you have renewed your personal relationship with the Great Spirit and your internal God. You have a function here. That function is to further the Elk Creek Tribe's interest, not just to accept dinner and social invitations."

They left a shaken but newly determined ambassador behind as they accepted the Governor's offer of ground transportation to the airport. During the ride, the steward told them the corporation behind the invasion was not Wearehauses but was instead just another mega-corp trying to muscle in on a rapidly diminishing resource. Wearehauses would almost certainly continue their legal battle as soon as it was reasonable to do so, considering recent events.

Chapter Nineteen

Upheaval

When Jamari and Terry returned from their whirlwind trip to Salem, the various chiefs and representatives were gathering. By the end of the week, there was a full Tribal Council underway. Jamari, as a newly appointed citizen, and as a solidly respected shaman, kept in the thick of the proceedings from the beginning.

Chief Elk Creek, while acknowledging the actions of his councilors as having worked out this time, met with the council. Initially, he proclaimed a need to replace all of his advisors. He claimed outright disobedience. "The Knight Shaman, so-called War Chief Jahangir, Chiefs' Scotts Valley, Milltown, Elkhead, and others deferred action when the time for decision was imminent. The Tribe should have responded with more force, with less quibbling. And Chief Elk Creek Tribe should have been the deciding force instead of a council of milquetoast advisors."

The council members were respectful about hearing him out. Then each approached him to wish him well in the next life. Chief Sutherlin was the first to mention the inevitable result of this course openly. "Will you specify an executioner so we will force no one to make that decision without your input?" he asked.

Chief Jacelyn took this one step further. "I think we need to determine if our Chief Elk Creek has lost his soul," she said. "Considering the circumstances we faced, with the understanding of our place in the wider world, the only obvious reaction was exactly what we chose. To have Chief Elk Creek," - she could build an exquisite level of scorn into the title - "insist on war as the first and only recourse does not represent at all what our tribe stands for."

Terry and Jamari exchanged glances at this comment. They had each noticed a diminishment of Chief Elk Creek's soul-spirit over the past year. Nodding in reluctant acknowledgment, Terry stood to speak.

"As shamans," he said, "we have noted some changes in the emanation of spirit-self from Chief Elk Creek. We can subject him to further examination if needed, with more than just casual observances to go by. I am certain, though, we'll find he's losing his spirit-self. The examination will be more than just looking for a soul, though. It will also be an effort to find the cause of such a thing and then see if it can be reversed or not. It will certainly leave him no opportunity to make a final, irrevocable directive in line with the practice established by Chief David James."

As he settled amidst a stunned silence, Peter Shaman stood next. Everyone saw Chief Elkhead sink back in his seat as Peter stood, as if he knew what was about to be said and knew the battle was over before Peter ever spoke a word.

"I've been Chief Elkhead's primary physician for over ten years," Peter told the council. "There will be no need to compel him to an examination." He paused here, looking at the dejected chief at the head of the council table. "Chief Elkhead is suffering from the early stages of Alzheimer's disease. We haven't been able to pinpoint a cause to learn if his is one of the dementia types which we can treat. That will take a trip to Roseburg and the more advanced medical facilities they have."

"I'm still here!" Chief Elk Creek yelled, leaping to his feet. "My spirit still lives in this body! I still have this beating heart!" He thumped his chest in emphasis and pointed to his temple. "I still have my wits! I can take action when needed!"

With the information from the two prominent shamans, the real debate was over. Yet Chief Elk Creek still insisted he was able.

Chief Matthew was the deciding voice in the end. "Will you choose an arrow, a knife, or a gun?" he asked of Chief Elk Creek. "These are the only options you're leaving us."

After all the representatives had spoken, Chief Elk Creek abdicated in favor of Jahangir.

The choice was a surprise, but near-universally accepted. It went against the standard selection process, but he had the broad acceptance of the council.

Then Jahangir stood. "I am honored and pleased at this honor," he said. "I will need some time to reflect before I can decide to accept or not." He paused and looked around the gathering. He gave one last, long glance at Matthew. "Please give me a week to consider."

They gave him three days. Then the next day, about two weeks after the debacle up at London, word came from the Governor of Lincoln. He wanted Jahangir to take command of the entire Lincoln National Guard as a Major General!

Once again, the council convened to hear Jahangir's thoughts on this other option.

"I can't help but believe the Tribe will be far better served with a member as the commanding general of the Lincoln National Guard," Jahangir told them. "This incursion and near-war seem to be only the first of many conflicts, as the broader nation once again brings their roads of death in and through tribal lands. From this position, I'll be in the Governor's council. I'll be able to advise him and others in ways to minimize the dangers inherent in that encroachment." He looked to where Jamari sat amongst the many voting members of the tribal council.

"I visited with Jamari Shaman after his trips up to Salem. He has shared with me some of his observations and thoughts of the spiritual state of that people. There are so many, and they are so far from God, with their soulless preachers building them into a frenzy of war against us, even as we recover from this first invasion.

"I will decline the honor of being chief of the Elk Creek Tribe. But only so that I can serve my tribe in a better way." Jahangir turned and took the few steps to his seat near the head of the table.

A slow mutter arose up and down the length of the long table as various village chiefs and council members shared their thoughts about this new situation. Most approved of Jahangir's decision. It was obvious he would better serve the tribe in the far more powerful position. The mutters rose in volume, each competing to be heard over the rising racket when the Knight Shaman stood and approached the head of the table. There, he stood in silence as each member gradually looked at him for his thoughts, awaiting his comments.

"You have abdicated your role," he said to the previous Chief Elk Creek. "Even if you specified an individual who has a better role to fulfill, you abdicated." He turned then to the council as the previous Chief Elk Creek stood and stalked from the room. Matthew signaled two guard members to accompany the fallen leader and keep him safe.

"We are seldom anything like a democracy," the Knight Shaman said once he had left the room, "except when we face the rare event of needing to select a new tribal chief. We selected the previous Chief Elk Creek long before I came up from my boy's hearth and into the young men's hall. Yet, I have known it as my responsibility to be the one who would preside over the selection process. So, I re-read the stories of our past selections and set in my mind how I would encourage this process to go."

He paused and looked around the room and down the long table of the Elk Creek Tribal Council. "First, I must remind you that any council member is eligible for consideration in this process. No one of us reached our positions absent the skills and abilities to lead this tribe." He again looked around, this time making eye contact with each of the members.

As he reflected, Jamari realized it would be an arduous process indeed. There were chiefs of villages who had long reigned over their fiefdoms and gained valuable skills and experience. There were war leaders among them, as well as a small smattering of shamans. *What is the possibility of a shaman leading?* he wondered to himself, looking at the Knight Shaman in a new light.

He was looking down at his hands folded on the table in front of him when he sensed a quiet anticipation build up in the room around him. When he looked up, he found there were many eyes focused on him, so many that it felt like a physical onslaught of anticipation and expectation. No one said a word as he realized the stunning import of their gazes.

Not a word, he thought to himself in quiet desperation. *Neither to encourage nor turn down, not a word to acknowledge the question in all these stares. How can they even contemplate it?* he wondered.

"I can see the looks," the Knight Shaman said into the silence. "Jamari Shaman has been growing in vast leaps and bounds in his role as shaman and as a man and citizen of the Tribe." He paused here, looking intently into Jamari's eyes. "I must apologize to young Jamari, though, as I say that he is not the best candidate for this position. He is still only a young councilor with only a few months as a full citizen. Yes, he has done some incredible things because of his stronger connection to the Great Spirit. Yes, he has been of such character that there are those who would unquestionably follow his guidance.

"I must remind you, though, never in the history of our tribe, or of any other tribe of the Pacific Northwest we know of, has there been a shaman elevated to the position of chief of Tribe. There may come a time when that legacy will be broken, but not in this case and not at this time."

He paused again as he put his hand onto the back of the empty chair at the head of the table, obviously caressing the innately carved wooden spokes jutting up from either side, letting his hand fall down to press into the soft cushioning of the chair back where a weary head would rest during a long council session. He lifted his hand from the regal chair, having emphasized some necessary points without saying a word about them.

"I propose we stand in recess for the noon meal," he said. "I think we should take counsel of each other over repast. I further propose we form groups as we now sit. Here is how I see these groupings." He stepped to the table by his own chair on the right side of Chief Elk Creek's.

"From the head of the table, down four spaces on each side, we have the first such group. This will be a total of eight. An even number, so we take one additional member from the women's side of the table for nine." He continued as he set up several groups, some with five men and four women, others with five women and four men. He looked around, seeing if there were any further suggestions or modifications.

"If each group offers a single suggestion which the group can support," he continued, "then we will have narrowed the pool."

"Let's break for a bit," he said. "We can talk over our ideas out in the main conference room as lunch is being set out. After lunch, we'll get the nomination from each group, with justification why their selection is the best choice for the position. If there is dissent, then the leading dissenter will state the objections."

Rather than join in the discussion right away, Jamari walked around the circumference of the main floor, what had at one time been the main gaming floor of the casino. Without really thinking about it, he entered past a hanging canvas wall at the far-left end of the vast room and looked at the scaffolding set up around the totem pole he had been working on for over six months. He worked his way through the labyrinth of poles and hangings to stand at the base of his work.

The salmon being formed from one pair of roots were easily identifiable, though still needing fine tuning to make them meet his plan. Up a little farther was an otter, twined around the pole itself, captured mid-slide in a playful slide down a mud bank, Perhaps expecting an easy strike on the salmon below, perhaps also simply hoping to trundle and hump back up the bank after this slipping adventure to have yet another.

Above the otter, a couple of deep slashes with inverted "V's" showed a ridgeline. Jamari craned his head back to look up into the murky dark to see Cougar, head lowered, forepaws digging into the tree beneath Her, hindquarters poised, tail held in a curl behind Her, prepared to strike. Above Cougar, on the bole of the tree, he could see the shadow of the hollows he had dug in to hold wings that would sway in the wind. Above that, out of sight from this angle, he knew was the crowning head of Eagle, looking regally down on His domain.

A scuffle at the outer edge of the scaffolding broke from him from his reverie. Turning, he started back to see who had stepped inside his work space. There had been a long understanding he would only reveal the totem when it was complete. And then only to those selected to transport it up the creek and to its designated platform on the south bank of Elk Creek at first. He wanted the tribe members to first see it as sunrise lit it up in its new home. Stepping out of the entry, he saw Chief Matthew perusing the scaffolding, and he looked up to see what he might be seeing. *Only the curtains*, he thought to himself. "Good afternoon, Matthew," he greeted his onetime teacher and guide, startling him from his perusal.

"Oh, hello, Jamari," Matthew answered quickly. "I was just going to call you in for lunch. I must confess to being very curious about what's going on behind all that mess and fuss."

"Well, it's coming along," Jamari answered amiably, turning as if to head back out of the canvas walling.

"Jamari, I'm sorry that they ruled you out of the running for chief," Matthew said quickly, pulling his attention back from the edge of canvas he had lifted aside.

"Don't be sorry," Jamari answered. "When I saw all those faces looking at me in anticipation, I had a very momentary sense of longing. Thankfully, it was very short, yet it was enough to tell me I seem to have a hankering for power. It leaves me feeling slightly soiled from the response itself." He held his hand up to forestall any further comment as Matthew opened his mouth to speak.

"The Knight Shaman was exactly right in saying I was not ready for the responsibility," Jamari clarified. "I haven't even the foggiest of notions of how to run a village, much less an entire tribe. It would only be a short time before someone recognized all my shortcomings, and then there would be a flood of 'advisors,' each hoping for a piece of the power in return for sage words."

Matthew nodded. "Do you think anyone should be shameful if they lusted after the position?" he wondered aloud.

"I can't speak for what is in another man's heart," Jamari answered. "This whole thing would be so much easier if I could. I know you have worked very hard to learn tribal management. I know you think you should be that next chief. If it is you, I think I would feel sorry for you, even if you think now it's what you might want. I think it's more of a sentence than a reward as I ponder it." He paused before they stepped out into the main spaces.

"Do you know that I've never seen Chief Elk Creek outside of Milltown Hall until he came down to the courthouse in response to our summons? Has he ever left the Milltown area since they selected him for this 'honor'?"

Matthew again pondered Jamari's words. "I can remember how young I thought you were only two years ago," he said, "when I first started showing you around the harvest operations." He paused as he remembered.

"You have matured," he said. "You have grown in ways I could not have imagined back then. Your words now bring me to wonder what I was thinking of wanting the role for myself. I'm sensing why Jahangir asked for a week of contemplation before accepting. I'm thinking if it's offered to me today, I'll ask for a week as well." He paused again before stepping up beside Jamari at the edge of a curtained wall.

"I came seeking you to ask for your support," he said. He lifted the canvas and stepped out into the dim recesses of a darkened corner of a vast room.

"If you are selected, and if none better are presented, you will have my support," Jamari answered as he stepped out as well. "And you will still have my sympathy as well."

They worked their way back around canvas-draped tables and other furnishings to reach the more public areas of the Great Hall in companionable silence.

Jamari joined the group of eight others he would work with. In this group was Lillian, the recently replaced Sophia Shaman; Chief Yellow Creek, a man of advanced years and weathered countenance; and Chief Sutherlin, a relatively youngish man.

As their group conversation developed, Chief Sutherlin had an interesting candidate to propose. Lieutenant Colonel Craig, the same Lieutenant Craig who had been Jahangir's aide in that conflict of eighteen years before. Colonel Craig currently commanded the Southern Division of the tribe's militia.

What a tangled day this is, Jamari thought to himself as he realized he would be the only dissenter in his group to this plan. Not because of any weakness Lieutenant Colonel Craig might have, but because he was the perfect candidate to assume Colonel Jahangir's command of all tribal forces, with a commensurate appointment as a full colonel in the tribal militia. It seemed a surety: with Jahangir in command of the Lincoln National Guard, it would soon be Colonel Craig in the state command structure as well.

If he had taken a moment to think about it, he too would have been as shocked as Matthew. He had become so sure of himself and his decisions of late. This Jamari was no longer the tentative Jamari who had returned from a coastal expedition over a year ago. He was truly Jamari Shaman now.

In the end, there were only four candidates nominated by the seven groups. Matthew, Chief Milltown, had three groups nominate him. Jacelyn, Chief Elkhead, had two. The other two, with one nomination each, were Lieutenant Colonel Craig and Chief Elkton.

Lunch was a very nice roast goat with roasted potatoes and carrots and once complete, it was a simple affair to winnow down to the top two candidates. Terry had everyone in the room write their candidate's name on a ballot and turn them in. The first count made it obvious that Matthew and Jacelyn were the final two candidates.

"I think we should rest on this decision through the night," the Knight Shaman proposed as the afternoon wore on. "We can almost certainly reach a decision shortly after breakfast in the morning. I know there are many here who have not visited the tribal seat up at Milltown Village in quite some time. Once we have our chief, there will be time to stop in for a visit tomorrow before the installation into office the following day." He stopped for a moment, looking at the two finalists, obviously considering saying something and then changing his mind.

I wonder if he's considering forbidding them from campaigning, Jamari wondered to himself. *Should they? It's such a tough choice! I think I'd like to hear what they have to say, but I can understand the reason we don't campaign. That would leave room for lies and deceit to enter the fray, and we could end up with a politician, someone who actually* wants *the position for power instead of one who will take on the duty in service to the Tribe. I wonder if I would even* want *someone in this position if they actually* wanted *the job!*

On the first ballot after breakfast the next day, Matthew became the next Chief Elk Creek. As he stood to acknowledge the honor, he looked at Jamari.

"I was talking about this eventuality with Jamari the other day," he said. "Jamari Shaman told me that if I were selected, I would have his support. And also that I would have his commiseration. I can't think of a thing to add to those comments. I will take on these burdens in the hope I'll have the support of all of you. If I ever look like I could use your commiseration, you can bring that to me as well." He looked at Jacelyn. "We've never had a deputy chief of the Tribe, but if we can build a way to have one, I'd have you in that position to work directly with me as we move our tribe forward into the future."

It was a short yet still very moving acceptance. Certainly nothing like the ceremonial pontificating they would present on the morrow for the whole of the Elk Creek Tribe to witness.

Jamari re-settled once again into his duties at the tribal court, but losing the spirit trees from the London groves still haunted his thoughts. Not all of them had been taken down since the villagers had discovered the invasion during routine patrols, but there was enough loss to serve as a reminder of an outside world, a world Jamari now recognized as much larger and more powerful than the small realm the Tribe had built. That world had set sights on the tribal forestlands. Those same lands the Tribe maintained and held in deepest reverence.

He had remembered enough of his long spirit sojourn over the last year to recognize his visions were indeed calling for him to act. He was being tasked to awaken the Founder's Tree. With the myriad of information, learning, and outright ingenuity he had been a part of over these past two years, he was still searching for his first clue as to just how to carry out such a daunting task.

Chapter Twenty

A Gathering of Governors

Human Quest

Our quest, our Earth walk,
is to look within,
to know who we are,
to see that we are connected
to all things,
that there is no separation,
only in the mind.

~Lakota Seer

With Winter Tide fast approaching, judges completed lingering cases and delayed opening new ones. Jamari and the other assistants cleaned and closed the court areas. The salmon run was an imminent event, with some early arrivals already caught by early anglers.

For many, it was a season of homecoming. Milltown Village welcomed any tribal members in this season when nature was setting in for the long night.

Jamari looked into the room he shared with Zach from the doorway. After much effort, the pair had finally declared it clean enough. With his bag of necessaries on his back, he looked over the neat sanctuary where chaos normally reigned. It was a smallish set of rooms to share with another person and easily mussed and cluttered. Located deep within the courthouse itself, with no windows to look out on the land, he still felt nostalgic as he recalled the times he and Zach had shared here.

Zach had elected to return to Yoncalla for the fall celebration, a puzzle to Jamari, who found nothing even like "home" in that primitive place. But it was where Zach saw home, where he had grown up in his boys' hearth, and where he first had been in a young man's hearth. Perhaps there was someone special there. Jamari hadn't asked, had only offered to have Zach share his rooms in Milltown Hall for the duration.

"I need to celebrate this season with my village," Zach had answered. "I'll be shaman for folks who rarely have one for the celebration." He had hugged Jamari closely. "I've learned a great deal from you," Zach had whispered quietly. "I feel like it's time to share out the spiritual renewal with others who can't make the trek here to Milltown."

Jamari had hugged him back. "I'll look forward to seeing you after the new year, then."

Now Joshua was hovering at his back, ready for the walk in the rain up to those warm and waiting rooms in Milltown Hall. Joshua surprised him as the one who wanted to stick with him so much. It wasn't even a "loverly" matter, though they did share eros regularly. Somehow, the level of devotion Joshua gave him felt more like an acolyte or a squire. Lon was already up at Milltown, where he was filling in an unexpected slot as a monitor in one of the boys' hearths.

"Okay, Joshua," Jamari said, "let's get on the road." He shut the door on one chapter of the year and they turned towards the main exit and the trek up the Elk Creek Valley for the next.

It still bemused him when he thought of the name as a "creek" when it was larger, longer, and with more presence than many "rivers" he had studied in his geography lessons. "There's already an Elk River," he'd been told, "so this is Elk Creek."

They emerged into a gentle fall of rain, tightening their fur-lined leather coats. The "creek" had greened up with the fresh influx of water, but had not yet risen as it would when the rains settled in for good.

The soft rainfall fully soaked both by the time they entered the main front door at Milltown Hall. There they sloshed water from their sodden shoes as best they could before squelching through the maze of halls and stairs to Jamari's permanent set of rooms.

As soon as they entered, and as soon as Joshua shut behind them, Jamari divested himself of the soaked clothing. Joshua hung each item up to drip at the door as it came off, helping when the jerkin, clinging wet, wouldn't come free of its grip on Jamari's shoulders. "Thank you, my friend," Jamari said, acknowledging the help. "Let me help you." He reached over to help Joshua get his jerkin unlaced and off as well.

Both were shivering and naked, yet at least not dripping, before they crossed to the bedroom and shower areas. There, they shared a warming shower. It reminded Jamari of his times with Shane as Joshua ran lathered hands over his body, sluicing off the last chill of the rain-wet day. The pain of those memories persisted. He turned to Joshua and held him in his arms as the warm water continued to bring each of them back to warmth and comfort.

"We should have dressed warmer," Jamari whispered into Joshua's ear. "We're both shrunken up to near nothing."

"Tonight after we're recovered," Joshua promised. "If we had dressed warmer, we would have been too warm for the walk. Maybe we should try to barter with Tahkenitch for some of their sealskin rainwear."

"Good idea," Jamari answered as he gently turned Joshua around to lather up his back.

Afterward, comfortably ensconced in the two-seater couch in the living room, adorned in freshly sewn sets of loungewear, they shared a warm mint tea. The lake water outside the glass was a dark roil, with a bit of wind stirring the rain-pattered surface. They both watched in vain for a salmon to pass by the view pane, talking of the upcoming fall celebrations.

The tribal fall celebrations centered on the salmon's return. Though they closely coincided shortly after the time of Samhain, the timing was coincidental. The tribe still honored those older ways of honoring the ancestors: the turning of the Wheel. Winter Tide was a newish thing, resurrected from ancient times.

This year seemed especially auspicious after Matthew's selection as Chief Elk Creek. Even though they didn't call it Samhain, and even though they didn't focus on the same services and rituals, the tribe carried out their observances under the ancient meaning: harvests are in; days are shortening; the veil between life, and after, is thinnest.

The salmon were the trigger that would kick off the most important of the celebrations. Depending on when the rains raised the river level up so the migration could ascend the last miles of their journey home, and then, holding the last service at dawn of the longest night of the year, the Tribe chose an older name: Winter Tide.

With November came the gathering of honored visitors. The surprise this year was the attendance of two state governors. The governor of Lincoln and the governor of Oregon had arrived in helicopters which had fluttered down to land on the flat rooftop of Milltown Hall.

It surprised Jamari to learn the founders designed the hall for just this purpose all those years ago, and the Tribe had once owned a small helicopter they had landed there regularly. With "the Fall," repair parts and capability had failed, and they had disassembled the bird for the base metals.

These weren't the deadly looking military birds Jamari had flown in earlier in the year. Instead, they were portly ladies, gingerly dancing down onto the rooftop to disgorge their passengers. It was just before noon when they arrived on a blustery, yet cloudless day. A young man apprenticing to Chief Matthew escorted the two dignitaries down to Chief Elk Creek's meeting rooms.

Once the day's festivities concluded, Terry invited Jamari to dinner with the dignitaries. He had only rarely been to Matthew's old rooms in the back reaches and upper floor of Milltown Hall. These new rooms occupied two levels. One level was above the level of lake and dam, with a veranda that looked out over the still waters of the lake. The other was one level down. The lower level had view windows, the same as Jamari enjoyed in his own smaller set of rooms. Chief Elk Creek's suite was much more expansive, though, allowing adequate space for moderately large meetings.

When Jamari came into the room with the Knight Shaman, he found the two governors seated in cushioned leather settees with a generous view over the lake. Sunset was just coloring the horizon and placid waters.

"You're here," Chief Matthew said from his own comfortable chair. "Gentlemen, I'd like you to meet Jamari Shaman and the Tribe's own Knight Shaman, Terry."

As they made the introductions, Jamari saw General Jahangir standing to the back of the room, resplendent in his major general's dress uniform, still sporting his long, graying braid, which was now bereft of his normal tribal decorations. *At least they let him keep the braid,* Jamari thought as he shook the somewhat clammy hand of the governor of Lincoln. He also noted General Tempson standing behind Oregon's governor.

When the two governors realized one so young as Jamari was going to remain through the dinner, Dean, the governor of Oregon, looked him over much more closely. "Have we met?" he asked Jamari. "I feel as if I should know you."

"I was with the Knight Shaman when we worked with you regarding the corporate takeover of our London area," Jamari answered.

He wore courtier's fancy clothing that day, supplied on order from the governor himself. He now wore leathers. Not the old and well-worn militia leathers, but a fresh set of elk leather jerkin and leggings. He always avoided the leather breech, and tonight was no exception. He was wearing a chamois loincloth and luxuriating in the gentle caress of that soft and welcoming fabric.

"Perhaps I was looking too much at how you wore the clothes then," Governor Dean said, running his eyes up and down Jamari's lean frame. Not a sexual glance, but somehow dismissive, as if the leathers made him something less than expected. "I wasn't aware you were also a shaman, though. That would have made some interesting conversation in the governor's mansion." He paused for a moment, looking over at Stephen, Oregon's governor.

"I don't want to seem overly rude, but we were hoping to discuss some weighty matters this evening, and I think you may not have a full grasp of what they might entail."

It was a clear dismissal, and Jamari looked to Matthew for guidance. Matthew simply nodded to Jamari to answer. *They're making me earn this right again,* he thought. *Yet,* he corrected himself, *I obviously already have their trust, and now they're asking me to pull my weight.*

"I am a full adult and citizen of my tribe," Jamari said. "I've completed the Manhood Rites and have earned full citizenship with the right to take part in tribal governance. What more would you require of someone invited to this meeting by Chief Elk Creek himself?"

"I was just thinking that you might be too young to understand the nuances," Dean answered.

"Well," Jamari replied, "I have had some opportunity to consider the act of politics and what they mean." He paused in reflection for a moment, watching the two governors and their two major general attendants, seeing Matthew and the Knight Shaman quietly listening to his words. Terry nodded his approval, bolstering his confidence to go on.

"I'll back up a few years ... actually, a few decades," Jamari continued. "I read of a U.S. election once which was fraught with pushes and pulls and fragile alliances formed and broken. There was talk of a foreign power deliberately influencing that election. What I remember most about it, though, was the description of the eventual winner. They designed his blustery speeches not to convey plans and hopes but to tear them down; they remarked on his garish make-up but ignored the lack of substance. Somehow, he had found a shade of orange, which hid the ugliness of his face and the soul inside.

"The masses he appealed to accepted the putrescence he brought to the election process as sincere. He appealed to the darkest natures of the populace, promising to put up a wall between two nations; promising to eject two distinct elements of the diverse population. He appealed to the darker natures so much that the other side completely discounted his ability to win. It surprised everyone when he won the election.

"When I read about that time, it compelled me to think of a troop of primates. The largest males, with the colors flaring in their bared asses: the brighter colors and the most offensive displays being the qualifiers for leadership of the troop. I don't see too much difference between 'politics' and a troop's battle for leadership. Perhaps one is that the primates will, when provoked, reach back to their ass and drag out a shot of shit to fling out upon their challengers." He paused for a moment.

"Though, that too seems somewhat similar to 'politics.' A superb politician will throw his shit into the mouth of an opponent, and when the opponent talks, the politician's own shit spews forth.

"Not too much difference after all, it seems."

Jamari watched the reactions of the two governors as Chief Elk Creek observed them as well. Matthew quietly sipped from his cup of liquor. Oregon seemed reddened from embarrassment at the near-accusation. Lincoln was near apoplectic with anger at having been called out so adroitly.

Jamari much preferred the embarrassed one. He looked to where Jahangir stood in the back of his own governor and was sorry that he had to serve the man he did.

"I guess I'm at a loss," Oregon's governor said, eventually. "Perhaps I need to know more about what exactly a shaman is and just what one does to get that title."

"Easily answered," Jamari said as Matthew and Terry continued sipping their drinks in silence, obviously working to disguise their humor by paying exquisite attention to those same beverages. "I spent my life seeking the God-within. I found him and have been able to show we converse in some rather unique ways. It's my education you're probably really noting, though. Shamanism has taught me nothing about the mud-sucking details of high-level politics. That has been history."

In the end, the discussion was not so weighty and complicated as suggested. They talked about the invading corporation, about the audacity of a corporate entity having reached out in an act of war. They discussed how to prevent and respond to any future incursions, and they set plans for joint military operations.

After the governors had departed for their rooms for the evening, Terry and Jamari remained with Chief Matthew. "Nicely spoken, Jamari," Matthew said of the points he had made at the beginning of the evening.

Jamari looked closely at his two mentors: Matthew, who had shown him around the valley area in his first weeks as a young man, teaching him the ways of the Tribe; Terry, who had been teaching and leading him as a shaman, who had been sometime lover, sometime disciplinarian, and now friend and fellow tribal citizen.

"Thank you, Chief Elk Creek," he answered solemnly, bringing their full attention to him with the use of the title.

"I think both of you are missing the main point, though," Jamari said to their silence as they looked out over the darkened waters of the lake from Matthew's veranda. "We need a bigger voice in the outer world, and we don't seem to take the steps to build one. I can see our population beginning to grow with the larger influx of younglings each year. I can see the other tribal villages growing and using the land under our control. Why do I not see any of us as representatives in Roseburg? Why are there no senators down at the capitol from our ranks? When we think about the oncoming deluge, as the outer world looks to devour us and our ways, why are we sitting here building more log forts, deploying our militia into defensive positions?"

Terry looked to Matthew for this answer. Even though he had been running a set of informers out into Oregon, monitoring the situation there, he had not yet considered tribal involvement in state government.

Matthew, too, looked a bit nonplussed. Yet he attempted an answer. "We don't have the population count," he breathed. If we insert ourselves into the political arena and fail, we'll never get a second chance. We were thinking of stepping into that field in fifteen to twenty years."

"What do you mean 'population count'?" Jamari asked.

"We've only got about five thousand voters," Matthew answered.

"Are you really not looking at how it works outside our borders?" Jamari countered. "The age of adulthood in Lincoln is sixteen. I'm certain we have far more than only a few thousand members who meet that criteria."

"But they're not all voters," Matthew answered shortly. "We've carefully identified a series of steps needed to show competence and rationality before they can earn that privilege."

"I'm not thinking of tribal voters," Jamari said stoutly. "I'm thinking of playing at their game, with their rules. How many tribal members over the age of sixteen are there?"

"Close to fifteen thousand," Matthew answered quickly. This was a number he was intimately familiar with, having taken on the responsibility of being their leader only recently, holding himself responsible for all of their welfare, all of their needs, keeping an adequate stock of food, medicine, and other necessities available.

"How many do we need to get a few state representatives, or a state senator?" Jamari asked, almost as a rhetorical question. "We already have the power and aren't using it!"

Both the senior-most leaders of the Tribe were silent in contemplation as they looked outside their self-developed paradigm. "It's something worth considering," Terry said to Matthew. "Sure, there are potential drawbacks. We'll need to step out into the world soon if we're to avoid the fate of our ancestors of the seventeen and eighteen hundreds."

"I only have one final thought," Jamari interjected. "How long until Lincoln's governor is up for re-election?"

"Surely, we couldn't aim that high yet!" Matthew exclaimed, for the first time beginning to doubt his new shaman.

"Why not?" Jamari countered.

"There are over a hundred and fifty thousand residents in Lincoln," Matthew answered. "We're not even close to having enough votes to take that position!"

Jamari considered for a moment as he saw the two of them watching him, wondering what he was thinking.

"I really was studying politics in those first few weeks under Rodney," he finally clarified for them. "Before I started training as a shaman, I was training to be chief or sub-chief of Milltown Village." He let this sink in. "I've continued to read some of the material Rodney recommended for me back then. What I am thinking is there's a good forty-five percent who will always vote for one side of an issue. There's another forty-five percent who will always vote for the other side.

"It's like a metronome with balanced forces at play. There are ten percent who actually carry every single election. Bring our fifteen thousand voters in and have every one of them vote the same way, and we'll have the governorship. But it'll be far over fifteen thousand in a couple of years. How many tribal members will be at or over sixteen by then?"

"We won't want to show our hand too early," Matthew said quietly as he contemplated. "State voters! Let's ponder this for a bit," he said, "and bring it up again in the spring."

"If you will," Jamari interjected as he and the Knight Shaman were standing up to head to their own rooms for the night. "I have some other thoughts. If, for example, you were thinking about using our numbers as I've suggested in some early and less important elective positions, it'll just give the opponents a view of what we can do, and they'll mount an offensive to counter our move on the governorship. If we are to do this right, we should be able to get a few talented members into the State House of Representatives and the State Senate at the same election as we take the governorship."

Chief Elk Creek looked intently at the Knight Shaman before looking at Jamari. "You've made some good and surprising points," he said in praise. "We'll definitely include you in the consultations when we get ready for that action. For now, though, we have Winter Tide upon us and then the long winter ahead.

"Let's get through those, and we'll be looking into the best candidates." He paused as Jamari started to speak and then lapsed back into silence. "I can see that triggered something," he said to Jamari. Have you thought already of who our best candidates would be?"

"Not for all the positions," Jamari answered. "The members from most of the outer areas of the Tribe, I just don't know enough to suggest. I have a couple of potentials in mind, though." He looked expectantly at the two tribal leaders.

"Go ahead," Terry urged him.

"Jahangir for governor," Jamari answered. "His actions with the outsiders at Hancock Valley, along with his most recent actions at the invasion of London, have put him in high regard and respect.

"Christian for the district of Elkton and Scottsburg. Maybe Andrew for Sutherlin and Oakland areas." It had been a while since Andrew's name had come up, and Matthew was obviously seeking to place him in his mind.

"Andrew was one boy rescued after the failed Calapooya Creek raid," Jamari said. "The tribe subsequently placed him to be raised by the members of Camp Calapooya. He was in the young men's hall with me."

Jamari saw Matthew's face light up with recognition. "He may form connections with the remnants of the outsiders still hanging on in the hills between Sutherlin and the Umpqua," he said in conclusion.

Matthew bid both of them a good evening as they descended from his upper-level rooms down and then out into the familiar hallways to walk the short distance to their own rooms for the night.

At dinner the next evening, Terry asked Jamari to join him in his rooms afterward to plan the upcoming festivities. Jamari looked over at Joshua with a question that Terry immediately answered. "There's no secret your good friend can't hear," he said. "Joshua can share the discussion with us."

In the Knight Shaman's rooms, Terry asked Jamari if he would take on a larger role in the festivities once the outsiders had gone and the Tribe could continue their observances without oversight. "I think it's time for you to conduct more of the ceremonies and sacraments. I'll keep most of the months' worth of ceremonials, but I'd like for you to build and conduct the first night's mass and invocation of the ancestors as well as to host the breakfast of the sun when mid-winter night passes. We've got a week yet before it all starts, so you and I can talk about what you'd like to do with your first service."

"I'm honored, Knight Shaman," Jamari answered gravely, thinking about just how young he really was for these many responsibilities he had been taking on. "It will mean more to me this year, with everything I've been learning than it ever has before. I hope I'll be able to carry this task out well, protecting and building the spirit of my people."

"Well, we can certainly work together to get the best plan in place," Terry answered. "I've been watching you grow over these last months. I think you're ready to *perform* as shaman now, in more than just name."

Chapter Twenty-One

Winter Tide

The salmon returned in stunning numbers in the third week of November, as if Gaia Herself was celebrating recent events. The governors and other out-landers had been gone for a couple weeks when the salmon return triggered the start of Winter Tide. Winter Tide arrived six months before the Spring Celebrations in May, which many of their ancestors had thought of as Beltane. The two seasonal events were the Yin and the Yang of tribal spiritual renewal. The first night of the Winter Tide also marked another looming date: Jamari was supposed to be done with the totem pole in less than six months.

Early afternoon prior to the first night's celebration, Jamari took a reflective walk through the grove of trees, mostly oak, which marked so many of the ancestors' graves. In the day's stillness, with just Joshua along, he felt the faint presence of those lingering ancestors at a level of nearness he hadn't experienced in this grove before.

He reflected to the one shared day last spring when Lon had informed him the three of them were becoming one. Joshua's supporting presence keyed the memory in this reflective time. He reached for those ancestral presences in thought, honoring them as was custom in this time of year when lore had the veils of life and after-life thinner and less substantial than at any other time. Even though he felt their acknowledgment, he also sensed a reluctance to share. He knelt in honor of them and the tribe they had built up. Then he turned down the hill to get ready for the evening's event.

In the Great Hall, deep within Milltown Hall, Jamari walked through the setting he had arranged. He looked at the altar where they would honor the ancestors, with its wreath and holly encompassing a small sprig of mistletoe. Jamari admired pottery pieces made from clay taken from the banks of Walker Creek, just up the valley from Lane Creek Village. He nudged a tray meant to hold the choicest bits of food into a better position beside a bowl for samples of the soup and a cup for wine.

They would use the enormous fireplace at his request. He had helped cart several loads of sawn wood into the interior of the hall in preparation. It had been many years since they had used the sacred fires in the Great Hall, but the rains didn't appear ready to let go their hold on the land for the night, and Jamari wanted to use the hall in the old way for the opening of the Winter Tide Observance. No one actually used their own fires in their homes in Milltown Village with the ready availability of heating and air conditioning. He wondered if the fires might be one draw that had called Zach to Yoncalla. There they still celebrated with an annual bonfire which was then used to kindle the hearth fires of the Men's and Women's Halls.

He looked at the arrangement of the tables. Not in the long line that was so often used for tribal citizen gatherings, but in a series of lines, as if the rays of the sun were radiating out from a central focus on the fireplace. He stood at the altar, just between it and the fireplace, and looked out along the radial arms of the sunburst arrangement. He had covered the tables in linen, not pure white, but that pale yellow of homespun hemp.

This was where he would center himself as he led his first set of rites. Not on the raised stage, which he would face as he opened the season. He adorned each table with center pieces of antlers cast off from local Black-tail Deer. Each centerpiece held a short and squat candle, awaiting a light to bring a comforting glow to the red and green table napkins set beside each pottered plate and bowl.

With everything ready, he made his way back to his rooms to dress for the occasion. His chosen outfit was simple yet gaudy at the same time. He wore a set of fringed buckskin leggings, unadorned. A belt held his clout up. Not an ordinary belt, but one made from a long cloth folded over lengthwise and sewn and then folded lengthwise and sewn again, then decorated with beads. These, he had taken garnered in trade from the coastal tribes and sewn them onto the belt in diamond patterns of various pearlescent hues. He decorated the front center like an enormous eye, a rounded diamond shape made of pearl surrounding a bright-brown iris and an obsidian-black pupil.

With no shirt, the belt became the sole focus of his lower body. On his upper body, he wore his Cougar cape with the two forepaws crossed over his chest and tied. He noted his own vanity when he saw that his once-rippled abdominal muscles from his days paddling canoes might have faded, but Joshua let him know the overall effect was of an attractive young man in his prime.

He was last to arrive for the dinner where the attendees were milling around at the foot of the stage, put off by the radial table arrangement with the altar and fireplace as the focal point. His entrance, walking rapidly around the outer edge of the room, with the loose back limbs and tail of the Cougar cape fluttering behind him, flung out at each turn. Cougar's head became the helm crowning his own head. He drew their attention almost immediately, and they followed his progress in gathering silence until they all looked along the rays of tables to where he stood at the focal point.

"Please, take a seat," he told them from his position at the front. "We won't assign seating. Just find a place near a loved one. Or simply a place where you will feel most comfortable."

Some looked around with curiosity, wondering where the Knight Shaman was, why he wasn't officiating this all-important opening session. Chief Matthew took the lead in finding a place to sit and gestured to others to sit as well. He wore the regalia of his new position, with so many beads threaded onto every available surface of his bleached-white elk-skin leathers it seemed as if he would falter under their weight, if not the weight of his recent promotion.

Others settled as Chief Matthew found a seat mid-way back at the center-most long table. Matthew fluttered his hands to shoo them away when other members attempted to settle around him under their rank in the tribe, thus dispersing them more evenly throughout the room. Gradually, everyone seated.

"Good evening, my friends and family," Jamari greeted. "I can see the curiosity. The Knight Shaman is administering these rites at Lane Creek, where the previous Chief Elk Creek has gone for retirement." He let the resultant muttering die down before proceeding. "Peter Shaman is serving the rites at Curtin, where a majority of the residents of London and others from throughout the Tribe are building the defenses and presence of Curtin beyond what it has ever been. They've already finished the first of two new long-houses and started on a Great Hall." He paused again to let the surprised exclamations quiet.

"We've decided," he said, looking to Chief Elk Creek, Matthew, "our northern border areas will need some attention in the coming years. We don't know how long before the masses up there will be spurred into action, but we know the churches are working on stirring them up.

"Oregon, like every other state in the union, still practices freedom of religion, so, even though the current governor, who is up for re-election next year, adamantly opposes the actions taken by the mega-corp last month, it looks like there will be further aggression by the corporate and Christian coalition." He had to pause again, even longer, before the agitated crowd settled once more.

"Zach Shaman is carrying out the Winter Tide ceremony in Yoncalla. The Sophia Shaman is in Oakland, and Paul Shaman is performing the rites down in Elkton. I hope that answers your questions. Now, let us proceed with the real reason we're gathered here tonight.

"I want to welcome all of you. Winter Tide is a special time for us. We take an entire month out of the year to observe and honor these celebrations. The Knight Shaman will be back tomorrow to carry out most of the Milltown Village services. For tonight, and the mid-winter sunrise service, you have me."

Jamari paused again as he looked around the hall, finally spying Rodney at the far back end on his left and Lillian near the center length of the second-right-most table. "Rodney, First of the Knight Shamans," Jamari spoke out, "will you come and assist me to open these ceremonies? And Lillian, Second of the Sophia Shamans, will you come forward as well?" Though seemingly random, Jamari had worked with both Rodney and Lillian to prepare this all-important first step in Winter Tide.

"Each of these has held the role of chief spiritual counselor to the tribe. Each has given the role up to another. Yet no one will never surpass them in knowledge or value to this tribe. Neither will they ever have their wisdom set aside or disregarded. In honor of their service, we let them open this ceremony. They will be the first to awaken the Winter Tide Fire."

Rodney and Lillian stepped to the stone-topped altar. Rodney brought out a flint, and Lillian a steel. Lillian held the rasp at the right angle as Rodney slid his flint down its length, setting off a chain of sparks, which they captured in a bed of tinder in a bowl of carved granite. The first onslaught failed to ignite, and Rodney ran the flint down the rasp again and yet again before Lillian leaned over to puff her aged cheeks to bring a gentle push of air onto the smoldering tinder.

A puff of smoke rewarded their efforts, and a small tongue of flame licked along the edges of the fuel. Rodney took up one of the fat candles from the stone altar and held it to this small flame until it, too, took up the light. Lillian picked up yet another of the candles from the altar and lit it from the tinder as well. When both held burning candles, they turned to the fireplace and the waiting kindling there. They knelt on either side of the pit and placed their candle flames against the dried wood and let it catch. In a remarkably quick time, the kindling had flames licking up it and into the larger staves.

As the hearth fire continued to grow, Rodney and Lillian turned to Jamari, who held forth the largest candle from the altar. The three wicks joined and made a brighter light against the crackling and popping of the resinous wood in the fireplace. Each taking one candle, Rodney went to the table farthest to the left, Lillian to the farthest right and Jamari to the center. The smell of fir pitch and the spicy apple fragrance of the candles followed each as they lit the first of the line of candles down the tables and then each table candle was used to light the next rearward until all the tables were alight with the softly flickering light of natural flame.

As Rodney and Lillian returned to the central focus, the three shamans took their candles to the altar. They set the lighted talismans around the two cast off antlers twined together as the feature for the table and then stepped back and knelt, facing the altar.

Jamari held himself on one knee at the altar itself, his head just above the height of the granite top. "We honor our ancestors at this moment," he said. "You who have prepared the way for us to grow and learn, closer to the Great Spirit, closer to our God, closer to you in this season, when the veil between life and death grows thin. We honor you, who have made our way of life possible, who have set the way forward for a proud and mighty people. Thank you, Grandfathers and Grandmothers, for showing the way."

He stood and turned, and during the turn, three-fourths of the main lights shut down, leaving the room awash in the flickering light of the ceremonial fire along with the scatter of candles. Each face along the table was glowing a dim yellow-orange in candle light.

"Your dinner is waiting on the table along the front of the dais," Jamari told them. "There are five different settings, each of which holds all the courses of the meal." He motioned to Joshua, who brought forth a platter of salmon. Jamari took the salmon and placed a generous portion onto the trencher on the ancestor's table before taking a healthy portion onto his own plate. Next, he motioned again, and David brought forth a tureen of goat soup in a rich and dark gravy base. This, too, he ladled out for the ancestors before placing his own serving on the table nearest to the altar. They proceeded through a rack of lamb, a platter of roasted vegetables; a bowl of mashed potatoes; and a peach compote for dessert. Once the ancestors were served, Jamari bade the attendees serve themselves and enjoy their dinner.

As the members were routing through the serving line, Jamari made as if to settle into his chair when he noticed a bobcat lumbering through the room and up toward the ancestor's table. Bobcats were a normal part of life in the labyrinth of Milltown Hall. They were the predators brought in to keep the mouse and rat population down. They fed them in regular places around the many hallways.

Other than in the youngling's crèche, though, they only rarely allowed themselves to be seen, and almost never volunteered a presence amongst the human residents. Joshua made as if to intercept this interloper, drawing a snarling response and raised hackles.

Jamari reached out with his familiar mental reassurance to the bobcat and found a greater presence instead. He motioned for Joshua to desist.

"We welcome the Great Spirit in the form of Bobcat to this celebration," Jamari said. He reached to his plate and picked up a generous portion of baked salmon, which he placed under the ancestor's table next to the fireplace to settle Bobcat into his meal. When he turned back towards his own plate again, he found himself the focus of a suddenly hushed room with many eyes darting back and forth between Bobcat and himself. *Will this be yet another tale to be told amongst the tribe,* he wondered to himself?

As the dinner was winding down, Jamari stood again, waiting for the general chatter to subside. "It was many centuries ago this celebration was first carried out," he told the crowd. "The yule fire was then a voice of resistance to the onslaught of the coldest time of year, the shortest days and the longest nights. It was a voice of defiance to the knowledge that many would pass into the next life during this season. There were many reasons for the season of dying, most of which we have cured in our modern society. I will mention only one of those reasons tonight, because it is an important lesson in life, liberty, and human spirituality gone astray.

"When the Christians began their march over the settled lands of the world, they carried with them some self-destructive beliefs and practices. One, which they enforced with the strictest of penances, was if a person were to see him or herself naked, then they had violated the law of God and had put themselves in a position of lust.

"This belief led to a hundreds-year-long practice of not bathing, except once a year, and then never allowing yourself to be nude while doing so. As we know in our current world, one in which we honor both spiritual and physical knowledge, lack of cleanliness leads directly to the spread of disease and contagion. I say this to you not so you will condemn Christians, which many of us are, but so you will understand the need for reason, as well as logical thought and process, in the lives of man. Even with the advent of science and reason, we still maintain this first night of Winter Tide as an opportunity to honor and remember our ancestors and those more recently passed. This is a genuine thing in the spirit world."

He paused for a moment of pained reflection before continuing. "Of all the many who are in that next existence, I feel the need to share about two in particular. Many of you knew Shane, my Night Studies mentor and the lieutenant in charge of training at the Young Men's Hall at Milltown Village. He who was taken into the next life long before his time."

He paused again to reflect on his relationship with Shane and the pain he had suffered at his passing. "What many of you don't know is Shane and I had declared our love for each other just before he was taken. We had decided we would become a bonded couple. When I held him in my arms that last night, we only thought of our future and all it had in store for the entity we intended to be 'us.'

"I want to remember him tonight. Not just for my love, but also for his sacrifice, which saved the life of Christian, our current ambassador to the Tahkenitch Tribe. And it was his sacrifice which kept the loss of life so minimal from that quick altercation. It was his skill and dedication, which trained many of the squads who responded. And of more recent note, his training of many of the militia members made our response in London a success.

"Someday, he will be thought of as an ancestor, when the children he left behind have grown and made children of their own, but for this time, I think of him as a lost friend and companion." Jamari reflected, wondering if he should add more before deciding he had said enough of Shane.

"Next, I want to talk about someone recently passed who we did not mourn, who is not likely to be remembered in tales our descendants carry down through the ages. I want to remember Lynn." He paused, as there were several near-shouts of protest amongst the diners, and he watched faces go red and near-purple in anger, with pursed lips and narrowed eyes. He held his pause with stoicism and patience.

Finally, Chief Elk Creek stood and faced down the dissenters. "You, all of you, know who this is," Matthew near bellowed. His face, in the light of the candles, was darkened fury itself. "All of you understand that any of the awakened has the full right to lead us in service, to share their thoughts and memories for the betterment of all. Who here will deny that right to Jamari Shaman, God Walker?"

"Thank you, Chief Elk Creek," Jamari said as the upset died down. He carefully ran his gaze over all the seated crowd. He noted some who still glared at him in anger, some who showed curiosity, some who wouldn't meet his gaze but lowered their heads to avoid contact with him. When his gaze had traveled from left to right across the entire room, he continued. "Oh yes, you all know Lynn committed an offense against a lad. You know he violated other customs and rules at earlier times in his life. You all know we declared him to be soulless.

"I want to share with you something I learned after his end. You all know Cougar is my totem. You all know I faced down a cougar attack in my third month in the young men's hall. What you may not know, at least the full details of, is Cougar, as the Avatar of the Great Spirit, God, has shared some of my travels and spiritual explorations out in the wild woods." He waited for a quiet susurration of murmuring to die down before continuing. "Cougar Avatar visited me once when I was alone in meditation. She sat guarding me while I learned something new and exciting about the world around me.

"Of course, when I awoke, and She was gone, leaving only a place where the grasses had been bent and bowed to cushion Her rest; when I saw the clear imprint of Her paws on the bare earth, I was frightened near to piddling." There were a few reluctant chuckles at this description and admission, which he waited out again before continuing.

"After that, the Knight Shaman decided I needed keepers to guard me during my meditations. I got to meet Lon," - he sought Joshua within the room and found him sitting at the table to the far right - "and Joshua.

"For the first few forays out into the woods with them, there was no spiritual peace. There was no internal awakening of the inner self which recognized the good God. And then there was a breakthrough. One morning, as I was settling into meditation, I felt a presence enter the glade we were in.

"I opened my eyes to see Cougar slowly approaching me, and I also saw Joshua, bow drawn, ready to slay Her. I called Joshua off, and his arrow went astray. That time, Cougar approached me and scented my hand and ran Her tongue over it before turning and bounding away. I'm sure Joshua will share his memories of the encounter with any of you who want to know more. Lon has taken on a role in Thomas's hearth, but he would also be glad to share memories of the encounter.

"Months later, after Lynn had met his end, I encountered Cougar yet again. This time, my companion was the Sophia Shaman." He sought the previous Sophia Shaman from the crowd and shared a glance with her. He knew his friend Sophie had shared this encounter with her predecessor. "Tonight, Lillian Shaman is with us. The Sophia Shaman has talked with her about the encounter. I'm sure she'll share any details relevant and necessary with you if you but ask." He paused here, realizing he might have been telling this story out of sequence and wondering how to remedy the error before going on.

"I need to backtrack a bit here," he said. "I was the representative shaman-judge with the patrol, which was Lynn's last journey. When he met his end, we covered him in large rocks and boulders to protect him from the ravages of the beasts. We found that to have been a vain effort, though. When our patrol came back through the same area, homeward bound, we found a cougar had rolled the boulders aside and brought out his carcass and, with other lesser animals, consumed him.

"Some of you will remember the night they inducted me into my role as shaman. I still bore the bandages over the wounds the cougar had inflicted on me as I walked up onto the stage there," he pointed to the stage and dais, shadowed and empty behind the dining area. "They inducted me into my service. I had recently dined on the flesh of the cougar. I had, in fact, shared out her heart with my hearth mates the evening of the attack.

"When the Knight Shaman inducted me into my role, he said something very important. 'Blessed is the lion which becomes man when consumed by man. Cursed is the man who is eaten by the lion and becomes a beast.' Verse seven of the Gnostic Gospel of Thomas.

"On the later encounter with Cougar, Avatar of the Great Spirit, I felt Her give up the spirit and soul of Lynn into the keeping of the ancestor's oaken glade, which looks down on Scotts Valley from the north. I felt his essence accepted into the glade."

Here, Bobcat, who had been slumbering under the ancestor's table, leaped up onto the table in front of Jamari, just beside the remnants of his meal. He scanned the room in mimicry of Jamari's earlier scan before leaping at Jamari, who caught Him in his arms. Bobcat nuzzled Jamari cheek to cheek before then turning and jumping down to saunter under the legs of the seated crowd and to the door, which was open to the halls. Jamari followed this progress quietly, smiling when some diners shifted themselves uncomfortably as Bobcat rubbed their legs in passing. He returned his gaze to the room when Bobcat disappeared into the labyrinth.

"I tell you this because of the truth of the matter. I do not have a feeling for what it means. I don't have any conclusions to draw, other than just this one: as Tribe, we declared a man to be soulless, and it turns out he actually had a soul. There is a lesson here. One we need to seek an understanding of.

"Now, I have told of two recently departed. This night is meant to share and remember those of significance in our past. Please, those of you who have stories to share of our ancestors and our recently lost, share with us on this evening of remembrance."

Through the evening, many tribe members shared stories of tribal ancestors, some who were not spoken of as often yet still had a great impact on the Tribe and its culture. Rodney, in particular, spoke of The Founder. As one of the few who knew him personally, he shared some tales of his lesser exploits and how even those more human moments made him more real and valued.

As the evening finally faded, the many awakened left the opening of Winter Tide, suitably impressed with their new shaman.

Later in the month-long celebration, Jamari was once again witness to the turnover of the year's class of young boys being brought down to Milltown Hall for the start of their life in the Elk Creek Tribe. He was but one of many out in the hall and could just make out a very broad range of boys in the twenty-five youngsters who were delivered into the hands of their new hearth master, Adam. He reflected on the number of boys as they settled them onto the stage; and on the fathers stepping in to greet them. When he came down the lake to Milltown Hall, he reflected, his own group of boys had been around twelve youngsters.

Over the last few years, the number had been growing with each presentation. It seemed the tribe was undergoing a population growth. Maybe some of the little valleys he had seen on his trip to the coast and back could become homes to some new villages in the next few years. Maybe they could begin to fill and utilize the broader lands they held hegemony over. Was there a second of the regal boats that brought the boys down the lake? If the classes grew any more, they certainly wouldn't all fit into the one vessel.

The Fall Plays dealt with the older-younger dichotomy presentation again. In the major play, a younger character was enticed into sexual congress with an older one. The older one started out visibly aged and decrepit. For the first scene, the younger character simply held and showed love and caring for the elder one. In the second scene, the older one seemed younger and more vital. In this scene, the two share eros in a limited fashion. In the third scene, the older is once again even younger and this time far more virile. He engaged in the dominant role of eros with the younger character, both fully enjoying each other's companionship. At the end of this scene, it was obvious the older character was now barely older than the younger. The relationship had restored him to his younger self.

After the play, Jamari had another recurrence of his repetitive dream in which the Stag-Man led him via visions to a specific place where the stag then faded into the soil. It was the same path each time, but there were no words spoken, so no explanation could be determined. After the third year of the Stag-Man visions, Jamari's dream had become so clear and specific about turns in the trail and the layout of canyons and ridges that he felt as if he could follow the path in real life and find the Founder's Glade. The only thing left to wonder was whether the monument would actually be there and whether he should offer his essence if he traveled to it. It seemed as if it would only take a couple of hours to walk it from the casino/courthouse.

In his dream, he was sprouting a small set of antlers and was the younger member of the play's cast. He had reveled in the sensation of antlers sprouting, fresh with new blood, from his brow. He had experienced the rush of rutting desire, but here, his dream separated from the plot of the play. The older character in the play became a Spirit Guide who led him on the path up into the woods.

He recognized the first part of the path as the road between the Courthouse and Milltown Village. Then the Spirit Guide led him south, off of the main path and up a series of ridges along a very dim trail until he found himself in the Founder's Glade. He'd never been here before in waking times, but in the vision, he recognized this copse of trees. The Spirit Guide faded away, and he faced the elder man of his prior dreams.

That personage was lying on a bier, wrapped in a canvas blanket, almost as if ready for the grave. As Jamari approached, still excited from the dream sequence where he had grown his tiny set of antlers, he could see movement under the shrouds. Jamari lowered his antlered head in challenge, and the man on the bier raised his own suddenly antlered helm.

These were the antlers of a stag in his prime, multi-pronged, broad, and tall. Somehow, this looming presence no longer seemed too old, but powerful, as he rolled to his feet. Jamari then bowed his tiny forked antlers in submission, and the stag man came to him and raised him up.

Then Jamari felt himself turned away from the stag and felt the first touch of the stag's embrace. First, it was sexual, and then it was not sexual. The sudden comprehension of "not" battled with earlier dreams, and this became more like it felt on the few times he had fully surrendered to the Spirit on his dream-walking sojourns.

That elder entity was in and of him.

As he filled him, Jamari suddenly recognized something important about all of his previous iterations of this same dream. The Spirit-Father had never meant the Vision as sexual. It was about a complete surrender to a greater power. It was about allowing his God to enter him without reserve, without shame, without remorse or fear. And his body, having no other way to express that exultation, had always responded sexually.

The Stag Man behind him released his hold and turned Jamari around to embrace him. There, Jamari found not the Stag Man, but the Founder, fully dressed in cloth pants and a button-up checkered

red and black shirt. He put his arms around the hero of his life. The presence overwhelmed him, and brought him to tears, somehow feeling not worthy of this honor. The Founder raised Jamari's head up and kissed him on the forehead, clasping him in his arms. As he concluded the kiss, the Founder reached his hand up and smoothed away Jamari's rack of antlers from his head.

The Founder slid a finger under Jamari's eye and picked up a tear. "This isn't necessary," he said. "You are, in and of yourself, worthy of me.

"I send you with a message now to the Tribe. There is a five-year-old child in the boy's crèche" - he looked deeply into Jamari's eyes, penetrating into his soul - "another son of my loins. This one, though, is being considered as soulless. He has been slow to learn, vicious to his playmates.

"There are also a couple of men there who are ready to dedicate themselves as partners. You know who they are. You will guide them to my Glade, where they will make their declaration. And bring that child with you. Your ability to guide them here will be your proof this message is real. Let the child explore the grounds as the lover-pair make the love offering on the monument which stands there. Then take the child back to the village and put him into the younglings' hall. He'll need more attention from the monitors, but he will have a soul and a future in the Tribe."

At the close of the Fall Celebrations, Jamari officiated the Winter Solstice, the acknowledgment that the longest night was past and that the spring would soon pry the land from the grip of winter's hand. At the dawn after the longest night, Jamari led the awakened of Milltown up to the highest gathering room in Milltown Hall. There, he had the doors to the east opened to the starry dawn sky, and they all watched the day struggle into being. Against all hope, there was a break in the clouds at the crucial moment, and the piercing rays of the rising sun streamed into the room.

Chapter Twenty-Two

Vision Quest

About four months after the Winter Tide, two months before the Spring Celebrations, the vision/dream came again. This time, the details remained clearly emblazoned in his mind, and he recognized it as a summons. He was being called to do something, and the time for that action was soon. "Remember this command, Jamari. Take this message and bring my child to me here in my glade."

Jamari awoke with the memory of the encounter imprinted into his mind, his night juices drying on his thighs, in his bed in the courthouse room he shared with Zach. He saw a slight reflective light glimmering in reflection from Zach's eyes. He was not asleep, but was watching Jamari.

"You were dreaming. I sense your dream was significant. Can you tell me about it?" he asked.

"I probably should," Jamari answered. "Even if I know you won't believe a word of it, I need to tell it now in order to cement it into my memory." He told Zach the complete story of the dreams after each year's fall plays, of this night's dream and what it felt like to sprout antlers, and, finally, of the culmination and the Founder's message.

"Do you think you should go there first, along the path you dreamed of?" Zach asked. "At least do that much to verify the truth of this dream?"

"No," Jamari answered. "I already know the truth of this dream. It is too clear in my mind. It repeats far too many times with more detail each time. I could go to the glade in the dark if need be. I've dreamed it for three years now. There is more clarity than before. The

Spirit Guide's words ring in my memory with the timbre of an alarm bell. How much longer to the dawn, do you think? This night seems far too long and yet far too short for all that has filled it."

"It's actually almost here now," Zach answered. "I was awake when you convulsed. I had hoped for a morning's loving before we were called to our duties, but you no need, I think."

"No, Zach. This vision may have tapped something of release from me, but I still have a great need for you this morning. Will you be with me?"

"Yes," Zach answered. He reached out a hand to caress Jamari's cheek.

While loving with Zach was always special, loving with anyone after the full sharing of that dream was a disappointment. Jamari satisfied Zach, but failed to find further release himself.

Later in the morning, during his discussion with Terry, Jamari told him about the recurring dreams.

"That's amazing, Jamari. The idea the Founder would visit you in a dream isn't too far off from what we believe about our inner spirit. We've long thought it should be possible, even likely for a strong inner spirit to return. Our shamans have always thought of the most likely avenue as reincarnation, though the best of them often rely on 'visions,' which they attribute as coming from 'the Other World.'

"I'm especially amazed at the detail about the young boy in crèche and the couple who are ready to make their commitment. You know about our Rule of Attachment. I know you do, since it has come up several times during your upbringing. Not as often as with some other youngsters, so don't be worried about it." Terry paused in bemusement, lifting his eyes to the ceiling above as he pondered.

"I will give you some more information now, though," he continued, his sharp gaze spearing Jamari to the core. "It is natural for some humans to bond solely with one other. We have, from the dawn of the tribe, known that truism. We also know the young are very emotional when encountering sexual expression and often mistake sexual attraction for love - love as the old-world romantic term which meant 'bonding.'" Terry paused again to gather his thoughts.

"There are natural processes inside the human body triggered by hormones, pheromones, and other chemical responses that are genetically programmed to encourage the continuance of the species. The intensity of these responses is often mistaken for 'love.' There is a purpose to this reaction in the development of humanity. When a male 'loved' the female mother of his children, he was much more likely to take part in the upbringing of those children. This most often produced the best outcome for the children, thus for the continuance of mankind.

"When we recognized the need for the complete alteration of how we built our culture, down to the most basic level, we built in a different propagation strategy." Terry paused again, reaching for his cup of tea, grimacing in distaste as he found it cooled and tepid. He placed it back on his desk. "We use the complete community to raise *all* our children instead of relying on individual sets of parents to do it on their own. What we end up with is a more cohesive community, truly built on common ground.

"If you think about it, there are many times you simply assume things to be true of your fellow tribe members and, more often than not, they *are* true. A specific example for you was your reaction to the judges' test three years ago on your Manhood Day. You *knew* no tribal member would ever force another to submit to their will. We taught all of you that truism. You *knew* what he was offering was *not* the route to manhood. You acted accordingly in how you responded to his offer.

"Well, in the society we've built, and in our recognition of the natural process of bonding, we have a process where two adults can declare their bonding. This doesn't mean they're entering a monogamous sexual relationship.

"I know you haven't encountered monogamy before. We don't have it in our lexicon anymore. A monogamous sexual relationship was one in which both partners agreed to have sexual relationships only between the two of them and to exclude all others from the sexual aspect of their lives. I know it seems insane, but it was the normal relationship for hundreds of years, and most of the rest of the U.S. still practices that method of bonding. It almost always ends up with one spouse cheating on the other. 'Cheating' was what it was called when a pair-bond member sought sexual interaction outside the designated 'couple' arrangement."

"We both know who the pair in this case is," Jamari interjected. "Elan and Haloki have long held their pairing to be permanent. They've often said, to me, and to any other who will hear them, they will always wait, one for the other, any time they part ways. Their attachment is real. And strong. Far more real and right than any other thing I can imagine."

"Yes," Terry answered, "we know who that pair is. I am forced to consider your subconscious may be putting details into a dream. If true, it would make this a dream and not a vision, as you seem to imply. My role, for now, is to help to determine whether you have been experiencing a repetitive and compelling dream or whether the spirits have given you a vision.

"You could think of my role as something the old Catholic Church used to employ in helping them to determine sainthood. The actual appointment, made in every one of their investigations, was 'the Devil's Advocate.' Along with the Devil's Advocate, there was his opposite, God's Advocate. The church sent these two out to investigate when rumor tried to build a saint." Terry stood and stepped over to the carafe of hot water, tossing the dregs of his lukewarm tea into the sink.

"No thanks," Jamari replied to a motioned question whether he'd like a fresh cup as well.

Terry mixed his cup before returning to his seat.

"Many times over the centuries various people have had strong and repetitive dreams which they convinced themselves were visions. When they acted as if those 'visions' were messages from God or some spirit or other, they caused great harm. Sometimes only to themselves and their reputations; other times, they brought death and mayhem all around them and even out to include the wide world in the two world wars. I'm not trying to question your integrity. I'm not trying to say or pronounce any conclusion just yet. What I am doing is trying to make some headway in determining just what this dream may represent."

He paused again. "Will you continue to be open and fully honest with me, even if you think I'm doubting the validity of your vision? It is a part of what I must do every time I encounter a dream or vision of this nature. It is even what you will be required to carry out in your future, as Jamari Shaman."

Jamari considered his words and the way he had felt when it seemed as if the Knight Shaman were doubting not just the vision, but Jamari himself.

"I will endure it," he answered. "And then I will take you to the Founder's Glade, even though I've never been there before. The Spirit Guide was very careful in showing me how to get there in every repetition of this recurring dream."

"I will be as gentle as I can as I keep questioning you, Jamari. Please don't hold it against me."

"I will try to view it as a process and not a personal affront," Jamari answered honestly. "If I can't maintain the separation, I'll tell you, and maybe we can take a break."

"I'll accept that," Terry replied. "Now, about the child in the crèche, I have heard nothing about a youngster doing anything so bad as to be in danger of being declared 'without a soul.' I really don't follow the activities in the nurseries so much."

Here, he looked at Jamari intently. "I know what you told the awakened about Lynn on the opening night of Winter Tide. I know what you experienced has resulted in a deep moral questioning. You need to recognize that the ability to question the strongest of beliefs is truly the power of the awakened. We are not meant to exist on 'belief' as a religion. Your experience with Cougar has opened a line of thought which many of us are pursuing as well." The Knight Shaman paused again. "I've let myself go astray from this discussion. We'll finish the 'soulless' discussion another time. I hope we can all learn and grow from the experience.

"So, back to the topic at hand. The most shocking part of your tale is the vision-Founder told you this would be 'another' child of his loins. I need you to be absolutely honest with me, Jamari. Will you promise you'll hold nothing back from me for the next few minutes? I'll give you amnesty for the next half hour. That means no matter what you say, or what I may learn from what you say, I will *never* use what you say against you and I will tell no one else.

"I can't emphasize enough just how important this is. Will you give me that level of openness and honesty?"

"Of course, Terry. I wouldn't do anything less given the tale I'm bringing you now and my genuine need to be believed."

"Okay, then. Here's the question. Have you ever heard anything at all about a way for us to have a five-year-old son of the Founder - who passed on over forty years ago - here in our nursery? Anything at all, even a hint or partially overheard conversation?"

"Nothing Terry. As I've thought about it, I remember the sample the doc took from me during my medical examination to determine if I was okay for full sexual contact, but I can't think of any way the collection of a semen sample could be associated with the Founder.

"I've been there when the vets take similar samples from stud stock, and I've seen them then insert those samples into the target female, but I don't think there's any way to reach back in time and get a sample from anyone from the Founder's time. And, I don't know of any way to preserve such a sample for transport. All the times the vets have done this insemination process, they've had the male and female right there together already. They told me it saved the animals from physical harm.

"I remember seeing one horse breeding another down at the courthouse when I was visiting there with my hearth mates when I was still in Jahangir's boy's hearth. There had been a gathering and apparently a stud horse had gotten into the pen with the mares. One mare seemed receptive. She squatted and peed, lifting her tail to the side for him as he mounted her. It was after his member had found its way into her and he had made several thrusts that she began to buck and kick. One kick connected with bone at the front of his back leg with a bang like a gunshot and pushed him out and off of her. When the owner got there, he settled the stallion down and took him over to a stall, where they stitched up his leg and put a poultice on him. It made perfect sense to me the vets would use artificial insemination for their prize stock after that.

"That's all I know about anything even remotely resembling what I discovered in that vision-dream."

"Everything?" Terry asked. "Do you have any memory of ever hearing of anything like this before? In any way at all. This is very important."

"No, Knight Shaman. I've never heard anything like it before."

"Well, if that's all you know, then that's all you know." He paused in contemplation again, taking a sip from his cup of mint tea.

"Now, there's another aspect we need to talk about. Do you remember when we told you we thought you were going to be a shaman? Do you remember what you said when we asked you to take on that role?"

Jamari remembered the day very well. He had recently had his encounter with Cougar, just after his first spirit-walking session with Hawk. It had shocked him when the group of adult advisors to the young men's hall in Elk Creek Hall had not only told him he was probably going to be a shaman but also that they were going to initiate him into an officer's rank in the tribal militia.

"I told you I was a Christian, so how could I be a shaman?" Jamari answered after some reflection.

"Do you remember what I told you after you said that?" Terry asked.

"You said, 'God speaks to all of us in the language, in the symbols, which we are best equipped to hear,'" Jamari answered. "And most of the tribe members are also Christians, and we, the tribe, follow the tenets of Gnostic Christianity and, as such, would never dictate to God what language or signs He can use to communicate to us."

"Very good," Terry said. "You're going to want to remember that observation and try very hard to live by it as you learn more about your dream, specifically about who, and what, you were communicating with. Another thing to remember is, for over two thousand years, Christianity has attempted to shoehorn God into one small image, all of which is contained in only one book: the Bible. In reality, what God is, the essence of God, couldn't fit into a collection of books with the mass and girth of the planet Earth. The Monad, the God who created the Aeons, one of whom was Sophia, is broader than the universe, in fact preceded the universe. All the universes. The Aeons were created and were expected to work in pairs of polar opposites. You'll remember they said Sophia desired to create something of her own, and by her own will. In her act of rebellion, she brought forth the Creator God, who then created the material universe.

"We can try to trace all the lineage, try to build an understanding. We can then allow ourselves some small way to define what it is to be God, but we should never try to act as if, from the multitude of expressions we have dreamed of as God, any of them is truer or more accurate or complete than any other."

"Where am I going with this?" Terry finally asked, in rhetorical fashion. "How much mythology have you read? Have you ever stumbled across the name 'Hermes the Hunter?' Or 'Pan?'"

"Almost none," Jamari admitted. "Remember, I thought of Christianity as a very narrow realm of possibilities which excluded virtually every other expression of God before I started down this road to shamanism." He stopped and looked closely at Terry. "What is it you're preparing me for?"

"Just ..." Terry started and then paused. "Just, your vision has elements embedded in it which those who study ancient mythology and symbolism would almost certainly recognize. In fact, any of them would instantly assume you had read the texts I'm going to recommend to you already, and your dream was a manifestation of having read them."

"Really?" Jamari wondered aloud. "My vision, a vision which has been a repeating motif for over three years now, has ancient mythology at the root of it?"

"No. At least not in that context, anyway," Terry said. "The imagery you've shared with me, the characters who are in your dreams, these have parallels in ancient mythology. Parallels so close they simply can't be dismissed." He paused again. "I'm going to dig out some of the old texts for you. I want you to read about Cernunnos. And about Herne, the Horned Hunter. And about Pan, the God of Nature. Then I want you to come back and talk with me."

Terry looked over at Jamari again, placing a hand on his shoulder for emphasis. "Do not tell anyone about this dream vision just yet, Jamari. I'm going to be going up to Milltown Hall right after lunch and talk to some folks. I'll let you know what I learn and when you can talk about this. I don't want to censor you or anything like it. I just need to know some things from the nursery master, another council member, and maybe even the Chief.

"Plus," he added, "the primary way in which shaman vision leads to out-of-control action has always been when someone hears of the vision and repeats what he understood of it and the tale carries on until the dreamed is unrecognizable in the popularized version.

"Sir, I've already told Zach about these visions and we talked about most of the details while I was waking up to help hold them in my memory. I think often of how much memory I had and lost after the episode with the extended dream walking with Eagle and the Founder. It was important to talk it out while it was still fresh, to help keep as much detail as I could. I didn't think to ask him to keep it private, but he seemed very concerned for my well-being and advised me to try the walk up to the Founder's Glade first, before telling anyone about the visions. I don't think he will have told anyone."

"Well, talk to him after lunch and find out. Tell him what I told you and ask if he'll hold it in confidence for a while."

"Okay, Terry."

Jamari was more troubled after this conversation than he had been with any part of the visions over the last years. He went back to his studies, but he couldn't really concentrate on the histories just yet. His mind was whirling with all the unspoken parts of the interview. And he hadn't even mentioned the realization it wasn't a sexual penetration at all, but an understanding that an entity, a force far greater than himself, seemed to want his consent to move its spiritual self into his physical body.

From the questions asked, it seemed as if it were actually possible there could be a son of the Founder over in the nursery right now!

With sudden inspiration, he started digging through the scattered papers and folders of past study sessions. He seemed to remember a really odd story that the Founder had written, one that wasn't widely shared. Eventually, he found the folder he was looking for hidden under a pile of other documents he wanted to read again someday.

Chapter Twenty-Three

Shocking Discoveries

*O*kay, *so I'm going to be a father. Just how could this happen? you might ask. As I did. I had told the council that every man of childbearing age should father a child in our first years in order to assure that we got our settlement off to a good start. The key here was the part where we all agreed to that proposal and those keywords "every man of childbearing age." Yeah. That part. Apparently, I was unaware that a sixty-three-year-old man was still "of childbearing age." My bad, I guess. So, this is the tale of how they made it happen.*

First, there have been studies that show that an older man is far more likely to produce offspring that have defects. The primary ones identified have been autism and Down's syndrome. They have identified Downs as a syndrome that is not because of inheritance, but simply an imbalance of chromosomal patterns during cell division of genetic material in either of the parents, though it's more common from the mother's side. It has been very unusual to have occurred in the father. That one wasn't a large factor.

What about autism, you may wonder? All the studies showed that the older a man gets, the more likely it is that he will produce children with autism. Not something I would want to contribute to. Well, it turns out that the studies only asked about the parents' age. They didn't ask about sexual behavior.

So, when the tribal folks got to looking around, they discovered some people fathering healthy children well into their nineties. Then they found some people from the studies and asked them the all-important question: how often did you ejaculate in the days prior to fathering your child? Turns out that the ones who fathered genetically normal children in their later years had maintained sexual activity, climaxing at least three or four times a week. A known bit of not-so-esoteric knowledge of male biology is that sperm, once generated, if they're not used in ejaculation, get reabsorbed into the body. The problem is that the longer those cells wait around for reproductive activity, the more likely they are to suffer some sort of breakdown that could lead to unhealthy offspring.

Suddenly, I'm a candidate for fatherhood. Who knew?

So now, how do they get past the fact that I'm unabashedly, unalterably, irrevocably gay and am completely repulsed by the thought of being with a woman? Sneaky. That's how.

I had been communicating with some beautiful young guys from overseas. The young gay guys in the Philippines actually like older men! Anyway, a lot of them turned out to be posers—guys looking for a chance to hit up foreigners for money or help to get into our country - or catfish—guys trying to collect pictures of other guys for their own entertainment or sometimes to sell as "porn."

The ones who asked for money were very inventive. At least, I thought so at first. I felt bad for those guys! One guy supposedly gave his entire savings to his mother when she got caught up in a terrible investment and then was getting evicted from his own home because she wouldn't pay him back. Another had a mother who needed surgery. Yet another was getting ready to be dismissed from school because he had lost his job and couldn't pay his tuition.

Amazingly sad stories. All of them. Until they started coming around again. This time from different attractive young men who seemed to have identical problems as all the others. And then came around again. I never got tricked into sending any money (I was getting all the attention I needed for free). But, I could stop feeling sorry for them. Getting money from men overseas was their primary income and the prettier ones seemed to get more (based on the quality of outfits and toys they had in their profile pictures).

All the undesirables I unfriended and blocked. Some others became special in my life. One that became really close was Clive. Well, that was his profile name, anyway. He was twenty when we first started chatting. He never once asked me for money. He told me a lot about himself. About his job at the local mall. About his schooling days. About his times with a girlfriend before he figured out that he was gay.

That was another unusual thing about Clive. He never tried to claim that he was a virgin, just waiting for the right guy before giving up that bit of ephemera. Just about every other Pinoy tried to convince me they would never have sex until they were with the right guy. Clive not only told me all about his times with women, but, over the two years we chatted online, he told me about his boyfriends. There were two: one who he was seeing when we first started chatting and another a few months later who stayed until the end of this brief story.

At one point, he told the boyfriend about me and then the boyfriend offered to hold the camera while we shared in a very special chat session together. Another time, they let me watch as they enjoyed eros together. This young man was very special!

So, of all the others I had tried, most failed, as I've said, but there were three others I chatted with regularly and a fifth I was just getting to know well when this little subterfuge happened.

I guess I should actually tell that part of the story now. When some snoops over in I.T. realized that I was chatting with some special guys, they also knew that I was having problems with performing with my fellow founding members. To be honest, I just wasn't a normal "gay" of those times.

I had a lover one time who told me that his motto was "Cock-a-doodle-do. Any-cock'll-do." He really meant that. He could, and did, get it up with any gay man who would let him get close enough to grope. I thought of him as a living satyr! Anyway, that wasn't me. The mores of our culture expected me to limit my activities to other men in my age range. Maybe as much as ten years younger, but our pre-tribal societal (unwritten) rule was that gay men had to stay in their age range. There were unkind names for some of the various gay men. Older men who chased after younger men were called chicken hawks. Just like older women who chased after younger men were called cougars.

Well, I wasn't a typical sixty-three-year-old man. By that time, I could stand beside my youngest brother (ten years younger than me) and people would ask if he were my father. I had longevity in my genes, with multiple grandparents surviving into the early hundreds. The oldest passing at 109. It looked as if I was going to either match or exceed that statistic. When I was in my sixties, I was often told that I only looked mid-forties.

I couldn't "get it up" for a wrinkled old man. I just couldn't. And let me tell you: folks in my age range were wrinkled old men. I had seen my old high school lover one time when I was fifty-five. I still didn't have a wrinkle on my face, and other than weighing a bit more than my high school football lineman self did back in 1982, they could easily recognize me from the strength of my yearbook pictures. He, Oh my god. When I saw him, it was he who recognized me. When he spoke to me, I recognized the voice, and then when I looked closer, past all the wrinkles around his eyes and mouth, I finally saw the same hazel eyes looking out past all that wrinkled and gray countenance. That was the first time that I actually recognized that there was something distinctly different about me. About how I was aging. It was appalling to see what the ravages of time had done to him.

Anyway, along with that, I just couldn't perform with men my age. They called it E.D. (erectile dysfunction). I suspect that the condition resulted from a lifetime of being told all the don'ts, and can'ts, and mustn'ts, associated with sexual activities. That society (and we're all glad to be leaving it behind as soon as possible) had been carrying out a war on sex for over two hundred years. The major result of which was a list of dysfunctions, phobias, and "conditions" that could have filled the phone book of any decent modern city just listing all the various names for the mental afflictions.

And, in my area of the world, the attractive younger men were reluctant, almost afraid, to be with an older man. Almost like it was contagious or something. I needed an outlet for a still-strong sex drive and wasn't getting it at home. So, I started looking on the internet. And found it in beautiful young Filipino men who adored me as a grandfatherly figure. I'm not even going to analyze that association. I'll only say that they liked to refer to me as their special grandfather and leave it at that. These young men shared some very special times with me.

Where was I going with this little maundering tale? Oh yeah. The tricksy bastards over in I.T. They put their heads together with some of the council they trusted to not let me in on the process and built themselves a plan. They sent a couple of guys over to the Philippines. There, those guys hired a local investigator and checked out the young men I was sharing special times with. A couple didn't pass muster, but three did. Clive, his boyfriend, Jhon, and another named Jere (the youngest at nineteen and the newest of my online buds).

It was very difficult indeed back in those days to get a travel visa for a Filipino into the United States. They talked to the three and, still keeping it a secret from me, arranged for two of them to marry the two travelers and the third to come and visit some family he had back on the East Coast. Of course, the plane landed in San Francisco as the first port of call and he got off the plane and met another couple of guys from the Tribe who drove him the rest of the way up to Scotts Valley. He was the last one to arrive, so they kept the other two down at where we were building the casino while they were waiting. There, they all got tested for various diseases and got several outfits to wear, and then they brought all three up to the camp at Milltown.

The dam was still under construction then, along with the steppes and both main halls. We were all living up above, in the hills, in teepees and wigwams. But we finished the first longhouse structure then, and I was just moving into a room in there when these three beautiful young men arrived.

I was amazed and thrilled and so happy to have them here. So why do I call those dastards tricksy and manipulative? Well, once the three lovers were in-house, they had me using a condom for the first few weeks. To make sure we were all safe, they said. When they asked for the used condoms and I asked why, they said they wanted to check my reproductive health. I should have been more suspicious. I really should have. They checked that. They reported back that I could safely father children. Whereupon I informed them I hadn't been able to get it up for a female person in over forty years. Not a problem, they answered. They'd just have one of my lovers (I chose Clive) in the room with me. It would be his job to arouse me enough to achieve impregnation with the selected female person. Didn't work. No sooner would I leave Clive to be with her than the bastard little cock would shrivel up and act like an earthworm burrowing back into the soil when it felt a footfall nearby. Embarrassing.

So, they added Jere to the mix as well. He was a hot little number, even if I hadn't gotten to know him as well as I did Clive. Between them, they would work me up and then I could consummate the coupling.

THIS WAS WHERE JAMARI had stopped reading before. He had understood the Founder's trouble with being with a woman. He had gone through his own doubts long before going through with it himself. What he couldn't understand was the Founder had admitted to masturbating. In writing. For all future generations to read and witness. What goal could there have been in that? Was it really so bad back in those days? That men had to masturbate because all the persnickety rules didn't allow them the opportunity to share eros as fitted their nature?

He hadn't been able to find the next pages after that point and had just let it drop. Now, though, his curiosity was piqued, and he worked to find those last words. He finally found them mixed in with text from the American Revolution.

I'M GOING TO BE A FATHER. The tricksy bastards.

End of cheerful story, right? Ha. Nope. Notice that I still call them "those tricksy bastards." You'll remember that insignificant detail of the condoms? Yeah. When an animal breeder needs to protect his prize stud, he'll collect samples from the stud and then use a process known as "artificial insemination" to spread that pollen out across his herd.

I'm going to be a father. Again. And again, and again. I do not know how many samples they stowed away back in the freeze labs in medical. I guess it's none of my business. We need our natural numbers to increase besides those that we're bringing in via adoptions, marriages, and such. Even as we seek those Native Americans who have been involuntarily "dis-enrolled" from their tribal affiliations because of their sexuality, we don't have enough people to found an independent community yet.

Yeah, that is an important part of our long-term plan. If we can keep the snoopy bastards from the government (we're here to help you) off of our backs for long enough, we're going to establish a self-sustaining gene pool and then tell the rest of this fucked up world to get lost and leave us alone. We just got recognition as an official tribe a couple of years ago. Mostly because no one actually believed that we could carry off this little community we're building here. More about all that later.

I'm going to be a father.

April 12th, 2013. At least the first one born to me, after a lifetime thinking I would never be a father, is an actual product of human congress. My son was born today. Rodney Alan Knight.

SO MANY PIECES BEGAN to fit together in Jamari's mind. The basis of the play the Tribe repeated every single year at the Fall Celebrations was right here in this brief story from the past.

Chief amongst the personal revelations was that Rodney was the Founder's son! The same Rodney who spent virtually every day of his life ensconced behind a desk in the young men's hall, setting up and delivering lessons to the young men who would hopefully be the future of the Tribe. The next revelation was that Jamari himself had allowed his sperm to be collected three different times over the past two years. All as samples to "test for any abnormalities or infections." He was a father as well. Of the four that he knew of. How many more might be out there? Had they already used some of his stored seed?

In the end, he decided, pretty much exactly as the Founder had, it was none of his business. There was a breeding council that made those decisions. Jamari wanted no part of that responsibility.

He wondered if he could bring it up with Rodney while they were setting up the trip to the Founder's Grove.

Next, he read up on Herne the Hunter; Pan, the god of nature; and the Celtic version, Cernunnos. And he realized just why the Knight Shaman had been preparing him for a bit of a shock. He had been dreaming dreams of the Old Gods! And he and the Founder both had been members of the host in this dream. A small part for himself, surely, as a simple faun to Cernunnos' satyr, and a seemingly bigger part for the Founder if he represented Herne, as Jamari was suspecting.

What is going on? he wondered. He had been having this dream for three different winters now. The dream always had some version of him as a faun (or some version of an antlered man-deer, anyway), meeting up with an older Cernunnos, which always morphed into a version of the Founder as Herne (or some generously antlered man-deer).

He had always thought of the antlered entity at the start of the encounter as the same antlered entity at the last of the encounter, but as he read up on the various myths, it seemed more and more like it was Cernunnos at the start, and through the sexual encounter, and then the dream morphed into Herne (the Founder) at the end of the encounter. Dreams were very unusual things without having the very confusing element of messages from beyond mixed into them!

They regarded Herne as a protector of one limited forest in England, first recognized at some point prior to the oldest remaining written record found in a 1597 play by William Shakespeare in which Herne was the antlered guardian of a very specific oak tree in Windsor Forest. It wasn't until many years later the pagans had celebrated him as one of the lesser god-spirits. In their mythology, he was also a predictor of dire circumstances for the royal line, appearing before major deaths or events that imperiled the royal line. They had regarded him as a protector of hunters and a protector of the prey. His influence in all the tales had him limited to only Windsor Forest.

Cernunnos was a much broader influence, having come into the mythos with the migrations of the Celts. Regarded as the God of Nature and wild things, most often portrayed as seated cross-legged on the ground, it didn't seem as if this deity had as much to do with Jamari's visions as did Herne.

Pan, though, was another matter. This mythological deity seemed much more representative of the sexual encounters in Jamari's repetitive dream. Also, a god of nature, and of the forest, Pan seemed much more likely to have a part in whatever was happening with Jamari and the Founder's Grove.

One thing was certain, though: all the research had opened a fresh memory from his time with the Great Spirit. He remembered Eagle settling Jamari's spirit onto the upper branches of a small oak. Small enough, it seemed almost weakened by its inability to capture the best light, which was being screened by the larger firs surrounding it. As he remembered his spirit-self clambering down the leggy limbs of the oak, he remembered sensing an entity trapped within its root structure.

One image in the research showed a depiction of Herne held in much the same way. There was no way this dream could be anything other than some representation of Herne/Founder. Was the dream Founder reaching out for help to free himself? If so, what could Jamari do to help the process? Would there be danger in awakening one of the Old Gods? He felt sure he was going to take Haloki, Elan, and the others up to the Founder's Glade as requested. That message was just too consistent and clear to be mistaken.

In his following conversation with the Knight Shaman, he voiced these thoughts, once again pointing out the repetitive nature and the sense of urgency that all the visions seemed to convey. He also shared the dream in which the Great Spirit seemed to have asked for permission to inhabit Jamari's body. This was a concern to him, yet not nearly as much as the Knight Shaman seemed to regard it.

"That's one of the most frightening aspects of this tale," Terry told him, his face suddenly gone white. "The thought of giving an entity, with no knowledge of its intentions or powers, permission to come into your actual body seems to be an invitation to disaster!"

"Can we think about that statement for a minute?" Jamari asked. "I've thought about little else since I realized it wasn't a sexual penetration at all, but my dream self trying to put the 'event' into some form my conscious self could perceive. Here's what I've realized: the entire role of a shaman is to allow the spirits to move inside of him, to seek that exact interaction as a part of divining the Great Spirit's goals in our lives."

"True," Terry reluctantly agreed. "I just can't ... Maybe it's how you worded it. Maybe it's a natural fear for one I've trained long and thoughtfully into the shaman you're becoming now. Let me see if there's any research in our files which would help us understand. And by all that's holy, please exercise extreme caution in this matter."

They moved on to the discussion of his recovered memory from his time in the Founder's Grove with Eagle and the Great Spirit. The addition of his additional memory of a trapped Founder under the root structure seemed to trigger something in the Knight Shaman.

"We've always interred our dead thusly," Terry said. "It was the Founder himself who started this ceremony after reading up on burial ceremonies from around the world. It would be the most painful thing to think the result would be the entrapment of a soul, held there in one spot forever. Prevented from returning to Heaven as we believe all of us do."

"Remember," Jamari said, "we both felt the release of the souls from Bryan's Grove when we gave them the benediction." His expression was thoughtful, brows beetled together in contemplation. "I deeply regretted when those spirits accepted the release, but I still understand it.

"I think it is one thing which will become clear if I'm allowed to carry out the instructions I brought back from this most recent vision," Jamari answered. "There are elements we can confirm, though. Specifically, if I can identify if a 'son of my loins,' as the Founder refers to, actually exists."

"I've already confirmed it," Terry answered. "There are some things we'll let you in on because of this vision." He paused here. "Make no mistake, they confirmed this as a vision. We've all experienced vision before. In little ways, when a totem spirit visits with a message. To use care in an endeavor. To understand an omen that was presented. Your vision goes far deeper, far beyond anything any of us can comprehend, and we decided to let you follow through with your request exactly as it instructed you to do."

"I may know more now than I did when I talked with you yesterday," Jamari said.

"How's that?" Terry asked.

"I remembered running across an old document from my first days under Rodney's tutelage," Jamari answered. "I had never actually read the full text because it had gotten mixed up with some other loose papers at the time and I couldn't find the last few pages.

"When I remembered having read something about how the Founder could finally have a son, I could connect with the substance of this vision.

"Did you know Rodney is the Founder's first son?"

"Yes," Terry answered. "That was but one thing that we decided to share with you." He paused, looking keenly at his protégé. "Tell me about this document, though."

"It was a part of the Founder's historical stuff Rodney gave me very early in my studies. I had no idea why, or even what significance it might have, so when I couldn't find the last pages of the story, I set it aside and forgot about it. Until after our last conversation, when you drilled me so carefully about what I did and didn't know about the possibility of the Founder having a son over in the youngling's crèche.

"When I finally found the last pages was when I learned Rodney was the Founder's son and the Founder had unknowingly contributed to some sort of sperm storage system which could conceivably have held his seed in stasis over a very long period. I still have my doubts about just how long, though. Ninety-four years seems like a huge stretch, but. I don't know enough about the mechanical systems available over in medical."

"It's not just possible, it's true," Terry said. "There is a boy over in the youngling's crèche who is from the direct seed of the Founder."

"They have sperm from me as well," Jamari said. "Is it their plan to use my seed in that way also?"

"Possibly, but not as likely as you might think," Terry answered. "The reason this boy even exists is the cryo-storage system was failing. They either had to use what they stored or lose it. There is no longer any genetic material from the Founder available. I don't have any idea if they can still store specimens long term. Nor do I want to know. I've given samples in their annual exams as well. I'm going to follow along in the Founder's thoughts and say it's none of my business unless they make it my business."

"That's what I decided as well," Jamari said.

"So, when can I go up to Milltown Hall and see this boy?"

"I'll give you tomorrow. I'm going to be tied up in court, so I'll let you go up and see him on your own."

Jamari spent the rest of the day working around the spawning salmon aspect of the totem. They, and most of the totem itself, were roughed in, and he was starting with the smoothing and polishing that would bring them out of the mass. At one part of clearing out the excess, the point of his chisel spanged on something hard contained in the roots. He dug out a small rock that would have interfered with the visual flow of the buck salmon in its place just down and outboard of the hen. He would have to shave more off the entire length in order to maintain proportion. More labor added to the year-long project.

Once he had the impediment out and cleared, he sharpened his next larger chisel to prepare for shaving off some now excess surface wood. It was near the last part of this process, one final tap of the mallet against the wood's surface, when the chisel skipped and flew out of his hand. Instinctively, he reached out and grabbed it as it spun away.

Lucky, he thought to himself. *Very lucky catch*. He transferred the chisel from his left to his right hand and ran that left hand down the buck salmon's flank. And watched it come to red-gold life, colored almost exactly as a live salmon would have been. Wondrously, he reached up to rub the gill plate of the hen, and it, too, shone forth with a pinkness of color. Then he felt a sharp pain in his palm. A delayed pain from a deep cut that had suddenly registered as he ran his hand over the gill plate and was now dripping blood onto the floor below. Not so lucky a catch as it had seemed.

He turned his hand palm-side up and looked to find a puncture wound which welled up a small but steady stream of blood. The drip was steadily dripping onto the leather chaps he wore to protect his legs as he maneuvered up and down the totem. Damn, he thought to himself. Just what I need. He left for the infirmary area, his hand closed in a fist and wrapped in a cleanish rag.

They used three very awkward stitches just up from the bend of his palm. The cut penetrated the base of the lifeline like the dot of an exclamation point. Stern warnings to be easy on the hand, no grasping. Some snide chuckling as the doctor made this admonishment. Yuck, yuck, yuck. He followed up with an order to come back in four days to have the stitches removed.

Chapter Twenty-Four

Lucas and Jim

Jamari went up to Milltown Hall early the next morning. Carrying his hand awkwardly as he walked, he experimented with comfort. If he let it dangle naturally at his side, it ached more. Held up higher, the ache went away, but his arm soon tired from the effort. He tucked it into the laces of his tunic and walked on up the trail, feeling awkwardly off balance and vulnerable.

At the youngling's creche, the newest boys had been settling in for the last few months since the transport boat brought from the Women's Halls up at Elkhead. He looked into the brightly colored room from outside an open door. He pondered the primary colors and the oversized alphabet letters ringing the room as wainscoting. Looking to the corner where he used to play with his favorite bobcat, he spied a young one snoozing. The room seemed so much smaller than he remembered. Shortly after he entered the playroom common area, Jamari heard a piping childish voice shout.

"Jamari!" the voice called. He turned and saw a blond boy rushing across the room toward him, dodging desks and chairs with his arms held wide for a hug. Jamari spread his arms to capture this wayward child, looking around to see what might be wrong, wondering how this little boy knew his name. He seemed very young compared to the other boys, who were between five and six years old. What was this one doing here with the rest?

The boy hugged him with an intensity that made absolutely no sense to Jamari, who was still looking around to see what the joke was. The hearth leader and mentors were standing slack-jawed, gaping at the pair.

"We didn't believe him," Adam, the hearth leader, said. "I thought he had to be delirious when he told us he knew you from the past. We assumed he had heard some tales of your exploits and built himself a dream from them. How can this be?"

"It's easy to understand," the boy answered in piping tones that belied the seriousness and tone of his words. "I told you Jamari was my friend. And that he would take me away with him once he knew I was here."

"But I didn't know you were here," Jamari said quietly, looking the youngster in his bright blue eyes. "I don't even know who you are and can't remember having ever met you."

"They called me Jim this time," the boy said, "but I was Shane."

Jamari's universe went blank and silent for a moment of stunned shock. The lights were too bright, and his legs were not really coordinating to stand him up. He sat down on the floor. Jim took advantage of the position and crawled into his lap. Jamari looked up at Adam.

"How long has Jim been telling you he knew me?" he asked. "How often has he told you he was Shane?" It seemed completely impossible. This boy looked to be four years old at the most, and Shane had passed only a couple of years ago. A year and a half, come to think of it. It had been late August of the year before last, when the battle with the Outsiders had flared up. Two Winter Tides were now behind them since then.

"The Eagle Spirit brought me to this body when he took me away from the streamside," Jim said. "I remember seeing you hold up the salmon strips to me, and then He carried me to this body."

Jamari felt weak from shock. Flashes of vision ran through his mind as Jim continued to cling around his neck. Looking into Eagle's eye. Watching his body fade below as he rode Eagle up into the sky.

Seeing the spark of spirit darting off ahead. He had a sudden flash of understanding. The spirit had been Shane-now-Jim, being carried up to Elkhead Hall.

Adam looked uncomfortable. "The attendants at the crèche told me he had been telling them he was Shane ever since before we heard the news of Shane's death. When they heard about it, they counted back and realized it had been the day after the attack when he had said it. Far too early for such complete sentences through a still unformed tongue, and easily discounted as a dream from having heard tales of your doings."

"Is there no guidance that you should bring a shaman into a matter when something like this occurs?" Jamari asked in obvious annoyance.

"It's okay, Jamari," Jim said. "I remember our love, and now that you're here, you can take me with you."

Jamari, recognizing the potential pain of rejection, stood Jim on the floor and stood on shaky legs. He took his pistol out of its holster and, being careful of the recent stitches in his left hand, removed the magazine from the base of the handle. He racked the action to verify there was no round in the chamber and handed the weapon to Jim. Jim immediately had to use both hands to hold up the weight of the pistol.

"Aim it at the wall," Jamari directed Jim, "where no one is at." He watched as Jim's small arms shook from the effort as he lifted the gun in both hands, trying in vain to hold it steady on a dark spot on the wall.

"Cock and fire it now," Jamari ordered. Jim simply couldn't carry out the order. His hands couldn't simultaneously hold the weapon up while also reaching for the hammer to pull it back.

"You probably remember when you were the marksmanship expert for the young men's hall," Jamari said. "You could put three bullets into the same mark faster than most people could blink."

The hearth leader and his assistants were ringing around the pair now, the rest of the youngsters forgotten as Jamari and Jim dominated the entire room in their slow dance between acceptance and rejection.

"I remember," Jim said in his piping five-year-old voice. With regret showing in his every move, he let the pistol settle to his side.

"This body is too small and not trained to it," Jamari said, reaching out and taking the heavy weapon from Jim's reluctant fingers. "You say you remember our love and I would take you away as soon as I found out. From that, I know you remember all the mental things about *how* to take aim, *how* to release the trigger, *how* to hold the gun so you can get multiple shots at an enemy in a brief period. But your body can't actually do those things yet. You'll need years of growth and training in order to re-attain the same level of competence.

"In the same way, you'll need years of growth and training before your body is ready to carry out the relationship you remember us having." Jamari looked into Jim's eyes, seeing the pain of recognition, the pain of knowing the memories of another time; knowing another body couldn't be in this new reality. He reached over and took Jim in his arms for a firm hug.

"Grow up," he whispered to Jim. "Learn what this body can do, and what it cannot. Train yourself with the intensity you brought to your other life, and you will be an amazing member of our tribe again someday."

Jamari could feel Jim's silent tears dropping onto his neck, and it took every bit of willpower he had to keep from crying out his frustration and loss all over again. "I have to go now," he told Jim quietly. He meant his words only for Jim, though he knew others would hear. "I came here for another reason altogether, and I must finish that task.

"Will you work hard for me? Will you be patient with the body you have now and teach it all the things it needs to learn before you ask it to take on the tasks and activities of an adult?"

"I will, Jamari," Jim answered, his voice thick with tears. "Will you wait for me? Will you be there when I come into the young men's hall again?"

"I will do everything in my power to be there when you do," Jamari promised in the same low voice. Then he put his arms fully around this young boy, holding him tightly before letting him go.

"I will check on you and see how you're doing whenever I can," he promised Jim/Shane as he stood from his embrace, wiping a sleeve against the sudden blurriness of his own eyes. In his heart, Jamari knew he had made his promise to Shane as much as to Jim.

Jamari looked at Adam. "You need to get word to the Knight Shaman as soon as possible," he instructed him. "He needs to be here before the afternoon is out so he can talk to Jim about what we just learned. Hopefully, the Knight Shaman will have some idea of what has happened and if there is anything to be done." He watched as they led Jim away and was smitten by the teary face when Jim turned back towards him to say goodbye. Jamari looked at Adam again.

"We have to figure out how to raise someone in as normal a manner as possible while remembering he knows, remembers, things these other boys won't even be thinking about for another six or seven years.

"You should have told someone as soon as you had any idea something was out of the ordinary," Jamari admonished again.

"We didn't believe it was possible," Adam answered. "I am sorry, Jamari Shaman. I can see what this has done to you."

"It was quite a shock," Jamari admitted. "It's going to be a challenge to raise him up while also trying to keep him from pushing his little body to do too much too soon."

This was definitely not the boy he was there for.

"The Knight Shaman should have sent word to expect me this morning," he told Adam after a quick effort to re-gather himself. "I was expecting to meet another youngster, for an entirely different reason."

"We have Lucas in another room," Adam said. "It's been more and more difficult to leave him with the other lads. It seems every time he is unwatched, even for a moment, one boy has an accident. Something gets dropped and broken; someone is hurt to tears; or someone just loses a valued trinket. I won't say he is evil, because I think we would sense an evil spirit. I have to say there is something wrong there, though. When any of the others gets hurt, he seems fascinated, but not the least bit sympathetic. Almost as if it's all for his specific entertainment."

When Jamari met Lucas, his fears from his dream met the reality Adam had described. This was a walking, talking, breathing human body that carried no scent of an internal spirit. Not evil, as Adam had mentioned, but neither fully human.

Jamari thought of Lynn and how he might have been in his younger days. He remembered the faces dancing in Vision when Lynn lay dying in the ferns. This was the boy he had seen in that vision and Jim carried the other face he had Seen. His dream, his vision, of the Founder's Grove seemed to show far more portent than he could have expected.

The next day, when Jamari talked with the Knight Shaman about everything he had encountered and learned during his visit to the boy's hearth. He had a difficult time trying to settle it all into words. Shane was occupying a four or five-year-old's body and was now called Jim. Lucas seemed completely unrestrained and unrestrainable, not just a hylic, but a soulless one like Lynn. Yet Cougar had finally shown Lynn to have a soul in the end. Was there hope for Lucas, too?

Chapter Twenty-Five

The Knight Shaman

A team of villagers carted Jamari's totem in overnight secrecy up to Milltown Village. There, they placed it on an outcropping of rock on the north side of Elk Creek, almost exactly midway between Milltown Hall and Elk Creek Hall. It was late April 2118, and he finished it just before the May-Day festival.

He had carved it so that when placed just here, with the salmon dangling over the flow, the crowning visage of Eagle would look up to Milltown Hill and the Founder's Glade to the south.

The tribe had agreed to use their airplane to buy and deliver concrete to hold the unusually shaped totem in place. Jamari watched as the install team mixed the powder into concrete as others used "A" frames to tip and hold the totem in position. In directing the installation, Jamari was careful to make sure the three remaining intact roots, all on one side of the tree, were in contact with the soil behind the rock formation he had designed the base to mount onto. As the installation began, he saw the spawning salmon adorning the other three remaining root sections being posed in infinite spawning. He almost fell into the stream as he assured they hung perfectly above the edge of the creek below. The streaming salmon roe, he depicted along one whole root as hundreds of individual eggs. Night shadows made it difficult to view, but he intended some eggs would seem to settle into rocks. The rocks which were suggested by the roundness left in the root that housed them.

When the village came awake the next day, there was a gradual gathering as folks stood around the totem pole and looked with awe at his creation. "Why, that otter is just as if it's truly alive," one member said, leaning forward only to be pulled back from a near-fall into the icy waters below.

The comment brought Jamari's attention to the sliding otter, and he remembered the care he had taken in settling a small piece of obsidian into the eye socket, the hours he had spent watching otters at play in the stream beside the courthouse, studying their behavior in the hope he could capture their essence.

"How are the salmon so real?" another asked, pointing out the color and sheen. Jamari remembered the sanding and scraping to get the glossy finish and then the blood flowing from his palm to color salmon and roe.

"And Cougar, that snarling countenance exactly reflects a cougar who is angry she has missed a kill." Jamari remembered all the contacts he had had with Cougar Avatar, along with the one short, but very eventful, attack that had marked him as a shaman.

Of all the totem spirits included in the work, he was most disappointed with Eagle. Eagle had ended up looking very like an old-style totem, lifeless, wooden wings, squared with a down turned beak to allow for it to be carved in bas-relief. Yet others noted that detail with admiration. "Didn't change it all up. Jamari didn't. Left the top bit exactly as it's always been."

On the spring evening, replete with watery skies, Jamari saw his totem pole safely installed. All the oohs and aahs were behind. Terry pulled him aside and asked Jamari to spend the evening and night with him in his rooms.

As quiet as they wanted dinner to have been, they found themselves constantly interrupted as one tribal member after another stopped by to congratulate Jamari on the totem. Jamari noted many an exchanged look between the well-wishers and the Knight Shaman, thinking they were justly congratulating him on a pupil well-taught.

Over a year's worth of mornings, evenings, and various other odd times, and the long effort behind him, Jamari felt a let-down somehow. Not disappointment, but almost as if it represented the loss of a good friend. He would no longer spend evenings until well past dark, climbing up and through the catwalks to get one last detail just right. Inspiration would no longer wake him in the night. Telling himself the detail he had just dreamed of would be a great addition to the work. He would never again wander out to the workroom before breakfast and be called back in for lunch.

He missed the project already. He missed the whirlwind of creation his mind had become when thinking about what to do next. Perhaps Terry saw all this. Perhaps not, but the invitation to spend an evening with Terry seemed the perfect cap to the day. They reached the Knight Shaman's rooms just before sunset on the hills above. They silently watched the interplay of light dancing through the view window through the water to prism on the floor beneath the window until it had faded away.

They were enjoying a superb pressing of the Tribe's pinot gris from the Scotts Valley vineyards when Terry looked over at Jamari as the lake waters darkened outside the view window. "I think it's time," he said quietly.

Jamari turned his gaze from the window to look at the Knight Shaman, noticing his own lengthening hair was flailing about and getting into his eyes and tickling his ears. Still not long enough for a braid, his blond locks were growing out into an adult's length, and he would soon need to use a headband. "Time for what?" he asked reasonably.

Terry set his half-full glass down on the stand between them, careful to not slosh the liquid amber within. "Time for you to take over as Knight Shaman," he answered.

Jamari spilled his own drink a bit as he hurriedly sat it onto the table between their two chairs. "What?" he gaped.

"It's not like anyone other than you could be surprised," Terry said lightly, smiling at his protégé. "To be honest, it's long past time you took on the title and the role. I've been getting looks and questions for several months now."

Jamari simply continued to look at Terry, slow realization dawning as he remembered a long-ago discussion when he had learned the position of Knight Shaman always transferred based on demonstrated ability and adeptness in the shamanistic arts. He had always thought he had more time. A year, maybe more, before the post would be his. But then he reflected on the things the teacher had been learning from the pupil and looked Terry in the eye.

"I realized in a conversation with Peter Shaman on the way to Curtin for my first time that it's long been assumed I'd be taking over the position from you. I finally came to accept I would take the position. Just much further off. I don't possess your wisdom or experience. Or the simple panache you bring to any situation."

"I've heard tales of the night you conducted the opening ceremony of Winter Tide," Terry answered. "It was after that night when folks first started looking at me as if I were the past Knight Shaman. Asking me how you were doing. Wondering behind veiled eyes how long I would force you to wait before taking your due. The night with the two governors up in Chief Matthew's rooms set it in Matthew's mind as well."

"It wasn't like I've been waiting, champing at the bit," Jamari answered. "I'm perfectly happy with you in charge and me still learning from the master."

"Do you think I'm the best advisor for the new Chief Elk Creek?" Terry asked. He looked intensely into his student's face. "When Chief Matthew quoted your words on his acceptance of the position; when all present recognized Chief Elk Creek was taking and heeding advice from you; when you conducted the ceremonies of Winter Tide so well; when you simply took over and actually, rightfully, chastised a hearth leader in his own hall just the other day. These things us you are the Knight Shaman."

Terry paused and picked up his wineglass, looking out at the dark waters. Jamari looked as well, seeing they were still faintly backlit, with a touch of orange as the last rays of light were leaving the day. Terry looked over to Jamari again, still seeing the innocent youth of three years back who had first stumbled across the path of a cougar on the mountains above Elk Creek Hall, yet also seeing the stern countenance developed over those years, with an increasing awareness of himself and his position.

"We've actually been wondering if you'd realize it on your own," Terry continued.

"I don't want to displace you," Jamari answered quietly. "I'll never be the advisor you were and are, regardless of whatever leaps I've made as a shaman. Anytime a new situation arises, I'll always hold myself up to the standard of 'What would the Knight Shaman do?'"

Terry's eyes crinkled in mirth as he heard Jamari's words. "What the Knight Shaman would do," he said with a smile, "is only ever what Jamari the Knight Shaman would do. It's been you for several months now. The only thing remaining is to make it official before the Tribe." He paused again, motioning Jamari to take up his glass and have a sip.

"You know I'll always be there to offer 'wisdom' if you need it. I think, though, the Spirit talks to you much clearer than It ever has to me. You need only listen. And if the Great Spirit doesn't offer you anything, fall back on what Jamari Shaman thinks. You've been pretty good at that lately, too." Here, he reached his glass out to Jamari, clinking the edges together before sharing a sip of the clear nectar.

He looked over at Jamari again. "The most important thing to remember is, if you don't have a thought on a matter, staying silent is often regarded as the greatest part of wisdom itself.

"And it's not likely that I'll be without an occupation with the many other duties I'll still keep."

The next night, nearly a year after Jamari's acceptance as a full citizen, Terry, the Knight Shaman, stood from dinner at the table of the gathered awakened, and presided over the ceremony making Jamari the Fourth Knight Shaman of the Elk Creek Tribe. It was much the same as transferring the Sophia Shaman post had been only eleven months before.

"I accept this posting," Jamari said as he stood in full regalia before the tribal gathering in Milltown Hall. He wore the hawk mask for the first time, with its close-swept wings and trailing feathers giving a fierce countenance. Pieces of rare and valuable turquoise beaded on the band along the front gave color to his ceremonial garb. The cougar pelt rested on his shoulders with the head hanging behind. The pale, near-white leathers beneath shone out and highlighted his youthful build. Both of his personal spirit totems adorned his body. "I'll always value your input and will certainly call on you for your advice as I seek to carry out this role," he told Terry Shaman.

"Please take your seat amongst the most honored of tribal leaders," he directed his mentor. Jamari watched the Third Knight Shaman move several chairs down the table. Then the Fourth Knight Shaman took his place in the seat to the right of Chief Elk Creek. The cushion was still warm from his mentor's time in it. He looked across the table to where his counterpart sat and locked eyes with the Sophia Shaman; his learning companion; the mother of his first-born child; friend, and confidante of the last few months.

Chapter Twenty-Six

Founder's Glade

Lucas was still small enough he had to be carried pick-a-back up the switchback trails. The various members of the expedition took turns at this burden.

"Can't you hold on without pulling so hard?" Jamari heard Haloki, as the first carrier, exclaim.

"Sorry," he heard Lucas' young voice reply in an off tone. When Jamari turned to look, he saw Lucas' small fist held up so his intent face could quietly admire some strands of hair he had pulled away.

"Let me try," Rodney offered. He held Lucas's hands in his own as they walked. It was uncomfortable, but doable. The others followed this strategy in their turns. Other than the small chin still jarring against their heads, they completed the journey with fewer bruises.

They were all sorely tired of his mischievous ways before the trip was over. He somehow always poked someone in an eye with a finger, grasped onto an ear, or "accidentally" bumped his chin into the backs of the various heads.

Jamari led via memory of a dream given by a Founder who had last walked these lands over forty years before. The roads and trails that existed in the dream had grown faint, either overgrown past the point of recognition or having fallen away to the incessant decay of gravity, rain, sun, and time.

He could steer his way around these unexpected obstacles because of the clarity of the vision. He drew not only on the recurring dream he had been experiencing for three years, but most importantly, he now fully remembered his flight over these lands and hills as Jamari Spirit, soaring with Great Spirit as Eagle Avatar. Even if none of the roads or trails had been visible at all, the vivid memories of that flight would have guided him to the eventual aim.

When they reached the grove immediately surrounding the Founder's Tree, Jamari and Sophia both stopped in surprise at the sense of welcome and spirit-presence. After all the various trips to different sections of forest, with success ranging from none to limited, this sudden sense of self they experienced in this glade was surprising and welcome. Jamari looked at Sophia to see if she could feel it as well. Her eyes were closed and her face was slack as she turned her head slightly as she experienced the thrill of the connection.

Jamari could almost connect to the thought-presence without slowing down his own consciousness. This was a tangible presence, much like the scattered memories he held from his sojourn in spirit-land from two years earlier. He remembered the Founder's presence in that time and place as trapped, though, as it was now. The presence seemed more open, more accessible, now than it had in his visions from before. This was the Founder-self, which had communicated to him in his dreams for over three years!

"Why are we stopping here?" Terry asked. It was clear it still surprised him that Jamari's visions had led them this far, but also, he seemed suspicious that this was the end of Jamari's knowledge and that it was not the destination.

"I was surprised," Jamari answered while still looking at Sophia, "at the strength of the spirit-self I feel here." He closed his eyes in concentration. This had indeed been the last bit of memory-guidance he'd had from his dreams, but the strength of the presence found here was a bright beacon. He turned, his eyes still closed in concentration, until he faced the center of the emanation.

Then he opened his eyes and stepped unerringly towards where he knew he would find the Founder's Tree.

The strength of welcome grew with each step as he maneuvered around one fir tree after another. The species raised doubts in him since his vision showed the Founder's Tree to be an oak. Not just a common scrub or white oak, which were the most common oaks in this region, but a California Black Oak, the largest and longest living of all the western oaks. Given the impact the Founder had imprinted onto the Tribe's spiritual identity, it would surely have been huge, at least three feet across the trunk and tall as the firs. But Jamari knew the Founder's Tree was only fifty-five years old, given he had reportedly been growing it for ten years prior to his death forty-five years ago. He didn't know what to expect, really, but he could feel his way to it from the edge of the glade he was in now.

When he finally rounded the last fir tree, the tree he saw appalled him. It was an oak. Likely a black oak. But this tree was scraggly and lean, a whipcord of a tree with few limbs on the rising trunk until near the top, where those highest limbs seemed to have finally penetrated the cover of firs surrounding it.

At its base, there was a gnarl of knobby growth almost totally ringing the bole. It looked as if some errant buck or bull had used it for an antler scrape at some long-ago time. In the dim light under the canopy, the shadows playing along this protuberance seemed to form a face. A face of surprise, with the eyes set high in the frame. A couple of valiant limbs had grown from the upper part of this face-like area, resembling the antlers of a buck deer.

The welcome Jamari felt from this tree nearly put him to his knees with its intensity. Sudden tears leaked from his eyes, embarrassing him until he saw Rodney's eyes were brimming with tears as well. This was Rodney's father's tree. The place of burial where Rodney had helped place him all those years ago.

Sophia placed her hands on Jamari's shoulders from behind, empathizing with what he was feeling, perhaps feeling it as well. Lucas wriggled down from Elan's shoulders, dashing from one side of the tree to the other, seemingly unaffected by the emanations from the spirit site.

Haloki and Elan both stepped toward the oak in awe, but Jamari couldn't tell if they were experiencing the same emotional outpouring that was nearly overwhelming the shamans.

And such was his awe at the group of shamans surrounding him - Rodney, the First Knight Shaman; Terry, the Third Knight Shaman; Sophia, the third Sophia Shaman; the only one missing was Peter, the Second Knight Shaman - a thought swam up in his mind: he, himself, as the Fourth Knight Shaman, was the least of this gathering.

"We should get started on the enclosure," Sophia said, being the first to regain her aplomb.

They had all agreed that, even if they had never used an enclosure before during the dedication ceremonies, they would not expose Lucas to the full experience of the ceremony.

Sophia pointed to a moss-laden altar that stood a few feet from the Founder's Oak. "There would be the place to build it."

All of them began digging for the shelter portions in packs and carry bags. In short order, the table-like carved granite structure became the center of an impromptu chapel. They let the leafy green forest itself provide for a roof.

Jamari looked to Terry, who was having his patience tested holding the boy-child, son of the Founder. "Lend us the strength of your blessing," Jamari asked of him.

"I wish you well," Terry answered, his brow pinching into three horizontal lines. He handed Jamari his personal smudging bowl, a large oval carved from the dark wood of a walnut tree, along with a bundle each of sage and sweetgrass. "I bless this endeavor to bring about a hoped-for awakening and restoral of a soul." He tried to catch an escaping Lucas before giving up and letting him run about the glade yet again.

He may not comprehend exactly what *he felt,* Jamari thought, *but hyper-activeness has never been one of his traits, so it seems as if he surely feels something.*

"I can do no more," Terry added. "You have your training and your vision to guide you. I will be here in support, but the next steps need to be amongst the four of you young folks."

Jamari held the entryway aside for Sophia to enter the enclosure ahead of Elan and Haloki. Together, they all worked to remove clothing from each in their turn. All three of the men were tentative with Sophia, but she handled it with humor and berated them at the first hesitance. In no time, all stood naked before the spirits at the shrine.

Jamari had been dreaming this dream for so long it had never occurred to him that others before him may have developed prayers and blessings specific to his need. When he had shared all the details with Sophia, she had immediately seen the parallels within Celtic lore and helped him dig up a copy of the blessing used at the Celtic spring celebrations of Beltane. Together, they had gone into the deepest recesses of Milltown Hall to the ancient I.T. Center. The room was old, but they kept the technology up to date since they built the hall almost a century ago. They were both slow on the keyboards, so they requested an I.T. acolyte to assist them in their investigations.

The versions they had found were non-specific, yet still of a kind: simple blessings, calling on simple spirits. What the two built together was a blending of old-world mysticism with modern Gnosticism. They hoped to return one of the lesser avatars of the Great Spirit into the world.

Once they were all disrobed, they joined in a circle around the altar, hand in hand, the monument as the center of their calling. Jamari, with Elan and Haloki on either hand, looked across at Sophia. They lifted their joined hands into the air and chanted out their prayer.

Beltane Blessing

Bless, O threefold true and bountiful,
Myself, my spouse, my children.
Bless everything within my land and in my power,
Bless the herds and crops, the flocks and corn,
From Samhain Eve to Beltane Eve,
With goodly progress and gentle blessing,
From mountain to sea, and every rivulet,
From fount to wave, and base of waterfall.
Be the Maiden, Mother, and Crone[1],
Taking possession of all to me protecting.
Be the Horned God, the Wild Spirit of the Forest,
Protecting me in truth and honor.
Satisfy my soul and shield my loved ones,
Blessing every thing and every one,
All my land and my surroundings.
Great Spirit and Avatars
Who create and bring life to all,
I ask for your blessings on this day of spring renewal.

---

1. *https://www.thoughtco.com/maiden-mother-and-crone-2562881*

Chapter Twenty-Seven

Miracles in the Glade

Jamari and Sophia turned to Haloki and Elan to anoint their bodies with oil. They had to use care here since the two young men were deeply attuned to the circumstances and to each other. They appeared very near to releasing their offering before they completed the rite.

Wordlessly, they decided Sophia would be the one to anoint the lower extremities. This stratagem worked as each showed a lessening of ardor at being touched there by a female person. She smiled in mirth at their response, but held back her wit to complete the anointing. Once the blessing and anointing were complete, they each gestured Haloki and Elan towards the intricate stone bench, which was the ritual offering place.

In shape, the founders carved it to perfection, with curved rises and careful indents, including an indentation for the receiving lover to rest his head if needed. Men of an earlier time would have recognized the basis of design as that of a chaise lounge, one with an open end, yet elevated to allow the offering to be made while standing. On a warm day, it could even invite one to lie back on the cool stone, letting it soak away the day's heat. They carved pillars for legs with an opening at the lower end for the receiver's manhood to stand freely while the active partner carried out his role.

Haloki took a position before the altar after placing a deer skin rug over the moss-laden stone. Elan approached Haloki, reaching around to hold his lover in an embrace that placed both of their bodies into full-length contact, Elan's manhood resting just inside of Haloki's glutes. Elan slid his hand down Haloki's belly to grasp him. Then he nudged Haloki forward and into a bend where he lay on the altar with his derriere still cupping Elan's rise, only now, by bending over, positioned such that Elan could enter. He was careful about entering his lover, yet they dared not tarry. This offering of fluid had a purpose far beyond their human pleasure, and they made their offering, each spilling his seed onto the mossy carpet under the altar.

Outside of the enclosure, Terry watched as Lucas tried to tempt a chipmunk into his reach. He was hopeful upon seeing the interest the lad displayed in the cute and furry little denizen of the wood. When he felt the first quakes of response to the ceremony inside, he looked away, hearing nothing of import but somehow sensing a surge from the Founder's Oak.

He sensed in the way Jamari had taught him a racing of energy along the fungal roots. He could barely sense, in a way more closely compared to "see" than the other four senses, the lightning synapse of Jamari's God Walking Vision spreading out to the far edges of the glade.

The leaves were springing from their buds at this stage of spring, but they suddenly seemed fuller and more vibrantly green. Terry felt a shivering shudder through the ground itself before looking back at the boy.

There it appalled him to see that Lucas had captured the 'munk and had crushed it in his small hands. Blood was still dripping from the poor creature's nose. It was obviously dead, absent even a twitch of its lax limbs. He was just reaching out with useless hands to take the creature from the errant boy when the next surging of life overwhelmed him with the fierce suddenness of an unexpectedly large breaker dashing onto an otherwise calm shore.

The maelstrom engulfed him in images and sensations. He could feel the Founder's Oak stretching out its senses. He lacked the sensitivity Jamari held in communion with the forest self and couldn't contemplate what Jamari felt in this gushing lift. Yet even he could sense the lightning dance of neurons sparking new messages along a tracery of root and fungal web, almost like sensing a human spirit, until he felt the Glade become aware of itself. Then there was a sudden rush of spirit essence, and it lifted him into an ecstatic high of well-being and bliss.

When he next looked at the boy through tears of joy, he watched as Lucas felt the impact of the awakening spirit as well. He saw the tears that formed as he looked in open-mouthed horror at the dead thing in his palms.

Terry was pulled into the awakening again, like being drawn into the center of a tornado, watching as life itself glowed from within the oaken bole to flash in synaptic dance up through limbs and leaves.

It left him gasping as the leaves blossomed out to full and he looked once again to where Lucas, obviously awakened to the world around him, wailed at what he had done. The life force surging through the tree reached out a part of itself to lick the furred body, to caress the face of the crying boy. Then the 'munk twitched and twitched again. Shortly, the awakened chipmunk scampered up Lucas's clothes to balance on hind legs on his shoulder, near his neck.

Terry watched as Chipmunk reached up with a front paw to touch the tears overfilling the young boy's eyes. He felt a moment's sudden fear as Lucas reached his arms up to Chipmunk, praying the revived animal wouldn't simply be crushed again. But Lucas cradled his new friend to his cheek, where they nuzzled each other in welcome.

Could he be sure the chipmunk had indeed been dead? He thought so. He was certain he had mortally injured it. Now, though, it was an obvious companion. Perhaps even a spirit animal, as Otter was to him and Cougar and Hawk were to Jamari.

Rodney, on the other side of the living tree, also felt the burgeoning life essence blossom against his years. He, too, felt the resurgence of life within and was uplifted on the tide of awakening spirit. Years dropped from his countenance as his often-stooping back suddenly was upright and strong again. He thought he heard a whispering voice.

"These are my sons in whom I am greatly pleased." Then the tidal surge of energy ebbed back into a new awareness, one not yet fully whole.

Back in the enclosure, when Jamari sensed the surge of awakening throughout the glade subside, he realized the offering so far hadn't been enough to achieve his goal. He remembered a line from the poem read at his Ceremony of the Awakened.

"I can't let it go, because then the night will own me!"

It was in this moment of revelation when Jamari, the newest Knight Shaman, looked over at Sophia, the newest Sophia Shaman, and without words, they agreed to make their offering as well.

Jamari felt the God Spirit swelling within him and experienced a completely reasonable fear of being subsumed into that greater consciousness again. With determination, he set aside this reawakened fear of losing his self into oblivion. He committed himself to this ritual he and Sophia were to perform. He knelt and swept the carpet of moss clear of twigs. Sophia, in apparent agreement to use the green blanket as their boudoir, lifted a small section of the moss away to reveal the lacy riddle of fungal root intertwined amongst the black soil.

Haloki and Elan, seeing their intention, moved over to them and anointed each of them with the same oils of their own offering. Haloki applied the oil to Sophia, bringing her already glowing skin into vivid life and giving one last, light swipe to her mons, noticing her moisture made it a moot action in the physical sense, yet still necessary as a part of deepest ritual.

Elan applied the oils to Jamari's lithe body, bringing the skin into a lustrous glow before running a careful layer over an eager rise.

Sophia, answering an internal rhythm, settled herself onto the thick blanket of cushioning moss, placing her opening over a small window she opened into the fungi. She maneuvered herself into a comfortable position on the lush and soft carpet, opening herself up in welcome to her partner. Jamari settled himself down into position over her and let his own rise shift into a position where she could guide it into her deepest self.

"We are the Fertility Ritual," Sophia informed him. "Haloki and Elan offered their seed to Earth. We will offer your seed to Life."

"You are my field," Jamari agreed as he felt the God slip into him as if he were a skin puppet. He let himself fall into the godhood of the moment, surrendering his ego and will to a greater consciousness. In surrendering to the moment, he realized, in fully offering himself up to sacrifice, he became a guiding force to the power of the God. Not a puppet, but an Avatar.

Exactly as Cougar had been over the last few months. In full realization, he understood the vision that had haunted his sleep for over three years. It hadn't been the Founder entering him in a sexual sense in those dreams. The vision all along had been God entering him in full form, lending His power to a human hand. His dreaming consciousness had simply put it into a context that his intellect could comprehend.

"Turned and plowed, my seed flows into your fertile soil." He didn't know where the words came from, nor the ritual feel of them. Just that as God surged into him, this moment was greater than any other in his life. Greater than his induction as the Fourth Knight Shaman. Greater than feeling the awakening of the Glade above Scott's Valley. Greater than the partial and hazed remembrance of his time walking in the realm of the Great Spirit.

As she guided him into her warmth, he realized this would not be an unconscious action. Unlike previous sessions with meditations with the inner God, when he'd had to surrender himself to the chaos of impressions and later work to make sense of the limited memories as he returned to his lesser human body, he knew this Offering would become a part of who and what he was for all time.

"I feel the goddess moving within me," Sophia-Moon-Goddess whispered in a voice which shook the Earth.

"I would think that you're feeling something manlier than that," Jamari-Sun-God's combined selves jested.

They became magic itself in that one moment.

"I am Thunder," Jamari-Sun-God whispered in a voice that smote the Heavens.

"I am Lightning," Sophia-Earth-Goddess agreed in a paroxysm that shook Earth.

They danced in rhythm with the Gods for both an eternity and only a few moments. Deep in rapport with God, Goddess and themselves, both convulsed in shuddering release before falling, still joined, onto their sylvan bed.

Jamari-Sun-God saw that the energy of the God was more than even the mass of this glade could hold, and he used his guiding will to direct the excess outward.

Justin Earl Knight awakened in spirit form, resident in physical space, yet still anchored in the Other World. They felt his pain as a being of multiple planes, of the universe, and not. Bound by time and freed from it. Saint Justin was now the patron saint of Milltown Hill.

There was yet energy to control. The tiniest mote when viewed by a God. A vast reservoir of destruction if not guided by human hand.

Where to focus the excess? Jamari wondered. And then he remembered his totem, the tribal totem, newly consecrated, standing forlornly at the river's edge. There, he sent the power, which was too much for him, Jamari-Sun-God; too much for Sophia-Earth-Goddess; too much for the Founder and his Glade. As that vast field of power blazed up into the heavens in an arcing full-sun rainbow, brightening the sunny day for a four-mile distance, he felt his freshly intertwined selves separate into the individual parts and, sensing the same great loss in Sophia, fell into darkness.

To go into that union is to face a little death, he remembered from his first Celebration of the Awakened as he subsided.

Their action fully awakened the Founder's Oak, and even the surrounding glade, into awareness, and the Great Spirit looked down on them with favor as they completed their offering of two-become-one.

It surprised Jamari to come back to full awareness just a short time, and a full eternity later. Still joined in love, he looked into Sophia's eyes and beheld the universe reflected at him in twinkling gleams.

"It will be a boy-child," she said, voicing their sudden knowledge. "Like no other boy-child ever before."

Sophia of the Gnostic Aeons had looked down on them with favor as she had teamed with her assigned pair-member and righted a wrong from her first ill-begotten action, which had spawned the Creator God and the entire physical universe. The Monad would have been proud had that one ever been able to perceive at such a basic level as the fundament of space-matter.

Jamari Human and Sophia Human, though, could recognize and *be* their separate selves again.

"Are you two okay?" Elan asked huskily from where he had fallen to the carpet himself. "We were struck by Thunder."

"And smote by Lightning," Haloki agreed. "I thought I had fallen into death. I saw the Great Spirit, and He was stirring the land into chaos."

"You but shared the leaking of Shaman-Vision," Jamari the Knight Shaman assured them. "The Great Spirit blessed us this day. I can't wait to see just how widespread this blessing was!"

"THIS IS MY SON, IN whom I am well pleased."

Jamari had lost most of the scarring from his encounter with Cougar, and the scar on his hand from carving the totem had faded to near invisibility. The Yin and Yang punctures where Cougar had marked him with Her claws, lying side by side, remained as spent lovers, but they faded, too.

THE QUICKENING OF THE Founder's Glade awakened a soul in the boy Lucas.

THE TRIBE RECOGNIZED Justin Knight as Saint Justin the Wise and honored Jamari the Knight Shaman for his part in the Awakening.

OUTSIDE OF THE TENT, Terry's attention was drawn away from the boy and his chipmunk as he felt the fresh surge of spirit-magic permeate the glade in rainbow iridescence one more time. *A physical impossibility*, he thought wildly, watching that great arcing flash of rainbow ascend up and over towards Milltown Village. This time, though, that light, energy, power spread out in near-unbearable intensity, yet his dazzled eyes aside, he sensed the burgeoning awareness spreading out into the Glade. With so much to behold, every sense near-stunned, his eye was drawn to the center of coruscating power, to the Founder's Tree, which expanded as it awakened.

He witnessed young buds blooming, and he knew the leaves, when they fully opened with the advancing spring, would hold a special shine beyond any oak leaf ever before. He saw the face of a spirit come to life at the burl he had noticed earlier, and the awakened tree looked about with eyes of bark and soil before spreading out its awareness in a visible web through the under-soil and air.

When the intensity died down, the face remained embedded in Oak, but not so visibly mobile. He could still sense it there, ready to emanate again at need. It felt as if a Herne-like presence had come into being here in this Glade, and he could sense the spirit-soul reach out to encompass a broad swath of forest.

With sudden clarity, he remembered Jamari's ramblings as he was coming out of his weeks-long Walk-With-God.

The forest awakens as slow lightning runs through the roots. Only where the fungi are missing are there still trees not awakening. All in the lightning realm are awake and answering the call. The animals are listening too!

And he looked up and beheld Eagle circling the Founder Tree, Elk, in stately march ringing the small clearing and Buck and Doe tiptoeing into their midst. And, among still others, Cougar, greater than he had understood from Jamari's telling, stalked up to him where he stood in frozen stupefaction, pushing Her nose against him until he stumbled to a seat on the mossy verge, whereupon She rubbed Her face alongside his own, letting him feel the bass rumble of Her contented, thunderously rumbling purr.

DOWN AT THE VILLAGE, tribal members summoned to witness by an unseen force were jolted by a sudden strike of lightning that blasted down from the heavens at the end of an impossible rainbow and smote a twin set of spiraling black furrows from top to bottom of the tribal totem pole. This lightning lasted a short eternity, sizzling the totem up and down its height.

Many fell senseless to the ground. All were shaken by the paroxysm of Thunder. Some swore they had seen Eagle fly down to land on His carved face on the totem just as the strike occurred. Others could only say, once they had picked themselves up off of the ground after the crashing flash and roll, that they had seen Eagle soaring away from the totem, adjusting wood-like wings into a semblance of feathered lifts, larger than ever seen before, seemingly capable of carrying off a full-grown man He was so vast.

Everyone near watched as the roots of the dead totem came to life and dug down into the rocky base in which Jamari installed it. Jamari's carved-leaping salmon dove into the flowing waters below, following their trailing strings of fertilized roe, which seemed to settle into the rocky crevasses underneath the silt-laden waters.

The freshly blackened twined furls formed into green-skinned bark and the outspread wings of the carven Eagle became limbs that reached into the sky and sprouted silver-green leaves.

The playful Otter finally found his freedom as He slipped into the flowing waters of Elk Creek and dove and splashed and cavorted His way down to disappear around a bend.

JAMARI RETURNED FROM his efforts with a more enhanced awareness of the surrounding glade. He only had to pause a moment and set his hand under the carpet of moss, to touch the lacy fungal roots, and there sense the life and awareness of the Glade. This communion would let him know when danger approached. He and Sophia would always feel a sense of desperate separation any time that they were called too far away from the Glade's boundaries. Those boundaries were large, though, encompassing all of Milltown Hill, down to the oak glade that fringed Milltown Village, and back west to encompass the Adams Creek basin as well. The scar from his gashed left hand remained, but the internal damage had been repaired and he had full range and function again. He had a fresh scar on his side, right where Cougar had first broken his rib during their first violent encounter over three years before. It seemed the mild pain he had been experiencing over the past year had been from a couple slivers of bone that had been mildly grating against each other as they worked their way out of his system. They had been ejected in an instant of healing as he swooned.

RODNEY, STILL REVELING in his new strength and heightened awareness, was talking as they set about gathering their possessions for the journey home, "I once said of Jamari, when Terry was telling me Jamari had gone so far beyond anything Terry himself had ever conceived, that we had finally brought God back into the lives of man. I think I was far short of expressing the reality of that eventuality.

"God has come to us in real and tangible form and it frightens most of us to piddling, and rightly so." He paused in consideration as he folded a section of hide, which had seemed to come to life during the Awakening, yet was now just tanned deer hide once again. "It took one son of the Founder to make it happen, as taught and led by the first of the Founder's sons."

"What do you mean, 'one son of the Founder?'" Jamari asked. "Did Lucas have something more to do with the awakening than I was aware of?"

"You still haven't figured it out," Rodney answered. "You, too, are a son of the Founder. We had hoped for a powerful leader when we used his seed with your mother. What we got was something so far beyond our hopes as to be unfathomable in our understanding."

"I'm the Founder's Son?" Jamari asked incredulously. He remembered the many times he had dreamed the vision that had eventually brought him to the Founder's Grove, and the times they had burdened him with protectors from the Tribe. He wondered at how slow he had been to pick up on the truth.

"I've got to be the slowest of slow-coaches in history," he said. "All the happenings that just didn't seem to add up. My 'apprenticeship' to Matthew in my first weeks in the young men's hall, my unexpected visits to outlying villages which other young men weren't getting to do, the constant presence of Peter at my side during the entire coastal expedition, and finally, Captain Eric shepherding me to safety in the log jam instead of rushing up to the battle site when they killed Shane. All these things I was a part of. And simply didn't realize the significance."

"Well, it has taken all our plans far beyond anything we ever expected, little brother," Rodney answered. "You will be far more than just a chief of the tribe as we had aimed for. I don't know for sure where you're going, but you'll never be asked to step down from there to be Chief Jamari of the Elk Creek Tribe as we had hoped."

"Brothers!" Jamari realized. He reached his arms around his older brother, and they shared a closeness never expected.

Chapter Twenty-Seven

Avatar of God

Many from surrounding villages had witnessed the bright-sun rainbow. They had seen the arcing display on a sunlit day and had marked the blasts of light ascending to the Heaven above. They had marked where it had landed near Milltown Village and gathered themselves up to attend.

They came from Yoncalla and Lane Creek the very afternoon of the Awakening, and from Oakland, Curtin, London, and Drain by evening. As the next morning dawned, others were streaming up from farther reaches.

Jamari asked all the villagers to be gathered at Milltown Village the next day, near the base of the tree that had once been a totem, the one he had sweated and bled over and into. He planned a very special message, including much he had learned from his journeys, what he had learned from Hawk, Cougar, and Forest. Even things he had learned from the People, including a very important aspect of humanity he had learned from Lynn. This address would be to the masses of the Tribe.

He asked the Sophia Shaman and Terry Shaman to participate in larger roles and had Zach Shaman and Rodney Shaman take roles as well. He had Sophia gather some of the best women chanters and then had them practice with the men Terry identified as the best male chanters. He had a bass drum fashioned from the bole of the largest tree the timber company had slaughtered and brought it thrumming to life with the tanned hide of a young bull elk stretched over the hollow.

He dressed in his ceremonial best, which was much more ostentatious than ever before, in his role as the Fourth Knight Shaman. He had elk-leather breeches with fringed seams, bleached near white in their curing, held up with a beaded belt that also held a ten-inch blade modeled after the Bowie knife of old. His breech clout was also studded with beads. It was leather even though he generally hated the feel of the coarse leather in that area. This set of leathers was different, far softer than any others he had ever worn. It had been a gift from Matthew on his ascension as Knight Shaman.

On his head, he wore the visage of Cougar. On a staff at his side, was a hawk-feathered banner made up of feathers given to him in Salem. The knife was scabbarded in beaded leather, with blue and white beads shaping the visage of Eagle and adorned with tessellated fringe, each strand of which was strung with even more beads. He left his torso bare for the occasion, covered only by his Cougar cape which he wore with the head in place as a hood.

The people regarded him with awe as he approached the gathering. Tales of what had transpired up at the Founder's Grove had spread faster than wildfire on a dry autumn day. The greening totem they stood under confirmed so much. Many villagers seemed afraid, and this saddened him. Even as the sometime Avatar of God, messenger of the Great Spirit, he was still at heart the same young Jamari, still wondering what his future held. Perhaps with a bit more wonder now than before, yet still Jamari.

In the forefront, he noticed Scott, the former corporal from Yoncalla, now a full man, still emanating so low a spirit he seemed dead to seeing eyes. Life and spirit force abounded in the gathering, though, and he steeled himself to his duty and faced the throng from the base of the totem tree, with the chuckling river at his back.

It was then he put the techniques of his enemy, the church, to use against them. He signaled Zach on the bass drum, Rodney with a kettle drum, and other drummers on lesser timbres to begin their performance. He brought chanters in with the message in song, a wordless song in which the shrill voices of the women ki-yi'd and yodeled up the scales, one in which the bass voices of the men stirred shivers down the villagers' spines as they ululated their entreaty to the Great Spirit.

He signaled the women to a simple hum and then the men to join them in their bass hum until he could fully sense the villagers falling into trance similar to what he had undergone that long-ago day in the church in Salem. It was trance that many had never been able to enter before, a trance they would never reach on their own. He connected his full village with God.

Jamari the Knight Shaman opened himself up to the Great Spirit and wore God again as raiment, as puppet without strings, as guiding force and Avatar of the one true God.

"I need to tell you a story," he told the gathering once the drummers had softened their beat to blend with the singers. "This is the story of our God. Of how he was taken away from us and held in thrall by an organization which portrayed itself as seeking to save human souls. This is the story of that God awakening and tearing himself free of those human bonds. This is the story of the Great Spirit as revealed to the Tribe." He signaled to the drummers, having Rodney on the kettle and Zach on the great bass continue a dissonant beat, so low that it was felt deep in the bones, rattling teeth if they were held together, forming a common heartbeat amongst the gathered souls.

"Out there in the world, away from the True God, they are gearing for conquest and war. They've made their first steps in razing London's wood. They've made their first filings in courts of law. They are aimed at extinguishing our light."

Jamari-Sun-God sensed his moment as the unified whole resonated with his pitch. He reached into them as Lynn had shown him, as Cougar had revealed. He accepted but a trace from their energy selves. Each was tiny alone, but they were massive in one gathered collection of spirit energy.

He brought this Life into focus on the living tree, not striking with thunder this time, but drawing a deep well of new root, pushing up columns of sap into long-dormant pathways. The tree, which had been stunned to a false life, was given birth to a fullness of spirit.

Some, too, he spuriously directed to Scott, hoping to affect a cure here as had been made with Lucas earlier.

Each tribal member had a tiny piece of his or her spirit settled into that tree. This was not a tree of an awakened spirit, as the Founder's Tree was. This was the Spirit of his People made incarnate and whole. This Tree was budding with new leaf. This Tree was being girded about by bark in a healing and wholeness never imagined. This Tree was the Elk Creek Tribe.

And in the forefront, Scott shed tears as he too was able to connect with the World Spirit; as he too could be sensed to be suddenly feeling true connection with "Other."

Perhaps, Jamari thought, *there need never be another Lynn.*

Epilogue

The Founder's Grove settled into slumber and somnolence. For a time at least. Until one day, a group of invaders armed with axes and saws found their way into the midst of the tribal lands and entered the protected glade. The spirit of The Founder awakened and, to the animals who listened, he called.

No one ever knew that that particular group of outsiders had ventured into tribal lands. No one ever knew where to look for the bones. None knew the awe those adventurers felt upon seeing a man horned as a stag leading the throng that descended upon them.

All in the lightning realm are awake and answering the call. The animals are listening too!

The forest is talking!

The End

M any people will look at the last pages of a book to see if they're interested in the story itself. I beg you not to do that in this case. I've built an intricate work, one with many supporting sub-plots and revelations that all build to a stunning conclusion. If you skip the labor of building the ladder and then forego climbing it to the top, you'll very likely pass over the work itself because you'll simply be unable to believe the view from the top of this particular ladder is possible!

Don't miss out!

Visit the website below and you can sign up to receive emails whenever R. Roderick Rowe publishes a new book. There's no charge and no obligation.

https://books2read.com/r/B-A-LESY-FTVMC

BOOKS 2 READ

Connecting independent readers to independent writers.

Also by R. Roderick Rowe

Jamari and the Manhood Rites
Jamari and the Manhood Rites Parts 1 and 2
The Founder's Sons

Lost In Legend
Heretic

Standalone
Cernon, The Genesis of Paradigm Lost
Cernon, The Genesis of Paradigm Lost